Once Upon a Christmas Kiss

COZY CHRISTMAS COLLECTION

CHERRY CREEK HOLIDAY ROMANCE

CIARA KNIGHT   BRENDA LOWDER   SUSAN CARLISLE

TERRA WEISS   SUSAN SANDS   CHRISTY HAYES

Everything
love...
Susan Carlisle

This book is dedicated to all the amazing readers who inspired us to write these stories of Christmas love.

Cover Design by The Killion Group
Continuity Edit by Rachel Brown

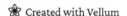

Reader Letter

Dear Reader,

Welcome to the world of Cherry Creek!

We know you'll enjoy the town of Cherry Creek and all its amazing and unique residents. Each of the books in this collection offers something unique. One might have a touch of mystery, another comedy, and another drama. Although the heat levels of these stories are low, one may be super sweet while another one has a touch of heat.

These stories do not need to be read in order but we encourage you to enjoy them all.

From all of us at Cherry Creek, we wish you the happiest of holidays full of friends, food, and family.

Sincerely,

Ciara, Brenda, Susan C., Terra, Susan S., Christy

Once Upon a Christmas Reunion

CIARA KNIGHT

One

COFFEE.

The elixir of life and an escape from the insanity of caring for a bed-bound aunt who thought giving up bungee jumping would be her only restriction post-hip replacement surgery.

Scarlet Cherish poured coffee beans into the fancy machine with enough buttons to control a top-secret underground elf network well beyond the borders of Cherry Creek, Tennessee.

Another unnecessary expenditure that her aunt couldn't afford. The piles of receipts and bills overflowed the tin basket on the desk at the other end of the humble café kitchen. A café that had been in her family for three generations but might be lost by the end of the year.

Her heart ached at the thought, but the fresh, smoky aroma of dark roast filled her lungs with a soothing coat of a good morning promise. She'd tackle the financial issues after the morning rush, which would be even busier than normal with only twelve days until Christmas.

The machine screamed, choked the beans through the grinder, and spit out liquid with a steam-rising crescendo. Scarlet slid her cup out and cradled it to her chin, sniffing the caramelized, nutty scent, but she didn't take a sip. The first sip needed to be savored while standing in her favorite spot, so she shuffled from behind the register counter and settled at the red-painted bistro chair in the center of the large picture window.

With a view of the distant snowcapped mountains, a backdrop to the colorful awnings dotting Main Street, she held the cup to her lips. The majestic site provided the perfect oasis to enjoy that first luxurious sip. Add a dash of Christmas lights glowing in the pre-dawn grayness, and it looked like a holiday movie set. From the sky, she thought, the red and green dots must make the street look like a runway for Santa Clause to land his sleigh.

Her eyes landed on the cute chalkboard sign on the sidewalk, inviting friends and neighbors in to try their holiday special. *Try our new Chocolate Cherry Coffee special, a perfect blend of rich and sweet goodness to celebrate love. Add a dash of peppermint for the holiday season.*

Small-town life had little to lure her into permanent residence, but Atlanta could never offer this kind of peaceful, quiet calmness and simplistic holiday cheer from friends and neighbors.

She tipped the Cherished Café mug up. Steam coated her skin and tickled her nose. One more inhale would seal the taste like fine wine.

Chugga-chugga-pop. Chugga-chugga-boom.

The old diesel truck grumbled like a toy soldier tooting an announcement of Duke Trenton entering town. She lowered her mug and glanced at the cuckoo clock her aunt had brought back from a backpacking trip through Bavaria a few years ago.

Why would Duke be making deliveries fifteen minutes earlier than normal? The two-foot-tall pile of organic vegetables flashed past along with the handsome man-that-could-never-be.

She pressed her cheek against the chilly window, but the truck disappeared around the corner. Of course, he wouldn't stop. He knew she'd been here for two months and not even a drop-by for a cup of Joe. What did she expect? She hadn't spoken to him since Christmas Eve ten years ago.

It didn't matter. She'd be back in Atlanta soon enough.

Atlanta.

A far and loud, distant city with smog and noise and job and boyfriend.

Perhaps this had been a respite from life, but she needed to return.

Maybe next month.

She took a whiff of coffee, closed her eyes, and brought the decadent promise of bliss to her lips. Finally ready for that first sip.

Kerplunk. Bang. Smash.

Scarlet jumped. Hot liquid splashed onto her white shirt like an antiquing technique gone horribly wrong. Heat assaulted her chest. She plucked the wet shirt from her stinging skin with a loud groan and hiss.

Abandoning her coffee on one of the white-topped red bistro tables, she grabbed the stapler from the register. She slid along the short hallway to the kitchen with the weapon high over her head.

"Who's there? I'm armed."

"Put the stapler down and help me. This ain't the big city, no one's gonna be stealing bad food."

Aunt Laura's muffled voice drew her gaze to the open refrigerator. Fruits and vegetables littered the white-tiled floor while her aunt's butt peered from behind the silver door, one hip higher than the other.

"What on earth?" Scarlet croaked.

Aunt Laura popped up and held out a black and mushy head

of lettuce with white hair growing between the dark spots. The odor of rotting, festering vegetables and fruit that sparked a memory of digging through a dump to help Duke fish out an alleged discarded part for his 1967 Mustang they'd restored didn't give her any warm, fuzzy feelings. Not even the thought of hot, humble teenage Duke Trenton could overwhelm this stomach-churning scent.

She gagged and held her knuckles to her nose.

"Save money, order in bulk, you said." Aunt Laura tossed a radish over her head, smacking Scarlet in the middle of her forehead.

"Don't use the fancy and expensive local organic farms," Aunt Laura said in her sugary, southern, sarcastic tone.

"Did the refrigerator cut off?" Scarlet retrieved the broken head of lettuce and all the dead, decaying leaves and placed them in a crate already a quarter full of veggie carcasses.

"Probably couldn't handle all that junk in there." Aunt Laura straightened to her five-foot-two commanding stance. Her tight-lipped expression could make the Grinch feel ashamed.

Scarlet let out a strangled sigh. "Another sign we need to cut our losses—"

"Not selling." Aunt Laura hobbled over and leaned against the tin food-prep surface. "You might not have pride in our three-generation, family-owned café, but I do."

"It's not that." Scarlet rubbed her forehead and eyed the mess and then pointed to the stack of bills on the desk in the corner. "You're bleeding money. This place can't stay open much longer. That's why I tried to reduce costs. It's business."

"Business? This ain't Atlanta. In Cherry Creek, Tennessee, we don't settle for subpar quality so people can be seen in the trendy places."

"It's not like that." Scarlet threw up her hands. "I'm not

going to argue with you. The damage is done. We'll have to offer baked goods and coffee today, not lunch. I'll shut down early, and we'll get someone out to look at the refrigerator."

"Got it handled already. No need to shut down." Aunt Laura hobbled toward the café. "If you wouldn't have been avoiding Duke, this would've never happened."

"What? No. I canceled the farm fresh veggies and fruits because it was too expensive. Told you, it's business." Scarlet grabbed a crate and set it in the middle of the floor, avoiding eye contact. Aunt Laura saw everything, even things someone didn't want to see about themselves.

She halted her retreat and hobbled like a windup toy to face Scarlet. "Riiight. Well, you want to help me so much. Clean this up while I prep for the breakfast rush."

She straightened and lifted her chin. "You're not supposed to—"

"Don't tell me I need to go rest or I'll lock you in that refrigerator with your cheap produce. I haven't closed this place since I took over from my father. I'm not starting now." Aunt Laura shook her head but leaned against the counter and offered her signature half smile, raised brow, and her when-are-you-going-to-get-it nose flare. "Listen, I appreciate everything you've done. Maybe if you moved back, we could work this all out together. We could use your business education with my hometown knowledge."

Warning bells chimed in Scarlet's head. "Don't start. My life's in Atlanta. I have a job, a boyfriend, remember?"

"The man who hasn't come to visit you for two months? The same one you haven't spoken to on one of those video call things?" Her gaze traveled to Scarlet's coffee-saturated shirt but snapped back up without a word about her clumsiness.

Unlike Henry, she never concentrated on Scarlet's inadequacies. But Scarlet shook off that thought and told herself that he made her better. He molded her into a potential director of his company. "He's busy and doesn't like telephones or texting." Scarlet shrugged and tossed a tomato into a crate next to the head of lettuce with a splat.

"I thought he was in business?"

"As I said, he's busy."

Aunt Laura didn't understand big city life with big city responsibilities. People weren't interested in excuses and ailments. Life happened. Get over it and get to work.

The idea filtered into her world, though. Was it strange that they didn't talk more? Was it even stranger that it didn't bother her? No, it's life when you have jobs and commitments, not gossip and girl time.

Aunt Laura pushed from the counter, her eyes twinkling. "What would you do if he wanted you to return now?"

"I can't leave you." Scarlet scurried on hands and knees like a blind bull on ice skates and face-planted. Her fingers scraped the rolling orange before it disappeared under the center island.

"What if I can't ever run this place on my own again?"

Scarlet opened her mouth to argue, but she'd never win a direct assault. "Less talk; clean up. If this odor reaches the café, we'll lose business. And we can't afford that."

"We?" Aunt Laura shoved Scarlet's phone in front of her eyes. The screen lit with one text.

Come home by Christmas and I'll agree to marry you, or we're done.

"Guess I better look into hiring a nurse. With that romantic of a proposal, I'm sure you'll be in the car by nightfall."

Scarlet sighed, stood, and gawked at the text message. A tickle of resentment flickered. "What are you doing snooping?" She snatched the phone from her aunt and slipped it into her pocket. Flickers of resentment ignited, but Scarlet doused her doubts at his ultimatum. If she were honest with herself, she'd admit she forced a smile to avoid Aunt Laura's judgment more than facing his abrupt and demanding words.

The last thing she wanted to do was talk to her aunt about her love life, so she grabbed the crate and headed for the back door. "Ready to sell? You're right, there's nothing keeping me here except the fact that you're drowning in debt and can't reach the canned goods on the top shelf. Not without a ladder which you can't climb."

"I think you can't avoid facing life with Humdrum Harry and are using the sale as an excuse to stay longer."

"Henry, not Harry, and he's hardworking, not humdrum." Scarlet corralled a rolling grape.

Aunt Laura kicked an onion. It bounced off the crate and followed the orange to the far-reaching underbelly of the island. "Marriage ultimatum via text message. Classy. Really. You know who's a real southern gentleman—"

"Stop."

"Why? You used to follow that boy around all over town. Your crush was bigger than 1980s hair. You'd fall at his feet if he'd ask you to."

"Not falling at any man's feet, especially his." Scarlet shoved open the back door. "I don't live in La La Laura Land. You might live carefree, but I live in the real world. I've built a real life with a real foundation with a real future. I'm not falling for another dreamer that has no future." She shoved her backside against the door, but it stuck at the door jamb. She heaved her body weight into it, and it swung ajar but bounced back and slammed against her. "Duke Trenton means nothing to me."

The door flew out from behind her, and she tumbled against a roadblock.

Vegetables and fruits and her sneaker-clad feet took flight. Produce and her body landed in a puddle on the icy asphalt.

Pebbles ground into her palm and her hip throbbed from

impact, but nothing startled her more than two size eleven men's dress shoes pointing at her.

Khaki pants belted a thin waist, white button-up shirt was instantly stained with red tomato juice.

Don't let it be. Don't let it be.

She forced her gaze a little higher to the distractingly delectable Duke Trenton.

§

Duke dabbed at the red smudges marring his pressed button-up. The sticky goo clung to his fingers, so he flicked it to the ground. His pulse hammered. "No. Not today." No way he'd get his business loan dressed like this.

He could hear Mr. Marwood now. "Another prank gone wrong? Didn't you learn anything in high school?"

Dainty hands pressed to his chest, smearing the foul, gut-curdling aroma into some impressionist painting. "I'm so sorry. I didn't know you were there."

He clasped her fingers, halting her assault. Perfect green fringed by long, dark lashes stole his focus. They were not just any green eyes. They were Scarlet's leaf green that matched the color of their childhood secret tree.

His pulse gushed through his ears faster than the creek down beyond the parking lot after last night's rain.

He'd thought of a million different ways he could bump into her casually and strike up old conversations since she'd returned, but this wasn't what he'd imagined. One more reason she'd never take a chance on a has-been baseball star turned worthless rancher.

His hands tightened, holding her closer to his chest. Breath abandoned him. "Scar?"

"Don't call me that. I'm not twelve." She jerked away,

breaking their connection, yet the static remained in the air around them. Did she feel it?

Obviously not, because if she did, she wouldn't be on her knees tossing rotten produce into the cracked wood box along with his perfect organic pieces. He squatted by her side and picked his nutritious produce out of the garbage. "Stop."

She rested back on her heels, blinking at him as if seeing him for the first time. It had been ten years. Not much about her had changed. Heart-shaped face. Full, kissable lips. Small shoulders, thin waist, long legs. The only difference was her straight, perfect hair.

He preferred the messed and less pressed version of Scar... Scarlet. Nothing in the world stirred him more than her sitting up after a long reading session lying by his side under their tree, leaves and sticks in her hair that he'd pluck out one by one. Such beauty.

"This is just great." White puffs of air flew from her mouth.

He wanted to offer her his coat, but he'd left it in the truck figuring he'd only be a minute or two and that it wasn't that cold with the snow only dusting the rooftops and cars. He'd planned on leaving the produce at the back door since he didn't have time to stop and chat. When he spoke to her, he wanted it to be perfect; he wanted to get the business loan first so he could promise her he wasn't the boy who blew his future on a prank gone wrong. A man who behaved like his father.

"What are you doing here?" She grumbled.

"Your aunt called shrilling about a desperate need for produce, so I rushed over here. I didn't know if you were still here." Liar—he'd kept tabs on her remotely through Laura since she'd arrived.

She bit her bottom lip and stared at a grape bumping along over pebbles then bouncing off the brick wall.

"Me and the bruised and bloodied fruit still reside here for the moment."

A nervous chuckle broke through which opened the floodgate of stress-relieving laughter. He threw his head back and howled, releasing all the tension. He'd always laughed when he was nervous, which got him in a lot of trouble back in school.

"How's this funny?"

He pointed at the mess. "It's like a vegetable massacre. A ravenous Bunnicula must've gotten loose."

She chuckled and joined him with a bent-over, arm-around-her-stomach outburst. Did that mean she remembered reading that book together when they were nine?

Laura burst through the back door. "What's wrong? You need a new hip now, too? I know a guy."

Tears dripped from Scarlet's eyes. "No. I mean...look at this."

"Oh, dear Lord, I broke her. She's cracked."

"I'm fine." Scarlet swiped the tears away.

"If you're smiling, let alone laughing, you've either been invaded by mutant elf dust or you've lost your ever-lovin' mind." Laura looked to Duke and her eyes shot wide. "Oh no. And you. I'm so sorry, Duke. You've got that big meeting at the bank this morning."

"Bank?" Scarlet offered him an apple and an eyebrow raise.

Laura dropped her hands and shuffled into the circle of wreckage. "Our resident organic farmer is working on expanding, so he was on his way to apply for a loan."

"Great, now I feel worse." Scarlet's tone tugged at his own disappointment and tossed it out of the way so he could focus on making her smile again. To hear the laugh that once echoed through the woods, making the cloudy winter days bright. "Don't worry about it. The interview was a fool's errand. Mr. Marwood's never going to give the son of a scoundrel a loan."

Scarlet tossed a smushed grape at him. "Shut up with that talk. You've never been and never will be your old man."

"And you'll never be your mother," he said, finishing the mantra they recited at the end of each book club meeting. He only hoped she remembered those times together. "I should stick to the gifts I've been given in life and be happy." Duke didn't want to leave. In seconds, he swore she'd stolen the only piece of heart he'd held onto all these years. She'd taken his love piece by piece with each kind gesture and word. She'd believed him to be more than a worthless Trenton when everyone had given up on him. The boy who only found town pride through baseball until he blew it like a true Trenton.

That's why she'd never see him as more than a friend. If he knew one thing about Scarlet, she'd never take a chance on being a small-town wife who ran off like her mother.

He tilted his head toward the carnage and eyed Laura. "No wonder you needed an emergency delivery. What happened?"

"You should go." Scarlet snapped, warning him he'd stepped on something more sensitive than the rotting pear. He wasn't sure how he'd offended her, but he knew what that crooked, forced grin meant. He'd stepped in something. The way he always stepped on his own words when around the most beautiful girl in Cherry Creek.

"I'll finish cleaning this up. You get to that meeting. Hard work and determination are always the key to success." Scarlet stated like she was reading from a manual.

Laura snagged his arm and edged him toward his truck. "I'll walk with you. Doc says I need to move more."

She snagged him by the crook of his arm and escorted him away. His mood slipped into grayness.

"No getting mad at me now, but I might have sacrificed some supplies to get you here. That niece of mine is in serious trouble, and I need your help. I love her too much to let her make the biggest mistake of her life." Laura tightened her grip like a nutcracker around a nut.

His gaze drifted over his shoulder to Scarlet. Her golden-fire hair fell over her face, and he wanted to tuck it behind her ear so he could see her beautiful features.

"And you love her, too."

His skin heated. His breath caught between *once upon a time* and *happily never after*. "What? No. We're friends. She belongs with some rich man from a good family."

"She belongs with you."

Four words had never caused any man to spontaneously combust, but the way his insides hummed and strummed he felt an explosion building inside his stomach. "Please, I'm a legendary Trenton. The most hated family in three counties."

"You're not your father, and this isn't high school. You don't have to worry about tarnishing Scarlet's reputation. I know that's why you never asked her out and why you kept your book club a secret. Not to mention you disappearing on Christmas Eve ten years ago."

His gut clenched and curdled. "You can't know why. No one does."

"Except the mayor and his secretary that put the call through from the sheriff," Laura nodded.

His nerves cross-fired in a symphony of relief and dread. "Then all the more reason you shouldn't want me to be anywhere near your niece. I thought you were supposed to be her guardian. How could you not stop her from meeting alone with the worst boy in town back in high school?"

"You were the safest man for her to be alone with. You've worked your entire life to prove yourself beyond the Trenton name. You've never let a drop of alcohol pass your lips or cast a bet on any horse or dog race. You're not your father or your uncle or your grandfather. You, Duke Trenton, are your own man."

"I proved my reputation solid. If you really know what happened, then you know I don't deserve her. Maybe before that incident, I had a plan to be worthy of her, but that sunk to the bottom of the icy lake along with the principal's car." Duke gripped the handle on his truck's door and yanked the driver's side door open with a loud squawk. "Besides, I'm just a poor farmer with no real prospects. Scarlet deserves a comfortable and fulfilling life."

"Maybe this is your chance to prove yourself to the town. Scarlet needs you." Laura touched his shoulder like a mother to a son. A touch he hadn't felt since he was six.

"Is this one of your games?" Duke brushed off Laura's comfort and hopped up into the driver's seat.

"No. I'm afraid Scarlet's in real trouble, and if we don't do something, she's going to suffer for the rest of her life."

His muscles tightened. "What're you talking about?"

"Scarlet's about to make the biggest mistake of her life, and I think you're the only one that can stop it."

His inner voice screamed for him to close the door and drive away, but he couldn't. No matter how much he tried to stay away from Scarlet, he'd always felt some sort of pull to her. More than anything, he always wanted to protect her. From other boys at school, mean girls, and most of all, himself. "What mistake?"

Laura stomped her foot telling him that hip had healed, but he'd keep her secret. "She's going to marry the wrong man."

Instinct nudged him to help, but his experiences told him to drive away. "It's her life and her decision. You need to learn not to meddle and let her make her own choices."

"The way your mother made hers, staying with your father

despite ending up in an early grave? Do you want that for Scarlet?" Laura's words sliced and diced his soul.

He swallowed a lump of regrets and gripped the door handle to slam the door shut on Laura's manipulation, but he couldn't. Not if there was even an inkling of truth to her words. He clenched his jaw and watched Scarlet disappear into the café. "How bad's this guy?" he asked in hopes he'd uncover her devious plot and see nothing worth getting excited about.

"The worst, and you and I both know that if Scarlet marries someone, it's for life. She'll never run off like her mother did."

He pushed his shoulders back and clenched his fingers around the door handle. The weathered door cracked with protest. "What makes you think he's so bad? Rumor says you've never met him before."

"He hasn't spoken to her or checked on her in two months and then sent a text ultimatum that she returns home to marry him by Christmas or they're done. It's like one more business transaction from a heartless, ruthless man."

He slumped and released the door. Images of being too tiny to help, sitting in his little white rocking chair listening to his father yell at his mother echoed louder than normal in his head. The tension in his neck knotted his muscles and his determination. "You should talk to her."

"Talk won't work. Already tried that. Can't you think of something to remind her of happier times? Make her admit how she feels about you. Show her that life doesn't have to be all numbers and work, that she can be happy."

"I let her go for her own good. But you're asking the impossible. I don't know if I have the strength to let her go again." Duke pinched the bridge of his nose and an idea popped into his head, but it would only prolong the inevitable. "Besides, it would take a miracle to get her to stay in Cherry Creek. And I don't believe in miracles."

"I've got a Christmas miracle up my sleeve in the form of a legendary book." She lifted her spotted hand and pointed toward the academy Scarlet had attended beyond the creek.

"The book from the academy about how a man and woman will fall in love by Christmas if the book finds them? That's no more than a folk tale or a legend. It doesn't exist." Despite his words, a part of him welcomed the possibility of reconciliation and romance. "You...have it?"

"Not in my hands, but—"

Warning bells chimed louder than Cherry Creek Community Church on Sunday. "That book's a legend. It doesn't exist. It's something some girls from the academy dreamt up to believe in happy endings. This isn't a story. It's real life."

"That book is real. And I'm going to prove it. Because this Christmas you're going to be in Scarlet's life story cast as her legendary romantic hero."

Two

THE RUSH OF PATRONS CONSUMED SCARLET'S THOUGHTS UNTIL SHE flipped the café sign to closed. Not that she stopped working after the lunch rush, not with the stack of bills she needed to get through. They weren't going to pay themselves.

She tried to focus, but the smell of vegetables kept eliciting visions of Duke on the ground with tomato innards on his shirt. The thought of doing that to him tore her up inside, yet why did she care? The man played a disappearing act greater than Houdini with an invisibility cloak.

Light faded in the office, forcing her to look up long enough to notice the clock. As if on cue, Aunt Laura hollered down, "Time to call it a night. I think there are town rules about working too late. This ain't Atlanta."

Scarlet stood and stretched the kinks from her neck and back. She grabbed her phone and remembered Henry's proposal which broke through her vigil to save the café. Exhaustion fogged her brain, so she lumbered up the back stairs to their second-floor apartment where she settled in at the settee next to the front windows to watch the clouds roll in and the moon hover at the edge of the mountain peak.

When she heard the shower cut on, she knew it would be safe to pull out her phone and text Henry back. Her thumbs hovered over the tiny letters, but she didn't move them. This should be an easy answer. They'd been together for two years. Sure, she didn't like the tone of his message, but she had left him to run the business on his own. Besides, Aunt Laura had never met him, so she didn't understand how he communicated. He was a strong man who only showed his real self in private, certainly not over a text message.

Texting didn't offer tone or inflection, and she couldn't think what to type. Besides, this subject required a real conversation. She tapped. *Can you talk?*

Her eyes were heavy, but she knew they needed to speak about getting married. Certainly, a proposal came with a discussion about the future. They'd never talked about the important things like children and religion and all of the things engaged couples should know about each other. For the last 730 days, they'd only concentrated on the future of the business, not their personal plans.

Her phone chimed.

Nothing to talk about. See you by the twenty-fifth or not at all.

Perhaps the day had zapped all her energy because she didn't feel anything. No anger, resentment, sadness, aching to be with him. She didn't have a desire to hop in her car and race back to Atlanta. Sure, she'd go back, but she had two more weeks. They didn't have the epic relationship of teenage dreams and hopes. This was real, and she appreciated something solid and dependable.

Maybe because she understood Henry, and that was a good thing. He was a reliable, direct, and driven man who would always stick around. His word meant something. When he said they would marry, she had no doubt he'd walk down the aisle and spend the rest of his life with her. That meant something.

She'd never have to worry about him running off and abandoning her.

Not like mother had.

Only fantasies promised passion and happily-ever-afters. Real life didn't offer both.

Scarlet tossed the phone to the cushion by her side and watched the moon rise higher like a beacon in the night. The quiet soothed her, and she propped her head up on the back of the couch. How many nights had she looked up at the sky and talked to Duke about her mother and his father? He'd held her while she cried when her mother didn't show at Christmas year after year despite receiving a postcard promising that she'd be there. Then he'd sit by her side after Christmas as she penned a letter expressing her disappointment and hope for the next year. And after a month, he'd cradle her in his arms again, her cheek pressed to his strong chest, when no reply came.

"What's got you entangled in such a mental war?" Aunt Laura's voice echoed like Santa's laughter.

"Nothing. Just tired." Scarlet curled her knees to her chest allowing Aunt Laura to sit in front of her on the couch.

"Denial. How long can you hold on to that?"

Scarlet opened her mouth to protest, but she snapped it shut. No use, the woman would never listen.

"Can I ask you something, and you'll give an honest answer? If not to me, then to yourself?"

Scarlet sighed. "I already know what you're going to ask."

"Maybe, but I promise to make you MeeMaw's famous chicken pot pie if you indulge me for a minute."

Scarlet's mouth watered. "You fight dirty."

"I'll sling mud any day if I know it's good for you." Aunt Laura tapped Scarlet's knee in that loving way she'd perfected over the years. Not that she had known much about being a mother when she gave up world travel to be home with a child, but she'd developed more maternal instincts than Scarlet's own mother ever possessed. She owed her everything.

"Go ahead. I promise to listen."

"I think you and I both know you left for college because you didn't want to be a burden to me any longer."

Scarlet shot up and dropped her feet to the floor. "I never said that. I'm thankful for all the years you gave me."

"That's just it. I never gave you anything, yet you gave me everything. To be honest, I never felt more complete than when I had you come into my life. I should've told you before you left for school, but I didn't want you to go. I love you. I know I'm your aunt, but in my heart you'll always be my daughter."

Tears pricked at the corner of Scarlet's eyes. "You didn't want me to leave? You didn't say anything."

Laura settled on the sofa by Scarlet's side. "I didn't want to hold you back. Part of me hoped that if you went to college, you'd prove to yourself that you're nothing like your mother. By finishing your degree, you'd realize that you finish what you start. Then I thought you'd come home and marry Duke and settle down."

"Duke? We're just friends." Scarlet let out a nervous sound, something between a hose with a leak and a laugh.

"So you both keep telling yourselves, but I see it. You love him. You always have."

"Me?"

Aunt Laura did the I'm-calling-you-out head tilt. "To yourself if not to me, remember?"

Silly ideas floated like fairies in Scarlet's brain, but who had time for fantasies when they were living in real life? "Fine, maybe I once or twice hoped something might happen between us, but it never did. And trust me, Duke had plenty of chances. We spent every day together, and I thought we were growing closer."

Scarlet tightened her knees to her chest, wanting to curl into the fetal position and never come out again. "Do you remember my last Christmas Eve here?"

"Yes."

"That night," Scarlet closed her eyes remembering the green dress, the hours of perfecting her makeup, the nervous energy, "I thought we were going on our first real date. Having our first real kiss. But he never showed." Her voice cracked.

"I know. But it's been ten years, and I know he loves you." Aunt Laura's words sent a flash of hope as bright as the north star, but it quickly burned out.

"Trust me, he doesn't. He might flirt with me now and then, but he thinks of me as his sister or something. We've been alone together, at night under the stars, holding each other with no supervision, and he never once tried to kiss me or anything else."

"He has his reasons for that."

"Like what?"

"Not my business to tell you. Talk to Duke. Ask him what happened."

"You've got it wrong. Trust me. I'd know if he really liked me. Besides, why would his childhood friend ask why he didn't show up that night when I had no reason to believe it was a real date?" Scarlet scooted from Aunt Laura to put distance from her manipulation. "I won't humiliate myself like that. None of this matters anyway; I'm engaged to be married so the past is the past."

"You accepted?"

"Not yet, but—"

"Good, then it's not too late." Laura shot up into perfect posture. "Promise me you'll give it two weeks before you decide to return to Atlanta. Talk to Duke, spend some time with him."

"No. I need to get back to Henry."

"Ask yourself what you're afraid of. If you truly love Henry and you plan to marry him, then you shouldn't feel anything for Duke."

Scarlet fidgeted with the pull in her shirt hem. Marriage was about more than fanciful notions of love and emotions. "It's wrong to spend time alone with another man when I'm in a relationship."

Aunt Laura shrugged. "Is it? I thought you were just friends."

"Subtle, really."

Aunt Laura rose from the couch holding her bad hip. "Besides, doc says I need help for a couple more weeks. I had a total hip replacement, remember?"

"I told you I can pay for a nurse when I leave."

"No, not having a stranger help me. I didn't pawn you off on no nanny."

"Don't hold any punches there, auntie."

"I won't when it comes to protecting you, niece."

A hammering sound outside drew Scarlet's attention. She rose up on her knees and pulled the curtain back but couldn't see anything with the awning blocking her view.

"Let me ask you something else. Do you trust a man because he says he'll never leave you or a man who's never left?"

"He might have physically remained in Cherry Creek, but he was farther away than Atlanta from me."

"And you never asked him why." Aunt Laura popped one hip out with southern attitude but then straightened as if remembering the pain.

"Besides, no red-blooded man is going to keep his hands off a woman all those years. And Duke Trenton is as red-blooded as they come."

"You have a point. He was once the most sought-after bad

boy, star baseball player, gorgeous guy in town. Many a swooning girl trailed after him."

"Exactly."

"Then if he didn't like you, why didn't he ever snag one of those?"

"He dated; remember prom?"

"I do, and the disappointed little girl who wished she was his date. But you weren't. You were off limits back then for many reasons." Aunt Laura brushed Scarlet's hair behind her shoulder. "Tell me something, all those nights you sat on the front porch watching for shooting stars, what did you wish for?"

Scarlet shrugged not wanting to think back to those years.

Aunt Laura raised a brow, but without another comment, she disappeared into the kitchen leaving her words to echo in Scarlet's head.

The front porch wasn't the only place she made wishes. How many times had she been under the stars at Duke's side? He'd point out a swoosh of light with a tail and then look at her, but never did he grant her the one wish she truly wanted.

A kiss.

The hammering turned to sawing, and by the end of their conversation, Scarlet's curiosity won and she marched down the steps to chastise whoever was making such a racket. She flipped on the light and flung the door open. "Do you know what time it is?"

Duke lifted a paint brush dripping with red paint onto a tarp.

She froze. Her gaze swept the area to decipher what he was doing and discovered a miniature version of Cherish Café.

He rose to his towering six-foot-two. His dark waves pushed to one side like some sexy workman from that old Coca-Cola commercial Aunt Laura insisted on showing her over and over again when she learned how to use the internet. "That's twice in one day you've scolded me." His smile quirked into an oh-so-sexy grin.

Her pulse bu-bumped at the speed of a reindeer on Christmas Eve. "You? I-I'm sorry. I mean…" Snowflakes melted on her heated face.

"I'm joking. I guess I was making too much noise. I'll probably get a visit from Sheriff Lomack at any moment.

He dropped the paint brush into a bucket and joined her at the door. "You shouldn't be out here without your coat."

His hands rubbed her arms. She shivered. Not from the cold but from his touch. She backed away, retreating from him and empty promises. This wasn't right. *Fiancé. Life in Atlanta. Nothing for me here.*

But no matter how hard she tried to focus on the right thing to do, her eyes betrayed her and looked to his lips. And all she wanted was to finally have that elusive kiss.

Three

DUKE FORGOT ABOUT HIS LOST LOAN, HIS BUSINESS, AND ALL HIS GOALS in the time it took for Scarlet to take a breath. She bit her full bottom lip, drawing his attention to his one true desire in life.

He knew that look. He'd longed to see it ever since the night she told him she got into the University of Georgia on a full scholarship. He'd planned to tell her on Christmas Eve how he wanted to follow her anywhere, but he couldn't follow her there. Not after he'd lost his baseball scholarship and all his dreams.

If he kissed her now, it could cause her to run. He knew her too well. She was in a relationship with another man. A man not worthy of her. A sobering thought that gave him strength to back away. "I should be going. I'll come back in the morning to put a second coat on before your breakfast rush."

She brushed past him, her arm grazing his. Even through his jacket, his hair stood at attention as if to pierce through his coat to touch her the way he longed to touch her since he first saw her this morning.

"Is this..." She shook her head. "You built this?"

He shrugged. "We always said we wanted our own free

library where people could enjoy our favorite books. A place where we could swap our favorites without having to set up a secret meeting. I can take it down if you want."

"Don't you dare." She wrapped her arms around her middle and looked at him. "It's the most amazing thing I've seen since returning to Cherry Creek."

With those few words, he stood a little taller, not feeling like such a failure after his loan meeting. "I'm glad you like it. I wanted to make it in a different shape, but if I didn't follow zoning, they'd rip it down."

Scarlet snapped her attention to him. "They better not."

"There it is."

She tilted her head, blinking and brushing snowflakes from her lashes. "What?"

"The fire in your eyes. You were such a force when we were kids. Fearless and bold and adventurous."

She touched the scar at her temple. "Right. All that got me was a nickname."

His insides twisted. "Wait, is that why you thought I called you scar?"

A light flicked on across the street and he knew they were being watched by a friendly neighbor. "Of course."

He wanted to run over and pull Scarlet into his arms and hold her tight, but instead, he tried to form words to express his emotions. Not easy, but Aunt Laura had been working with him on communicating instead of grunting and waving so that he'd have a chance to secure a loan. "I called you Scar because you were tough and original and fearless. You got that mark on your temple when you saved me from falling from our tree. I thought you knew."

She shook her head. "There are a lot of things I never understood."

He couldn't hold back any longer. He slid his coat off and

wrapped it around her shivering frame. "Come on. I'll get you inside, and I vow never to call you Scar again."

"No, I like it. I hadn't realized." She took a long breath and eyed the library box in front of her. "I think there is a lot I hadn't realized. Come inside with me, and I'll make us both some hot chocolate to warm up."

What hadn't she realized? Her words were weighted with subtext based on the low tone of her voice. He made quick work of cleaning up so he could get inside with her to find out what she meant. He knew gossip could fly about them being alone together, but maybe Laura was right and he had to stop worrying about what people think and do what he thought would be best. And saving Scar from a bad marriage would be best.

He tossed his gear into the back of the truck and found Scarlet at the bistro table with a cup waiting in front of an empty chair with his coat slung over the back across from her. The dim under-cabinet lighting and the streetlight outside filtering into the space gave a romantic feel to the place.

Aroma of fresh hot chocolate welcomed him to sit.

"Tell me about your loan meeting today." Scarlet tilted her head at the chair across from her.

He plopped down, grabbed his mug, and took a gulp of too-hot liquid that made him cough and his eyes water. She scooted her chair next to him and patted his back followed by slow, comforting circles.

Heat rushed through him from toes to throat, from spine to heart. "Excuse me. I should've realized hot chocolate would be hot." He chuckled, but he'd burn his tongue a second time if it meant getting her to touch him again.

Her fingers abandoned his back and swiped his nose. "Dot of whip there."

Her chest rose and fell. The space shrunk to millimeters

between want and self-control. It had always been that way between them. The attraction nearly drove him mad, but he waited because he knew Scarlet could never be a high school fling, she would only ever be a forever love.

"Your loan?"

Rich chocolate lingered in his mouth but not as long as his disappointment. "Not happening," he shrugged.

"Why? Your vegetables are amazing and inexpensive compared to the big stores. I'd pay three times what we do here for that in Atlanta and they wouldn't be as fresh."

He tapped the rim of his glass. "Said I didn't have a solid business plan, but we both know my reputation's the real reason."

She smacked him on the shoulder. "Get over yourself already." A sip of coco and a huff sounded before she spoke again. "You're not your father, and the bank doesn't care about reputation, they care about a solid business plan and numbers. Bring what you submitted to the bank tomorrow morning before we open, and I'll take a look."

"I can't ask you to do that," he argued, but he loved the idea of an excuse to spend more time with her.

"What? Don't trust me?"

"It's not that." He wanted to tell her that she should leave the loser that sent her a proposal via text, but like ten years ago, he remained silent, keeping his feelings to himself. Aunt Laura would call him a shmuck.

"Terry College of Business grad not good enough? A girl who co-runs a successful tech business in Atlanta not a strong enough resume?"

"I didn't say—"

"Relax." She sat back giggling and raised her drink to her lips but lowered it again. "I'm only teasing. I think you forgot how to laugh."

"No, it's just that I hadn't seen that beautiful smile until now to remind me how to be happy."

She hid behind her mug for a long gulp, but he saw the way her eyes were wide and full of mischief.

They sat silent for a few minutes listening to the hum of the fridge in the back room. "Fixed the fridge already?"

Scarlet's nose crinkled in a cute *Bewitched* kind of way. "Doubt it was ever really broken."

Soft steps overhead reminded him they weren't completely alone. But they were good at this. The teasing, flirting, dancing around everything while having fun. "Aunt Matchmaker strikes again."

She averted her gaze to her fingernails the way she always did when she wanted to avoid answering a question.

"Can I ask you something?" He dared to nudge into dangerous, black-diamond-level conversation. "What is it about the guy back in Atlanta that won your heart? Why does he deserve Scarlet Cherish?"

"Deserve?" She set her mug down and lifted her chin. "Maybe I'm the one that has to work to deserve him."

"I doubt that," he said in his firmest tone.

"It's not a matter of deserving someone. It's about compatibility. Wanting the same things. Making a lasting bond over what each of you wants and needs."

"You mean he's a big city guy, and you have no desire to return to Cherry Creek." Thoughts of giving up his land, his business, his life to run off to the big city pinched him.

"That's not it. I mean, there isn't any work for me here. I need to be in Atlanta so in that sense, yes, that is a contributing factor."

His heart ached to have a purpose and a place in her world. "What about love and romance like the books we used to read?"

"Stories. That isn't real life."

He scooted his mug away, his stomach churning with uncertainty but he had to be bold to break up a soon-to-be bad marriage. "What about the legend of *Once Upon a Kiss*?"

Scarlet waved off the notion. "It's just that, a legend."

"Laura says the book's real. I doubt it. I don't believe in miracles, but I do believe in work and dedication and love. Doing things for people to show how much you care. Love isn't a transaction, it's a feeling."

"That sounds like my aunt." Her gaze narrowed. "Wait a minute. The library box." She stood, scooting the chair out with a loud squeal against the hardwood floors. "That was her idea, wasn't it?"

Warning alarms blared. "I only wanted to show you what kind of life exists here. The one you left behind where friends and family care about you."

"So she told you to make that." Scarlet stabbed a finger at the window.

He stood. "No."

"Duke Trenton, don't you lie to me." For the first time since they spoke, she dropped her big city pretense and used her country twang on him. A warning if he'd ever heard one.

"She might have hinted that I should show you how much I care. As a friend, you know."

"I'm such a fool. I thought—"

Hope swelled. "Thought what?" He cupped her elbow, willing her to talk to him, but she jerked away and swung open the front door. Aa blast of chill rushed into the room and dropped the temperature almost as fast as her cold stare. "I think it's late and you should leave."

Her dismissal stirred his anger and pride. "Right. I won't bother you again." He swung his coat over his shoulder and walked out the door.

"Wait."

He stopped at the curb and about-faced, finding her leaning against the door jamb, her gaze on the stars in the sky. "We're friends, and friends help each other. Be here at 5:30 AM. I'll look at your stuff while I do prep."

"Friends? I guess I should've checked the zoning permissions on our relationship. I won't overstep again. I'll be here. Thanks."

"Don't be late." Her voice softened to a teasing tone.

"No, ma'am." He saluted and winked.

He'd be here, first thing, along with a plan to figure out how to prove to her that she deserved better than that boyfriend in Atlanta. And he knew just the way to show her how he felt. It might not be the legendary book promising love at Christmas but a book that would prove how much he cherished her. A book he'd clung to for a decade. A book that would show her small-town living was much better than big-city life. Especially with him. A man who always had and always would love her.

Four

SCARLET TIPTOED FROM HER ROOM AND DOWN THE HALL. NO NEED TO wake up Aunt Laura this morning to twist her thoughts. After a night of tossing and turning with intermittent dreams of silly love legends and kissing under the stars, exhaustion threatened to take her back to bed at this ungodly hour.

The *Ain't Too Proud to Beg* soundtrack echoed down the hall from the kitchen. "Aunt Laura?"

No answer, so she peered through the swinging kitchen door to spot her dancing with hips swaying and gyrating. "What the?"

Aunt Laura spun; a wooden spoon covered in cake batter dropped to the floor as did her expression. "What are you doing up so early?"

"What are you doing dancing when you couldn't walk straight yesterday? Surgery complications, huh?"

She bent down and retrieved the spoon without limitations. "Gig's up I guess."

"You've been faking it all this time?"

"No, I did have hip replacement remember?"

"And the doctor said it would be months before you could

return to work. That's why I'm here. To take care of you. Why I'm not back at home with my fiancé."

Aunt Laura's lips folded down. "Then you told him yes."

"No. I mean, yes. I mean, I haven't told him anything yet, but I'm going to now." Scarlet spun on her heels, returned to her room, yanked her suitcase from under the ruffled bed skirt, and tossed it onto the mattress.

"What are you doing?" Aunt Laura stood wearing the apron Scarlet made her in the fifth grade. The ruffles on the arms were crooked, and there were moth holes in the skirt, but the woman never wore anything else in the kitchen.

Scarlet yanked open a drawer and grabbed a load of sweaters and tossed them into her luggage. "I'm packing."

"I can see that, but why? You have two more weeks."

"Because you don't need me, and it's time for me to get back to my life." She scooped her T-shirts out of a drawer and tossed them into her bag, then went to the closet to grab her dresses, but when she returned the shirts were gone.

Aunt Laura stood with her mischievous, twitching eye.

"Stop that."

"What?"

"Manipulating and lying and using anything you can think of to get what you want." Scarlet tossed her dresses into the empty suitcase with hangers and all.

"You don't need to leave. You were ordered to return within two weeks."

"Ordered?"

Aunt Laura crossed her arms. "It's what it was. You say I'm manipulating, but whatever trickery I choose is because I'm doing what I think's best for you, not myself. Can you honestly stand there and say that this man—"

"Henry."

"That your Harry is what you really want in life or what you tell yourself you deserve?"

The clock chimed in the hall, so Scarlet decided her non-packing could wait until after she met with Duke and helped with his business plan. The minute she finished, she could get out of here and far from her meddling aunt.

"You know he loves you. Always has. And I'm not talking about Hank."

"Harry. I mean Henry." Scarlet threw her hands up in the air and stormed out of her old room, but Aunt Laura trailed behind her all the way down the steps. Steps that she took like a three-year-old chasing after a candy cane. "And you're wrong."

"Am I? Then why'd he make that special library box for you? Do you know how many women in this town would fall at his feet for such a gesture?"

Scarlet spun around to face her. "I know you told him to build that. You manipulated him just like you manipulated me. No matter how much you try to keep me here, it isn't going to happen. He doesn't love me."

"What if I can prove it?"

Breath caught somewhere between Scarlet's throat and words, so she clamped her mouth shut in faux anger.

"I never told him to build that for you. He came up with that all on his own. I simply told him that Harold told you to get home by the 25th or you were done."

"Har-Henry. What's your point?"

"My point is that Duke Trenton is a good man."

"So is Han...Henry."

"He's a man who knows you and what you like and dislike, what your childhood dreams were, and what you adored. That man wanted to marry you."

"You're wrong." Gooey emotions stuck to her insides, but

she'd take a Clorox wipe to her heart if necessary to escape false hope.

"Am I? Ask him about this." Aunt Laura pulled a folded piece of paper from her pocket and handed it to Scarlet.

She opened the note and read one line. "Meet me at our tree at midnight." Scarlet blinked at her, trying to decipher the one sentence as if it were a secret code. "Yeah, and we used to leave notes like that all the time."

"This one he brought on Christmas Eve ten years ago." Aunt Laura gripped her shoulders. "I didn't see him leave it, but I saw him retrieve it from under the pot on the front porch and throw it away in our outside garbage. When I saw a broken man leave, curiosity won, and I retrieved what he'd tossed in there."

Scarlet shook her head. A tingle danced up the nape of her neck. "It means nothing. He was supposed to be over at eight and never showed."

"You and I both know it means everything."

"Why? What do you know?"

"I know he asked you to meet him that night for an important reason."

"What reason?"

"That's not for me to tell you." Aunt Laura curled Scarlet's fingers around the note. "Ask him. If you dare to face the truth. The truth you've always run from. A truth that he knew, and that's why he let you go even though he loved you."

Scarlet shoved the note in her pocket and turned to face the window in the café, to look out at the mountains where she always found peace in a storm. "More manipulations."

"Believe what you want. I won't force you to stay. He's not going to abandon you, Scarlet. You deserve real happiness no matter what your mother's parting words were. She was a sick and selfish lady, and you deserve better."

Conviction hugged Scarlet's resentment away and she

reached behind her; Aunt Laura took her hand soothing her emotions. "I got better."

The old diesel truck backfired its announcement of Duke coming down Main Street, shattering the early morning quiet with a pulse-jumping bang.

"Ask him. If you dare. But you better be ready to hear the truth because that boy deserves a happily ever after, too. And between the both of us, he doesn't believe in miracles. And you, hon, are his only desired miracle."

Five

CHRISTMAS.

It had been a long time since he had any warm feelings toward that holiday. He patted the old, worn book on the passenger seat.

Last night, he tried to explain his feelings, but conversation had never been the strongest tool in his relationship belt. Not that Scarlet and he had ever been in a relationship.

Fat snowflakes stuck to the trees and dotted his windshield just like the night he'd come to tell her he'd chosen to take the scholarship at University of Georgia instead of Stanford so they could be together. The night he'd planned on telling her how much he loved her.

He twisted his hands around the steering wheel and eyed his wrists. The ones that had handcuffs slapped around them before he could knock on her door.

Puffs of air escaped his tight lungs. He smacked the dashboard hoping to jostle the heat into working or pound out his frustration. Either way, it felt good to let out some nervous energy.

Duke pulled around back and parked his truck. The produce could freeze out here, but he found himself caring less about his business plan and a little more about the woman who promised to help him.

Was Laura right? Could he believe in Christmas miracles?

No. But he could believe in telling the truth. If he even had a shot at saving her from a horrible marriage, even if she didn't want him, he'd embarrass himself to take that chance.

All night, he'd tossed and turned thinking about the way Scarlet's hair framed her angelic face. Her perfect curves and perfect lips and perfect heart. And he knew one thing—she deserved more than a text proposal.

He grabbed the folder with his business plan, his laptop, and the small, worn copy of their favorite book he'd kept all these years. The one that had remained on his nightstand ever since he watched her board that bus out of town.

He hopped out of the truck, took a deep breath, and marched ahead to face his fear of rejection. He didn't even make it across the parking lot before Scarlet stood with the door open for him to enter the kitchen. "Good morning."

She smiled, the kind that warmed a man coming in from a long, cold day working on the farm.

"Good morning." The muscles in his mouth twisted at the sight of her uncaffeinated expression. "Waited for me to have your first cup?" He was honored. Scarlet never waited for anyone before her coffee, not even when she was twelve.

"Why do you think that?" she asked.

"Because your eyes aren't wide and full of mischief."

Scarlet slammed the old metal door behind him and ushered him to the café. "That's observant of you... or am I that easy to read?"

"No, not at all. I just know you." He set his stuff on a bistro table and dared to toss a comment to home plate. "I'm sure your fiancé notices things like that all the time."

She turned on the espresso machine causing a squeal that ended their conversation. A foul ball, obviously. Once she placed two cups on the table and sat down across from him, he knew she'd try to hide behind business.

"You're doing it now, aren't you?" She raised her armor of warm beverage to her lips and peered over the mug.

"Doing what?"

She took a sip then set the mug down, leaned back in her chair, and folded her hands on the table. "You're so good at reading me. What's your observation?"

He lifted his chin, his nerves jolting like he'd had twenty espressos already. "I'm not sure you want to know what I have to say."

She rested her hands by her sides as if she was relaxed and didn't care, but the way her right eye twitched told him it was a forced posture. "Try me."

"I would, but I need your help, and I don't want to send you running from this table." He leaned forward and clasped his hands in front of him, daring her to run.

She matched his position with hands only inches from his. "I promise not to run away until after I help you with your proposal. Now tell me."

He captured her gaze and hoped never to let it go. "You're going to remain professional with a rigid stance and distance between us to avoid any type of friendliness."

She lowered one shoulder, then the other, and he had to fight his knowing grin from showing.

"Okay, Sherlock. Let me deduce your actions." She sat further forward, leaning on the table, daring to edge her hands closer. "You're nervous that I won't be impressed by your report and that I'll judge you for your work."

He leaned in, matching her distance, yet still not daring to cross the line by touching her. "I guess we both can read each other."

"We're both good readers," she snickered.

This is the opening. Go for it, man.

His muscles tightened, but he forced his arm to move to his side. He retrieved the book and handed it to her. "Then maybe you'd like to read this again."

A blizzard of emotions caused a white-out expression on her face. It took several seconds of her eyes doing an elf jig around the cover then snapping to him then back to the book before her face animated into a childlike grin. "You still have this?" She turned the book, brushed her delicate fingers across the title, and sucked in her bottom lip.

"Of course. It was our favorite. Out of all the books we bickered about, this one we always agreed on."

She shook her head. Tears shining in her eyes. "Wow, I didn't think..."

"Didn't think what?" He dared to push.

She cleared her throat and opened the book, but he covered her hand to shut it. "Don't. You're not ready."

"Ready for what?"

His heart thu-thumped with apprehension. "I wrote a note inside to you."

She curled her fingers around his, sending heat up his arms.

Her lips parted and her chest heaved in; her eyes darted to his hand. "I thought you wanted me to read your note."

He shook his head left, then right. "I don't think you're ready to read it."

"Why?"

"Because I wrote it on Christmas Eve ten years ago," he said in a distant, strained tone. His throat threatened to close and never allow him to speak again. "I was going to give it to you at midnight when we met at our secret spot."

Her chest rose and fell, her eyes wide and yet distant. She quirked a brow at him and tilted her head in that way only Scarlet could manage. The tiny scar winked at him. "The night you never showed?" Her voice sounded barely above a whisper as if she feared to say the words aloud.

"Yes." He swallowed the walnut-sized lump in his throat and sat back to try to suck in some air. "I can get another copy to go in the library box. I know it was always your wish to share that book with everyone, but this one is for you and you alone."

She held up one finger, slid her hand from under his, stealing his joy, and then disappeared from the room.

He crumbled over the table, his head in his hands, forcing himself not to hyperventilate. What would she do when she read his message? Would she disappear and never speak to him again? This could backfire and she could run from him straight into the worthless boyfriend's arms.

Soft steps echoed from the stairs, then overhead. His breath came in short, lung-constricting gasps.

Her gallop down the stairs was bold and loud before she reappeared in the hallway. His neck muscles tightened, threatening to choke him. She stood with a goofy grin and her hands behind her back.

He swallowed and willed himself to remain calm. "What'cha got there?"

She held out her own copy of *All Creatures Great and Small*.

Like he'd been taken over by the mind of a fifteen-year-old girl, he questioned why she had that book here with her—what did it mean? Was it only because she loved the story or because she pined away for him? He shook out the wayward thoughts and cleared his throat, willing himself to say something. "Guess it's still your favorite book, too."

She sat and moved in close as if to whisper a secret. "Do you remember when we read this for the first time?"

"Do I? Of course." He brushed his thumb over her scar. His pulse jumped and pumped. She leaned into his touch but then sat back in the chair out of his reach.

She toed the floor and kept her gaze downcast. "That was the day you kissed my cut to make it better."

"You remember that?"

"I remember being in a teenage body. The type that couldn't breathe or think when your lips brushed my temple. I remember willing your mouth to travel lower to my cheek... to my mouth." Her mouth twitched. "Foolish teenager, right?"

"Then we were both foolish because all I wanted to do that night was kiss you." He breathed out the words that he'd been holding for all his life.

"Then why didn't you?" she asked.

"Because I thought I wasn't good enough for you."

She shook her head. "You were too good for me. You were the most popular boy in the county school. A ball player—the girls threw themselves at you. I always thought I was your secret friend that you didn't want anyone to know about because the geeky little bookworm would ruin your reputation."

He wanted to sweep her into his arms and kiss her now, to show her how wrong she was, but that wouldn't solve anything. She had to choose. He'd never ask her to stay here for him. And she never would. Not even after she read the message —he knew that—but perhaps it would make her think twice about marrying a man all wrong for her when she knew there were other possibilities.

After a long, calming breath where he allowed his brain to function past carnal thoughts, he stood and took her hand. "All I ever wanted was to have you on my arm, but I didn't want to risk your reputation, afraid that hanging out with the town's most depraved family would tarnish you."

She chuckled. "Boy we were dumb teenagers, weren't we?"

He dropped her hand and let out a stress-relieving laugh.

"I miss that."

"What?"

"Your laugh. The kind that is so jolly it makes others feel elated even in the darkest of times." She fidgeted with the book he'd given her, and he saw the mental war going on—her jaw tightened and her lips pressed into a thin line.

He held his breath, waiting to see what she'd do. Would she open and read it now?

She stood and swiped her copy from the table. "Tell you what, let's put my copy in the library now."

"You sure?"

"Of course, what harm could that do? The box needs books, right?"

"True." He forced himself not to mention the abandoned copy on the table. The one that confessed his love and told her he wanted to be with her forever. And when she strung her fingers between his and tugged him toward the front door, he didn't care about words; he never wanted to let her go, to give up the warmth of her skin. He didn't care about any bank or gossip in town with her by his side.

Without even donning their coats, they made it to the box. Despite the heavier snowfall now sticking to the sidewalk, the cold didn't drive them inside.

"Look, someone's already put a book in it. How cool is that?" Scarlet opened the door and pulled out a forest-green hardback book with frayed edges. Her face went snow white.

"What's wrong?"

Scarlet held out the book to him. "It's the Christmas book."

Duke took it and eyed the title, *Once Upon a Kiss* written in gold lettering with a mistletoe imprint below the title. "This is THE book? The book that promises Christmas miracles? The book that promises true love by Christmas?"

Six

THE BOOK.

The legendary book.

The guaranteed happily ever after with the man she loves.

Snowflakes melted on Scarlet's heated skin. Her breath escaped in small white puffs.

Duke slid her copy of *All Creatures Great and Small* into the free little library box. "It doesn't look like much. I thought with the legend it carried, it would be more... ornate."

"It can't be. I mean. It's only a legend." Scarlet studied the plain cover with mistletoe under *Once Upon a Christmas Kiss*. She opened the book and slid her fingers over Ms. Chamber's inscription written in perfect cursive looping with graduated brilliance. The words sang like a childhood lullaby whispering in her memories.

To my dearest friend Charlotte. May your heart be filled with joy this Christmas season. I leave you with the long requested true love story of my parents from years ago. May it bring you the happiness and peace it has always brought to me—and maybe a love of your own. I will miss you sweet friend. Yours Affectionately, Elizabeth Chambers

More messages from women who'd found their true love were scribbled in various handwritings and ink colors.

True love does exist.

Once upon a Christmas, I found my husband thanks to this book.

Y'all, this book is the real deal! After reading this story, I met my forever love at the Cherry Creek Post Office...

A heartfelt thanks to Miss Chambers for the romantic Christmas magic she weaved into this story. I thought I would never find that special someone, but I truly believe this book made it happen.

Dozens of inscriptions littered the opening pages, but her gaze snagged on one in particular.

Don't settle. Find Mr. Right.

The streetlight flickered, calling her attention back to the present. "Is this authentic?"

Duke covered her hands with his and scooted into her side, stealing the remaining breath from her lungs. "It looks like it's real. I can't believe the legend's true. I've heard about this book. Women have been trying to find it at the library for years, and the librarian laughs each time someone enters the building asking for it. People say you can't find the book, the book has to find you."

Scarlet spent too much time skimming the messages from front to back, shivering in the cold. Not that she felt a hint of chill, but apparently her body did because Duke closed the little library door and cuddled her into his side, her shoulder easily fitting under his arm and her chest pressed into his side.

The warmth she once felt when they'd snuggled watching the stars shot through her like a reindeer flying after consuming three Monster drinks.

He ushered her inside and held her to his chest, the book blocking their connection, but she felt his arms around her, his strong, reassuring, I-believe-in-everything embrace. His breath grazed the top of her head.

She stood there, swaying, clinging, aching to move the book out of the way and feel him against her.

Footsteps overhead jolted her to reality, and she nudged out of his arms. "Coffee should warm us up."

He remained standing there with his mouth downturned and his eyes soft and longing.

Great, the book already played with her head.

"What exactly is the legend?" Duke asked.

She realized she was still holding the book and tossed it onto the table like a bad fruitcake. "That whoever has possession of the book will find true love by Christmas Eve."

Duke cleared his throat. "Then I guess you'll be married by Christmas to your true love back in Atlanta."

She didn't respond; she couldn't. Harry... Henry... true love? "That's just a silly lie people tell to give hope to those desperate to find someone. I bet Aunt Laura put this in there. It's probably a fake."

The bitterness in her voice coiled around her heart. She collapsed into the bistro chair knocking into the table. The dark liquid sloshed over and seeped into the tiny dents and nicks the way thoughts of this book eked into her mind and solid life plans.

No, she wouldn't be like her fickle mother and run out on her vow to be with someone. She'd committed to Har...Henry. Darn Aunt. She swirled and twirled Scarlet's feelings faster than her expensive espresso machine brewed perfect coffee.

"My papers!" Duke snatched his white papers but not before the brown liquid scarred the corner.

"Sorry. Oh goodness." Scarlet jumped into action, retrieved a rag from behind the counter, swiped up the mess the way she swiped away her wayward feelings, and took their coffees to dump. "I'll get us fresh drinks, and we'll get started."

"It's okay. I have deliveries to make before my produce

freezes out there. The temperature is dropping quickly, and they are saying a real snowstorm might hit us. I need to pick up the damaged produce and take it out to Johnson Ranch on my way back, too. Not to mention the fact I need to fix the barn roof so it won't cave in when it snows." He studied the papers for a second. "You don't want to marry him. You just believe it's the right path. A path you drew up the minute you found yourself alone on your aunt's doorstep when your mother didn't show to pick you up from boarding school that fateful Christmas." He locked gazes with her. "Don't do it."

"Not any of your business. You best go get to that work of yours."

"I won't bother you again." His words pierced her resolve, and she abandoned the coffee and rushed to his side without a thought.

It had been so long since she'd been around such friendship, she'd forgotten her manners. "Wait." She grabbed his hand to keep him from leaving her again. They'd been lifelong friends. She couldn't throw that away. "I promised to help, and I don't break my promises. Please, sit. You still have time. Heck, I can come help you with the roof. Remember when I helped when you tried to repair the attic floor in eighth grade?"

"You mean when you didn't step on the beam and fell through the roof, making it so I had two spots to repair." He chuckled. His thumb grazed her hand and her chest swelled.

"Hey, I still helped." She missed this. Their fun. Their connection.

"That and the fact that your aunt warned me that she'd have me put out to pasture if I ever let you get in the attic again."

His thumb dancing over her skin dizzied her. She needed space but not too much space. Having him here was like having a Christmas hug. Was it wrong that she wanted him in her life as a good friend? "My point is, we've been friends a long time. I know you avoided me when I arrived."

"I avoided you?" He stepped closer, but she retreated behind the counter. His hand was one thing, but that hungry look would tease any woman.

"I'll make us some fresh cups; get your stuff organized. I won't take no for an answer."

He joined her behind the bar, crowding her and her emotions into the corner. She attacked the espresso machine like a barn cat after a field mouse. And she knew he wasn't leaving until he got an answer to why she hadn't visited him.

"I didn't mean to avoid you, it's just that my aunt needed me. And this place has been slammed. And—"

"And you're engaged."

She closed her eyes, feeling the steam rise around her face. "No. I'm not."

He edged closer, causing her to jerk the cup. The scalding liquid scorched her skin. The ceramic mug flew from her hand and smashed against the hardwood floor.

His arms shot around her, ushering her to the sink. The cold water splattered full blast over her burning wrist, cooling the fire.

They didn't move for several seconds. He stood behind her, resting his chin on her shoulder. "How's that?" His lips brushed the edge of her ear and set fire to her entire body. His warm breath kissed and teased her friendship doctrine.

"Fine. I'm fine." She shut off the water and turned to retreat but instead found herself in his embrace. His gaze transfixed on her lips.

Her pulse pitter-pattered like children's feet on Christmas morning, running to unwrap their presents. Did he feel how hard her heart beat against her chest?

The smell of coffee faded. The lights glowed in romantic

hues. For over a decade, she'd dreamed of his lips on hers, and when he edged closer, she melted into him.

His mouth brushed her forehead.

Her cheek.

Her lips.

Seven

DUKE PULLED SCARLET TIGHTER. HE DARED TO OPEN TO THE possibility that miracles might still exist in the world. Because the minute he slid his lips softly across her mouth and she gasped, he knew life would never taste sweeter.

A light flicked on overhead, shattering the cozy kitchen in blinding rays.

He blinked and turned enough to catch a glimpse of Laura standing with her mouth dropped open and her eyes wide. "Oh, um. Sorry. I didn't know." She waved both her palms at them and backstepped to the light switch, flicked it off, and disappeared.

But when he turned to reengage, Scarlet bolted. He caught sight of the golden-red flames of her hair retreating. Standing on the other side of the counter, she shifted between feet and kept her gaze on the ground. "Right, um. I didn't realize how late it is. I'm sorry, you do need to go make your deliveries, and I need to open up shop. Listen... leave your papers here and I'll look them over and get them back to you this afternoon."

He looked down at the sludge of white papers saturated In brown brew on the floor—vital documents he'd abandoned to go to her aide. "Doesn't look like you have much to work with here."

She gasped and rushed back, collapsing onto her hands and knees in front of him, swiping the mess into a puddle of worthless, saturated, torn papers.

"Stop. There's no saving them."

"Maybe some things aren't meant to be saved," she whispered, but he heard every word. Words that popped his hope balloon.

She flung her hair back and eyed the mess. "Please, tell me you have this on your computer."

The hair slid right back over her face. He didn't dare brush it out of the way or help her up because he knew the moment had ended and there was no recovering it right now. Not the way she kept her distance and her lips far enough away not to engage again. She was doing that looking-everywhere-but-him move Duke had perfected long ago when he'd be on a bad date.

But he wouldn't give up. He'd taste her lips, and when he kissed her, she'd finally believe how much he loved her. Had always loved her. "Yes, of course. I can drop another copy off later."

"Or you could email it." She shrugged but didn't stand.

He stepped around, allowing her to stay on the floor despite his inner Southern gentleman screaming at him to help her up. "I'll email them to you, but if you really want to help, I need you to talk me through your changes."

It wasn't a lie—he wasn't good with written notes; he'd found out long ago that he was more of a doer than a visual learner.

"Right, sure."

He about faced and ran smack into Laura hiding in the shadows.

A giggle sounded, and she held two thumbs up at him. "Way to go," she whispered.

All the way to his truck, down the street, and through all his deliveries, his mind rested back on their almost kiss. It wasn't until he reached Ramen Johnson's farm to deliver the damaged produce that he realized he didn't remember half his morning.

The old yellowed farmhouse and brown barn stood out against the fallen snow. A pretty plot of land in the winter. Duke pulled up into the circular dirt drive and shut off the engine.

The weathered posts and front porch needed work before decay set in, but it wasn't his place to say anything.

Duke got out and heaved the bag from the truck and tossed it on the ground before he stretched and inhaled the fresh scent of pine. A woodpecker hammered a steady beat nearby. And darker snow clouds drifted closer to Cherry Creek.

Ramen came out of his barn, removing his gloves but tipping his hat lower on his head as if to hide the scars that kept him hidden away from the world. "Hey, you. Told you not to go out of your way."

The man around the same age as Duke stood a couple inches taller and several inches wider in the shoulders.

"It's no bother. I enjoyed the extra drive before getting back to my place." Duke scooted the bag of food scraps to the grassy knoll. "Besides, I knew you wouldn't leave here to pick anything up."

"They still calling me the Haunted Hermit?" Ramen chuckled.

"You know it." Duke ran a hand through his hair and eyed the man who'd avoided all relationships for so long he could be labeled a hermit easily.

"I go into town on occasion." Ramen grabbed the bag. "I don't have a reason to go in town every day anyway. Not like you. How's Scarlet?"

Duke leaned back against his truck and crossed his arms. "How's a recluse able to get intel from town?"

"Gossip travels on the wind 'round here. You know that."

"Maybe you should get a woman in town; then you'd break everyone's assumption about you."

He took one hand and jimmied his hat a little lower on his head. No matter how far he tugged the hat down, it wouldn't cover the scars along the side of his face. "Only way I'm getting a woman is if it's Halloween and I can wear a mask."

Duke thought about all the right things to say. Words dozens, if not hundreds, of people had already used to try to bring him out of his self-imprisonment. None of that would work, though. Like nothing anyone told Duke after his failure would change his mind about himself. "Nowadays, you don't need a pretty face. Women are all into broad shoulders and strong arms. You got that in multiples."

Ramen laughed. Good. That's what the man needed in his life. "Thanks, man. I'll keep that in mind."

Duke's phone buzzed so he slipped it from his pocket to see a text from Scarlet.

Meet me at the café in the morning.

His heart beat faster than the woodpecker burrowed into the tree.

"I know that look. I'll let you go." Ramen dared a glance up, startling Duke for trusting him with eye contact. His scars had faded, and they weren't that bad anymore. The skin had been grafted, but his features were still off a little, and one eye was white like cloudy glass. Duke didn't blame him for hiding out here far from the paparazzi since the accident that took him from his famous *Truth or Legend* show and his fiancé.

"Thanks, man. I'll bring you a load again tomorrow."

"Don't go out of your way."

"No trouble. But you ever want to stop by my farm and pick

up anything, feel free." Duke didn't want to give him an opportunity to refuse. Not when he understood falling from grace in the eyes of the town. But Ramen fell from grace in front of the eyes of the world.

Ramen didn't stand around to say goodbye. He disappeared into the barn leaving Duke to realize that no matter how much trouble he thought he had in life, he could always meet someone else that had it worse.

He shoved his truck into gear and bumped and bucked the old truck down the long, rocky driveway until he hit the main road.

He'd be meeting Scarlet tomorrow morning. Perhaps she'd read what he'd written and wanted to see him. If not, he had another way to remind her of what they once shared. He swung a U-turn in the middle of the road and headed out to the creek near the lake. He shot down East and West Main Street and didn't pull over until the secret trail beyond the dip in the road.

The snow covered their trail, but he'd been down it so many times when they were younger that he knew the way. It had been ten years since he'd visited their spot. It never seemed the right time. That's a lie. He never wanted to see it again without her.

He climbed over a fallen tree and pushed back some brittle brush and skidded down the embankment landing at the water's edge. Once he found his footing, he about-faced and looked up the hill to find bottles and cans and waste scattering the once-beautiful spot under the big oak tree.

His heart skipped and slid into a damp spot. How could this happen? He couldn't let Scarlet see this. His hand rubbed the ache from his chest, but he tightened his coat around his neck, trudged up to their spot, and dropped to his knees.

The sound of rushing water provided nature's music for his work. He tugged his gloves up, splayed his fingers, shoved garbage toward the tree, and then moved around to another spot and bulldozed more toward the tree.

An owl hooted his displeasure at the noise, but Duke didn't stop. He worked and worked and worked until sweat beaded on the back of his neck despite the icy chill in his fingers.

The debris became a junk pile, but he didn't have anything to put it in, so he'd have to go rummage through his truck to see if he had any bags or crates left. He got to his feet and shuffled back to his truck where he found one small crate.

This was going to be a long night, but he couldn't walk away from this. It was time for him to clean up the mess. The way he needed to clean up the mess he'd made out of his life. If there was even a chance the legend was true, then he'd work all night to make this place special again. Special enough to bring Scarlet tomorrow night. He'd leave her a note to meet him here like the old days. And when she arrived, he'd be ready with candles and wine and kisses.

He'd once and for all tell her how he felt, but he wouldn't ask her to stay. That would be her decision. If all this only ended up with her not marrying the wrong man, he'd have to live with that.

For now, all he could do was work. And work never frightened him.

Twenty trips and three cuts later, he managed to dump the last load into the truck bed. He went back and pushed around the snow to get rid of any stains from soda and beer.

Still not special enough. But it would be. Candles, lanterns, blankets. By the time he finished, it would be the perfect replication of a fictional setting.

When he stepped back, he could see it again.

He might not believe in miracles, but he could still wish for one. Better yet, he could make it for himself and for Scarlet.

Eight

Predawn sunlight cast faint streams of fiery golden rays. She ran her fingers over the cracked and worn cover of *All Things Great and Small.*

"You gonna stare at that book all day or you gonna open it to see what he wrote inside?" Aunt Laura sauntered into the café and settled in the seat across from Scarlet.

She'd been up all night thinking through everything, trying to figure out why she hadn't returned to Atlanta despite figuring out that her aunt didn't need her anymore. "Snoop much?"

Aunt Laura shrugged. "Happened to come down when you two were talking."

Scarlet shot her a sideways glower. "Eavesdropping, then."

"Doesn't change the question."

"I have a better question for you. Did you put that book in the free library box?" Scarlet shoved the *Once Upon a Kiss* book across the table, but Aunt Laura retreated from it.

"What? You really believe if you have that book you'll be in love by Christmas? That's insane. I'm going to prove the legend isn't real. Duke is headed here now, and when he gets here, I'm going to show him how to get his loan and then I'm going to return to Atlanta. I've worked too hard to make a life for myself; I'm not going to abandon it because of some stupid legend."

"Of course not," Aunt Laura said in an alarmingly convincing way.

"But?"

"But it isn't about how hard you've worked. You shouldn't have to work that hard to love someone."

"I'm not my mother. I won't walk away from something real to chase the next breeze. Nothing you say will change my mind."

"I can see that." Aunt Laura stood, smoothed out her shirt, and lifted her chin. "My words shouldn't weigh into your decision. I'm all healed up, so feel free to go."

"Fine, I will."

"But forget about the legendary book and open the one he gave you. Read his words."

Scarlet eyed the physical reminder that the man didn't even say goodbye to her before she left for college, never wrote, and never told her why he didn't want to see her again. "Nothing he says now can change my mind."

"Then open it."

Scarlet eyed the book and part of her knew Aunt Laura was right; she was scared to face whatever waited on the other side of that front cover. Because if something kept her here then she'd be no better than her mother, running out on someone she was supposed to be with. Then why hadn't Scarlet left yet? The question rolled through her mind once more and bumped into the truth. "I'm my mother."

"What?" Aunt Laura rubbed Scarlet's arm as if rubbing the cold from her limbs. "No, hon. You're nothing like her."

"Yes, I am. Think about it. My boyfriend tells me he's ready to marry me and I'm still here. That's exactly what my mother would do."

Aunt Laura shook her head. "No. You've got it all wrong. Your mother always ran from something good, you ran toward something good. Your life, your home, your family, your one true love."

"He was never mine to love." Scarlet shot from the table and paced the floor. Her fingers laced together behind her head, her elbows out, back straight, she tried to find air. "I'm leaving as soon as I help him with his loan. I won't be her." Scarlet's voice choked and she thought the grief would spill out of her. "You know, I don't know why it still hurts. I don't even want to see her again at this point."

"It hurts because you're not your mother. You have a kind and loving heart. There isn't a narcissistic bone in your body. Your mother craves attention. You crave love, so allow yourself to be loved." Aunt Laura never sounded so desperate. Her pleading tone clawed at Scarlet's determination.

She closed her eyes and allowed herself to go back to that moment when she sat on the school steps waiting to be picked up for Christmas break all those years ago. She should've known then that her mother would never return, but she clung to childish wishes for years.

"Christmas is a commercial holiday that makes people believe in happy families and bright futures. I'm not falling for that anymore. Life is real and hard when you live for the impossible things you can't control. My life might not be what you want, but it's perfect for me, and you need to respect that." Scarlet straightened the papers the way she planned to straighten her life.

Aunt Laura grabbed Scarlet's arms and spun her. Face-to-face, she trapped Scarlet into listening to her. "I see the way you light up when Duke enters a room. The way you flush when he looks at you. The smile when he touches you. I saw the way you lost yourself in his attention before I interrupted."

"Flashes of empty promises and broken dreams." Scarlet shoved from Aunt Laura, grabbed *Once Upon a Christmas Kiss*, and marched outside. She shot a glower over her shoulder. "This belongs to someone else, and if the legend is true, a person who wants true love will find it. I don't want such fanciful things in my life." She opened the glass doors to the beautiful free little library Duke created, shoved the book inside, and closed the door.

The unmistakable backfire of Duke's truck announced his arrival. "I ask you not to interfere any longer. I promise to visit you twice a year. If you truly believe I'm not my mother, then you take my word for it. That is the best I can offer. However, you're always welcome to move to Atlanta. I'd help you get set up and I'd take care of all your bills. I love you, Aunt Laura, and I'm grateful for everything you've done for me, so stop worrying I'll abandon you."

"Oh, dear child, I don't worry about you abandoning me. I worry about you abandoning yourself." Aunt Laura disappeared into the café leaving Scarlet to prepare to be strong and do the right thing.

His truck came into view, so she straightened her spine and her resolve and headed inside. Chopping sounds and banging warned Scarlet that Aunt Laura wasn't pleased.

Scarlet would prove to her next year that she'd spend Christmas with her, but this year she needed to be with Harris... Henry. Ugh, Aunt Laura had really done a number on her head.

The back door slammed shut followed by angry whispers from the kitchen filtering down the hall. Scarlet made sure her chair sat on the opposite side of the bistro table. Chin up, she offered a business smile when he entered the café. "Please, sit. I'll go over the notes with you like I promised."

"What happened?" Duke slid into the chair and reached for her hands, but she yanked them away and held them together in her lap.

"I've gone over everything, and the notes are on the page. The numbers are strong, but they are buried under a bunch of frivolous information that a bank doesn't care about. You have a strong business, stop trying to convince them with lengthy explanations that you're worthy of expansion and show that you are already doing well. Facts are all a bank will care about."

"I see." Duke leaned back, stretching his legs under the table until his foot raked along the side of her shoe. An instant flash of excitement clouded her plan for a moment, but she shook it off and bent her legs to tuck her feet under her chair. "Don't do this," he said, his voice low and longing.

"I'm not doing anything you didn't ask. Listen, stop trying to apologize for your family name and start focusing on what you have to offer the world. No one cares about where you came from, they only care about where you plan to go."

"I plan to go with you tonight to our spot. We need to talk, Scarlet."

She clasped her hands tighter, digging her nails into her skin. "There is nothing to talk about."

He shoved the chair back and knelt by her side, taking her hand in his and squeezing it tight enough that she couldn't pull away but without hurting her. "You're right. I need to stop worrying about being my father."

"Stop." Tears welled in her eyes, but she blinked them away. "Look at me."

She snapped her gaze straight to his and forced her voice to be calm and cold. "It doesn't matter what you say."

"It does." He abandoned her hands and cupped her cheek. "Listen to me, and when I'm done, if you still want to leave, I won't stop you."

She swallowed the Christmas miracle with a Grinch chaser reminding herself that today might be fun, but tomorrow is what matters.

"My senior year, I lost everything, but the worst thing I did was lose you. I pulled away, feeling unworthy, when I should've fought harder."

Her face muscles softened, and she drew her brows together. "What are you talking about? You decided to stay and take care of your father out of some sort of sick obligation."

"No, I lost my ball scholarship because of a stupid prank."

Scarlet's world tilted. "I don't understand. No, that's not true. I would've heard about this. Small town, remember?"

"It was hushed because it was the mayor's son. I agreed never to speak of it to anyone to avoid a felony charge. The mayor paid off the principal with a brand new car better than the one he owned, but the principal put the incident in my record and sent notices to the schools that had accepted me. The man was bitter because he signed a gag order, and when the papers reported the accident, it blamed him for reckless driving. He took it out on me. I thought it was personal then, but it wasn't. He was bitter and needed someone to punish, and I was the easy target."

Scarlet's hands trembled, her lips trembled, her heart trembled.

"I wasn't even the one drinking that night, but I was the last one in the car. I'm the one that set the emergency break. I didn't know it didn't work." His hand dropped lower, his thumb brushing across her lips. "My father had to come bail me out of jail for a change, but he didn't take me home to punish me. He drove me to the local bar, and I bought us both a beer knowing my life was over. I didn't drink it that night, but I still have it on my shelf to remind me never to be that stupid again."

She shook her head, tears streaming down her face. "No. not true."

"It's true. All of it."

Scarlet flipped through everything in the past decade—college, work, relationships. But she stopped at that night, Christmas Eve ten years ago. "I thought we were supposed to go on a date. I sat on the front porch for hours, waiting, and you never showed. No explanation. Only distance and an occasional wave from that night on."

Her chest tightened and tears spilled out of her eyes. She shot up, trying to find air to breathe. Dizziness churned her stomach. Distance, air, something. She needed to get away from this.

His arms wrapped around her from behind, but she didn't fall into them; she stiffened like they were the arms of a stranger. "I love you, Scarlet Cherish. I always have and I always will. Please, meet me at our spot tonight. Let me show you that I'm a new man. A man worthy of your love."

She slipped from his arms. With all the strength she could manage, she faced him with the most sincere expression. "I'll never forgive you. You abandoned me just like she did." She took in a stuttered breath. "I'm leaving. I'm marrying Henry. He is a man who speaks the truth. A man who would never leave me waiting on the front porch like my mother and you did. He's reliable, dependable, perfect for me. You, Duke Trenton, were never more than a high school crush. Take your business proposal and go."

"Wait. I won't let you go. I choose to believe in the legend. We belong together. We'll be together by Christmas. Take a chance and believe me."

"Goodbye, Duke. This time, it's for forever."

Nine

SCARLET SHUT THE DOOR ON A POSSIBLE FUTURE AND LOCKED HIM OUT. "You don't mean that."

"I do," Scarlet said in a hoarse whisper. "I trust you as much as I trust my mother, and without trust, you have nothing." His emotions bubbled to the surface, and he feared he'd lose his mind at the realization that this was it. The end of his lifelong dream of being a good man. Good enough to marry Scarlet, have children, and grow old together on the farm where he would provide a great living.

He struggled between wanting to pull her into his arms and never wanting to see her again. "And you're as disturbed as my old man." The words slipped from his lips. Anger, something he'd spent his life overcoming since that night ten years ago, seeped out of his atrophied heart.

The refrigerator in the back hummed. Strange thing to think about while his heart was being ripped from his chest and stomped into squishy pieces.

Scarlet didn't say another word; she ran upstairs, leaving him in the café alone. He rubbed his chest, refusing to allow the sob welling up inside him to escape. Men didn't cry. Not over a girl. Isn't that what his father taught him with a switch and angry words when he was thirteen?

"That's the funny thing about childhood best friends who fall in love. They know how to hurt each other in an epic way no one else can. But they can also love like no other couple." Aunt Laura's words were no longer welcome.

Duke faced the window and swiped his face, refusing to show his weakness in front of her. "You can stop using me to get Scarlet to stay. I failed."

"No, you just broke her down, and now she realizes how much she can't bear to be without you."

Soft sobs leaked through the ceiling from Scarlet's upstairs bedroom. The sound a replica of his mother's cries. A theme song for any woman living with a Trenton man.

He grabbed his papers. "You're delusional."

"Really? Then why did she run with tears streaming down her face? Why is she upstairs crying, shaking, longing for you?"

Laura placed a hand on his shoulder. "Because son, she's in love with you so much it hurts. You're the one person she could give her heart to, and that's what scares her."

"We're all scared. But you're wrong. I messed up by not telling her the truth back then. She's right, I abandoned her the way her mother did." His voice cracked under the realization that he had harmed her in a way that couldn't be undone. "I've proven myself unworthy of her love, so let it go. She deserves happiness, and although we disagree with a man who sends a marriage proposal via text, he's a man who won't fail her. One that doesn't hurt her." He wrenched open the door receiving a blast of cold air chilling him to his core.

"Duke, don't do this. Stay. You've proven yourself worthy time and time again. You are a better man. The best Trenton that ever lived." Aunt Laura blocked his exit. "You have never touched a sip of alcohol. I know about that bottle on your shelf.

It's not a symbol of your failure but of your success. You could've drowned your sorrows when you thought you lost her, but you didn't. Doesn't that prove something to you?"

"I've spent a decade pining after Scarlet. But I did the one thing I tried so many years not to do. I hurt her. The way my father would hurt my mother. She's upstairs crying now because of my actions. I always said I should never be in a real relationship because I have too much of my old man in me, and now I know it for sure. And not even some legendary book will change that. I'm not worthy of her, so, because I love her, I'm going to let her go. And Laura, you have to let this go and let me move on with my life. I can't take another minute of living with the torture. I know that I'm the one who caused all this pain. If I can't have her, then I want her happy but far away."

"Duke. No." Laura pleaded.

"This will not and will never be fixed. I'll make sure of that because I'll never hurt Scarlet again. That dream flew away with the blizzard of our lives."

He slid past Laura and closed the door, walked to his truck, started it, and drove away. Away from the pain. Away from the sorrow. Away from the woman he loved.

Soft knocks at Scarlet's bedroom door made her pace and pack faster. The squeal of the hinges warned of Aunt Laura's next assault, but it wouldn't work. "Save your breath. I know you're going to tell me how he made a mistake. That he did what he did to protect me. As you would say, it's hogwash."

"I think you should leave." Aunt Laura's voice sounded foreign and strange.

Scarlet pushed her clothes down into submission so she could close her suitcase. "What is this? Reverse psychology?"

"No. I think it's time for you to go. I thought you two belonged together, but I was wrong," Aunt Laura's cold and distant tone chilled Scarlet.

No warm hand touched her back or kind words. She wouldn't fall into the trap. "Right. Sure. You're not going to try to convince me that he left me that night to protect me unlike my mother who abandoned me for her own happiness. That he didn't leave me physically and he never left. He's been waiting for me here all these years."

"No."

The single word drew Scarlet to face Aunt Laura, wanting to discover her next play, but all she found was a sorrowful, defeated, downcast expression. "You should go."

She held the book *All Creatures Great and Small* in her hand. "Surprised you don't have the *Once Upon a Christmas Kiss* ready to remind me about how I have no power over this. That I'll end up with Duke no matter what because some legend says so."

"I didn't put that book in the free library that Duke built for you with his own two hands and heart."

The way she said "for you" convicted Scarlet. He'd been out in the cold creating something special for her, and she barely thanked him. "Right, well, I didn't ask him to do that." Her argument sounded weaker by the minute.

"You didn't have to, but it doesn't matter because you need to go and never return."

Scarlet's mouth dropped open, but she recovered, straightening her shirt. "Right. Like you don't want me to come home for holidays," she snickered.

"I don't." Aunt Laura's eye didn't even twitch. Her serious, tight expression sent a warning zap through Scarlet.

"What are you saying?"

"I'm saying that I'll come visit you in Atlanta if you want, but you never need to return to Cherry Creek because it's not fair."

Scarlet let out a nervous chuckle. For the first time, she found herself imagining holidays in Atlanta, and she no longer wanted to be away from home hiding away in a big city. She wanted to sit at her bistro table, watching the mountains, waiting to hear the backfiring of Duke's truck entering town. "You hate Atlanta. I know you want what's best for me, but I said I'd come home for the holidays, so I will."

"You don't get it. I don't want you here for the holidays." Laura stepped forward and dropped the book onto Scarlet's bed. "I don't ever want you to return."

"Why?" she asked, her voice trembling.

"Because I just saw something I never thought I'd see. That man—who loves you more than himself, who did everything for you since the day you met, who managed to never take a sip of drink despite four generations of drunks—just flinched when I mentioned alcohol. In that moment, I knew one thing."

"Alcohol? He'd never." Scarlet dropped her sweater to the floor; her head rushed with a thousand thoughts at once until she couldn't make any but one out. "What did you know?"

"That if you hurt him again, it'll be too late to repair the damage. And I'm not going to peel his butt off a bar stool because you broke him." She shook her head, lips tight. "I've never seen you act more like your mother than today, and that boy deserves better than you." Aunt Laura's words erupted inside Scarlet like a dry pine tree going up in flames.

"I'm nothing like her." Anger, resentment, defiance rammed each other at once.

Aunt Laura pulled a stack of letters from her pocket in Scarlet's handwriting in a progression from childhood scrawls to mature teenage script, all of them stamped with *return to sender*. "I tried to protect you from her, but I guess I should've let you know the truth. She never read one of your notes. Never wanted to face her failures in life. I think she loved you in the only way she knew how, just like you love Duke in the only way you know how."

Scarlet's stomach knotted. "That's not fair."

"Isn't it?" Laura dropped the letters on top of the book. "Like mother, like daughter." She about-faced and walked out the door.

Her words percolated and soured in Scarlet's belly. She collapsed onto the bed and eyed the dozens of unopened letters in her childlike handwriting. Every year after Christmas, she'd send a note to her mother. She didn't need to open one because she knew what each of them said. It would always start out angry and hateful, then turn to pleading and promising to be a good girl.

Conviction cut deep. Aunt Laura's words sizzled in her mind. Her face heated at the sight of *All Creatures Great and Small*. She owed it to Duke to at least read his note. A note from someone who wanted to tell her how he felt, the way she'd tried to tell her mother.

She swallowed a decade of regrets and tugged the book closer. The worn cover made it look unassuming, but she knew better. Whatever he'd written inside could change everything. That's why she never wanted to read it. Because if she did, she'd have to truly face her own feelings. Emotions she'd buried for so long she didn't want to remember them, ever.

Scarlet cleared her throat and eyed her suitcase. "I won't be you, mother, but this won't change anything," she whispered to a ghost. That's all her mother had been, a ghost with an occasional postcard.

She flipped to the front and saw a paragraph in Duke's handwriting. Her pulse tip-tapped at her neck.

She took a long, deep breath and read.

. . .

My Dearest Scar,

I don't know if this will shock you or if you've always known, I've always wanted more than friendship from you. You're the most beautiful, kind, loving, and breathtakingly generous person I know, and I'm in love with you.

I've been holding back, so I feel like I'll explode if I don't tell you the truth. Every night we could meet, I raced to our spot, waited for you to appear, and savored every second with you. But it was torture not to cross a line. A line that would bring you down to my level, but now I have a shot better than I dreamed. I can earn the right to have your love.

I'm taking the scholarship for University of Georgia instead of Stanford. I can't move that far from home and from you.

Meet me at our spot tonight at midnight so I can tell you in person how much I love you. How much I ache to hold you and kiss you.

How much I want to spend the rest of my life with you if you'll consider giving me a chance to earn your love.

Forever Yours,

Duke

Tears streamed down Scarlet's cheeks. She choked and gasped. A river of emotions rushed through her. He would give up his top university, most prestigious pick, to be with her?

"No. No. No." She held the book to her chest and shook with rage. He had no right to give this to her now. Everything was settled and organized. The life ahead was certain and right not full of possible disasters, but this... This changed everything.

Her head spun, her eyes stung. All these years, she'd wanted to know why he left her. He tried to tell her, but she didn't want to hear it. But this. He didn't leave her because he didn't want her. He left because he wanted more for her.

That's not my mother.

She let out a strangled cry, but how could she trust this... this legendary love? A love that could bring disappointment and disaster.

Is this how her mother felt each time she saw a letter from her? Had she loved Scarlet enough not to want to face opening one?

Scarlet stood and paced until she found herself in the living room facing Aunt Laura.

"So, what are you going to do?"

"I don't know." Scarlet plopped down next to Aunt Laura on the couch, willing her to make the pain go away, but that wasn't her job anymore.

"Do you love him?"

The last twenty years of her life flashed. Swimming in the lake, hiking the trails, reading by their tree, climbing, falling, kisses to her cut. A rush of emotions stole her breath. She clutched her chest trying to breathe. "Yes."

"Then go tell him."

"What about Henry? Shouldn't I text him or call him or something?"

"I think he made his point clear. Be home by the 25th or don't return. Which do you want to do?"

"I know you're right." She choked back the sobs, but she knew Henry never loved her and she never loved him. They were a business arrangement, a team, but never marriage mate-rial. It was safe but unfulfilling.

"No matter what, it's over with Henry. It's been over for a long time. If it ever even began." She shook her head. "But I told Duke I never wanted to see him again. I was awful, accusatory, mean. I hurt him profoundly. I accused him of being his father."

"And he hurt you. But when are you both going to get past your pain and open your hearts to greatness? Take a chance. Go tell him. Go to the farm and tell him everything. Go tell him you love him."

Scarlet let out a knowing chuckle. "He won't be at the farm."

Aunt Laura smiled. "Wherever he is, go to him. He's waiting for you even if he doesn't know it himself. Get to him before he does something stupid over a broken heart."

Scarlet stepped to the stairs. "What if he won't listen?"

Aunt Laura flung Scarlet's scarf around her neck. "Then make him listen." She grabbed snow boots from the hall closet and tossed them on the floor in front of Scarlet.

She plunged her feet in and tightened the laces.

Aunt Laura kissed Scarlet's cheek. "It's time to heal, Scarlet."

She ran down the stairs and out the door. Snow came down in crystal puffs. The aroma of fresh roasted nuts wafted in the air from some nearby festive gathering. With arms pumping, Scarlet made it across the street, down the road, slipping and sliding with each step from ice forming in roadside pockets.

Duke's old red truck, parked at the trailhead, shone like Rudolph's nose in whiteout conditions. She followed it to the path to their secret spot. She trudged through the snow, feeling his presence before she saw him. The hair on the back of her neck stood at attention. She prepared herself to beg his forgiveness.

Her stumble down the embankment, splashing into the water's edge, garnered his attention. But he didn't run to her.

He sat in the snow—on a blanket surrounded by candles and lanterns in some romantic scene—hovering over a brown bottle, a brown beer bottle in his hands.

.

Ten

"WHAT ARE YOU DOING HERE?" DUKE DRAGGED HIS GAZE TO THE SKY, but he didn't dare wish on any shooting stars.

Scarlet shuffled through the snow. "I made a mistake. A huge mistake."

His pulse double-timed. Did he dare believe she came to tell him she ended things with her boyfriend? Life wouldn't be that easy. He closed his eyes and willed himself to be strong. She said it herself—she wanted a life beyond this town. "You should go."

"I'm not going to marry Henry."

Her words filled him with warmth. At least she wouldn't be in a loveless marriage. That was something, but it would never be enough. "I can't say I'm sorry to hear that, but it doesn't change anything. You were right. I don't belong in your world."

"That's not true." She dropped to her knees in the soft snow. "You could belong anywhere. But I don't want you to move to Atlanta."

He ran a hand through his hair, his shoulders tight with apprehension. "Listen, I know we said some things and your aunt probably manipulated you into coming here to try to make up with me so we can continue to be friends, but it's too late for that. We're not teenagers. I don't want or need you as a friend."

Harsh, but honest.

"I see." Scarlet eyed the bottle in his hand, and he realized why her face was tight with fear.

"I didn't drink. Not that I didn't think about it. This is the bottle I've held onto for ten years as a reminder of how I couldn't afford to make stupid mistakes in life."

She let out a soft exhale and smiled. "Everyone makes mistakes, especially when they're teenagers. But I know what you were willing to do for me. You were giving up your dream to be with me."

He smiled, if only a little. "You read my message."

"I did."

"Then you know why I can't be your friend, because all these years I've been stuck waiting for you. Keeping you in my life, and that has kept me from living." He turned away in fear that his tears would betray him again. He hadn't cried like this since his mother died. Grief for the loss of the woman he loved weighed his heart down so heavy, he thought it would drop to his gut if he moved.

"Then we shouldn't be friends.".

Her words caused the night temperature to drop somewhere between cold and glacial. "Don't."

A soft touch pressed against his knee. A simple touch that provoked so many complicated emotions because he wanted more. "I'm sorry. I know you won't believe me, and I don't blame you. I've been horrible, but I'm telling you from my heart how sorry I am. I'm whole-heartedly, unequivocally sorry for hurting you."

Her words drew him to reciprocate an apology, but he couldn't because he'd have to feel something, and right now, he liked the numbness of not only his frost-nibbled fingers but his deadening emotions. "Doesn't matter anymore."

"But it does. You told me you loved me, and I didn't answer."

"It's fine. Don't worry about it."

She tugged his arm, but he wouldn't look at her; he couldn't because if he saw her full, red lips he wouldn't be able to hold back. Didn't she understand he's a man despite how many years he held back his passion?

"I didn't respond because I love you too much." She shimmied closer and took his cheeks between her hands. "I'm scared because I lost you once and I couldn't bear to lose you again. I used to drive by the farm slowly in hopes you would come out to see me. I came here every school break and every holiday for two years until I finally had to face that you would never be mine. That's when I met Henry."

His hands fisted, but he released them and stretched his fingers. "I should've told you the truth at Christmas, but I didn't. I missed you so much that I couldn't face this tree anymore, so I abandoned our spot. Heck, I couldn't even have a Christmas tree in the house because it would remind me of you."

"I'm so, so, so sorry, Duke."

A car passed by, but she didn't pull away. Instead, she raised up on her knees to be at his level. "If you'll give me another chance, I'll spend the rest of my days making it up to you."

"What about your job in Atlanta?" He dared to ask, knowing he had to have all the facts before he could ever consider opening his heart to her again.

"I've enjoyed helping you with your proposals. I'll work to help other small businesses or startups. For the first time, I'll do something I enjoy instead of what I think is safe."

After all these years, it couldn't be possible. It had to be some fairytale or crazy dream. But her lips pressed to his in a tentative yet heated kiss.

He pulled back and looked at her tree-green eyes to see the truth. And he saw it. Her love. The way she looked at him with soft eyes showed how she felt. "I didn't think miracles were possible."

The End

About the Author

Ciara Knight is a USA TODAY Bestselling Author, who writes clean and wholesome romance novels set in either modern day small towns or wild historic old west. Born with a huge imagination that usually got her into trouble, Ciara is happy she's found a way to use her powers for good. She loves spending time with her characters and hopes you do, too.

Get to know Ciara at www.ciaraknight.com

Once Upon a Christmas Treasure

BRENDA LOWDER

One

"Twenty-five is a very important number," my best friend, Ginny, says as she stomps the snow from her boots and leaves them at my front door. She hands me my birthday gift and beams. "A quarter of a century is *substantial*."

I laugh and twist the curled pink ribbon around my finger as she takes her coat off. Even though my birthday is just five days before Christmas, Ginny treats it separately. She makes it special, just like my mom and dad used to do. "I think anything sounds substantial once you start throwing the word 'century' into it. But you're right—like Marilyn Monroe said, a quarter of a century makes a girl think."

We sit on the couch, and Ginny claps her hands in a flurry, bouncing the cushion next to me. "Open your present!"

I tear into the pretty polka-dotted paper and suck a breath in. "Wow!" I turn the large book over in my hands. Now that's substantial. "This is beautiful." I flip through the pages. Gorgeous glossy photos of Paris, Shanghai, Rome, Sydney, Hong Kong, and pretty much every place I've ever wanted to go leap out at me. I trace my fingers over the image of the Taj Mahal at sunset. "I love it, Ginny, thank you."

"You're welcome. I know how much you want to travel and see the world."

"Oh, I really do." *Did*, anyway. I'm trying to be more practical now.

"And here, let me show you." She takes the book and turns to the last pages of the Paris chapter. "There are recommendations for restaurants and shopping and all kinds of things to do in each of the different areas. They keep it all up to date on the app. See? You can download it and get access with the code. You know what that means?" She watches me expectantly.

I give it a beat. "What?"

"That we should plan our big trip soon—for this summer." She knocks my elbow with hers. "I found a great Groupon deal on a flight and hotel package to Paris. We've got the world at our fingertips." She lays her fingers on the cover for emphasis. "We should just go."

When I don't say anything, she passes the book back to me. After a minute, I say, "This is so great, Ginny. Thank you. I love it." I reach out to hug her, but she leans back and gives me a look.

"What's up?"

She shakes her head. "You totally sidestepped my suggestion of traveling this summer."

I put my unhugged arms down. "Oh. You're right. Sorry. It's just...you know we don't really have the money even with a Groupon. And I can't leave Felicity and the boys." Ever since my older sister's husband abandoned her and their one and a-half kids—she was eight months pregnant with the second one— I've helped take care of my nephews. Felicity married Mark right out of high school and never made it to college. Since our parents died in a car accident five years ago, Felicity has had only me to lean on. I've become the other half that makes her life function. In the time since Mark ran off to LA to be an unemployed actor, we've had to work hard to support ourselves and the kids and keep the house our parents left us.

As she so often does, Ginny reads my mind. "You've been so supportive of Felicity. You've been there for her and for the boys one hundred percent. But she's your sister, not your life partner. This situation was never meant to be permanent, was it? I'm sure she wants a future with new adventures and love. And so do you! Felicity needs to find her own person to build a future with so you can start living yours."

I lean back against the couch. "It's not like that, Gin."

"Come on. It's *exactly* like that."

"Not exactly."

"She needs someone else in her life. She needs to move on. And so do you."

I hadn't thought about anything like that in a long time. "Maybe."

"But you know what? We can help Felicity. Right now. We can help her find a man. A man who has a real job and will love her and the boys."

I bite my thumbnail, thinking. "Felicity really could use some love and romance in her life. You know, last weekend she was watching an animated movie with the boys, and she spent twenty minutes telling me how hot the cartoon fox was and what a kind, sensitive father he'd make."

Ginny's eyes go wide. "Wow. She's worse than I thought."

I nod. "Yeah. Now that I'm thinking about it, she got a little too into Toad the other day when she was reading *The Wind in the Willows* to the boys. She told me he had a rakish handsomeness that was very appealing."

Her eyebrows furrow. "Your sister's very into the cartoon animals lately. That's a little disturbing."

I bat a hand. "She's a mom. Cartoons are all she sees. Besides, Toad is a total bad boy. Felicity's always been a sucker for a bad boy." Like her ex-husband.

"Or in this case, a bad toad."

"Well..."

"All the more reason she should start seeing *human* men."

Felicity and I are so into the daily grind of work and taking care of the boys that neither of us has the time or energy to think about a human man. We stagger our schedules so one of us is always home with the boys. I'm a teacher at the middle school—just like Ginny—and Felicity works nights waiting tables at the Cordial Diner. It's hard to juggle everything so finding someone to date isn't high in either of our priorities. More than that, Felicity was a bit traumatized by Mark's desertion. She hasn't wanted to risk her heart again.

But it's been four years, and things are getting better. It is probably time she got back out there. "I guess you're right. After all, human men are the best kind of men."

Ginny shakes her head. "You could probably both use a man, but we can work on finding one for Felicity first."

"That's easy to say, but there aren't that many Mr. Toads walking the streets of Cherry Creek, Tennessee."

The corner of her mouth twitches. "You'd be surprised. There are a lot more toads than princes."

"What am I going to do? Stand on a corner and ask men to date my sister?"

A glimmer appears in Ginny's eyes. It's a look I recognize from late-night slumber parties and Ginny shenanigans. "What about the book?"

My heart flies over a beat. "Oh, *the book*. Huh." The memory of the book descends on me like a half-remembered dream. Fifth grade. Ginny and I learning about Cherry Creek's own legend: the book *Once Upon a Christmas Kiss*. The story was written by Elizabeth Chambers, and a single copy of it is filled with notes in the margins and inside covers with wisdom from Cherry Creek residents who'd found their one true love while the book was in their possession at Christmastime. Ginny and I made endless lists of where we'd go to find our true loves. Paris. Zurich. Rio de Janeiro. Auckland. But I hadn't thought about the book in years. We've never seen it, and it's not registered at any library or bookstore that I could ever find. It's practically a fairy tale. "Do you think this book is even real?"

"Oh, it's real. I've seen it in action. Mrs. Atchison's daughter Jenny had never dated in her life. She got the book, and then boom! Met her true love at Christmastime and is married with two kids now."

"But will it work for Felicity?"

Ginny shrugs. "I've never heard of it *not* working, have you?"

"No. But then again, we probably wouldn't hear about the times it didn't work."

"Yeah. But it's worth a try, right?"

"Auntie Meelie! Auntie Meelie!" My four-year-old nephew, Hudson, barrels into the living room and throws himself onto my lap, squeezing me hard with his little arms. He's such a sweetie. I've never seen anyone give themselves so completely over to a hug like he does. It's boundless excitement followed by a total physical collapse until he's a human blanket pinning me in place. I squeeze him back. "Hello, my little Muddy Huddy Buddy."

His seven-year-old brother, Trace, lingers by the Christmas tree, but when he sees Hudson on my lap, he strolls over, too, with much more reserve. As if he's debating with himself, he glances at his brother before also giving me a big, collapsed hug. Trace isn't as demonstrative as his little brother, but he doesn't like being left out of anything.

"Auntie Meelie!" Trace pops his head up and regards me with his serious gray eyes. "Did you buy our Christmas presents yet?"

"I sure did, buddy." I got really good ones, too. I'd saved up for a new gaming system and some games they could share.

"We think we need a bigger present." Trace sends a side glance to his little brother. "Maybe you'd better tell her, Hud."

Hudson emerges from the snuggle pile. "We need a new daddy!"

Trace sighs as if he'd have eased into the subject better. "We do. We decided we want a new daddy for Christmas. That's more important than any other present. So it's okay if we don't get any toys this year. We just want a dad instead."

"We still like toys!" Hudson pipes up. "But a daddy probably comes with toys, too."

Ginny catches my eye, and we share a smile over his head. "It doesn't really work that way, buddy. But you have good timing. Ginny and I were just talking about that very thing."

"Yeah!" Trace says. "Like Huddy said, make sure he comes with good accessories. Like a car."

"And toys," Hudson adds.

"I'll keep that in mind. A car and some toys are a good idea. It takes time to find a new daddy, though."

Their faces fall. I hate disappointing them. But I also know firsthand what short attention spans they have. They'll forget about it pretty fast once they've unwrapped their new video games. "Don't worry. You guys know how lovable your mom is. She'll find someone sometime. And maybe we should help her *start* looking. I'll see what I can do."

"Yay!" They get down from the couch and start jumping up and down, the ornaments on the tree shaking violently. Before I can corral them back, Trace stops.

"Auntie Meelie, if you get us a daddy, maybe Santa can still get us toys," he says.

"That sounds fair," I say, laughing. They both jump on top of me again.

Felicity comes into the living room and laughs when she sees her sons blanketing me. "Sorry, Meelie. I tried to keep them out, but they snuck past me when I was cooking at the stove."

Ginny and I share a look, her alarm twinned with my feelings exactly. Things don't generally go well when Felicity cooks. Fire, catastrophe, mayhem—and people running away screaming—are the likeliest results.

"I'll take over in the kitchen." I roll Trace and Hudson gently off my lap and get up from the couch.

Felicity exhales with visible relief. "Thanks, Meelie. Sorry. I was trying to make you something nice for your birthday, but, uh, it's not really turning out. In fact, sorry. There's nothing in there that you could call dinner."

It's so kind that Felicity keeps trying to cook despite all evidence that she should cease immediately. I squeeze her arm. "Thanks, sis. You didn't have to do that."

She smiles and shrugs. "You do so much for us. I wanted to do something to show our appreciation." I know she appreciates me, just as I appreciate her. She and the boys are my family. I'd do anything for them. And the truth is we lean on each other. We've had to. We'd already lost Mom and Dad, so when Mark left her before Hudson was born, I ended up being the one holding Felicity's hand in the delivery room. We've been there for each other ever since.

And Hudson stands a better chance of seeing his father on TV than actually meeting him.

Ginny jumps up. "Actually, I'd already planned to take the whole family out to dinner tonight to celebrate Amelia's birthday. How does the Cordial Diner sound?"

Trace and Hudson shout, "Yay!" Hudson bounces in place, clapping, and after a second, Trace does too.

Felicity's eyes dart around in alarm. "Y'all can go without me. I mean, I'll have to show up there later tonight for my shift."

"Oh, come on." Ginny beams her winning smile all over Felicity's objections. "It'll be fun for you to get waited on for once." Her eyes gleam with mischief. "You can make your coworkers jump at your beck and call. Make huge demands. Be really high maintenance."

Felicity's face fills with horror. "Oh, I couldn't do that."

"Sure you could," Ginny insists.

"I'd never want to make anyone's job harder." Felicity turns plaintive eyes to me, wordlessly imploring me to call off the eager watch dog that is Ginny.

"That's okay," Ginny says, catching the look. "We'll just do it for you."

"She's kidding!" I bend to help Hudson tie his shoes. "We'll be model diners. Your coworkers will barely even know we're there."

Two

Oliver

They cause a stir the minute they step through the door.

All the diners at the Cordial Diner turn to regard the energetic little crew. A young boy jumps from one black tile to the next white or black one and then backward according to some game of his own that doesn't seem to have any discernible rules but has a lot of loud positive affirmations for himself. His older brother follows. There's Ginny Thompson. Of course I remember her from elementary school when she was always hanging around. She's no doubt the architect of tonight's excursion as she herds the group and directs the proceedings with her pointer finger aimed at employees and diners alike. She's practically pulling Felicity Taylor inside as Felicity tries to cling to the edge of the doorway.

I crane my neck to peer past the other diners, hoping she's with them, straining to catch sight of the one person my eyes are hungry to see.

And then she's there.

Amelia Taylor.

She emerges through the doorway after her sister. The overhead light dances on her long, glossy, auburn hair, which is no longer in the ponytail she favored in high school but instead falls in soft waves around her shoulders. She tilts her head, listening to something her nephew is saying to her, and her eyes flicker with sparks as she laughs. She takes off her coat and drapes it over her arm, her cheeks rosy with the heat inside after the cold outside, her skin bright, almost glowing. She's ten years older than when I last saw her, and she's even more beautiful.

A lump forms in my throat, and a sharp needle of pain lances my heart—completely unrelated to the double bacon cheeseburger in front of me.

Amelia Taylor. The girl I've loved since we were fifteen. The woman I've come back to Cherry Creek to see because in the ten years since we last saw each other, I haven't stopped thinking about her.

My feet move before I tell them to. I'm up. I'm walking. My heart jackhammers against my ribs, and I've closed more than half the distance between us. My gaze is targeted on Amelia, but Ginny spots me first. Her eyes widen, and she elbows Amelia in the side as I approach. Amelia glances at her friend before following Ginny's eyeline to settle her gaze on me.

My breath chokes. In that unguarded moment, I see every emotion as it crashes behind her eyes. Surprise. Delight. Warmth. *Friendship.*

She smiles, her full lips stretching wide into a dazzling curve that manages to blaze a fire so hot it heats my skin.

"Oliver!" She steps forward but then hesitates, a sudden cloud descending on her brow as if she's deciding how best to greet me. A hug? A handshake? A wave? They're all inadequate for the former best friend who hasn't been seen in ten years. I should be thankful she remembers me at all.

She settles for standing in place. I lean toward her, past

Ginny, the kids, and Amelia's sister, Felicity. "Happy birthday, Amelia."

She puts a hand to her heart. "Oh my gosh. You remember it's my birthday?"

I laugh. "Of course. We were best friends, right?"

I catch a glare of resentment from Ginny, who must have become Amelia's replacement best friend in the time since I'd left.

Amelia's oblivious to Ginny's annoyance. "Get in here!" she says and finally grabs me in a big, friendly hug.

I hug her back gently, my heart jumping around, skipping over itself. My packed-down crush is threatening to combust. This hug, this contact—even *seeing* her—means more to me than it does to her. I never told her how I felt.

"Good to see you," I say into her hair. It smells like coconut. I hold on a second longer before wrenching myself away.

She laughs. "It's good to be seen. It's been way too long, Ollie! I catch your posts on social media now and then, though. I heard your parents moved back here, but I thought you were some fancy lawyer in Chicago now."

"I don't know about fancy, but yeah, I'm still in Chicago. I'm here for Christmas. Came to see my parents." *And you*, I don't say.

A blink of her long lashes. "That's great. We totally need to catch up for real."

I nod. "Absolutely." I tear my eyes from her and glance at the rest of her gang who've all been openly staring at us. "Sorry, I don't mean to interrupt your party."

She shrugs and puffs her lips out, making her duck face. I love it. I remember the first time I noticed her doing that. It was on the playground in second grade. That may have been the first moment I fell in love. "You're not interrupting anything. This was a last-minute plan."

Her younger nephew—I recognize him from her social media posts—tugs on her pant leg. "I'm hungry, Auntie Meelie! Make the man stop talking."

Felicity reddens with embarrassment and peers down at him in horror. "Hudson! That wasn't nice. Apologize to your aunt and her friend."

He lifts his chin, a glint of rebellion burning in his eyes. It's a look I remember seeing on his aunt, and it means trouble. "I'm sorry, Auntie and boring friend, that you're talking so long when I'm hungry."

Amelia stifles a giggle, and I clamp down on a smile.

"It's okay," Amelia says, resting her hands on her nephew's shoulders. "Would you like to join us, Ollie? Some of us are a handful, but it's been too long since I've seen you."

Her nephew looks like he's hating me more by the second. "No, thank you. I was just here to get some of the Cordial Diner's famous fried chicken. They have the *best* fried chicken. I've been craving it for years. But I should really get back to Mom and Dad. I said I'd help them hang some pictures tonight. Gotta go."

"Oh, sure. If you've got to go." Her lips turn down. Is she disappointed? The thought buoys me. I start to leave. "Hey." She catches my arm. It's my imagination, I'm sure, but the warmth of her touch radiates through the layers of my sport jacket and shirt. I resist the urge to cover her hand with mine.

"Yes?" My antenna goes up, and I stop myself from rushing to fill the pause with a declaration of love. Or a proposal.

"I have this idea I've been looking into, and I might need your help. Would you have time to meet up tomorrow? Around four? I'd love to run something past you."

I feel myself beam and recognize that I have zero game when it comes to Amelia Taylor. I never have. "Run away!" I say.

Her eyes narrow, and she frowns as she tries to process my comment.

I shake my head. "No! I mean, please run anything you'd like to say by me." That still isn't quite right. I am a buffoon.

She smiles, though, obviously understanding me despite myself. "Great. Meet you for cookies at Smart Cookie Bites? It's new since you left. My friend Abby owns it. They have the most delicious cookies in the world. They're made with fresh fruits and vegetables locally sourced from Trenton Farms. They're fantastic. You're going to love it."

"Perfect."

She grins. "Great. See you then."

"Wonderful." I stumble past her and the rest of her entourage, waving goodbye awkwardly. In the last ten years, one would think I'd have gotten smoother. Not when it comes to Amelia.

But we're meeting tomorrow. And there's something specific she wants to talk to me about. As I open the door and step out of the Cordial Diner, my chest puffs out, and my heart *cha-chings* with hope. This is what I've come back to see. This is exactly what I hoped would happen.

As I glance around the snowy street in search of my car, I realize I've already made two crucial mistakes. The first is that I'm freezing and have left my coat inside. The second is that I didn't finish my dinner or pay my bill.

I turn around to go back in. There's always hope that I'll find a way to up my game tomorrow.

Because tomorrow I have a date with Amelia Taylor.

Three

AMELIA

"Oliver Jameson sure grew up good," Felicity says, waggling her eyebrows at me as we shepherd Trace and Hudson down Main Street together. We just went by the big Christmas tree in the square to visit the ornaments we hung at the tree lighting. Now I'm on my way to meet the grown-up-good Oliver Jameson himself, and Felicity and the boys are going Christmas shopping at Gifts and Bits, a fun little shop that sells local crafts and jams, novelty T-shirts, and Cherry Creek branded merchandise. Trace and Hudson like it for their extensive candy selection. I haven't pried, but with the shifty way the three of them are acting, I think I'm the one they're doing their Christmas shopping for today.

"You think so?" I ask, though of course I'd noticed. It'd be hard not to notice a man who'd grown at least a foot taller since I'd last seen him and filled out the shoulders of his suit coat like Superman.

"Oh, yeah. Don't you think?" She pauses to pull Hudson back from the curb he's poised to jump off.

"I guess." When I saw him, it hit me that he'd be the perfect person to help me with my plan for Felicity. But he might be useful in more ways than one. Especially if Felicity's noticing a man who isn't a cartoon character. I glance at her, watching for her reaction to what I'm going to say next. "If you're interested in him, I could talk to him for you."

Felicity freezes mid-step. "Amelia, that's not funny."

I fold my arms, and my purse and messenger bag slide down my shoulder. "I wasn't making a joke."

She bites her lip and rescues Hudson from a muddy snow pile he's attempting to jump into. "You know I don't date. Not *after what their father did.*" She whispers that last part so Trace and Hudson won't hear. My sister may be bitter about love and relationships and her runaway ex-husband, but she wants to give her boys a healthy outlook and doesn't say bad things about their father in front of them. "Besides, I'm too busy for any of that. You know this. And even if I wasn't, I wouldn't be interested in Ollie."

"What's wrong with Ollie?" She was the one who'd just commented on his attractiveness. And she wasn't wrong.

"He took drama with you in middle school, right?"

"Right."

"Yeah, there's no way I'd date anyone who has anything remotely to do with acting after Mark."

"Point taken."

"And Ollie is such a *good* guy."

"What's wrong with that?"

She tilts her head. "You know I like a bad boy."

"That's not a good thing."

"Still. But most of all, I'd never be interested because he's one hundred percent *your* guy. I mentioned him, though, because I was thinking of *you* and Ollie."

"*Me* and Ollie? Nope. Can't picture it." Ollie was my first and best friend in kindergarten. And kindergartners don't date. I'd never thought of him that way. "We've always been just friends."

She gives me a pointed look. "He didn't *always* look like Superman."

She surprises a laugh out of me. "That's scary. We obviously share a brain."

Her answering smile is smug. "See? That's because he does. And you like it."

I shake my head. "We weren't talking about me and Superman."

"Yes, we were."

"Well, we shouldn't be. We should be talking about you and moving on."

Felicity's eyes glaze over, and there's a sudden rigid set to her jaw. "We don't need to talk about me. I've got everything I need in my life and more." She gets a pinched look on her face as she gestures to Trace and Hudson, who are now both jumping into a mound of dirty snow.

"I get it," I say. And I do. Neither of us has any time because it's taking both of us to support these boys. The difference between us is that Felicity's past has her closed off to pursuing a future. While I'm just...regular busy. "We have a little more time than we used to, though."

"What do you mean?"

"I'm just saying the stage the boys are at now is a lot easier than when Hudson was teething and Trace was peeing in the closet." Trace had an epically difficult time with potty training.

"Yeah. Wow. That's the truth. Things are easier with them now."

"And it'll get even easier when Hudson goes to school next year. They won't need quite so much help."

"But that doesn't mean we've got a ton of free time now."

"Life is busy. You're not wrong. I'm just saying maybe you should start opening your mind to possibilities."

"Okay. I will open my mind. And I'll start looking around when I have the time." Her brow unfurrows and the pinched look retreats from her face. She may only be telling me what I want to hear, but I think it's doing her good already. She seems calmer and more hopeful. Which lasts about two seconds until she runs over and tugs Hudson away from a bell-ringing Salvation Army Santa. Huddy was trying to stand on the donation bucket.

We stop in front of Gifts and Bits. "Have fun," she says with another knowing grin.

I wave her off. "You too."

She grabs the boys, and they head into the store. I continue on to Smart Cookie Bites and Superman—I mean Ollie.

He's already there, seated at one of the cute bistro tables by the window under wide strands of sparkly gold garland. A loose strand of the shiny stuff has fallen onto his head. He's playing on his phone, but he stands when he spots me. "Amelia, hi. Good to see you."

I pluck the bit of garland out of his hair, showing it to him so he won't think I'm randomly grooming him. "You too, Ollie. Thanks for meeting me. Now we've got no time to lose. We have a lot to do."

He blinks at me. Whatever he thought I was going to say, this wasn't it. He should hang on. It'll get worse before it gets better.

"Okay. Do we have time for a cookie?"

I set my purse and messenger bag on the floor and take my coat off. "Well, yes, of course." I drape my coat on the back of my chair before sitting down. "There's always time for a cookie. That's why we're here."

He sits across from me and smiles. He still has his dimples.

Two of them. He always had a bit of a baby face, and now that he's all grown up it's endearing to see he still has something left of the boy I knew.

"So what's up?" He pulls a white pastry bag toward him. He must've already stood in line to get them. How early did he get here?

"I have a project that requires a...person like you."

"Oh? Like me how?"

My heart rate picks up its pace. I don't know why I'm nervous to tell him. It's just Ollie. And yeah, I don't really know Ollie anymore, so that might be why. "Let's have a cookie first."

He opens the cookie bag. "Which one do you want? I got us a couple of their specialty cordial cherry cookies, a carrot cake cookie, some Christmas cookies, and a raisin oatmeal chocolate chip."

"Oooh. I'll take the raisin oatmeal chocolate chip, please."

He hands it over with a doubtful look. "Really? I would've thought—"

"And I'll take a cordial cherry cookie, too, if you're willing to part with one," I interrupt.

He chuckles and hands it over. "That's what I thought. I ordered you a cup of milk, but only because I didn't know if you'd acquired a taste for coffee in the last ten years."

"You remembered!" I smile. "But I like coffee now, too. I already had a big cup though, so milk is perfect, thanks." I eye his giant mug. "I see that you're fully embracing adulthood as a coffee drinker."

He picks up his coffee. "That I am. And I take it black."

"How manly."

"Extremely. Upped my manliness since we last hung out." His tone is light, joking...flirtatious? I find myself leaning closer. "You don't know the half of it. Come watch me bench press at Fitness Train later, and you'll really see how manly I am now."

He wiggles his eyebrows. "I've got muscles that didn't exist in middle school."

We both pause at his comment. It doesn't make sense, and I review it in my mind. Is he being suggestive like I should want to examine these new muscles? I decide to let it pass and seize on practicalities. "You got a gym membership when you're just here for the holidays?"

He blows a breath out, probably glad I didn't call him on his facetious boast. "My dad got me a guest pass so I can spot him. See? Super manly. Helping my dad workout." He sports those dimples again alongside a self-deprecating smile. "But you should come. You could help, too."

I groan. "I almost want to take you up on that. It's been so long since I've been to the gym. I used to love to work out there, but now with Felicity and the boys, I just don't have time."

"You're like a second mom to them," he observes.

"Well, kind of. It takes both of us working to pay the bills, and we take turns with the boys. She's at home with them during the day, and I take the nights. But I'm just filling in the gaps for Felicity."

He nods, watching my lips. I worry I have some cookie crumbs hanging and grab a napkin.

"I'm glad I ran into you again. The way we used to talk, I thought you'd have left Cherry Creek long ago. All you ever talked about was seeing the world. The lights of Paris. The museums of London. The sunset over the pyramids in Egypt. Are you still hoping to travel?"

My chest tightens. I used to want to see all those things. But I hadn't thought about it in years—until Ginny gave me my birthday present. I sigh. "Maybe in a few years. My family needs me too much now." I shrug. There are more important things in the world, and Trace and Hudson are two of them. I tap my fingernail on the table. "Impressive memory you have there."

"Of course, I remember. Traveling the world was your dream."

"Yeah." I give a half laugh. "I guess it's still just that—a dream."

His eyes are sad, and I want to tell him not to look at me like that. I'm fine. He doesn't need to feel sorry for me. It's so not a big deal. But Oliver and I aren't close like that anymore. I can't just tell him I know what he's thinking.

"You'll get there," he says quietly, like it's important.

The gentle sincerity in his voice kills me. It's like he knows who I am and what I want, even when I'm trying hard not to show it. How does he still know me after all these years apart? I've been trying to focus on my family, not myself. Even this much attention on me is unnerving.

"Anyway!" I pull my messenger bag out from under the table and unload my notebook and pen. I open the cover and the pages stick together with newness.

Oliver leans forward and rubs his hands together. "A brand-new notebook? Oh, we are in for an Amelia adventure, aren't we?" His tone virtually crackles with delight.

I can't help but smile at his enthusiasm. "Yes. It's an adventure. But it's not for us."

He sits back with a scowl of disappointment.

I weigh my words. "But we're involved. Don't worry. We're just not the focus or the goal."

He gives a micro nod like I haven't lost him completely yet. I pick up my pen and put it back down. Yep. I'm definitely nervous. It's Ollie, but it's grownup Superman Ollie, and I'm about to impose on him big time. I wipe my palms on my jeans.

"It's Felicity," I tell him. "We have to help her."

His dark brows come together in concern, and he leans over the table. "Sure. Anything."

I swallow. "We've got to find her a man."

"Here?" He casts his gaze around the room.

"No, of course not. This'll take more effort than that."

His eyes widen in alarm. "Are we creating fake profiles for her on dating apps, or would you rather we go door to door?"

I laugh. "Neither. It's a lot more complicated and clandestine than either of those."

His smile falters. "So just what are we doing?"

I squeeze my hands together in preparation for my grand declaration. "We're going after *the* book."

His forehead furrows. "*The* book? What book? The Bible?"

"No, don't be silly. The book Cherry Creek is famous for."

He stares at me, obviously waiting for me to clue him in. I give him a minute to see if a memory will surface.

He shakes his head. "Amelia, I've been away for a long time. If Cherry Creek ended up being featured in some bestselling book, I must've missed it."

I skewer him with a look. "You seriously don't know what I'm talking about?"

"I really don't."

His expression is blank. I can't believe he doesn't remember. He was there in fifth grade when Ginny and I were making our plans for the book. "You *really* don't remember?" At his head shake, I clear my throat to tell the well-worn tale. "Many years ago, the director of Cherry Creek Academy wrote a Christmas fairy tale book. It was a love story, inspired by her parents' own courtship. She fell in love and got married while writing the book at Christmastime. When the book was published, she moved on from the academy and gifted a copy to a dear friend who was a teacher there with an inscription saying she felt like the book had helped her find her own happily ever after and she wished the same for her friend. The really incredible thing is that her friend met and fell in love with the man she'd marry that next Christmas. After that, the book gained a reputation for helping people fall in love at Christmastime, and it's been circulating ever since."

A light of recognition comes into his eyes. "It sounds like that story you and Ginny made up in elementary school."

"We didn't make it up. It's real. We found out about it then. It's the book that helps a person find their true love."

"Why? What's the book say?"

"It's not about what it says. It's just like a talisman or something. It makes it happen. People think it does, anyway."

"How does it work?"

I rest my arms on the table. We're inches apart. I drop my voice. "Well, I don't know *how* it works. It just does. Having the book in your possession at Christmastime will guide you to true love. Then the book moves on to someone else."

"Is it supposed to have feet or something?"

I gape at him. "Oh my goodness. Don't be ridiculous. It's not *alive*. And before you ask, no, it isn't magic either. It's just a rumor. But it's a rumor that *has always come true*." I sit back and let the impact of my words land.

"That's...amazing." He leans back in his chair.

"You don't believe me."

"Of course I believe you. I just don't necessarily believe in the rumored powers of the book. It's like winning big at a casino—the rumors only spread about the wins. But if you believe, I'm more than happy to believe with you and help."

I can't really picture how one would believe *with* someone something when they don't actually believe it. It's like saying you're believing *near* someone so that should count, but it's not the same thing at all. Not that it matters. I'll take his help whether he believes in the book or not. I need him, or this won't work at all.

"Okay, well go ahead and believe *near* me. I appreciate your help."

A thick eyebrow goes up. "How exactly am I helping now?"

"Well, the book makes a pretty random path through the population of Cherry Creek. Some people try to keep track of it in case they might want to find their true love one day at Christmas."

His head pulls back. "And you're one of these people?" I can't tell if he's interested or terrified.

I roll my eyes. As if I didn't have enough to do. "Of course not. The last thing I need on my plate right now is true love."

"Oh." His full lips turn down into a thoughtful frown.

"Yeah. Besides not having the time, I've always thought I'd just find my other half on my own someday. Like fate. He'd show up exactly when I was ready—and not before."

He breaks his small cookie in half. "He'll just show up, huh? Like someone new? Not like someone you already know."

I pull my notebook toward me and click my pen. "Huh? No. Someone new, of course. Cherry Creek is way too small. Maybe I'll meet him in Paris or Prague or Singapore or something. Somewhere exotic I'll be someday. Anyway, no one I've talked to knows where the book is right now." I scan my eyes down the list of Cherry Creek residents Ginny and I brainstormed. I'd called the whole list.

"And that's bad."

"Very bad. We need the book. So I can give it to Felicity, and she can find her true love."

Ollie chews his cookie while he drums his fingers on the table. He's got large hands with long fingers. Man hands. His nail beds are wide, and his nails are neatly trimmed. "Is that what she wants?"

"Not consciously. But it's what she needs. She's still so bitter over Mark leaving her like he did that she doesn't believe love and happiness are even possible anymore. That's why she needs the book to bust through all her defenses and deliver her the love and support she needs."

He jerks his chin. "But doesn't think she wants."

"Exactly."

"And you need my help for this?"

"Absolutely. Hold on." I put my pen down and take a bite of my cordial cherry cookie that I can't wait another second for. I close my eyes at the luscious, rich taste of chocolate ganache and maraschino cherry. "*Oh*, these are my favorite." I open my eyes to find Ollie staring at my lips again. He licks his own.

"I'm going to buy another one of those for me." He jumps up and gets in the order line, and I can't fault him.

"Get two!" I call out to him. He nods in acknowledgment.

Five minutes later he's sitting back down across from me. He slides one of the new cookies over and bites into the other one. I watch him like he watched me. His eyes roll back with pleasure the moment the taste hits his tongue. As he moans, there's a jump low down in my stomach that has nothing to do with eating cookies.

"Wow, that's good."

"It really is," I agree. "Thanks for getting more."

"No problem. Though if I was smart, I would've bought a dozen. Maybe I still will." He shifts in his chair.

"First I have to finish telling you why I need you."

He stretches a leg out. "Yes, please tell me why you need me. And exactly how."

There's a low lilt to his words and part of me wonders if he's being suggestive. But it's Ollie. I'm sure I'm imagining it. "Well, as I was saying, no one knows exactly where the book is, but really someone has to know. *Someone* had the book last. Someone knows where it ended up. And I came across someone who said there's a clue."

He cocks an eyebrow. "A clue?"

I nod and break off half a cookie and pop it in my mouth. "Mrs. Atchison said Sadie Foster has a clue."

"Sadie Foster? Who's Sadie Foster?"

"She's the town matchmaker. She's been around forever."

He pulls a face. "Town *matchmaker*? Is that a thing?"

"Yes, it's a big thing—her business is booming. She's had more clients than she can handle after all those matchmaking shows started streaming."

He rubs his jaw. There's a small patch of stubble on the left side that he must have missed shaving. Ten years ago he wasn't capable of producing such solid stubble. "Why would this matchmaker have a clue about the book?"

"Maybe professional interest?" I suggest with my pen in the air. "I don't know why she has the clue or if it's even real in any way, but it's the closest to a hint I've been able to find, so I have to pursue it. Mrs. Atchison, whose daughter found her true love when she got the book, told me Sadie Foster has the clue, but she's also got stipulations about who she's willing to give it to."

"What stipulations?" Ollie eats the carrot cake cookie in one big bite.

"She says she'll only give the clue to a couple. She says if anyone's looking for true love, they need to hire her. Matching people is what she does for a living. She's not going to assist a book in stealing her clients away. But a committed couple looking for a little extra insurance on their happily ever after can get the clue from her. She also seems sympathetic toward looking for the book to give to someone else."

Ollie tilts his chin and gives me a soul-piercing look. "Can I ask you something?"

I stare back with equal seriousness. "Sure."

"Has Cherry Creek always been this odd? Or is this a recent development?"

I laugh and lean my elbows against the table. "Oh, I think

it's always been like this. People have believed in this book for more than twenty-five years, and it's been connecting people with their true loves. We've at least been odd since then."

"Right. And you want me..."

"To be the other half of my committed couple, yes. I know you've got the acting chops. You rocked drama with me in seventh grade. Don't you see? It's perfect. The book is worth a try. It won't hurt anything to get it, and I really want to see my sister happy again. I know she's lonely and broken in a way that's only getting worse with time. And here you are, right before Christmas, and apparently the clue will take both of us to get. You're here just in time. My Christmas miracle." I beam at him like he's the biggest gift on my list, tied up with a red velvet bow on his head.

I may have gone too far. Ollie's eyes widen like a deer in the headlights of a Range Rover.

He leans back and runs a hand through his hair. "I don't know if I can do it. Pretend to be a couple with you."

My heart sinks, not to mention my vanity. I have a sudden ache inside that he hasn't been feeling this little spark of attraction for me that I've been feeling for him. I guess once you're just friends, you're always just friends. Or maybe he's already in a relationship. Or in love with someone in Chicago. I swallow the sudden lump in my throat and scramble for the words to persuade him.

"It wouldn't be real. It'd just be pretend. And not even for very long. Just long enough to convince Sadie and get the clue and the book. I promise I won't get in the way of your normal dating life."

He stares at the table for a long moment. Finally he blows out a breath. "All right. I'll do it. But just to get the clue. No pretending after that."

I want to clap and jump up and down, but I settle for

making a check mark next to *get Ollie to be my fake fiancé* in my notebook. "Of course not. Why would I want to pretend longer? This is all about getting the book."

He nods, though the slight pout of his lips makes him look less than swayed. "Sure."

"Great. Thanks." My happiness that he's agreed evaporates. Instead I feel like I've done something to offend him, though I have no idea what it could be.

"Anything for you," he says in an even tone. Is he being sarcastic? The look he's leveling at me makes me squirm. I don't know why he's being reluctant. This is a temporary situation. It's not like I'm committing him for life.

But he said he'd do it, so it's a win. "Thank you. All we have to do now is go over to Sadie Foster's house and ask her for the clue." And make a plan. And agree on our cover story. I bite on the end of my pen. I may've made the task sound simple, but I have no idea what her screening practice entails. Just how will she know if we're a couple or not?

"Super. Let's go. Now." Ollie stands and steps away from the table.

"Wait! What about the cookies?" I gesture to the Christmas trees, angels, and Santa faces we didn't get to.

"Oh. We'll save them for later." He picks up the cookies with a napkin and puts them back in the pastry bag. "Hold on a minute. I'm going to get that dozen of cordial cherry cookies. Sadie Foster might have a sweet tooth too."

Four

I don't want to give my cookies to Sadie Foster. I only said that to buy time alone so I could try to come to terms with this pretend-relationship thing. But I've got my box of a dozen in hand, and I'm following Amelia to her car. She said she'd drive because she knows where Sadie Foster lives.

Amelia glances at me twice on the drive when she thinks I'm not looking. She's biting her lips and tucking her hair behind her ear—two characteristic gestures I recognize from elementary school that reveal she's confused and doesn't know what to think.

Join the club. I have no idea why hearing that I have to pretend to be her boyfriend has gotten under my skin. Scratch that. Of course I know why. Pretending to be the thing I actually want to be is giving me a rash. It's an insult to the real thing. It also shows how far we are from reality. I might as well be a stranger. Amelia doesn't have feelings for me like I have for her. The only thing these last ten years did was make her forget me... and make her see she never needed me in her life. All she needs me for now is pretend.

And I'm the willing schmuck who'll take pretend over nothing.

"What side of the bed do you sleep on?" Amelia suddenly blurts out.

"Uh...the right side."

Before I can ask her why she's asking, she says, "Is that right when you're facing the bed, or when you're in it?"

I think for a sec. "When I'm facing the bed."

"Great! I mean, that's good. I sleep on the left side—that's the right side when I'm in it. We fit perfectly."

I pause for her to explain, but she seems to be concentrating on the icy patches on the road. Of course I have to ask. "Are we going to start sleeping together? You haven't let me sleep over at your house since second grade. And then it was only because we both fell asleep when my mom was visiting yours."

A rosy blush comes into her cheeks. It's adorable, and I want to say more things that'll make her blush.

"I just don't know what Sadie will ask to prove we're a committed couple. I figure it might be an interview like they do for immigration marriages. Like in the movie *The Proposal*. So, just in case, here's some more about me—my favorite song is "Starlight" by Muse. My favorite color is red. And I use Olay moisturizing cream before bed every night."

I scratch my jaw. "Is she going to ask all that?"

Her shoulders go up around her ears. "I don't know. I'm freaking out. I have no idea what she's going to ask."

"Well, don't worry about it. We've known each other forever."

"And yet I'm worried. But I photoshopped us an engagement picture last night, so we have photographic proof we're together."

I bark out a laugh. "What did you use as our picture?"

"I put our heads on Miley Cyrus and Liam Hemsworth."

"Nice. But weren't they only married for, like, five minutes? And didn't they get divorced a long time ago?"

"Well, yeah, but they've got *our* heads, so it's us. Not them."

"I don't know. Seems like bad mojo for our fake engagement."

The corners of her mouth pull upward. "Maybe I should be fake worried then." She pulls the car up to a small, well-kept house in the Cherry Creek Homes subdivision. "You still up for this?"

"Sure. Just pretend, right?" Ugh. Why do I sound like a sore loser? I should look at this as an opportunity, not a rejection. She could've asked any guy to help, but she didn't. She asked me. This scheme is giving me a chance to be close to her, which is what I wanted in the first place.

Time to square myself with my new role. I stick my elbow out and nod for her to grab it. "We should look like a couple, right?"

She bobs her head and loops her arm in mine. "Good thinking."

We stroll up Sadie Foster's front walk—without the cookies. They were too good to share—and Amelia rings the doorbell. She leans her head against the top of my arm and snuggles into my side as we wait for the door to be answered.

My heart beats a jangly rhythm as I catch the coconut scent of her hair. The situation's messing with my perception of reality. My body is starting to think we're an actual affectionate couple, even though my head knows we're not.

An older woman opens the door, but just a little. She wedges herself into the slice of space as if to say she'll come out before she'll ever let anyone in.

"Mrs. Foster?" Amelia turns a bright smile on the woman and tightens her grip on my arm.

"Yes, dear?" the woman says sweetly.

"Hi, Mrs. Foster. I'm Amelia Taylor. We spoke on the phone?"

"Ah, yes, dear. I remember. The sweet girl who's looking for the *Once Upon a Christmas Kiss* book for her sister."

"Yes, ma'am. My...fiancé...and I are here for the clue, please. We were told you were the person to see."

Mrs. Foster inches out of the doorway onto her top step and lets the screen door slam behind her. She scans us up and down and crosses her arms. "I'm only giving that clue to a committed couple. You two don't fit the bill. Scram."

I gape at Sadie Foster. She'd seemed so sweet. I get ready to turn and scram as asked, but I have to hand it to Amelia—she doesn't falter.

"We *are* a committed couple." Amelia's voice is strong, and her gaze is steady. "*Very* committed."

Mrs. Foster's eyes narrow. "Really? Prove it."

What proof is she looking for? Even married couples don't go around carrying their marriage certificates on them. Are we supposed to show her our matching tattoos?

"I could show you our engagement picture—" Amelia starts.

"Pictures can be faked!" Sadie Foster snaps. This woman missed her calling as a drill sergeant.

"Then what—" Amelia starts again.

"Kiss her!" the woman barks at me.

Something in the deep recesses of my mind or my soul or my heart has prepared me for this eventuality without any conscious planning on my part because instead of gasping or dropping my chin to the floor, I'm instantly turning toward Amelia, registering her slight nod of encouragement, and capturing her mouth with mine.

My arms wrap around her back, clasping her to me. My mouth coaxes hers as I pour ten years of missing her and uncounted years before that of repressed puppy love into that kiss full of longing.

Her lips are sweet and full. They mold against mine lightly at first, then with increasing pressure. I deepen the kiss and her hand grabs a handful of my shirt, crumpling it. She flattens herself against me. More parts of me than my soul wake up at the tender aching she coaxes in my core.

When I pull away, Amelia stumbles and I catch her, supporting her back with my arm. Her cheeks are pink. She's only a little breathless when she steps away and stands under her own power. She faces Mrs. Foster, looking as dazed as I feel. She raises her chin. "My fiancé and I are *fully* committed."

Sadie's answering laugh is a cackle. "I can see that. Okay. Y'all can come on in. I'll get the clue for you." She holds the door open, and I grab it and help Amelia through before following.

"Let me see." Sadie looks around. "Where did I leave that very important clue?" She glances back at us with a wry look.

I feel Amelia stiffen beside me, probably fearing—like me—that we're going to be here for hours as Sadie Foster searches her house for a clue that doesn't exist, but the matchmaker walks over to the hutch in the kitchen, opens the first drawer on the right, and pulls out an envelope.

"Here it is!" She holds it up in the air with a triumphant smile.

Amelia's hand twitches, and she reaches for it. Mrs. Foster hesitates with a shrewd expression, but after a beat she releases the envelope to Amelia, and all of us start breathing again.

"Thank you," Amelia says and runs out of the house.

Five

AMELIA

Oliver follows me out to the car. I'm glad I was fast and he's a step behind, because I don't want him to see my face. Since the moment he placed his lips on mine, my skin has blazed. I'm sure the vast confusion of my emotions, churning wildly as they are, are written all over my flushed face.

Oliver was my childhood friend. As an adult, he's a perfect stranger. But that *kiss*. That kiss was *something*. A flame. A fire. An awakening.

What do I think of this? Of Oliver? Of Oliver's lips? I absolutely shouldn't think of Oliver's lips. I'm finally holding the clue to the location of the legendary book in my hot little hand. The book is my focus. Felicity's happiness is my priority. Not Oliver's lips.

"Do you have a girlfriend?" I blurt.

His eyebrows twitch. "No, I don't. Why?"

"No one waiting for you back in the Windy City?" I press.

"No. Why are you asking?"

Because I've started to become preoccupied with your lips... but I don't say it. "Just making sure we're not disrespecting anyone with this, uh, fake relationship we just staged."

"Ah. No. Free and clear. Like you, I think you said."

"Yeah. Okay. Good. No one to worry about then." Just the miles and miles of space between the two places we each call home. Not that I should be thinking of that. That kiss may have been knee-buckling, but it was fake. I need to remember that. Often.

"What does the clue say?" Ollie opens the driver's side door for me.

I stare down at the unopened envelope in my hand. "I don't know yet. I'll open it in the car."

"Oh." He goes around to the other side, and we both get in. I feel like this is a big moment, and there should be more cere-mony, more fanfare, as I unveil the clue. But if I wait to build up to something like that, my mind will stray back to Oliver's lips while I'm waiting. No more picturing Oliver's lips.

I tear into the envelope. There's an index card inside with a few lines typed onto it.

I have six sides
But I'm not a die
Inside a ring of envy, I'm black and white.

Oliver leans over my shoulder. I can smell his aftershave. Something like the sea and...spice? Cotton? The mountains? Whatever it is, it smells good. "What do you think it means?"

I frown. "Well, it's probably a location for the book, right? Not an object like I'd be tempted to think with the mention of dice." I fan myself with the index card, thinking of all the build-ings and landmarks in Cherry Creek. There are a lot of white buildings and black shutters and black roofs. But there aren't any six-sided buildings that I can think of. Not real buildings, anyway. And what about the ring of envy? Envy is the green-eyed monster. Or maybe that's jealousy. Same thing? Green with envy is a thing, I think. Green. Aha.

I clap my hands. "It's the gazebo in Cherry Creek Park. It's white and has a black roof. It's got six sides, and it's ringed by a circle of *green* bushes." I pause as Oliver applauds me. I laugh. We don't even know if I'm right. "But why would Sadie leave such a valuable book exposed to the elements like that?" I start the car. "It doesn't make any sense. Unless she's purposely trying to destroy her competition."

"Maybe drive fast." Oliver buckles up. "Or maybe don't. There's still some ice."

"I'll try for safe and fast." I never break the speed limit, but we still make it to the park in record time.

Without further discussion we're out of the car and running to the gazebo. After hunting around the bushes ringing the white building with their green envy, I finally find a metal lockbox between a bush and the bottom of the structure. "Got it!" I yell, though when I pick it up, it feels far too light to contain the book. It's also got an added complication in the form of a three-digit combination lock. "Maybe I don't have it. It's too light." I hold the box out to Oliver.

"Is it locked?" He gives the numbers each a whirl and tries to pry the lid up while I study the index card for clues I may have missed. "Yep, it's locked. What's Sadie's birthday?"

I blink at him. "I have no earthly idea."

"Last three of her social?"

I laugh. "Yeah, right."

"Street number of her house?"

"12527."

"Okay. Too many numbers." He rolls some combinations of

the house number. None of them work. "Maybe the answer's in the clue."

"Well, there are three lines of text to the clue. Maybe it's the number of words or syllables or something. The first line has four words, the second has five, and the third has nine. Try four, five, nine."

Oliver rolls a four, five, nine into place and tries the lid. It doesn't open. "Try it backwards."

He rolls a nine, five, and four next. It opens smoothly. "That was easy."

We both peer inside.

As I suspected, there's no book. There is, however, another white envelope inside.

"Well, hello, you two!" My sister's voice rings out behind us as two squishy human balls hurl themselves at my lap, knocking me backwards onto the snow.

I come up laughing and wrestle my bundled-up nephews off me. "Hey, sis!" I smile up at Felicity, who's standing over us with a knowing grin.

"I brought the boys to the park to run off some energy, and it looks like you and Ollie here are doing something similar...?" She lets her words hang suggestively as if we might rush in to explain why we're huddled close together by the steps of the gazebo. I shoot an apologetic look at Ollie. I'm sure she's embarrassing him.

"No. We've been making out. We came here to rest," he answers with a straight face.

My sister's jaw drops. "Oh."

I feel my face catch fire. "He's joking, Felicity! Just joking."

She regards him with a thoughtful smile like she trusts his explanation more than she trusts mine, but she doesn't pursue it.

"What's 'making out'?" Trace looks up from the snowball he's packing between his hands.

Oliver has the grace to cringe. "Sorry," he whispers to my sister.

"You'll find out when you're twenty-three," Felicity tells Trace firmly.

Trace nods. "Must have something to do with work, then. That's when I'm supposed to get a job after college."

"That's right," Ollie says in a serious tone. "Get a job making out, and you'll be set for life."

I close my eyes, afraid to see my sister's reaction to Ollie's career advice. But I can't keep myself from adding, "Because it pays so well."

I sneak a look at Ollie, and we both bust up laughing.

Felicity shakes her head with a rueful smile. "You two are terrible. I'm going to have to answer *so* many questions about this. You just wait and see what I tell *your* kids." She nods at both of us, and we freeze. *Our* kids? There's joking and then there's going too far. "It'll take you years and multiple diagrams to help them figure it out. Boys!" she bellows. "Let's hit the swings!"

Trace and Hudson brush the snow off and race to the swing set. Felicity turns to follow them and pauses. "You two be good now. But not too good." She winks. Oliver laughs. And suddenly I'm fifteen again and completely embarrassed in front of a boy.

Six

AMELIA

We open the white envelope to find another index card with a second typed clue.

> *I'm a person not a place.*
> *I meddle, but I'm kind.*
> *My last name's at the beginning,*
> *But my house is hard to find.*

Oliver blinks when he finishes reading. "How are we going to figure this one out? It could be anyone in Cherry Creek."

"Anyone in the first half of the alphabet."

Oliver nods slowly. "And I guess also knows Sadie Foster."

I brush the snow off and take a seat on the top step leading up into the gazebo. Ollie sits next to me, his long, hard thigh brushing mine. I tap my lips with my finger, thinking about the clue and definitely not about the man sitting next to me.

"And you can't throw a stone in this town without hitting a kind person."

His lips quirk up. "I don't think you should be throwing stones at anyone, least of all kind people."

I smile and knock my knee into his. "That's not what I meant."

"I know. Just kidding." He leans against the gazebo wall. "And I suppose everyone around here meddles?"

"Oh, yeah. You can count on it. You may have left Cherry Creek before you started paying attention to what the adults do in this town, but meddling is the official local pastime. Though there are some people who are worse about it than others."

"Who's the nosiest one out there?"

I pinch my lip, thinking. "Mrs. Atchison. For sure." I sit forward. "In fact, ever since her daughter fell in love and got married while she had the book, Mrs. A. has been up in everyone's business and almost always knows all the gossip on who has the book. You know she was my first call last night. When I asked her about where the book was, she's the one who told me Sadie Foster was the only one who'd know and that she'd give a clue to a committed couple. She's all about the meddling. And 'A' is at the beginning of the alphabet."

"What's Mrs. Atchison like? Is she kind?"

"Very. She collects strays of all sorts—cats, dogs, humans, houseplants. No one in Cherry Creek will go hungry on her watch."

"That's nice."

I nod. "And she lives on Red Oak Drive. That street has no visible numbers on any of the houses or curbs. People are always getting lost over there. And her house is at the very back of a series of twists and turns. It's like a maze."

Oliver stands and extends a hand down to me. "Sounds like that's exactly where we should go next."

I take his offered hand and get up very slowly, suddenly less excited about getting to the next clue. "Yes, it does sound like that, doesn't it?"

Oliver cocks an eyebrow at me. "But you're hesitating for some reason."

"Yeahhh," I draw out the word and rock on my feet. "You caught that, huh?"

He smiles, and a glimmer of amusement dances in his eyes. I don't think I've noticed before what a truly beautiful shade of brown his eyes are. Warm and liquid. A color I'd like the chance to observe more closely...while taking my time. I pull my brain back to the present and the topic I'm avoiding.

I spit out all my words at once. "Mrs. A. asked me to do something, and I haven't done it. Truth be told, I don't want to do it."

His smile grows with my mini-fit, and he crosses his arms. The seams of his coat strain at containing the well-developed muscles within. "What exactly does she want you to do?"

I rub my forehead. "Introduce her to my new boss, Principal Bourne. She thinks he's cute."

Seven

OLIVER

I laugh. Since the day we met in kindergarten, Amelia Taylor has been surprising me. "And is Principal Bourne, in fact, cute?"

"I don't know," she says, half wailing the words. "That's not the point. He's my boss. And he's new to the job, so I don't know him very well. I'm not sure how he'd take my meddling in his love life. I don't want to risk the security of my job. He's a nice-looking, older gentleman, but he's in charge and can impact my whole entire career. *Cute* isn't a word I'd use for him."

"Ah." I nod sagely. "I get it. Awkward."

"Sure is. And the last time I spoke to Mrs. A, she strongly suggested that I get the two of them together. Luckily I got off the phone last night before she could ask, but if we go over to her house, she's going to want to know. I don't want to be blamed if that whole situation blows up."

"Well, sure. No one wants to feel responsible for someone else's relationship."

"Exactly."

I fold my arms. "What are we going to do about it?"

She pinches her bottom lip between her thumb and forefinger. "I don't know. I'm still thinking."

"Well, we're not going to give up on the next clue, right?"

"Um...right."

"Maybe we should drive over there while you're thinking."

She tilts her chin and gives me a blank look. "I can't drive and have a serious think-fest at the same time."

"If it's *serious*, can it really be called a *fest*? Isn't that short for festival?"

A faint smile tugs at my lips. Oliver has always been so literal. It's adorable. "I don't know. But anyway, I can't think and drive at the same time. It's a personal failing."

I shrug. "Okay. I'll drive."

"Okay, then. You can drive my car." She hands me her keys, and her fingers brush my palm. The hairs rise on my arm, making me wish she'd touch me again. Apparently all the nerve endings in my body are craving her.

I suck in a deep breath and pretend I don't feel it. I'm getting better at pretending. "Great. Let's go."

Amelia navigates, and I drive to Mrs. A.'s house. Amelia was right—the path to get there is remarkably maze-like. But Cherry Creek is pretty small, and it only takes us ten minutes to get there despite feeling like I've twisted through some magical forest to arrive at our destination.

The house is simple and plain for all the loops and turns it takes to get there. It's a tidy, ranch-style home set far back from the road. But what the house lacks in drama, the front lawn fully makes up for.

A giant inflatable Santa—taller than the house—stands watch in the center of the yard. Around him are more plastic Christmas decorations than on display at all the big-box stores combined. There are reindeer and a sleigh, Gru and his minions, Trolls, the Grinch and Max and Cindy Lou Who, Snoopy and

Woodstock, Tweety Bird and Sylvester, and the entire Bob's Burgers family all wearing Santa hats. There's even Nemo and Dory, though why they're out of the water for Christmas is anyone's guess. "Wow."

"Yeah. Mrs. A. really goes all out. It's a commitment. And an enormous electric bill."

"I guess so." I drive all the way up the long gravel driveway and park behind a rusting old station wagon.

Amelia unbuckles her seatbelt. "Here we go. Let's get that book."

I follow her to the front steps, but Mrs. Atchison opens the door before we get there.

Her smile stretches wide. "Amelia Taylor! And her loving beau. Sadie told me all about you two, kissing like a house afire on her front step."

I wonder at the speed at which that info exchange would've had to happen. Gossip is faster than the Wi-Fi in this town.

Amelia blushes bright red, and I resist the urge to pump my fist in the air. Apparently I'm not the only one who thought that was the hottest kiss in human history. I just hope Amelia's rosiness isn't only embarrassment. Or regret.

I mean, I know she can't have felt what I did. For her, it wasn't the culmination of a ten-year-long crush, but she kissed me back. I want to think she liked it too. And that little bit of unbalance following the kiss gives me hope that maybe, just maybe, she felt a little something for me.

It certainly felt like she did. I smile just thinking about it.

Mrs. A. laughs, looking right at me. "He's really smitten, isn't he?" She steps out of her house and comes closer. "Tell me. Are you Clark Kent, or are you Superman?"

"Excuse me?" I don't get the non sequitur. I look around, but I don't see Superman decorations on her lawn.

Amelia clears her throat, her face as scarlet as it was a

moment ago. "Mrs. A., I'm sorry. We're kind of in a hurry. We solved this clue in Mrs. Foster's treasure hunt for the book, and we think you're it." She holds the white envelope out as proof.

Mrs. A. laughs again. "Yes, I am. Although I wasn't lying to you on the phone earlier about not having the book. You're right that I do have the next clue."

She scurries back inside and returns a moment later with another white envelope. She strolls past Amelia without looking at her and places it directly in my hand instead.

"Thank you," I tell Mrs. A.

She smiles. "Any time." She pats my upper arm. "Oh," she says in a low voice, curling her hand around my bicep and squeezing. "You do have some nice, solid muscles there, don't you?"

"Mrs. Atchison!" Amelia's voice squeaks. She stalks over and physically pulls me out of Mrs. A.'s grasp by my other arm. "Oliver and I have to go. Thank you for your help."

Mrs. Atchison crosses her arms. "Amelia Taylor. Don't you dare leave here and pretend you don't remember what you agreed to do."

Amelia freezes in place with a guilty look. "You're right. I'm sorry, Mrs. A. I haven't spoken to Mr. Bourne yet."

"What's the holdup?"

Amelia takes a deep breath. I can see the moment when she decides to be open about her fears. The corners of her eyes unpinch, and the furrow on her brow smooths. "I really, really need my job. It's important that I take care of my family and don't do anything to jeopardize it. My family is the most important thing to me. That's why I want the book. I want to give it to my sister Felicity so she can get over Mark and get on with her life. I'm sorry. Principal Bourne is new, and I don't know him well enough to know how he'd take being set up. And he's my boss. I don't want to risk the stability of my job if something between you and Mr. Bourne doesn't work out."

"Love is always worth the risk," she says then holds up a hand. "I mean when you're going after love for yourself. For me? Well, I'm sorry I put you in that position. I'm letting you off the hook. I'll find a way to introduce myself to Mr. Bourne, and you can bet your behind it'll be memorable."

Amelia cracks a smile. "I'm sure it will be. But I think I can still help a little."

Mrs. A. raises an eyebrow. "Oh?"

"What if you made one of your wonderful pecan pies for the PTA bake sale? You'd be there...he'd be there...it'd be natural for me to introduce the two of you."

The older woman beams. "Now that sounds like a plan!" She rubs her hands together. "Okay run along, you two, and go get that book for Felicity. She needs that thing more than anyone I've ever known. And Amelia?"

"Yes, ma'am?"

"You take care of that Superman of yours, okay?"

Amelia's face blushes crimson this time, and she sneaks a sidelong glance at me. "Yes, ma'am," she says again. "I will."

My mouth goes dry, and I bite down on a smile.

Amelia just agreed that I'm hers.

Eight

AMELIA

Oh, will the indignities never end? This wacky treasure hunt has been one embarrassment after another. I don't see how Oliver isn't on the next plane to Chicago with everything he's been subjected to today. Apparently Cherry Creek is pulling out all the stops to showcase our eccentricities—and our obsession with other people's love lives. Even the pretend ones.

I'm driving my car now instead of letting Oliver drive, but only because I wanted to escape from Mrs. A.'s house as quickly as possible. I haven't opened the next clue, so I don't actually know where I'm driving to.

The way Mrs. A. was handling Oliver like she wanted to eat him with a spoon was just...well, it was just...it was quite simply *relatable*, but that doesn't make it any less inappropriate.

"I apologize for Mrs. Atchison and how she acted back there with you."

Oliver chuckles. "Don't apologize. She was sweet, and it's nice to be appreciated. Even if it is just for my arms."

I'm sure she was appreciating him for more than that. "You really do have nice arm muscles." Did I really just say that out loud? I feel another killer blush suffuse my face and neck. If only my coloring didn't give away my *every* stray thought.

Ollie's laugh sounds surprised. "Thanks. So do you. They seem to hold your arm bones together nicely."

I laugh, too, shaking my head. "This has been such a weird day."

"I know, and it's barely started. Hey, by the way, where are we going?"

"Anywhere." I slow the car as we pass the courthouse. "I just wanted to get away. I'll pull over somewhere so we can look at the next clue."

"I can read it."

"Go for it. What have we got?"

Oliver opens the envelope and reads as I pull into the parking lot of the public library.

Hold me up, take me down.
I might be a ninja, or I might be a clown.

Oliver shakes his head. "This is the worst one yet. What's that supposed to mean?"

I snap my fingers and start the car back up. "I know exactly what this one means. Ginny and I took the boys there last weekend when the ninja was fighting the clown. But they were both wearing Santa hats—it was a Christmas-themed bout. And they hugged at the end, because, you know, peace on Earth and goodwill toward men. And ninjas and clowns. Anyway, our next clue—or the book itself—is at the Cherry Creek Wrestling Entertainment school."

Oliver laughs. "Cherry Creek has a wrestling entertainment school? Seriously?"

"We do. And it's very popular. People come from all over to see their weekend shows. They're very entertaining. That's why it's in the title."

"I guess so. Good for Cherry Creek then."

"I take it your parents haven't attended a show yet?"

He shrugs. "If they have, they haven't mentioned it."

I put on the blinker to turn left. "They'd mention it."

"Then I guess not. They probably don't even know about it."

"Well, you should take them some weekend. I think they'd really enjoy the show."

He shifts in his seat. "Maybe you could take me."

I shoot him a sidelong glance. His expression is smooth, even. This isn't a casual comment. He's genuinely waiting for my answer.

"I could do that. We're old friends. Why wouldn't I?" I don't know why I feel the need to qualify my answer like that. Actually, I do know. It's because Chicago and Cherry Creek aren't next door. He's leaving after Christmas. And when he's gone, he's gone.

He nods slowly and exhales. "Yes, we're old friends. That should be fine."

His words fall flat, and disappointment plunges in my gut. I don't know what I wanted him to say, but something more than bland agreement would be nice. Even bland *disagreement* would be better.

We don't speak again until I pull up to the wrestling school, which is a large warehouse-type building on the outskirts of town. It used to house a paper company, but when that went out of business, Waylon Moffatt bought it and turned into the wrestling school he'd always wanted. Now a respectable-looking brick sign sits out front announcing it to be the Cherry Creek Wrestling Entertainment School.

"Huh," Ollie says, frowning. "It's real. I almost didn't believe it."

"It's real, all right." I get out of the car. "Now let's just hope Waylon has the book itself and not just another clue for us."

We end up disappointed on all counts. Waylon isn't even there, so we don't know what he may or may not be in possession of. The custodian, Bud, tells us class is done for the day and we might be able to find Waylon at his favorite haunt, The Cheery Cherry Bar, so we move on.

The Cheery Cherry is all decked out for Christmas. I haven't been here in years, but it looks the same as it always has with the exception of the large, decorated Christmas tree taking up half of the dance floor in front of the jukebox. Boughs of greenery and holly hang from every rafter, and a scarecrow dressed as Santa sits alone at the back corner table.

We ask the bartender, but Waylon isn't there either. Oliver glances at his watch. "Do you want to call it quits for today? Pick up the search tomorrow when the wrestling school opens?"

It's true that nothing else can be accomplished tonight. More than that, I don't even need Oliver anymore because only the first clue required a committed couple as far as I know. Really, Ollie could ditch me any time, and I'd probably still be able to get the book for Felicity. But I'm not ready to part with him yet.

"Are you hungry? I'm hungry. We could get dinner," I say hopefully. "Felicity isn't working tonight, so I don't have to hurry home."

Oliver looks around with obvious skepticism. "Have dinner here?"

I'm sure The Cheery Cherry is nowhere near as nice as the

fancy Chicago restaurants I assume he frequents, but we're already here, so the convenience can't be beat.

"Yeah!" I take his arm and pull him over to one of the booths. "They've got good bar food. Burgers, sandwiches, onion rings. Basically anything fried is a specialty here."

He glances at his watch again. "Okay. But I've got to text my mom and tell her not to wait on me for dinner."

"Okay."

Oliver texts his mom, and I drum my fingers on the table in rhythm to the pop song I'm barely registering playing in the background. That song ends, and my fingers pause. The opening notes to "You're Beautiful" by James Blunt float through the air, and my head snaps up. It's a song I love, a song from the past, and it always makes me think of lost connections, of what might have been if things hadn't turned out differently. If Oliver hadn't moved away. If his whole life wasn't somewhere else entirely right now.

Oliver's eyes go to mine, and I realize he's feeling the same way. The hungry look in his gaze says that he's right there with me.

"Do you want to dance?" he asks.

"Definitely." My voice is almost breathless.

Two couples are already out on the floor. This song means something to more people than just me...and Oliver. We leave our coats on our seats. Oliver holds a hand out to me, and I take it, his touch inciting an electrical current that zings up my arm. We step out onto the dance floor. He puts his arms around me, and we start to sway. I tip my chin up and find his eyes on mine with a studied, deep look in their clear pools as he watches me. I'm suddenly aware of every molecule of contact between us. My arms around his neck. His arms around my back. The press of his body against mine as the music and lyrics dip and swirl around us.

I feel myself melting. More than just my body, which seems to be a mass of excited sparks in his arms. My heart is melting too. Memories of Oliver meld with the very real man in front of me. The boy who was always there for me. The man who's here with me now. My will starts to melt too. My determination to make good decisions for the future—to avoid having feelings for someone who is geographically unavailable—seems to retreat behind my growing desire to enjoy the moment here with Oliver now, even though he'll be gone after Christmas. Maybe taking my heart with him.

That can't happen.

"I've got to go," I say, leaning back and stepping out of reach, out of touch.

Oliver's lips turn down, and his eyes swim up from a dazed expression. "Uh, sure." He combs his fingers through his hair. "You're not hungry anymore?"

Not for food. And I definitely shouldn't be hungry for anything else. I don't have time or space in my life for an attraction to Oliver. And we're miles apart, geographically. My greedy little desire to be held and to dance with him is impractical and completely unproductive. "No, thanks. I'll drive you home. You can tell your mom the disruption in dinner plans is all my fault. I'm sorry." I start back toward our booth.

"Amelia," he calls, and I turn. "Can I join you in the morning to go after the next clue?" His eyes appear uncertain, and my pulse stutters.

I take a deep breath. "Sure."

He smiles, and there's an answering flutter in my ribcage that I quickly try to squash.

Oliver and I are just friends, I tell myself sternly. He lives in Chicago, and I live in Cherry Creek. Friends are all we'll ever be.

Nine

Oliver

I don't know why Amelia freaked out last night. One moment we were having a great time, planning a greasy dinner and connecting body and soul on the dance floor, and the next moment she's barely slowing her car down as she drops me off at my house, speeding away so fast her back tires kick up gravel on the way out.

Things were going well last night. Very well. With that song playing, I was ready to bring up how I felt about her back then. How I still feel. And how that might lead to something starting between us now. For our future.

But she'd have to stop running away in order to have that conversation.

I take a sip of coffee just as Amelia's car pulls into my driveway. I pick up her cup and take it to her, pausing as she rolls down her window. She accepts it from me gratefully before I move to the passenger side and get in the car.

"Thanks." She squeezes her coffee cup between her hands and takes a sip, her eyes closing with blissful appreciation. "I hadn't gotten any yet. I was hoping to pick some up on the way. You read my mind."

"No problem."

She shoots me a side glance. "Sorry about running out like I did last night."

I almost ask why she did, but I don't want to push her for an answer she might not be ready to give. Better to pretend that I don't care. "No worries. My mom made lasagna, so I was glad I didn't miss it."

She nods. "Your mom's lasagna is great. I remember." She looks like she wants to say something else, but I glance out the window.

"We should get going," I say.

She bites her bottom lip, her straight teeth sinking into its softness. I remember her braces in sixth grade, and her front teeth losing their slightly beaverlike bite. Sometimes I miss it. "Yeah. Sure."

She backs out of the driveway and drives us to the wrestling school. This time it's open.

We enter Waylon's office, and the man behind the desk looks up. He's got a solid build and is definitely more muscled than the average guy, but he doesn't look like the pro wrestlers you see on TV. A CCWE T-shirt stretches tautly over his chest. "Hey, you two. Sorry I missed you yesterday. Bud said y'all were after your next clue."

"That's right." Amelia stands up straight like she's prepared if he asks her to audition.

He nods and grabs an envelope from the shelf behind him. "Here you go."

She sticks her hand out and takes it from him.

Waylon scratches his scruff of a beard. "Say, would you two like a wrestling entertainment lesson while you're here? Free of charge. I'm working up these date packages now—couples can take a lesson. I'll even have Groupon deals. It'll be a fun date."

"No, thanks," Amelia says without looking at me. Her cheeks turn pink. "We're in a hurry to get to the next clue."

Sure, she's in a hurry. To get far away from me. Guess we aren't past whatever drove her off last night. It puts an ache in my gut.

Waylon nods. "I get it. Don't have too many left now, do you?"

Amelia perks up. "Don't we?"

Waylon chuckles uncomfortably. "Not quite sure. Best get to the next one, I suppose." He jerks his head toward the envelope in Amelia's hand. "Good luck with that."

"Thanks," Amelia and I say at the same time. We wave goodbye to Waylon, and Amelia practically skips back to the car.

"Not too much left to go, it sounds like." She smiles.

My gut churns. Once we have the book, Amelia will no longer need my help. Then I guess it's extreme disappointment, heartbreak, and hanging with Mom and Dad until it's time to go back to Chicago. Maybe I can think of a way to make the hunt last longer. Or maybe I should just enjoy it while I can. At least she's smiling now.

Amelia waits until we're both back inside the car before opening the envelope. She holds the clue between us so I can read it along with her. I lean in close until I can smell the coconut scent of her hair. I never knew how much I loved coconut.

I'm handy, but I'm not soft.
I'm no biker, but I love a loft.

I have no idea what the clue means, but I see the wheels turning behind Amelia's sea-green eyes.

"Okay, there aren't too many lofts in Cherry Creek." Her head leans side to side as if weighing the options. "There are some barns and haylofts outside of town. We don't have a ton of loft apartments like NYC or other big cities. But there are a couple of lofts over a few of the stores on Main Street." She stares out the window. I give her time to think.

After a minute, she hits the top of the steering wheel with the flat of her hand. "It's Harley at Harley's Hardware. It's got to be. He lives in the loft above his store, and hardware isn't soft."

I rub my hands together. We're back in the chase. "Sounds like that's it."

She puts the car into gear, and we speed off toward the next clue—and the end of our adventure together.

Ten

AMELIA

"Sorry, Amelia. I have no idea what you're talking about. A clue? About a book? At a hardware store? This sounds like some kind of trick to me."

I stare at Harley, wracking my brain for any other person or location in town that could possibly fit the clue.

I'm coming up blank.

Oliver shifts his weight from one foot to the other. He doesn't say anything, but I wonder if he's got faith that I'll figure this out. Or if I've hideously embarrassed him by dragging him to the wrong place on my wild goose treasure hunt.

The corner of Harley's mouth twitches, and before long he's full-out laughing. He slaps the checkout counter with glee. "Man, you should see y'all's faces. Thanks for that. It was hilarious."

Oliver and I trade looks as Harley beams at us. We're not nearly as amused as he is.

"Harley, can—" I start.

"I've got your clue right here, darlin'" he interrupts me and heads toward a shelf behind the counter. He holds the envelope out to me, but when I go to take it, he snatches it away.

He giggles. "Not so fast there, Ms. Taylor. Sadie said anyone on the hunt has been bona fide in love and stamped with approval by her." He raises his eyebrows and gestures between me and Oliver. "Y'all don't look so stamped to me, standing there scowling."

"I didn't know you needed proof, too," Amelia says as she crosses her arms in front of her.

Harley shrugs. "I don't. At least Sadie didn't say anything about me needing to verify anything. It's more what you'd call... a *personal* interest." He eyes Oliver with a head-to-toe look.

Great. Another Cherry Creek resident who's far too appreciative of Oliver's looks.

And Harley's always been interested in everyone else's love lives. I pull my features out of my supposed scowl and turn adoring eyes on Ollie. "Oh, we're very much in love."

"We certainly are." Oliver puts his arm around me. "So in love I forget to breathe. She has to remind me."

"Uh-huh." Harley looks unconvinced. "Y'all walked right under that mistletoe when you came in, and neither of you so much as glanced at it. That to me does not proclaim hearts full of love." He purses his lips and shoots us a look. I take it for the challenge it is.

I pull both of Oliver's arms around me. To his credit, he picks up on my cue and wraps me in close, molding me against him. After a beat, he leans down and kisses the top of my head. "We're very much in love," he says, his voice low and rough, convincingly hitching on the last word. I beam all my pretend happiness at Harley like I'm on a teeth-whitening commercial, even as I'm wondering why Ollie didn't lay another showy kiss on me.

"Uh-huh," Harley says again, folding his arms and leaning his side against the counter.

"Yes. I've just been so preoccupied with finding the book for Felicity that I haven't been thinking about anything else. Believe me, if I'd seen that mistletoe over there, I definitely would have been all over this guy." I pat Oliver's chest with the back of my hand. It's remarkably solid.

"Uh-huh," he says for the third time. I'm striking out here. Harley's going to call Sadie and tell her he can't give us the clue because Oliver and I being a couple is a total fraud.

I glance toward the giant festoons of red velvet ribbon surrounding the perfect dangling branch of mistletoe. "In fact, now that I do see the mistletoe, we're going to make good use of it, posthaste."

I raise my eyes to Oliver in a silent plea. He nods to me, and in no time, I'm steering us under the supposedly unmissable mistletoe. I rise on my tiptoes and kiss Oliver for all I'm worth. He's rigid at first, as if keeping part of himself in reserve, but after a moment, he leans into the kiss. He cups the back of my head with one large hand and the other holds my back as he bends over me.

Lights, music, and fireworks all explode in my body at the same time. The pressure of his lips on mine is tantalizing, perfect. My fingers stroke through his short hair. A satisfied sigh escapes me, and my eyes go wide as I realize I'm having very real physical and emotional reactions to a kiss that's not supposed to be real. I pull away.

"Love that mistletoe!" I stumble a bit, and Oliver catches me. I just can't seem to keep my balance around him.

Harley claps wildly. "Okay, I believe you! No one could fake that level of chemistry. Here's your clue." He lifts the envelope in our direction. Oliver strides over to the counter with more balance than I have and takes it. Harley rests an elbow on the counter and props his chin in his hand, openly ogling my pretend fiancé.

"Did anyone ever tell you that you look like Superman?" Harley bats his eyes.

"I don't—" Ollie starts.

"We've got to go!" I put both hands on Oliver's back and push him toward the door. Harley sighs with disappointment, but I don't let go of Ollie until we're safely out on the sidewalk.

I fan myself with my hand once we're outside. I catch Oliver watching me with an amused expression. "What?"

He smiles. "It's freezing out here, and you're fanning your face. Just trying to understand why." His tone suggests he knows exactly why. It sends a frisson of longing through me.

I look at my hand. "I'm just flushed or hot or something. I don't know." My face is probably Santa-suit red, but I stop fanning myself. "It was really hot in there."

His gaze is steady on mine. The corners of his lips edge up. "It certainly was."

My stomach dives toward my feet, but I refuse to think about that kiss. Or the fireworks. Or the longing. I won't acknowledge anything in any way. "Now what does our next clue say?"

Oliver fumbles for it even though it's already in his hand like he forgot he was holding it. I smile. That fake kiss got to him, too, even if he's a little better at hiding it. He opens the envelope, and we read the clue together.

To find me next, be in a natural state.
Come for the kissing, and don't forget the bait.

"Oh, no." Oliver visibly pales. "Does this mean we have to get naked for this one? Nudity is a hard thing to pretend."

"What?" My mouth falls open, and my eyes bug out. "What makes you think we'd have to get naked?"

His cheeks redden. "The...um...'natural state' part of the clue. Not that I'd mind seeing you naked. I mean, I bet you look great. It's just that it's so cold out. So very cold and—"

I hold up a hand. "It's okay. Don't worry. Nobody has to get naked. I mean, we definitely won't, no matter what Sadie might say."

"What?" Oliver looks alarmed again.

I wave it off. "I'm just kidding. I'm sure the clue's about something else."

"Like what?"

"I don't know. Let me think. Natural state. Nature. State of Tennessee. Anything there?"

Oliver shakes his head. I go on with my brainstorming. "Then there's the kissing..." I don't want to talk about the kissing. I scan to the rest of the clue. "Oh, the bait! I bet that's something to do with the lake. There's great fishing at Cherry Creek Lake and a bait shop not far from the..." I trail off as I realize what the clue means.

"The what?"

"The kissing tree. The clue's talking about the kissing tree. It's on the edge of Cherry Creek Lake."

"The kissing tree? How did I miss that?"

"Well, you did move away before your prime kissing years."

Ollie shakes his head. "Wow. The things I've missed."

He's missed a lot of things in Cherry Creek, and I've missed all the time I could've had with him if his family hadn't moved away. I wonder if we would've stayed friends in high school or if we'd fall into different crowds and drift apart. Or if we'd have dated.

I unlock the car and get behind the wheel. Ollie slides into the passenger side as I start the engine. He leans toward me, and for an incandescent moment, I think he's coming in for another kiss. But he adjusts the air vents and sits back in his seat.

"So how did the kissing tree get its name?" he asks.

I pull the car out onto Main Street, wondering if he's baiting me, but I answer anyway. "It's where people go to kiss—teenagers, mostly. It's a misnomer because there are lots of trees around there that are just as good for kissing under, but this particular one is the most famous."

"Why's that?"

"Personally, I think it's because it's open to the clearing, so more people have been caught kissing under it than any other tree, but it's also probably the most comfortable tree to sit under."

He cocks an eyebrow at me. "Ah. So you have first-hand knowledge."

"Tons. An incredible amount, actually."

Before he can look too scandalized, I add, "I'm a middle school teacher. I hear all the rumors. And most of them are true."

"So does the kissing tree have special powers like the book?" He lifts an eyebrow.

"You know the book doesn't have any powers—it's just the belief that it works that makes it special."

He shakes his head. "But no one knows that for sure."

"So you're a believer now?"

"I'm reserving judgment. I want to get a look at this famous tree."

I park the car at Cherry Creek Lake, and we stroll to the kissing tree. Fortunately no one's there right now, so I don't have to face the embarrassment of someone thinking Oliver and I are there for our own kissing reasons. If one of my students got ahold of info like that—or, heaven forbid, photographic evidence—I'd never live it down.

"I found it!" Ollie says, pulling a metal lockbox out from behind the kissing tree.

"Great! Is it another combination lock?"

"It is." He holds it out to me. "Should we check the previous clue for the code?"

"Yeah. I left it in the car." I take two steps in the direction of the parking lot. Oliver doesn't move.

I swivel back to him. "Are you coming?"

"It'd be a shame to waste the trip." He gestures at the tree. "Test the powers of the tree?"

I laugh, thinking he's joking.

His feet don't budge. "You're not interested? I could've sworn you were at least a little bit interested."

Oh, I'm interested, but I shouldn't be. I have a puzzle to solve and a sister to save from a lifetime of bitterness.

But Oliver's waiting.

"I'm not *not* interested." I take a single step toward him. "But what about all that pretend kissing we've been doing for the hunt? Aren't you sick of kissing me yet?"

He barks out a surprised laugh. "No. Can't say I'm sick of it. Don't think I ever could be."

I take another step closer. My heart is in my throat. "And this kiss would be...real."

He takes a deep breath. "Amelia, they were all real."

My body moves faster than my brain, and suddenly I'm in his arms, kissing him and knowing that this time it's really us. Our thoughts. Our feelings. Our reality. No more pretending. When we come up for air, I look around for the lockbox, which I managed to drop and lose track of when we entangled ourselves.

I pick it up from the ground. "Okay, we've still got to open this thing."

We head back to the car, and Oliver puts an arm around me. It's warm and comforting, and I'm absolutely not letting myself think about what that kiss and his arm around me could mean to the future. Together? Apart? We live in two different states. I can't leave Felicity and the boys. I draw in a steadying breath and tell myself to stop spinning out. It was a very nice kiss. But it doesn't have to be more than that. It can't be. And I can live with that. Can't I?

We get in the car, and I hand the lockbox over to Oliver and grab the previous clue. Maybe something about the number of words per line like before, or maybe the number of letters in certain words, or maybe the number of "E's," or some other letter will make up the combination.

"Hey! I got it open." Oliver flips the button, and the lock unlatches with a click.

"How?"

"I rolled them all to zeroes, and it opened."

"I thought treasure hunts got harder closer to the end, not easier."

"Yeah." He stares at the box as if it'll explode.

I lean over as Oliver raises a hand to lift the lid. He hesitates, then flips it. We both stare inside.

"It's empty," I state the obvious. "Why is it empty? This is ridiculous."

I start the car and throw it into reverse. Oliver scrambles to put his seatbelt on. "Where are we going?"

"To Sadie's house. This is her treasure hunt, and apparently, we've reached the end of it. She's got some serious explaining to do."

"Do you think the book's been stolen?"

I stop for a pedestrian crossing Main Street under the wide

arches of sparkling garland. "No, I don't. That box can't have been there more than a few hours. It snowed last night, but the box didn't have any snow on it. I think Sadie never put the book in there. I think this whole thing is a giant trick."

Eleven

Oliver

"I admit it was a trick." Sadie Foster shrugs as she takes the empty metal lockbox from Amelia.

"Aha!" Amelia jumps and jabs her finger in the air.

Sadie stares at her. "I already admitted it. You can relax." She shakes her head. "Yeah, I was trying to come up with another clue, but y'all solved it before I could. I put the box out there, but I hadn't quite figured out where to point the next clue to yet. And you just solved them all so much faster than I expected. I was hoping you'd maybe solve a clue a day. That would've taken us safely past Christmas."

Amelia and I regard each other with shared disbelief. "Why did you want us to solve it after Christmas?" I ask.

She gives me a look like I'm obviously not a Cherry Creek local. "Because then the book would be out of circulation for another year. I wouldn't have to worry about it bringing another couple together for a whole other year. It's not good for my business."

Amelia folds her arms. "Sadie, where's the book?" The glare

she levels at the older woman shoots switchblades across the room.

"I'll get it for you." Sadie waddles off to the dining room, and we follow.

"Are you serious?" Amelia says. "You're going to just give it to us now? Why didn't you hand it over the first time we were here asking for it?"

"I was delaying, remember?"

"And yet you didn't destroy it. You could have thrown it in the fire," lawyer-me feels duty bound to point out her inconsistent reasoning.

Sadie and Amelia both turn around and glare at me like I just suggested burning the Declaration of Independence.

Sadie pulls herself up to her full height of maybe five foot one. "I'm a businesswoman—not a monster."

She scrambles under her dining room table, pretty spry for her age. "I've got it!" She emerges a second later and presents the book to Amelia. It's a forest green hardbound book, no dust jacket, with gold lettering spelling out *Once Upon a Christmas Kiss* on the cover. A small sprig of mistletoe is imprinted below the title. Amelia takes it into her hands and holds it close, almost hugging it. I'm suddenly jealous of the thing.

"Thank you," Amelia says.

"Well, I guess it had to get back out there sometime." Sadie's voice is gruff.

Amelia flips the book over and gives the back a good look. It's not every day you get your hands on a legend. I wouldn't mind taking a look myself. "It's not much competition for you, really, is it? Maybe one Cherry Crook couple a year?" she asks.

Sadie sighs. "It's true. And my online business is booming. The book can't go online now, can it?"

Amelia and I glance at each other and try not to laugh. "It certainly can't."

"Well, good luck to your sister, Amelia. I don't mind losing the book to you. With all she's been through, Felicity is a tough case. It'll take more than my matchmaking powers to match her." Mrs. Foster escorts us both to the door.

"Thanks, Sadie. I think Felicity needs all the luck she can get."

We get into the car and wave at Sadie Foster as we drive away.

Amelia has the book now. Technically, our fake engagement is ended. But that kiss by the kissing tree means we're something now, even if that something is new and undefined.

When we get to Amelia's house—which is, of course, also Felicity's house—a scared look comes into Amelia's eyes. "I really hope this works."

"It's supposed to, right?"

"Right."

"And Sadie wouldn't have felt so threatened by it if it didn't."

"True."

I send her a bolstering smile. "So you've got this."

She smiles back at me, and a little fishhook in my heart gives a tug.

"Thanks for all your help, Ollie."

"Of course. I can honestly say I wouldn't have wanted you to do this treasure hunt with any other guy." There was far too much kissing.

"Me neither." She uses her key and opens her front door. I hesitate at the threshold behind her.

"Come in," she says. "You've got to see the payoff." She waves the book in the air. "This is our triumphant return."

Twelve

AMELIA

The decorative wreath bangs against the door as I let Ollie into the house behind me. "Felicity!" I call. I shut the door against the cold and tuck the book behind my back like the surprise it is.

"Hey! What's up?" She jogs into the living room and skids to a stop when she sees Oliver's with me. Her smile grows. "Well, hello, you two. Been out having fun?"

"We certainly have." I beam at Ollie and don't even blush. I've been having a ton of fun with him, and I don't care who knows it. As long as he does. "And I have an early Christmas present for you. I didn't wrap it because I wanted to put it in your possession right away. It's probably the best gift you've ever gotten or ever will get in your entire life. I hope. Or maybe it'll do nothing. We don't actually know."

Felicity glances from me to Oliver and back again. I can almost see her expectations amping up. "Okay. Wow. Lay it on me."

I squeal and hand her the book.

She stares down at it. "It's a book."

I'm so excited for my sister I barely register her lack of enthusiasm. "It's not any old book."

"It *is* an old book."

I jostle her arm. "But not *just* any old book. It's *the* book."

She holds the cover up to her face like she may have missed something. "The Bible? It doesn't look like the Bible. It's too skinny."

"No." I glance at Oliver. He'd thought *the* book would be the Bible too. "I have to say I'm disappointed in you, sis. That right there, in your very hands, is the most famous, most beloved book in all of Cherry Creek."

She's flipping through the pages, frowning, as I wait through the silent drumroll in my head. I add a mental trumpet flourish too.

"That is the legendary book *Once Upon a Christmas Kiss*," I announce.

She looks up. "And?"

"And it's the book that makes everyone who has it in their possession at Christmastime find their true love."

Felicity drops the book.

My mouth falls open. Her eyes are wide. Oliver, Felicity, and I all stare at the book on the floor.

"*The* book?" Felicity breathes.

I nod. "So, you *have* heard of it."

"Of course, I've heard of it. That book's a Cherry Creek institution. It's our claim to fame. It's practically proof of the supernatural."

"Uh-huh," I say. We all continue to stare at the book on the floor.

"I'd forgotten all about it," Felicity says in a reverent whisper. "I haven't thought of it in years." She swallows. "So, it's really mine now?" Her voice squeaks on the last word.

"It's all yours," I confirm.

She bends and gingerly picks it up. Now that she knows what it is, she holds it in her arms like it's an hours-old infant. "Wow. So *the* book is in my possession now."

"Yup."

"And I...might...find my true love at Christmastime now that the book is in my possession."

"That's what people say."

Her forehead creases. "This Christmas or next Christmas?"

I glance at Oliver. "I don't know."

"And what if I don't want true love?"

I shrug. "Then I guess you can give it to someone else before Christmas."

She bites her thumbnail and nods absently, the book firmly clamped under one arm now. With a decisive nod, she pulls her hand away from her mouth. "Wait a minute. If the book is in my possession now, that means it was in *your* possession up until now, since you're the one who gave it to me. And it's Christmastime. Right now."

Her words hit me like a physical wall. *Oh my goodness.* The book has been in my actual physical possession for the last half hour. Sadie Foster handed it to *me.* I say the first thing that pops into my head, "Well, it belonged to Oliver, too, because we followed all the clues together, and Sadie even gave it to both of us, and he was holding it in the car."

Felicity's whole face lights up with a smile as bright as the star on top of our Christmas tree. "So did either of you fall in love while the book was in your possession? Or did you both?" Her eyes spark with mischief.

My heart gallops like a runaway reindeer, and I turn to see the same panicked expression on Oliver's face that must be plastered all over my own.

And then I see him for what he is—my best friend, the deepest friend of my soul, returned to me through space and time, by my side without question, up for any adventure I drag him on, helping me, supporting me, kissing me. Oh, boy, how he was kissing me.

The memory of our most recent kiss explodes behind my eyes. That kiss—and each of the two public ones that came before—was mind-blowing, earth-shattering, life-changing. Oliver's kisses have truly changed my life.

Because I am one hundred percent, from here to the North Pole and back again, in love with Ollie.

I tilt my chin and study his eyes. Is he remembering our kisses too? Is he thinking anything along the same lines as I am? Does he have feelings for me at all?

There's only one way to find out.

"I fell in love. I think...I think I've been falling in love with you this whole adventure," I say in a small voice. I'm out on a holly branch, risking my heart and pride, but as Mrs. A. said, Oliver's worth the risk.

His face seems to fold in on itself. I flinch, steeling myself for rejection.

"Not me," he says, and my heart plunges to the ground. "Oh, Amelia," he whispers as he puts his strong arms around me and pulls me close. "This isn't new to me. I've *always* been in love with you."

He tips his head, and our lips collide in a breath-stealing kiss. The back of my knees buckle, and my pulse jackhammers. I pull away, panicked.

"But Oliver! You live in Chicago. I live in Cherry Creek. I don't see—"

He stops me with another kiss and laughs. "My parents are here and the woman I love is here. I'm moving back to Cherry Creek."

My body floods with relief, and I beam at him. He bends his head, and our lips meet again for a slow, sweet kiss.

When we part, Felicity pretends she wasn't staring and drops the book again. "Sorry." She picks it up. "Congratulations, you two. Looks like the legend worked for you both. I guess the book's perfect record continues."

I grab Oliver's arm and hug myself to his side. I'm not letting go until Christmas. "And now it's your turn. Merry Christmas, Felicity."

The End

About the Author

Brenda Lowder is an award-winning author of lighthearted women's fiction and romantic comedy novels. She lives in the Atlanta area and loves pretending to exercise, whipped cream on coffee, and air conditioning. She's a big fan of fiction in all its forms—books, films, television, and the lies we tell ourselves. Her Special Agent husband and two princess-scientist daughters love her enough to insist she's still twenty-nine.

Get to know Brenda at www.brendalowder.com.

Once Upon a Christmas Promise

SUSAN CARLISLE

One

LAUREL MARSH'S HANDS SHOOK AS SHE STRAIGHTENED HER SUIT jacket. This was what she had been working toward her entire career: a promotion to senior art agent.

She entered the glass office where Joe, her boss and boyfriend, along with Mr. Antwan, the owner of the agency, waited. She offered them an apologetic smile. "Gene should be here any moment."

After courting the artist Gene McGivern for over three months, she and Joe had finally pulled off a coup by getting him to agree to let the Antwan Art Agency represent him. He was coming in today to sign the papers. Except he was fifteen minutes late.

She checked her watch, the one with diamond chips Joe had given her when he'd been promoted over her. He'd used it as a token of his promise to help her achieve a promotion as well. "I'll go see if McGivern is in the lobby."

Joe stepped out behind her. He hovered a hand over his immaculate hair without touching it. His eyes narrowed as he hissed, "Where is he?"

"I spoke to him yesterday and he said he would be here."

"You know your promotion depends on us signing him. I thought you had this." He stalked two paces one way then back

"I did. I do."

Joe leaned toward her, glaring. "Then where is he?"

"Laurel?" the front receptionist said.

"Yes." Laurel hadn't even heard the woman approach.

"There's a Mr. McGivern on the phone asking to speak to you."

"I'll take it in the conference room." Laurel reentered with Joe right behind her. She pushed a button on the phone sitting on the table. She spoke into the speaker. "Mr. McGivern, is everything okay? We've been waiting for you."

"I'm not signing." Mr. McGivern's voice boomed around the room.

Her stricken look met Mr. Antwan's then Joe's. She stammered. "Excuse me? Why?"

"A black cat ran under my ladder today."

"What?" Had the man lost his mind?

"It was a sign I shouldn't sign with you." He made it sound so matter-of-fact.

"Now Mr. McGivern. I'm sure it didn't mean anything. Why don't I bring the papers to you. We can sign them at your place."

"I'm leaving for Christmas out of the country. My taxi to the airport is waiting."

Everything she dreamed of was slipping through her hands. All because of some superstitious temperamental artist. "Please Mr. McGivern, I wish you'd reconsider."

"That won't happen. Merry Christmas." With that, he hung up.

Mr. Antwan stood and gave Joe a direct look. "Joe, I'll let you handle this." He went out the door without even glancing at Laurel.

"Joe, you know I had this in the bag. You even spoke to McGivern."

"But it was ultimately you who was to bring him on. You didn't do that." Joe didn't meet her look. "I'm going to have to let you go. If I don't, I'll be out of a job."

She stepped toward him with her hand out. "Please don't let me go. When McGivern returns, I'll contact him again. I know I can sign him on as a client. I just need time."

Joe shook his head. "I'm sorry. Did you see the look on Antwan's face? I have to."

Disappointment filling her, she spat, "Thanks for having my back, Joe. After all the clients I've helped you bring in. Promises really mean a lot to you, don't they."

⁂

The next day, Laurel caught the flash of red out of the corner of her eye seconds before she slammed on her brakes. She jerked to a stop. The boxes on her back seat which held most of her worldly goods slid onto the floor. Not only was she out of a job but a home as well. Her heart thumped against her chest wall. The sound of a hand slamming against the metal of the car rang in her ears. Had she hit someone?

"Hey lady, pay attention." An arm waved back and forth. "This is a crosswalk."

She looked at the wooly mountain of a man glaring at her through the windshield. A knit cap was pulled down low over dark wavy hair sticking out in a wild array from beneath the cap. His blue eyes held her mesmerized. They reminded her of a clear mountain pond she'd seen once on a skiing trip. There was something familiar about them, but she couldn't imagine where she would have met this rough looking man.

Despite their beauty, the man's eyes flashed. Fear crawled

into her chest. She sank into her seat. A bush of beard with full lips surrounded by more hair made the man look uncivilized.

She winced, pulling a face. "Sorry."

He glared, then stuffed his right hand in his pocket. "Be more careful."

Laurel nodded, afraid to disagree. He had stepped in front of her. But she had been thinking about the fact she was homeless. She'd been living with Joe. That had been over the minute he fired her. She vowed never to work for anyone like Mr. Antwan or Joe again. What she needed to do now was find the Cherry Inn, then settle in for the night and nurse her wounds.

The man stepped to the sidewalk. She could see all of him now. His wide shoulders beneath his bright jacket hunched against the cold and wind. He wore jeans and well-worn heavy boots. He waved a hand as if giving her leave to go since he had moved safely out of the way. A hand still remained in his pocket. What was he trying to hide?

"Welcome to Cherry Creek, Tennessee," she mumbled. Laurel shivered and drove slowly down the street of the Christmas card picture town. Despite her shambles of a life and almost hitting someone, she could appreciate the quaintness of the town. There was even a Christmas tree in the square. Wreaths hung on the light poles with large red bows attached. Every store had decorations in the windows and on the doors. What would it be like to live here?

Cherry Creek had been the halfway mark on the way to her cousin's house for Christmas. At least she had a charming place for her stopover. She couldn't have found a quainter place if she'd been looking for one.

The shaking of her hands had eased by the time she pulled into the parking lot of the inn. The warmth of the Victorian home settled her nerves.

"Hello. Welcome to Cherry Creek Inn and Merry Christmas," a college-aged woman said from behind a table near a roaring fire.

"Hi. I'm Laurel Marsh. I have a reservation for tonight."

The girl shuffled through papers.

Laurel glanced around the lobby with its staircase that went up to a landing then up again. Against the wall beside it stood a chest. Next to it sat a piece of art made from wood twisted and polished to a gleaming shine supported by an iron stand. It looked out of place among the antiques, yet it fit in as well. Laurel knew quality work. This piece screamed excellence. She was nearly overcome with the urge to reach out and run the pad of her finger down the length of it.

She recognized this artist's work, but she'd never seen this particular sculpture. If she had she would've remembered the shape of its lines and the emotions it evoked. She had seen numerous pictures of this type of work and pieces in a gallery once. It was by B. Wheeler.

Hadn't she read something about his grandparents living in Tennessee? Could it be here? Her heart beat faster with anticipation. Could her luck be changing? If she could get B. Wheeler to come out of hiding and represent him, that would pave her way back into the art world.

"Ms. Marsh, your room is ready," the woman said.

Laurel stepped toward the desk pointing toward the piece. "Do you happen to know if the artist who produced this sculpture lives here?"

"No, I'm sorry I don't." The girl picked up a key off the desk and handed it to Laurel.

She wasn't giving up. Someone in town had to know something. Laurel took the key. "That is a B. Wheeler piece." By the blank look on the girl's face, she had no idea who that was. "He's an artist. This looks like one of his earlier works." Laurel couldn't help but gush.

The girl shrugged. "If you say so. It's always sat there as far as I know."

Settled in her room, Laurel checked her watch. It was still early for dinner. The girl had given Laurel a run-down on eating places in town. Laurel would ask around at the diner about B. Wheeler.

The artist had just disappeared. He hadn't been seen for almost two years. He had skyrocketed to fame then walked away. Laurel had read everything she could find about him. His picture in an art magazine had captured her interest enough she'd cut it out and put it in her wallet like a teenager with a crush on her favorite rock star.

She'd never met him, but she'd seen him once at an art opening. Laurel had been tempted to introduce herself, but a beautiful woman wrapped her arm around his, stopping Laurel from making a move. He had turned during the evening event and their gazes had met, held for a heart-stopping moment, before the woman drew his attention again.

Laurel reached for her purse. Finding the picture, she studied it. Those eyes reminded her of the ones she'd seen recently. The man she'd almost hit. Could it have been? But the man looked nothing like the clean-cut preppy in the picture. She shook her head. Those two men couldn't be the same.

The art world had no idea where B. Wheeler had gone. But her gut told her he was around here or someone who lived in the area knew him. She intended to find out. This was too good of an opportunity to ignore. She needed him as a client. Whatever it took.

Laurel looked around the period decorated room with its four-poster bed and floral satin bedspread and matching window dressings. Located on one wall was an armoire. On the other stood a dressing table, and next to the fireplace was a small bookcase.

She wandered to it. Maybe she could find a good book that would take her mind off her ills. She perused the books. Some were her old favorites. On top of a row, one book had been turned backward. She reached for it. The least she could do was put it on the shelf correctly.

Laurel ran the faded green cover with a couple of loose threads through her fingers. It felt old and appeared more used than she'd originally anticipated. That intrigued her. She read the gold print title Once Upon a Christmas Kiss on the cover. Opening it she found numerous notes like: The legend won't let you down. True love does come at Christmas.

Laurel made a tisking noise. Yeah, that wasn't going to happen. Not after what Joe the Jerk had done to her. She was finished with people like him. Letting someone take credit for her work then dump her when something went wrong. She deserved better.

Laurel sank into the only chair in the room. This might be interesting. She started reading about a boarding school-teacher's parents who found love. The author gifted her story to her friend, Charlotte when the author left the school. Whoever had the book at Christmas found true love. Laurel huffed. It sounded like a Sunday afternoon movie storyline.

Closing the book, she plopped it on the table beside the chair. She needed to get to the diner before it got late.

She bundled up, deciding to walk there. It wasn't far and she could use the time to clear her head. Strolling along she became caught up in the allure of the place. The people she passed smiled and spoke to her. The town had everything. A Cut 'n Curl, gym, and a sweet shop called Smart Cookie Bits – what more could a girl want in a place to live? Having cut her ties to the city, making a complete change to a place like this had its appeal.

In the next block, Laurel stopped in front of an empty storefront. She faced it and stepped back. This would make a wonderful place for an art gallery and agency. Her place. She could see it now: Marsh's Art Agency and Gallery. Being her own boss would leave her free of people like Joe and Mr. Antwan. If only she could make it happen. With B. Wheeler as a client, she could.

At the Cordial Diner, she sat next to the window facing the street. A server came to her table. "Hi, I'm Felicity. What can I get you?"

Laurel gave the woman her order. As Felicity turned to go, Laurel stopped her. "Hey, can I ask you a question?"

"Sure?"

"Do you happen to know a B. Wheeler? Or an artist who works with wood living around here?"

"I uh..." She glanced out the window.

Laurel followed the direction of the woman's look. The same man Laurel had almost run over walked by. Her heart fell. It just couldn't be.

"No, um I don't." The woman's expression quickly sobered before she hurried away.

Could he be B. Wheeler? The way the server had stammered over her answer and the shocked look on her face, it might have been. Regardless of her trepidation, Laurel had to find out. Her career depended on it.

Pulling on her coat and grabbing her purse, Laurel hurried out into the cold evening air. Searching the sidewalk, she located the tall man with the knit cap a block ahead. She moved as fast as her three-inch heeled boots would allow. Her purse swung on her arm while her fingers worked the buttons closed on her coat.

The man's long stride put more distance between them. She pushed herself to walk faster. When he turned a corner, panic bubbled in her. She mustn't lose him. Still, she could be completely wrong about him. What if this was a wild-goose chase?

She went around the corner. Where had he gone? She groaned when she saw footsteps leading to a path into the woods. Looking around the area and seeing nothing, she had no choice but to follow if she wanted to find out if her hunch was correct. She'd been a city girl all her life and stomping around in the woods in the snow and cold wasn't her idea of a good time. And her feet were already freezing. Her boots weren't made for hiking. The heels stuck in the damp ground causing difficult walking. Still, she refused to turn back.

The tall trees blocked the light, making it challenging to see. And the sun was setting. If she didn't locate shelter soon, she'd be in trouble. She thought about turning around and working her way back, then she stepped into an open area. To one side sat a small cabin. Smoke streamed out of the chimney. The appeal of a fire made her plod on.

She trudged to the door. Lifting her freezing hand, she knocked, wincing at the pain radiating through her arm.

The door swung open. The wooly-looking man filled it. His eyes widened in disbelief. Some heat worked its way around his mass to reach Laurel. She huddled in her damp coat.

He snarled, "What're you doing here?"

Two

BRANDON WHEELER HAD PUT ANOTHER LOG ON THE FIRE, THEN HELD his hands out to warm them. Since he'd been gone, he needed to warm the place and himself as well. It would snow again tonight.

The banging on the door had startled him. People didn't come to his cabin. He'd seen to it visitors were discouraged. Keeping his damaged hand out of sight, he whipped the door open. A gust of cold air hit him. The last person he expected to see again stood in his doorway. Still he had thought of her more than once in the last few hours.

Everything about the woman screamed big city gone wrong. She was inappropriately dressed for the weather. She wore an expensive looking red coat, but it appeared more for looks than function. Jeans covered her legs. Designer ones would be his guess. And heaven forbid, she'd worn some fashionable boots with pointed high heels. How had she managed the uneven ground wearing those, he had no idea. Her uncovered hair hung in wet ropes. She could compete with Rudolph for the reddest nose.

"What're you doing here?" He looked past her. "Come to try to kill me again?" Where had she come from?

Her teeth chattered. Her wide eyes held an appeal for help.

"Are you lost, or have you just lost your mind?" He took her arm and tugged her into the cabin, kicking the door closed. "We need to get you by the fire." After stationing her close to the heat, he asked, "Can you speak?"

"Yes." A word barely recognizable through the clink-clink of chattering teeth.

Brandon sighed deeply then nudged her toward the recliner. "Sit."

She fell back more than sat.

"Your boots need to come off. What made you think stomping around in a snowy forest in these would be a good idea?" Dropping to his heels, he used his good hand to take her foot by the heel and pulled, dropping a boot to the floor. He repeated the action with the other boot before he stood. "You need to rub them to help get the blood flowing again. "Now that you can speak, would you mind telling me what you're doing so far from town?"

"I'm sorry I almost hit you." She chattered. "Thank you for letting me come in."

"Today must be my knight in shining armor day." She still hadn't answered his question about why she was here. Was she dodging it? What was the woman up to? "And you followed me all the way up the mountain to tell me that."

"Well, no. You don't think very highly of me, do you?"

She looked around his one-room cabin.

Glad he had closed the curtains blocking the sight of his workroom, the space he never entered, he watched as her gaze returned to him. "Rub. While I find you some dry clothes."

Brandon couldn't believe she'd followed him from town. He didn't know what to do with company. Being in his cabin alone suited him just fine. Despite being on friendly terms with the community, he still kept himself on the outside as much as possible. At one time he was in the middle of the glitz and glamour of the art world, and now he lived a simple life in the mountains. Those closest to him accused him of hiding after the accident. His parents complained he had started to like living in the woods and not shaving too. Others thought he had become a hermit. It was easier that way.

It had been a long time since he'd wished things in his life were different. When he saw the wide green eyes of this woman through the windshield, something stirred in him. An emotion he'd not felt in a long time. Desire.

His disfigurement kept him from pursuing a woman. His ex-fiancé had seen to that. He had more scars than the long one on his hand. She'd shivered while she told him it made her skin crawl to have him touch her with his injured hand – that had been the end of their relationship.

To compound the matter, the accident had robbed him of his livelihood. Nothing he tried to produce after the accident looked right. Felt right. He crammed his injured fist further into his pocket. An action that had become a habit since his surgeries had been completed.

This woman sitting in his chair was so tiny, she only reached his shoulder height. Did he own anything small enough for her to wear? Going to his chest of drawers in the corner, he removed a pair of wool socks and returned to her. "Put these on." He moved the footstool closer to the fire. With the socks on, he cupped her heel and place her foot on the stool. He repeated the process with the other all the while making sure she couldn't see his wounded hand.

Once again, he went to his chest and rummaged around, taking out clothing. He might not enjoy having company but he couldn't stand to see her uncomfortable. Over his shoulder he said, "Take your clothes off." He heard a small gasp. "It's not what you think. You need to put on warm dry clothes." He laid the garments he'd picked out on his bed. "Change. I'm going to warm up some stew. I'm hungry and I assume you are too after that hike."

"Can I go behind those curtains to change?"

He snapped, "No." He adjusted his voice to something more congenial. "I'll turn my back." He went to the crockpot where he'd put all the stew fixings that morning.

"Oh, okay."

He glanced at her. She had stood. Her head moved as if she were studying the place. No doubt the obviously fancy-pants woman from the city wasn't impressed by the bed with a home-made quilt or rustic chest of drawers beside it. The pile of wood next to the fireplace and his kitchen in one corner of the cabin with the two mismatched chairs beneath it couldn't be up to her usual standards.

Her brows drew together as her gaze lingered on the black curtains.

"Go on. Anyone who follows a stranger home should be prepared for anything but I'm not going to attack you." No matter how tempting she might be. "Leave your clothes on the floor. I'll hang them in front of the fire after we eat. We'll eat by the fire."

A few minutes later, the woman sat in the recliner again. This time she had the quilt his grandmother had made around her shoulders. That seemed appropriate since his grandmother would've been proud of his actions. He would have liked to have slammed the door in the woman's face and been left alone. He handed her a bowl of steaming stew.

Brandon carried a chair from the table with one arm and thumped it down beside her. He returned to the kitchen for two glasses of water, setting them on the table next to his recliner.

Getting his bowl of food, he settled in the chair. They ate in silence. Finished, they placed their bowls on the table along with the glasses.

Twisting in the chair to face her, Brandon pinned her with a look. "Now you are warm and have eaten, tell me who you are and why you followed me."

"I'm Laurel Marsh." Her look didn't waver. That impressed him. "I'm just passing through for the night on my way to my cousin's house for Christmas." She looked around. "You don't have any Christmas decorations. This would really be a fun place to decorate."

Her décor comment gave him whiplash. What did that have to do with her being here? He chose to ignore her statement and stick to the point. "I don't mean in Cherry Creek," he pointed to the floor, "I mean here in my cabin."

She looked at him a moment as if formulating her answer. "Because I'm looking for B. Wheeler."

Brandon's worst fear had come true. His jaw tightened. His two fingers that were left tensed at his side out of her sight. All this time, he'd stayed hidden and now the outside world had come calling. He flinched. She suspected who he was. How could she possibly know from their brief encounter in the middle of the street?

"Thinking I was some guy you clearly don't know, you thought it worth taking the chance that I'm not an ax murderer. Did you think about getting lost in the woods or freezing to death? He must be an important fellow."

"Well, it does sound kind of bad when you put it that way." She gave him a sheepish look. "Generally, I'm more level-headed."

"That's reassuring." Oddly he liked her honesty. "What do you need this B. Wheeler for?"

"I'm an art agent from Atlanta. I saw a piece of his work in the Inn. I wondered if this is where he disappeared to. I read somewhere he liked to spend time with his grandparents in Tennessee when he was a child. I wanted to see if he was still working. His sculptures are so beautiful, touching."

Just his luck. Who would've thought of woman passing through a small little town in the mountains of Tennessee would recognize a piece of his artwork?

There were a number of his earlier works around town. They were from his starving artist period. His grandparents helped him by buying his work as gifts. It wasn't like he could go around collecting them when he returned to Cherry Creek.

He put his right hand into his pocket and picked up their bowls. When he bobbled them, she reached to help. Her fingertips brushed his. That slight touch clung to him. Being around Laurel had shaken awake his libido. Emily had dropped him like a hot potato after the accident. Since then, he'd stayed to himself, away from the art world, people in general, and female attention.

"You are B. Wheeler, aren't you?" A note of excitement filled her voice as she stood, the quilt dropping to the chair as she picked up their glasses and brought them to the kitchen.

Brandon placed the bowls in the metal tub that served as his sink. "Yes, I'm Brandon Wheeler."

"I would've never recognized you behind that beard."

"Have we met before?" He studied her a moment.

"No, but I've seen your picture." She came to stand close to him. "Before you disappeared."

He flinched.

"Why did you?" she all but whispered.

"Do what?"

"Stop showing your work."

Because he didn't have anything to show. Hadn't for almost two years. "Because I haven't done anything new."

Her eyes widened with disbelief. "Nothing? You have such talent. I was hoping you would agree to let me represent you. I heard you had parted with your agent."

"More like he parted with me. If you don't work, then you have nothing to sell." He moved back to the fire.

She followed. "You could start working again. I would love to represent you."

He turned. "Did you hear me say I'm not doing that anymore. You wasted your time tromping after me."

"What can I do to make you change your mind?"

"Nothing. Art is behind me."

"Then I guess that's the end of my career." She sank into the chair.

"What do I have to do with your career?" He had his own problems and didn't need hers added on.

"I was hoping to persuade you to start showing your art again. I've been a fan of your work for years. I've kept up with your career. I hoped maybe you would let me represent you."

"That's not going to happen." The words came out harsher than he intended.

"Why not? You're an amazing artist." Her eyes darted toward the curtained-off area. Raising her shoulders, she let them drop. "I don't understand why you're not working. You have such talent."

"Because I can't," he said sharper than he would have liked.

"Can't or won't? You're cheating the world by not sharing your talent." She watched him like a cat studying a mouse.

"Are you this pushy with all the artists you wish to represent?"

She settled back in a chair with a loud sigh. "No. I'm just desperate."

He put another log on the fire. "Why?"

"Because I lost my job with the Antwan Art Agency."

He waited for her to say more.

"With you as a client I could work for any agency. Maybe even start my own."

"So you want me to be an avenue to recover your career." He wasn't sure how he felt about that.

She sat forward. "I want to help us both."

"I don't need any help," he said calmly yet his heart beat faster.

She looked around, her lips tightening with skepticism.

He had the sudden urge to kiss that look off her face.

"It would be a mutually beneficial deal. I would represent you, you could have a great comeback exhibition. Your recent hiatus will increase the value of all your work. You could live someplace nicer than this."

His brow rose. "Do you have a problem with my home?"

"No. It's just that this doesn't look like the person B. Wheeler was nor do you." Her gaze dropped to his beard.

"Are you being insulting on purpose? Do you talk to all strangers like this?"

"No, somehow you bring it out in me." A slight grin formed on her lips.

It sent a tingle of awareness to places best left dormant. "I'm sorry about your job. But I can't help you."

"Can't or won't?"

She was pushing once more. Into a place he refused to go. He looked at the window and the darkness beyond much like his life. "It's too late for me to return you to the Inn and it's snowing. You'll have to stay here for the night. I'll get you back in the morning."

Her voice rose to a squeak. "I can't stay here all night."

He snarled. "You should have thought about that earlier. It's getting late. I'm tired. I know you must be from your hike through the woods. Let's go to bed. I'll get you back to the

Inn first thing in the morning. In time to run over someone else."

"Funny." She looked at the bed and back at him.

He pulled a purposely rakish grin. "No, we won't be sleeping together. Much to my disappointment." He rubbed his beard. "I already know you aren't turned on by my looks. You take the bed and I'll sleep in the recliner."

"I can't do that. I'll sleep in the recliner."

His smile went wider. "I might enjoy having you join me or in that case, we should share the bed."

Laurel's eyes widened. She swallowed hard. "I'll take the bed."

Brandon chuckled as she hustled out of the chair. It was fun to tease this woman who had literally forced her way into his life. He felt whole again for a brief moment.

Three

LAUREL WATCHED THE MAN WHO'S HOUSE SHE'D INVADED ON A WHIM from under the covers on the bed. She pretended to sleep.

Brandon gathered her clothes and hung them on the chair placing them close to the fire before he pulled his shirt off over his head. He turned, giving her a view of one side of his body. The warm yellow light reflected off his skin covering defined muscles of his shoulders and chest.

He pulled his boots off using his toes for leverage. When his hand went to his waistband, she held her breath. He pulled his belt from the loops with a whoosh. She was being a voyeur, but she couldn't stop herself. He was gorgeous. The man from the picture. Her fingers twitched to touch him. All evening he'd kept his right side turned away from her. Why?

That had also been the hand he'd quickly shoved into his jeans pocket when he reached the sidewalk. Hadn't he had it in his jacket pocket as he walked down the street? Was something wrong with it? Was that why he hadn't done any work in almost two years? The man was an enigma. A fit one, but a mystery nonetheless.

He flicked open the button of his jeans and her breath

caught. His head jerked up like a deer hearing a noise. She squeezed her eyelids together.

A soft chuckle rolled from his throat. He settled into the recliner which creaked under his weight. Reaching forward, he pulled a quilt over him. It hit her bag, toppling it to the floor. The contents went everywhere. A soft cuss word filled the air.

Laurel threw the covers back hurrying to where her purse lay. Brandon squatted on his heels picking up the scattered contents. He used both his hands. A lipstick rolled by him. Brandon reached to catch it. That's when she saw that three fingers were missing from his right hand. He tried to stop the movement of the round object, but he missed.

"I can get it." She reached for it.

"I can get it," he growled. He captured it with a slap using what was left of his palm against the floor. He didn't look at her as he said, "Now you know my secret."

She continued stuffing items back into her purse. Questions pushed at her lips but by his stilted movements now wasn't when she should ask them. She flinched when Brandon looked at her wallet that had fallen open. Brandon's picture stared up at them. Something about him had pulled at her then and it still did.

He picked it up and studied the picture then studied her. Slowly he closed the wallet and handed it to her. He stood.

Laurel finished putting things away. Brandon faced the fire, his back to her. Unsure what to do she returned to bed. She pulled the covers high under her chin. A few minutes later Brandon sat in the chair again and adjusted the quilt. He raised his feet and put his hands behind his head, his bare shoulders just visible from her vantage point.

The low gruff timbre of his voice cut the thickness in the air. "Why is my picture in your wallet?"

She didn't answer for a moment. "Because there was something about you that called to me."

"Called?" A note of humor mixed with disbelief hung on the word. He shifted so he could see her.

She saw the moment his eyes widened.

"I remember you." He stopped for a second then pointed at her. "I saw you at an art exhibit. You stood across the room watching me."

"Yeah. We had a moment. Silly, I know. There was something about you that I...uh found interesting." She couldn't have him knowing his picture made her middle quiver. "I know I must sound like a stalker."

"You were only interested because of who I was. I'm not that guy anymore."

Laurel had the distinct feeling he knew there was more to her explanation than she'd given. It was time to get the spotlight off her. "I would imagine under all that wooly bugger beard that same guy is still there."

"You'd be wrong." The harshness of the statement echoed off the wooden walls.

"You don't work at your art because of your hand."

The air grew tense once more.

"BINGO!" A sadness surrounded the word.

"That's why you disappeared and live out here all by yourself." She couldn't not ask. "What happened?"

His hands moved to rest on his stomach. His good hand over the damaged one.

Now it was his turn on the hot seat. She could feel his angst from across the room as if it were a living thing. The subject was one he didn't discuss.

His words came slow and low as if being pulled from him. "I was starting a new piece. One I was excited about. The wood I had chosen for the sculpture was a particularly gnarly piece. I had the vision of using the natural twist and turns to my advantage. To create a look of a rippling brook."

He paused, lowered the recliner and sat up. His elbows went to his knees.

Laurel's heart broke for him. He sounded and looked so defeated. She slid out of bed and padded over to him. He smelled of pine and wood smoke. It suited him. When she could see his face, she sank to the floor.

He remained hunched over. His good hand continued to protect the bad. As if he didn't realize she had moved, he continued, "The saw blade hit a knot that I hadn't seen. The wood jumped. By the time I could react, two of my fingers were gone and half of the third. After the doctors were through, I was missing all three."

"I'm sorry, Brandon."

He looked at her. "There's nothing for you to be sorry about. I'm the one who did it."

"It was an accident."

He clenched and unclenched his hands. "One that I should have prevented."

"So that's why you quit working." Now his attitude made more sense. Yet what a waste of talent.

"I had a couple of surgeries and some physical therapy. I was out of action for six months. When I started back, as you can imagine, I was hesitant with the saws. What really got me was I couldn't hold and move the chisels and sandpaper as I once had. I wasn't in the same place as I had been artistically."

He leaned back and looked at her, the firelight making the ridges of his cheekbones harsher. "Now you can understand why I'm never doing another sculpture."

"That's a shame. You do such breathtaking work." Her chance of getting her job back faded. Or maybe she could open her own agency. Excitement ran through her at the idea.

"I did."

"Have you thought that maybe your sculptures might be good but in a different way?"

He studied her a moment. "Is this an agent talking or an art lover?"

"Couldn't it be both?" She placed her hand on the arm of the recliner. "The difference might enhance your work. I hate to see you waste your talent."

"How am I supposed to work with this?" He raised his hurt hand and shook it in the air.

Laurel controlled her reaction to seeing the majority of his hand missing. The long red scar running the length of his hand hadn't faded. She clasped his hand between both of hers.

"Let go. You don't want to touch me."

His hand felt odd between hers yet there was warmth and strength there. A zip of excitement went through her at his touch. She'd experienced the same emotion when she'd seen his picture. Her reaction had propelled her to cut it out and place it in a safe place. This man needed her reassurance, the world's reassurance.

He lowered his hand, but she wouldn't release it.

"Do you know what I feel?" Her look met his.

He watched her.

"I feel strength, talent, and expression." She squeezed his hand. "All those qualities are here. They still exist. Just as they did before but in a different form. They need to be used and tried." She had his attention. He watched her with such intensity it was as if he were looking straight into her heart. Even in the dimming firelight, she could see his eyes questioning. "I can imagine the beautiful works this hand can create. If you would give it a try."

He pulled his hand from hers. "That has passed. Long ago.

Don't confuse me with the fame and fortune of before. That's over."

Laurel hesitated a moment, forming her words. "How long ago since you have worked?"

"Over a year."

"That long? Maybe it's time to give it a try again."

"And if I do, and I fail?"

The last word hung in the air. "I think you and the world would benefit from you trying."

"Are you just saying that because you want to represent me?"

"It would be nice to represent you in your comeback but I'm really encouraging you because your work spoke to me and many others. I believe it could again." She returned to the bed, pulled the covers up, and turned her back to him. "You know, there's something rare and special about the emotions you evoke in people with your art. I think you can do that again despite what happened to your hand."

Four

Brandon stared into the fire's flickering flames for a long time after he heard the soft sound of Laurel's even breathing. Enough. He mulled over her words. She had touched his hand. More amazingly, she held it without being revolted. How had the woman managed to have such a profound effect on him in such a short amount of time?

He knew nothing about her other than she was an art agent so desperate to meet him that she had taken a chance on following him on a hunch. She sounded so sincere about her appreciation of his work. And his picture in her purse. He wasn't sure what to think about that. In an odd way, it pleased him.

When she had taken his hand, his heart had almost stopped for the fear of revulsion he had expected on her face. Instead, it was a tender look, as if she wanted to take all his pain away. For a moment he'd forgotten his deformity and enjoyed a woman's touch. The feel of skin against soft skin. He longed to caress her cheek but didn't dare.

Could he believe her words? His parents had said much the same thing a number of times but had made no headway with

him. Yet for some reason, Laurel had managed to get through to
him. Had made him question his resolve to never do his art
again. She had rattled his well-order seclusion. For the first
time in months, he actually considered trying to create something again.

His mouth formed a line. No, it would just be wasted
time.

Brandon was up early the next morning. In reality, he hadn't
slept much. After his uncharacteristic spilling of his personal
life to a stranger, he had been unsettled. He buttoned his pants
then pulled on a T-shirt and flannel shirt over that. Still Laurel
slept. After adding a log to the fire, he looked at her for a few
moments. If circumstances were different, what would it be like
to crawl into a warm bed and pull her into his arms? Would she
be accepting? He shook his head. It had been too long since he'd
held a woman.

Laurel was a stunning one. Dark, wavy hair, large expressive
eyes in contrast to her creamy skin that had touched him with
compassion along with her soft soothing voice. She wore the
typical clothes of an up-and-coming woman in the business
world trying to prove herself, but he sensed a soul-deep pain in
her. One that understood and touched his. Yet she was big city
from the tip of her pink pedicure to the top of her finely arched
brows.

Would she be scared if he touched her hair? How had this
woman gotten under his skin so fast? He forced himself to move
into the kitchen. Pulling a pan from the shelf, he got the sausage
out of the refrigerator and put it on the stove. It sizzled and
Laurel stirred.

"Hey," she said as if testing his reaction.

"Sorry if I woke you." He focused on his cooking. "I'm not
used to having an extra person around."

She climbed out of bed. He glanced up. Laurel looked

around the place. She started toward the curtained-off room. "Where are you going?"

"I was hoping there's a bathroom through there."

"No, it's right this way." He directed her to a small door on the other side of him. Apparently, she hadn't noticed it last night.

She entered the bath with a sink and commode. Soon she returned. "No shower? Do you use the creek?" She crossed her arms and shook in mock reaction. "That would be cold this time of year."

"I have a shower outside. Cold at first but I have plenty of hot water. It's refreshing if you would like to try it."

She shook her head. "No thanks."

"It's especially nice at night to look up at the stars."

"I'll take your word for it."

He raised a brow. "Not very adventurous, are you?"

"Not really. Following you here was about as spontaneous and adventurous as I've ever been."

"How do you feel this morning?"

She moved her chin to the side in thought. "That might have been the best night's sleep I've had in a long time."

"We'll have breakfast then I'll take you back to the Inn. I know you must have plans for Christmas. By the way, your clothes are dry."

She walked over and fingered her jeans. "I'll put these on right now."

"No need to do it on my account," he quipped before he thought.

"I still think I should get dressed." Laurel returned to the bathroom. She came out wearing a silky-looking shirt that wouldn't keep her warm, her jeans, and his socks. She went to the fire and picked up one of her boots and examined it. "Well, these are ruined."

He couldn't help but feel sorry for her, she sounded so sad. "I'm not surprised having worn them in the snow."

"I know I got what I deserved. They weren't appropriate for the weather, I get that. But you have to take some blame. If I had slowed down long enough to buy other boots, you would've disappeared on me."

He chuckled. A rusty sound since it had been so long since he'd done it. "Interesting way of looking at it. I'm really sorry about your boots."

"Me too. They were my favorites." She dropped the boot to the floor.

He turned back to his cooking. "Maybe you can buy another pair."

"I doubt that. Remember I'm out of a job."

"I don't think you'll have any trouble finding a job." He looked over his shoulder.

Her gaze met his. "I think there was a compliment in there somewhere."

He grinned. "Maybe a small one."

She started toward him. "Can I help with something?"

"No. I'm almost done. Take a seat at the table."

Laurel did as she was told. "Will you be staying here for Christmas?"

"Yes. Why?"

She fingered a scar on the table. "You're not going to see your family?"

"No."

"You shouldn't be alone on a holiday. I think it's sad that you wanna be by yourself at Christmas." She watched him long enough to make him uneasy.

"Doesn't matter if you do or not." His tone sounded hard. His mother had begged him to come home for Christmas. He'd refused. All that attention he cared nothing about. Having people look at him with sad faces was better left not experienced. Some of that old toughness that had been eased with last night's conversation had returned. He sat a plate of food in front of her with a thump. "Breakfast is served."

Brandon went after the other chair. Moving it, he saw a small green book on the floor. He picked it up. "We missed something last night." He handed it to Laurel then took his seat at the table.

"I'm glad you found this. It's not mine. I picked it up at the Inn. It's a funny little book. It's a love story with notes in the margins from readers who had the book at Christmas and found their own true love. I've never seen anything like it before."

He huffed. "That's the book. I have heard of it. It's a local legend. I heard of women coming to town just to see if they can get a hold of it. I'm not a believer in that sort of stuff."

Laurel took the book from him. "I'm not surprised."

His brows rose.

"I don't put any stock in it either. So, you're safe."

"Good to know."

She held up the book. "It does make for interesting reading."

He scoffed.

"So you came here to hide out." Laurel filled her fork with eggs.

"Something like that." He refused to look at her for fear of her seeing more than she should.

"What do you do all day?"

"Mostly I stay busy doing chores and chopping wood. Occasionally going to town. And apparently getting almost run over every once in a while." He gave her a pointed look.

"I told you I was sorry about that." She gave him a syrupy smile.

"I don't go into town often because I don't want to scare women and small children."

A quizzical look covered her face. "What do you mean by that?"

"My hand bothers people. As much as I enjoy sharing my artwork I don't enjoy being stared at."

"No one would enjoy that. But the more you're around people the more they get used to your hand. They'll quit looking if you give them a chance."

"They didn't where my grandfather was concerned." Brandon had hated the way his grandfather had been treated but the man had taken it in stride. Somehow Brandon couldn't do that.

She put her fork down and placed her elbows on the table resting on chin on top of her clasped hands. "He was missing fingers as well?"

"No, his arm. His entire life people stared at him. As a kid I would go to the store and watch people point at him. Laugh and turn away."

"Did he say he minded?"

Brandon thought a moment. "No, I guess he didn't. If someone asked him about not having an arm, he took the time to explain he was born that way.

"As a kid I can remember other kids running up to him then squealing and running away. I'm not interested in being a freak. As much as I like showing my art. I don't want to be the center of attention because of the loss of half my hand."

"Fair enough. Will you tell me more about your grandfather?"

Brandon wasn't sure he wanted to let her further into his life. What would be the harm? At this point, she already knew his darkest secret. "He was a great man. Super smart and very successful. He never considered it a disability. A challenge sometimes but nothing more. He was even a scratch golfer. But few people recognized that at first. What they saw was a man with one arm. I don't want to be treated that way."

"You could maybe take a lesson from him."

Laurel had a way of making him think. "It could be he had a supportive family and marriage. I lost my fiancé," he raised his hand, "over this accident. She said she couldn't stand my deformity. Couldn't deal with my touch, but the truth was she couldn't stand the fact that I was no longer living the bright-lights big-city life. She enjoyed all that glitz and glamour. Being on my arm at shows and events. She didn't get to do that after the accident. And the idea of having to help me do simple things like button my shirt didn't appeal to her."

Laurel gave him an "I am sorry" look. She stood and reached for his empty plate and stacked it on top of hers. "I'll wash since you cooked."

He rose at the same time, brushing against her as they went in opposite directions. Heat washed through him. The urge to bring her close made him shove both hands into his pockets. "Sorry. This cabin is small for two people. While you're doing the dishes, I'll chop wood. Then I'll show you the way back to town."

"You have no trouble chopping wood?" She looked toward his hand.

"I've learned how to do it."

"Mmm." She nodded.

He could almost hear her thoughts. If he could learn to adjust to splitting wood, then he could learn to do his art again.

She asked, "Instead of showing the world your talent you're just gonna stay out here the rest of your life?"

Five

Brandon pulled on his jacket and placed the knit cap on his head. He opened the door, letting in a burst of cold air before he closed it behind him. Taking a deep breath, he filled his lungs with the crispness as he looked at the blue sky. The fresh snow had left the ground pristine.

He needed this. To get away from Laurel's questions. She had him tied in knots. He'd admitted to stuff he'd never said to anyone. Laurel had a way of getting him to share his feelings. This stranger who almost ran him over and showed up at his door wanting him to flip his life around, she'd shown more compassion and understanding than he'd ever known. Yet she dared him to do more.

Laurel filled his cabin and pushed in directions he didn't want to go. To make matters worse, he was aware of her, too aware. It had been so long since he had been with a woman that maybe he was just super sensitive to her. With every touch, his desire increased.

He went around the cabin to the chopping block. With a mighty swing, he split a log. This was part of his morning ritual. His way of getting exercise. Today it was about working off his frustration. The physical exertion helped him keep his emotions in check. He pulled back and slammed the ax into another log.

It was also his way of staying in touch with wood. If he couldn't create out of wood, at least he could enjoy the feel and smell of split logs and watching a pile grow. His shoulders burned. He stopped to roll them. His eyes went wide. He had left Laurel in the cabin alone. Had she looked behind the curtains?

He burst through the door.

Laurel looked up from where she sat in his recliner reading the little book.

Brandon glanced toward the curtains. They hadn't been disturbed. His chest lowered in relief. He looked at Laurel to see her gaze had followed his.

"Is there a problem?"

"No, no problem." He didn't want her seeing the horrible state of his work. She'd admired it too much to have her be disappointed.

He pulled off his jacket and tossed it on the end of the bed. To his surprise and pleasure, she had made the bed and tidied the cabin.

"I made a fresh pot of coffee, if you would like a cup." She put the book in her purse and moved to get up.

He toed off his boots. "That sounds nice. I'll have one before we head into town."

Laurel quickly poured and brought him a mug of steaming liquid as he sat in front of the fire. She even kept it going while he was out. It wouldn't take much for him to enjoy Laurel's kind of attention. He watched the fire trying to absorb that uncomfortable thought.

"It's time for you to go." That didn't sound nice, but he didn't try to retract it.

"Okay," Laurel placed her mug on the kitchen counter. "I'm

sorry but I need to borrow a pair of socks. I stepped in a puddle of water."

He went to his drawer, pulled out socks and handed them to her. She took them, her fingertips brushing his. The almost indetectable touch sent an electric current through him. This had to stop. He searched under the bed and found a pair of his old boots. "These will be better than those silly things you wore here. You can leave them at the Inn and I'll pick them up sometime when I'm in town."

Six

Fifteen minutes later, Laurel trudged through the woods behind Brandon. The sky was beautiful. The day clear with fluffy, white clouds hanging high above them. The crunch of the snow the only noise.

"Try to keep your feet in the same place as mine. That way it'll be easier to walk," Brandon called over his shoulder.

Why did he suddenly act as if he were eager to get rid of her? During breakfast, he had been talkative and congenial. Last night, he acted as if talking to her was cathartic. So why was he so uptight now?

He stopped before entering the woods. When she wobbled in an effort not to slam into him, a hand shot out to steady her. He didn't let go as he continued to follow the path. Her hand looked small in his but felt warm and secure. Joe had never created those emotions. Was she letting her long-time distant crush affect her?

She looked at Brandon in his plaid shirt, jeans, boots, and all that facial hair. Had the man he'd once been totally disappeared? Turned into this surly man? The loss of that dream hurt.

Yet she would bet there was a sensitive man beneath all that bluster. She'd seen his work. Admired the fine line of the carved timber. The one that made the wood come alive. All there because of Brandon's touch and talent. Even the small piece at the Inn had affected her.

She must figure out a way to get him to reconsider working again. To at least try.

Brandon continued to hold her hand as he led her to the corner of the building facing Main

Street. There he stopped and dropped her hand. He pushed his damaged one into his jacket pocket. His entire demeanor had changed. He'd closed himself off. In a gruff tone he said, "I think you can find your way to the Inn from here. It's just down that way two blocks and to the right."

"Would you like to have a cup of coffee at the diner to warm up before you head back?"

He said nothing for a moment. "No thank you."

Disappointment filled her. She wasn't sure what she'd been expecting but she didn't like this distance between them. "Thank you for taking care of me and giving me a place to stay last night. Showing me the way back to town."

Brandon nodded. His hand remained shoved in his pocket.

"Then I'll say goodbye. If you change your mind—"

He shook his head. "I won't."

"Still it has been nice to meet you."

He cocked an eyebrow.

"I see through you, B. Wheeler. You're not as tough as you try to act." On impulse she grabbed both his upper arms, came up on her toes, and kissed him. She wasn't sure who looked more shocked him or her.

Seconds later, Brandon pulled her into his arms. His lips found hers. They were cool, calculating, and delicious. The man knew how to kiss. He teased and tasted, creating a heat in her that had her reaching for more. His beard brushed her cheek along with his mouth before he stepped away.

Laurel rocked back on her heels. She stood watching as Brandon disappeared into the forest. With a sigh, Laurel turned and walked down the street.

At the Inn, she left her boots, Brandon's, on the front porch and climbed the stairs in sock feet, also Brandon's. The wooly-looking version of him had gotten to her just as the clean-cut one from the picture had. Standing under the hot water of the shower, she had the feeling she'd just lost something. Now she had found him, she couldn't just drive away. She had to try again to get Brandon to see he needed to work. If not for others, then for himself.

She searched through her clothing for something more practical to wear then she'd had on the day before. Choosing a sweater, jeans, and her thickest socks, which were more dressy than practical, she dressed. She stuffed what few things she had used into her suitcase then zipped and sat it beside the door. Branden's socks lay on the floor. She would stuff them in his boots so that they were returned as well.

Minutes later she told the receptionist goodbye and let her know that Brandon would be by to pick up his socks and shoes. It wasn't until she drove down Main Street that a plan formed. When Laurel passed the Five and Dime, she turned into the next parking place. She had to try one more time to convince Brandon to continue his art. Then maybe he would reconsider letting her represent him.

Just maybe if she helped to bring him back into the real world, he would see what he had been wasting. She would start by giving him a Christmas. She could get decorations to make his cabin festive. Also, it would be her way of saying thank you for him being so kind to her when she showed up at his door uninvited. Laurel called her cousin and told her she would be late.

With a plan in mind, Laurel pulled her bag over her shoulder and headed into the store. There she picked up everything she needed to make the cabin festive as possible, along with a pair of flannel-lined jeans, a knit cap with rabbit ears, heavy socks, and rubber boots.

She made a quick stop by the Inn and asked for her room back. She was told it was already booked for the night and the entire Inn as well. Laurel would have to drive through and arrive at her cousin's place late. While at the Inn, she changed into her new jeans. She picked up Brandon's boots on her way to the car. Those she would return herself.

Laurel parked her car in the last spot at the end of town closest to the path. She unpacked the matching duffle bag to her suitcase, leaving the items on the back seat. Stuffing the things she bought into the bag, she pulled on her new boots.

She put her arms through the straps and pulled the bag on like a backpack, shifting the weight until it was comfortable. Tying Brandon's boots by the strings, she picked them up and started toward the path. Hers and Brandon's footprints were still visible. She was careful to stay on the path he had created. After stopping twice to adjust her baggage, it was with relief that she reached the clearing. She stood watching the cabin. Was he there or outside somewhere?

She broke into a sweat that had nothing to do with exertion as she approached. Second thoughts swamped her. Would Brandon be mad she returned? He hadn't been pleased to see her the first time – what made her think he would be this time? Maybe that kiss?

What had seemed like a good idea a few hours ago didn't look like one now. But she had come this far. Laurel was no quitter. Her father had always told her, "Don't ever give up on what you want." She wanted Brandon to trust her.

Stomping through the snow across the opening, she practiced at least ten times what she would say when he opened the door. She dropped her bag to the snow while she knocked. No answer. Her anxiety increased. Her pulse raced. She called, "Brandon." Still no answer. She stomped her feet as she knocked again. She couldn't stand in one spot all day even if it was a beautiful one. Turning the knob, she found the door would open. She entered and closed the cold weather out, putting her bag on the floor inside.

Why was she really doing this?

Because she felt sorry for Brandon. Wanted to bring some happiness into his life. He didn't know it, but he needed to return to the real world.

She looked around. Everything was as it had been that morning. Except the black curtains had been pulled back. They had remained closed the entire time she'd been there. She'd had the feeling he didn't want her to know what was behind them. Now they were open, she couldn't resist looking.

It was a workshop of sorts. Not a very large one, but everything he needed to create his works was standing waiting on him, a bandsaw, a stand sander, and polisher. A long workbench ran along the far wall.

A couple of half-finished works sat on the workbench. Brandon's pieces were beautiful. He'd taken twisted pieces of wood and formed them into a man and a woman intertwined in passion and another was a large bird in flight. Both were stunning in their simple beauty. How could the man not see his talent and ability?

He'd obviously been doing some work. So why hadn't he shared? Because she was a stranger. Yet they'd told part of their lives to the point they were no longer strangers. Based on these pieces, Brandon's hand hadn't affected his work, if anything it had made it better. More passionate, thought-provoking. Could the problem be that he didn't think it was up to his standards?

She could help him regain confidence. He must recapture it for him, and her.

As much as she'd like to continue to admire his expertise, she had decorating to do before hopefully Brandon returned. Already this visit hadn't gone as she had planned. When Brandon entered, she would say, "Ta-da, I wanted to give you a little bit of Christmas." Or maybe better, she could decorate and be gone before he knew it. Somehow that sounded safer.

She sat down in Brandon's chair and removed her boots before adding a couple of logs to the fire. She unloaded the bag of stuff she had bought.

Laurel jumped when the door opened with a gust of wind that made the fire blaze. In stepped Brandon. "What in heaven's name are you doing here now?" He whipped off his knit cap then waved it toward the floor where all her purchases lay. "What's all of this?"

Apparently, her idea hadn't been a good one after all. Keeping her voice even she said, "I thought it wrong for you to spend Christmas without any decorations or company. So, I brought a little Christmas cheer to you."

"You know this could be called breaking and entering." He walked to the curtains and whipped them closed.

She stood. Her back went straight. "I didn't break anything. I just entered."

"And I thought I had sent you on your way," he murmured as he pulled off his coat. Brandon stood with his legs spread and hands on his hips glaring at her. "Are your feet frostbitten again?"

"No, I bought some warm pants and boots." She nodded toward her footwear. "Not very fashionable but my feet stayed dry."

"For once you showed some common sense." He looked down at the stuff on the floor. "What's all this stuff?"

"Decorations. You needed a little Christmas décor, spirit."

He glared at her like a bull in a fight. "And you came all the way back out here with all of

this stuff to give me 'a little Christmas spirit'." He all but spat the words.

"It doesn't sound like as good an idea when you say it."

A long loud sigh came from him. His look turned contrite. "I have to say it's the nicest thing anyone has done for me in a long time."

Laurel's chest filled with warmth. She smiled. "I'm glad you feel that way. Now I just need to get it all put together." Maybe if he participated it would help him get into the spirit. With half lowered eyelids she asked, "Would you like to help me?"

"I'm not much good at that sort of thing."

"I'll show you. First, we need to go cut a Christmas tree. Something I know you're good at. Also, I need some boughs to decorate with."

"That's in my wheelhouse." He moved to pick up his jacket.

She grinned. This could be fun. At least Brandon showed some enthusiasm. She pulled on her boots.

Outside Brandon said, "I don't want a big tree."

"You are grumbling again. I thought we got past that. I'm glad you don't want a big one because I only got miniature ornaments. I thought you could put it on the table."

"That sounds like the right size." He led her around the back of the cabin.

They passed a small pile of wood with a lighter center than the outside and others with very defined rings in it. "What are these for?"

"Nothing special." Brandon continued walking.

His tone told her they might mean more to him than he wanted her to know.

He kept moving into the woods. She hurried to keep up. He finally stopped in front of a tree. "Will this one do?"

"Isn't it too big for the table?"

He gave her a pointed look. "I can cut the top out for the tree and the rest you can use for decoration."

"What kind is it?"

"Norway Spruce."

She walked around studying it. "Then I think it's perfect."

"Do you give all Christmas trees that much attention?"

Laurel continued to study the tree. "I see things as a work of art. Worthy of attention and worth a real look."

He looked at her for a moment. "Why did you decide to be an art agent?"

"I always liked art. My mother was a lover of art. She took my brother and sister and I to museums whenever she could. There were books about art in our house. I majored in art history."

He started chopping down the tree. A few minutes later there was a crack and the tree lay on the ground. He finished cutting it from the stump. "Here. Carry this. He handed her the ax then lifted the tree to his shoulder.

Now, he really looked like a lumberjack.

"You lead the way."

Laurel moved ahead of him.

"Why did you lose your job?"

Brandon's question caught her off guard. She fumbled with the ax.

"Careful, you don't want to cut yourself."

She gained control of the ax. For a few minutes there was nothing but the sound of them breathing and the crunch of snow under their feet. "I set up a deal along with the help of a man who I thought cared about me. He stabbed me in the back. When the artist decided not to sign the contract with our company, Joe blamed it all on me. He kept his job and I lost mine."

"Why would he do that?"

She stopped, faced him. "Because I was the up-and-coming person who knew her stuff while he was hanging on my coat-tails, but I just couldn't see it."

Brandon looked at her for a moment. "You cared about the guy."

"Yeah. I thought he would ask me to marry him."

"That stings."

"Yes, it does." But for some reason not as much as if had before she'd met Brandon.

"I'm sorry that happened to you." He sounded sincere.

"I guess we have more than art in common. We have poor judgment in people."

She walked on. Brandon said nothing more and neither did she.

At the cabin he laid the tree at the front door. "How much do you want me to cut for the tree?"

She showed him. He took the top off.

"I'll cut the limbs off and bring them in."

"Okay. I'll get the tree set up." She headed inside.

Brandon said softly, "He was a jerk, you know."

"Yeah. I know." She gave him a tight smile. "But it's nice to have someone else think so too."

Inside she placed the treetop in an empty can of water she found under the sink. She put it on the table. She wrapped a bright red scarf around the can as a tree skirt. Gathering the packages of ornaments and a string of battery powered lights, she began to add them to the limbs.

Brandon entered with an arm load of boughs. "Where do you want these?"

"Just put them on the floor beside the door."

"What do I need to do next?" He added a log to the fire.

"Why don't you come help me?" He gave her a dubious look but shucked his coat. She had most of the ornaments on the tree. "You can help put on the tinsel."

They worked together placing the shiny strings, occasionally their fingers touching. She was too aware of Brandon. "You've gotten the hang of this. I'm going to start with the greenery."

"You're leaving me?" He sounded like a small boy who wasn't sure of himself.

She laid her hand on his shoulder without thinking. "I think you got this."

He looked at her hand. Then his gaze met hers.

"I better get started on that greenery. I have to drive to my cousin's tonight." Laurel placed limbs along the mantle and added some large red plaid bows and round gold ornaments.

"All done," Brandon announced. "I could use some lunch. How about you?"

"I am hungry."

He went to the kitchen while she continued working. She put greenery on the windowsills along with a bow. The fat candle she bought went on the table beside his chair with a bow around it. She placed a quilted Christmas pillow on the bed. The only thing left to do was add wreaths to the front door and the chimney.

Taking the wreath frame she bought, Laurel wrapped it with greenery using wire. She fashioned a bow and added it. Going outside she hung it on the nail already in the door then stepped back to admire her handiwork. With smoke coming out of the chimney and the bright red of the bow, the cabin reminded her of a Christmas card. One that she would like to live in.

That thought shocked her. She'd always been such a city girl but somehow the cabin, Brandon had grown on her.

At the spit of moisture, she looked up at the sky. It had darkened since she'd gone in. She would have to leave soon not to be caught in bad weather.

"That took you long enough." Brandon turned from the stove when she entered.

"I took a few moments to admire my efforts."

He raised a brow. "What did you think?"

"Pretty as a picture."

"I'm not surprised." He looked at her. "Pretty is as pretty does." His attention went back to the pan he stirred.

Heat ran through her. Brandon thought she was pretty.

Laurel picked up the other wreath frame. Soon she had it ready to go above the mantle. She pulled one of the kitchen chairs over close to the fireplace, she stepped up in it, and positioned the wreath over the mantle.

"My grandmother used to hang a wreath there too."

She looked over her shoulder at Brandon. Losing her balance, she grabbed the mantle, but her fingers slipped across the wood. Her foot shifted and the chair tipped. Strong arms caught her, pulling her against a hard wall of chest. She clung to Brandon's neck as her gaze locked with his, their mouths inches apart.

"I've wanted to do this again since I left you in town." His lips found hers with a pressure that heated her from the inside out. His arms tightened around her waist pulling her flush against him from chest to toes. He teased her mouth until she opened for him. Her fingers dug into his hair as she returned his desire. Tightening her arms around his neck, she hung on for the dizzying ride Brandon was taking her on.

Slowly his kisses turned tender. His lips traveled over her cheek to her neck then back to her mouth where he kissed her deeply, once again leaving her weak. All she could do was hold on and enjoy all he offered. Laurel moaned. She wanted more. More kisses, more Brandon.

The smell of something burning made her jerk away. "Food."

He said a harsh word under his breath before he let her go and hurried to the kitchen.

Laurel sank to the chair, her knees too weak to stand.

Seven

BRANDON WAS TORN BETWEEN AGGRAVATION AT AND APPRECIATION FOR Laurel. He liked her despite her pushy ways and her probing questions. Here she was in his home again. She should've been long gone. He had wanted to turn her away at first, but he couldn't stand the thought of hurting her feelings. She'd looked at him with so much expectation. What she had done to his place was nice. He particularly liked the moments before, when he'd been kissing her like there was no tomorrow.

He placed a bowl of soup in each of their places and added a plate of grilled cheese sandwiches between them. "Lunch is ready."

She picked up the chair.

"I'll get that." He hurried to take it from her. She said nothing. The last few minutes had been the quietest she'd ever been. Had he scared her? That's the last thing he wanted.

"This looks good. I hadn't planned on you feeding me. I was going to be gone before you got home."

"I'm glad you weren't." Brandon took his chair. "What's this?" He picked up a small present tucked under the Christmas tree.

"You need a little something to open on Christmas day."

His chest tightened. She had thought of everything. No other woman outside of his family would have shown him that much attention.

She shrugged. "I saw it and it made me think of you."

Now he would think of her when he saw it. He wasn't sure that would be a good idea. "I don't have anything for you."

"You could show me the work you been hiding and tell me about it."

He looked up from his soup. "I'm sure you've already seen it."

"I did but I'd like you to show it to me. You can trust me, you know."

His heart jumped. Could he really do that? The last woman he believed cared about him had disappointed him bitterly. Why wouldn't Laurel do the same? Because she'd proven herself better than that. But what if she was doing all this just to get him to do what she wanted? "I'll think about it."

She lowered her eyes and ate.

Brandon didn't want to show her his workroom. It had been days since he'd been in there. Those half-finished pieces haunted him. The idea of returning to his work terrified him.

But he felt he should honor Laurel's request since she'd been kind enough to give him a Christmas, even if he hadn't requested it. Would it be so bad to just show her around his workroom?

"I'll take your bowl if you're done." He took their bowls and put them in the sink. "I'll show you my workroom now if you'd still like to see it."

She smiled. "I would."

He pulled the curtains back and stepped inside what should be his sanctuary but had become a source of pain.

Laurel followed him. "Why do you keep the curtains closed?"

"Because I don't use it."

"There's not even a speck of dust in here." Her amazement surrounded each word.

"My family cleaned it and I haven't used it since the accident."

"When did you do these two pieces?" Laurel pointed to the workbench.

"They aren't finished." He looked down at the one he had started when he thought he was in love. "I began them before my accident."

"They're beautiful."

"I couldn't finish them. I have difficulty holding them at the right angle now. My hand won't hold the tools like they once did."

"Yet, it's still an amazing piece of work. And this one." Laurel stepped over in front of the bird in flight. "It's soaring. You caught the beauty of freedom." She looked at him with wonder in her eyes. "Tell me about your process. Do you sketch a form beforehand or just look at a piece of wood and see what it's supposed to be?"

Laurel sounded so engaged he had to answer or disappoint her. "A little of both. It depends on if I have something in mind I want to do or if I just like the piece of wood and let it speak to me. The couple I drew because I wanted the woman to be the lighter color and the man the darker."

She reached out as if intending to touch the sculpture but stopped short of doing so. "It's such a sensual piece. It makes my heart hurt."

The emotion on her face tightened his chest.

Her fingers moved as if to touch the bird's wing. Once again, she stopped just short of doing so.

"You can touch it."

She looked at him for confirmation. "I don't dare."

"You might as well. Nobody else will be seeing it."

Her fingertip caressed the length of the man's back.

Brandon's body heated as if Laurel touched him.

"It's not fair to the world to hide this from them. We need more beauty. And this one." She turned to the bird. "It makes me think of longevity. Of expanding. Pushing further. Past your limits. The possibilities in life. It inspires."

Brandon stepped closer. He hadn't heard this type of talk since his last show. It was gratifying. He'd had no idea how much he had missed having his work appreciated. But would the reaction be the same for the work he could do how? "That is kind but the days of that quality of work is over."

"If that's true then why is there a pile of wood like this behind the cabin?" She moved toward him.

"My father piled it there. I just hadn't moved it." He wanted to kiss her again. Hadn't it been forever since he'd been with a woman?

"Tell me what you would do first with a freshly cut piece of wood."

Over the next few minutes, he explained his process. The more he talked about it, a spark of excitement grew. He hadn't felt this fire in a long time. Moving to the workbench, he fingered the tools of his trade lined up in an orderly fashion. "I use these to tease out the form I want."

"It must be exciting to see your vision come alive." She looked at him with bright eyes.

An inkling of that feeling tingled in his fingers.

She returned to looking at the man and woman. "How long does it take for you to make an image come alive?"

Were they still talking about his work or something intimate? Whatever it was his mouth had gone dry. "It depends on how large it is. How much I want it."

She blinked. A hint of pink filled her cheeks.

Brandon dipped his voice low. "It's like any other thing worth having – it takes time and care to cultivate it."

She looked around as if more sculptures appeared from a cabinet. "Have you done anything since the accident?"

"I have but they weren't worth keeping."

Laurel faced him. "I'm not sure I believe that, and I've not even seen them."

"I only keep these to remind me not to bother to try."

She stepped in front of him and took both of his hands in hers.

Until Laurel, he'd never had anybody voluntarily hold his damaged hand outside of the medical staff. He pulled his hand back, but she wouldn't let it go. She ran her fingers along the scar where his fingers had once been. "There's magic in these hands. Such talent for producing beauty. So many people wish they had what you have. I wish everyone saw what I see."

"I only have half of what I used to."

"You're so wrong." Laurel let go of his good hand and brushed his hair away from his forehead. "No, the ability to create something and see something in a piece of wood is right here." She tapped his forehead. "You can still create. It may not be the same as it was. It can be different and still be amazing. Your work wouldn't be any less beautiful." She kissed the palm of his hand.

A sensation he thought dead shot through him. Laurel made him come live. More than that, she had him starting to care. But was he ready to face what could be? "Please don't do that."

"You don't want me to touch you?"

He wanted her to touch him everywhere. But he couldn't say that. "My hand. It looks awful."

"You don't believe that. You're using it as an excuse because you're scared."

He jerked his hand back and shoved it in his jeans pocket. "I've seen how people look at me. I've had a woman leave me."

"You're gonna let a few people and an idiot woman define how you live your life? Here you are, hidden away in this cabin in the woods looking like a bogeyman pretending that you don't want to work anymore when there's a pile of wood behind the cabin just waiting to be formed into something astonishing. I think your fear is holding you back."

"I can't even hold the sander like I did before." He picked up his hand-held sander. "See." He could barely grip the bar.

"Then let's figure out a way where you can. Maybe some sort of strap around the top. Or using your other hand."

"I can't get the same texture with my left hand." He put the sander down.

"Maybe that'll bring a new dimension to your work. It'll be different but still a B. Wheeler's piece."

"I don't want to talk about this anymore." He stepped out of the workshop and went to his chair. He sat, placing his elbows on his knees, and watched the flickering fire. So much of what Laurel had said was true. That was the problem.

"I'm sorry if I upset you." She went to where her boots sat beside his. There was something intimate about that. She pushed that thought away. "I should go."

"Stay."

She stopped with a boot halfway on and looked at him. "Why?"

"Because I like your company." He gave her a wry smile. "And it's sleeting. You can't be walking back to town in that."

Laurel went to the window. "It's really coming down. I

didn't intend to impose on you again. I was just going to spread a little Christmas cheer and be on my way."

She had taken the time and energy to do something nice for him. It had been a long time since anyone had tried, or he had let them. His parents had tried. Members of the town had asked as well, but he had refused them. Somehow, this one small woman had managed to get through his defenses. Brandon pushed her away as well, but she'd pushed back.

"Will your cousin be worried?"

"I told her this morning not to expect me until she saw me."

"Then it's settled. You can stay here again tonight." For some reason that put a genuine smile on his face.

Eight

Laurel wasn't sure she should be staying again, but she had no choice. Plus she wanted to. She liked Brandon. The more she was around him the greater her crush. But the man had deep-seated problems. The loss of his fingers dominated his life.

She huffed. Wasn't she one to talk. After all, she had no job. No prospects. She had been used by a man who had promised her a future. She should have known better.

"What was that sound for?"

"I was just thinking how gullible I am."

"How's that?" His face had turn to one of concern.

"I believed in someone's promise. Again."

His eyes narrowed. "You don't believe in promises?"

"I certainly do not." She dropped her boot on the floor.

"Who hasn't kept their promise to you?"

Did she really want to go into this? "My father when he promised he would come back. I haven't seen him in twenty-two years. My high school boyfriend who said he would stand by me when I got pregnant. He was gone before I lost the baby. My co-worker and jerk of a boyfriend who'd promised we'd bring in the client together. I hate promises. No one keeps them."

"I do. I don't make them if I can't keep them. If I make a promise, I'll do everything I can to make it true."

She smirked. "Isn't that what everyone does when they make a promise?"

"I don't know. Some people just say what others want to hear." He gave her a pointed look.

Did Brandon think she had been building him up without any truth behind her words? "I mean what I say. Especially about your work."

"I have no intention of returning to the art world. If I do anything it'll be for me or family and friends."

"I'm sorry to hear that. I think we'd make a great team."

"I wish I could help you but it's not going to happen. I've been thinking, I can talk to a few of my art buddies, like Ross Biggs. I know he's looking. I can send him your way."

"Ross Biggs! That would be great. He'd certainly help me get another job. I wish you'd contact him." Biggs might even be her ticket to starting her own agency.

"I'll do it." Brandon nodded.

"That's a promise?"

His look met hers. "A promise."

"Don't disappoint me."

"I don't plan to. Tell me about what happened with your father."

"He and mother divorced when I was seven. The last thing he said to me was he promised he would come see me. He never did. He's the one who told me from the time I started walking that he promised if I tried something I could do it."

"So that's where it comes from."

"What?"

"The full court press you've been giving me to do my art

again. You even said if I would just try. Sometimes it takes more than that. You have to want to try."

She pursed her lips. "And you don't?"

"I have tried. It's not there. I don't want that world anymore. I'm satisfied here."

Laurel knew better than that by spending the last twenty-four hours with him. She'd seen it in his face when he described his work. "I don't believe that."

He shrugged.

They were both quiet for a few moments.

He pulled his boots to him. "I'm going to get firewood before it gets dark."

"While you're gone do you mind if I see about supper. You cooked for me, so I thought I'd give it a whirl tonight."

"Sure. That would be nice. I get tired of my cooking. To have someone else do it would be great." He finished putting on his boots, picked up his jacket, and headed for the door.

With Brandon gone, Laurel let out a breath of relief. The past few hours had been intense. In more ways than one. They needed some time apart. She went to the kitchen to see what she could find. To her surprise, he had a well-stocked refrigerator and pantry. She took out a roast and gathered some vegetables. She could cook a nice pot roast with vegetables.

While she worked, Brandon made trips in and out carrying firewood. By the time he returned with the second load, she had the roast in the pot, and by the third the potatoes, onions, and carrots were tucked in as well.

He removed his boots. "Somethin' smells delicious."

"Pot roast and vegetables," she proudly announced.

"Sounds wonderful. Do I have time for a shower before it's ready?"

"Sure. Go ahead."

He gathered clothes and headed into the bathroom removing his shirt as he went. The small door clicked close.

Laurel threw a log on the fire and sat down in Brandon's chair pulling her feet beneath her. She checked her messages on her phone then sent a quick text to her cousin letting her no she would be there tomorrow at the earliest. Putting the phone in her purse, her hand bumped the little book. She pulled it out.

Opening it to where she had left off, she continued reading the story of a couple falling in love. As she read, she didn't miss any of the notes written in the margin. She'd never seen anything like this book. She had become engrossed in other couples' love lives.

The sound of the bath door opening drew her attention. When Brandon didn't immediately exit, she returned to the book.

All the people who had written in it had found true love. They had made promises to each other. What would it be like to have that in her life? She hadn't seen it in her parents' marriage, hadn't been able to maintain a positive relationship with a man. But she still believed in finding a happily ever after. Could she take that chance? Brandon had said with confidence he stood by his word. Despite her experiences, Brandon had her thinking promises had meaning.

Fifteen minutes later, Brandon stepped into view. Her eyes widened. He'd combed his hair back and had trimmed his beard to a fashionable length. She could now see his strong square jaw and his firm, full mouth. Heaven help her, he was gorgeous. In fact, he would make an excellent model for one of his own sculptures.

"Oh wow, this is unexpected."

He ran his hand along his chin. "I figured if somebody was going to make me a pot roast, the least I can do is clean up for the occasion. Do you like it?"

"Yeah." She liked it too much. "I'm not disappointed," she said softly. "Not at all."

Laurel stuffed the book into her purse. She wanted her own fairytale. Like those she'd been reading.

Brandon crossed to his drawers on bare feet, removed socks then tugged the chair closer to her. Somehow he made doing the mundane exciting.

"As you can guess, I don't get much company. If you keep showing up at my door, I'm going to have to get another chair." He grinned. "And more socks."

"A stuffed chair with tiny flowers like in a field. With a pillow. It would be really nice."

He studied her a moment. "I'll keep that in mind."

Brandon put an ankle on his knee. The man had nice long toes with a high arch. Strong feet. There was no getting around the fact she found him attractive.

"I'm sorry I can't follow your lead and fix up a little bit. My clothes are in my car."

His gaze started at her head and went down to her toes. Heat flashed through her at its intensity. "You look nice. Just the way you are. If you'd like to take a shower, now is a good time. The water is hot. Otherwise you'll have to let it run a long time for it to heat up."

She wasn't sure she should. "Didn't you say the shower was outside?"

"It is, but there's a frame around it. With good warm water you'll be comfortable. You might be surprised how much you enjoy it. Pretend you're at a ski resort going into an outside hot tub."

"I've never done that before."

He grinned. "Then you're up for an adventure. That's only if you want to."

Laurel debated the idea. She'd sweated getting to the cabin

carrying everything. Then she'd helped cutting the Christmas tree. She wouldn't have another chance at a bath until she got to her cousin's. She probably could use one. "I'm up for an adventure."

"Good to hear. Come this way and I'll show you." He led her through the bathroom and out a door attached that opened into the shower. Boards created the enclosure with knee-high sides. A rubber mat covered the floor. "Turn the water on, undress inside and hustle under the water."

Laurel shook. What was she getting herself into? This city girl liked a good soak. "If you say so."

"I'll leave you to it." He closed the door leading to the bathroom.

She might as well get started. Brandon was right. The water was hot. She stripped, took a deep breath, and ran to get under the water. The hot water flowing over her shoulders felt wonderful. While soaping up, she looked at the evening sky. The experience was intriguing.

What she wouldn't do for a little red dress to wear for the evening. She looked over the top of the enclosure toward the woods and screamed.

Brandon was there before she could draw another breath.

"Lion." She almost didn't get the word out. "Mountain lion."

He laughed. A full bodied one. "That's Herbert."

She didn't take her eyes off the large tan and white animal watching them. "You know a lion?"

"Yes. He comes around regularly. We try to stay out of each other's way."

"Do...do you think he and I can have the same agreement?"

Brandon chuckled. "I believe you can." He took her arm. "Maybe you should come in just in case he doesn't agree."

She took a step backward leaving the fall of the water. The

cold air smacked her back to reality. She stood there in all her naked glory in front of Brandon.

A towel appeared in front of her face. She snatched it out of his hand, quickly covering herself. Daring a look at him, she found Brandon watching her.

His hot gaze met hers before he blinked then reached around her to turn off the water. "You better get inside before you freeze." The words sounded forced from him. "Head for the fire. I'll bring your clothes."

She pulled the towel tighter around her and did as he said. Standing by the fire, she shook. The coolness of the air brushed her damp skin.

Brandon joined her. He dropped her clothes in his chair. "Get dressed, Laurel."

Something about his gruff tone and bad-tempered attitude made her want to defy him. "What if I don't want to?"

His look bored into her. "Don't play with me, Laurel."

She reached for his two-fingered hand, holding it against her cheek, cupping it.

"Laurel," he bit out.

"Is something wrong?" She cooed, turning her mouth so she could kiss his palm.

"Don't." He pulled it away.

"Brandon." She waited until his look met hers. "I want you to touch me."

"I should go outside for a few minutes. See that Herbert's on his way." Brandon's husky voice skidded over her skin.

Her eyes widened. "You're going out now?"

His jaw tightened and mouth thinned. "I need a few moments alone."

Why? Then it dawned on her. "You don't have to leave on my account."

"Laurel, don't tease a man who has been by himself as long as I have."

She looked into his eyes. "Who's teasing? I've had a crush on you forever. You're better than I imagined."

"That's not a good reason to go to bed with a man." He backed away.

"Now I've gotten to know you, I'm attracted to you for who you are. You're a talented man whom I've admired for a long time. More than that, you're an honorable man. Like right now. Those are hard traits to find. In anyone. You have a sense of humor. Do I need to go on?"

His focus didn't waver. "If I stay, there'll be no going back. No promises of tomorrow."

She wanted Brandon. This memory of the best days of her life. "Remember? I don't believe in promises. Let me turn off the pot roast."

His lips touched the ridge of her shoulder as the towel landed on the floor. "It'll wait. I can't."

Nine

Brandon picked up the largest of the wood chisels. Holding it in place the best he could with his thumb and index finger, he raised the mallet and took aim. The chisel slipped to the side then fell to the table. He tried again. If he only tried harder, he could get this.

He sensed Laurel beside him before she touched his arm then pressed against him. She was wrapped from head to toe in a quilt. His grandmother's handiwork had never looked so beautiful. For a moment he considered returning to the bed and getting under the quilt with Laurel.

"You're working." Awe filled her voice.

He kissed the top of her head. "I thought I'd try again. I had one piece I'd started on. I threw it out. It was under that pile you saw."

She touched the wood, a gentle movement. The form he had in mind had already begun to emerge. "What's it supposed to become?"

"Herbert." The long lines of the mountain lion were already there.

"May I watch you work?"

No one had ever asked him that before. "It's not much of a show. I'm only removing wood on one out of every three hits."

"I don't care. You're fascinating."

He grinned and winked. "That's always good to hear."

"Don't let your ego get ahead of you Wheeler."

He put the chisel in the place he wanted to remove the wood. "Yes, ma'am."

She pulled his work stool out of the corner and up beside him. "Will I be out of the way here?"

"Sure." He liked having her close. He'd never intended to get so involved with Laurel. What did he have to offer her? Nothing. He made a harder than necessary lick on the end of the chisel. This time it flew to the floor.

Laurel reached for it. He caught a glimpse of bare breast before she secured the quilt again.

He set the mallet down. "I'm hungry. How about pot roast for breakfast?" He'd gotten up in the middle of the night and turned the oven off. "But it might be a little tough."

"If you don't mind I won't either. First, I'm going to get dressed. It's Christmas Eve and I need to get going. I can't put off my cousin forever. I don't want her to worry."

The idea of Laurel leaving saddened Brandon. What could an artist who wasn't sure he had a future offer her?

He heard Laurel head to the bathroom. A few minutes later the water to the shower started. He grinned at the yip that burst through the air. Laurel must have stepped outside.

Ten minutes later, she dressed in front of the fire. He looked over his shoulder, watching as the firelight reflected off her back. That was a piece he wanted to do. He grabbed his sketchbook and quickly drew what he saw.

"Can I borrow another pair of socks? I hate wearing dirty ones. I'll mail them all back to you." She gave him a smile he couldn't refuse.

"Sure. You know where they are. Just keep them." She'd have something to remember him by.

He had returned to his piece of wood by the time she called, "Breakfast slash dinner is on the table."

"Go ahead. I'll be there in just a minute. I can't stop right here."

She laughed. "The artist at work."

The next time his thoughts strayed from his work was when Laurel dropped her bag near the door. He looked up. "I'm sorry, sweetheart. I haven't been much of a gentleman this morning."

"Don't worry about it. I'm just glad you're creating again."

He placed his chisel and mallet on the table. "I owe it to you."

"No, you don't. You would've gotten around to it. Your kind of talent begs to come out. I'll say bye now."

"Don't you move. I'm going to walk you into town." He pulled a fresh flannel shirt over his undershirt, buttoned, and tucked it in. He tugged on his boots. Minutes later they faced the cold morning.

He held her hand as they made their way down the path. The trip into town passed quickly. Too soon they stood next to her car.

Laurel turned to face him. "Brandon, I want you to consider trying a show. See how it goes. Even a small one before doing something larger. See how your art is received. I'd still like to represent you, be your agent."

"If it's not received well, I'm the one risking rejection." He'd had enough of that for a lifetime. "They'll say the man with two fingers doesn't have what it takes anymore."

"But you were working this morning. I was hoping you'd changed your mind. All you need is some confidence."

He put some space between them. "Did you sleep with me just to get me to work again?"

"I'd never do that."

His stomach turned sick. She'd taken pity on the man with half a hand. "That's how it sounds to me."

"You give me too much credit." Her eyes had turned pleading.

"You can be very persuasive. Was the decorating, the attention, and going to bed with me all about getting what you want?"

"No, uh...some of it. At first. Then I got to know you."

"You're no better than that partner of yours who left you high and dry." Anger churned in his belly. "I don't appreciate being manipulated. So long, Laurel."

Ten

BRANDON WALKED AWAY, FEELING AS IF HE HAD BEEN CRUSHED UNDER A boot heel. He'd been used. No matter how prettily or passionately. It was still being used. Laurel tricked him into believing she was better than that. He'd been as misled by her as he had his ex-fiancée.

It had never crossed his mind that Laurel might be one of those type of people. He'd known she'd was desperate to get her job back but never dreamed she'd sleep with him to get what she wanted.

He stomped back to the cabin but that didn't ease his pain. The place was empty and lonely without Laurel. He looked at the piece he had been working on with such intense anticipation. It was pure Laurel down to the finest line. He jerked the curtain closed.

He sank into his chair. His life had been desolate before Laurel and was more so now. She'd made it clear what she wanted and went after it. He shouldn't have been surprised.

The hours slowly rolled by. Brandon sat in front of the dying embers of the fire, the cold seeping in. This time he wasn't going to recover. How could he without Laurel?

It had turned dark outside and inside as well. His phone rang. The caller ID screen showed his parents. It was Christmas Eve. Of course, they were calling. "Hello."

"Merry Christmas," they recited in unison.

He didn't feel cheerful. "Thank you."

"Are you sure you don't want to come home tonight or between now and New Year's?"

His mother never gave up. This time the temptation to agree pulled at him, yet he held back. "Not this time."

"Brandon, we miss you."

His parents had worried about him for too long. It was time he faced them and the world. They needed to know their son had starting to see his way back to life. "Mom and Dad, I've started working again."

"You have." The relief in his mother's voice heaped guilt on him.

He'd done them wrong. "I started this morning." Pride filled his voice, something that had been missing for a long time.

"Whatever made you do it, hang on to it. Don't let it go."

Laurel. Their lovemaking had been intense, raw, and fulfilling. Everything he could have wanted and more. Laurel couldn't be that great of an actor. Had there been true emotion behind her touches and muttered words of desire?

He spent the next few minutes telling his parents about Laurel, leaving out some of the more personal parts.

"Son," his father said, "if this girl really means something to you, go get her. Tell her how you feel."

Not only had he let Laurel go but he'd shoved her away. Could she forgive him? He'd made her a promise to call Ross Biggs and he intended to keep it whether they were together or not. But could he do more to win her back? A grand gesture that would win Laurel's heart?

"I think I'd have a better chance showing her."

"You need to show her. Then bring her to meet us," his mother stated.

Brandon grinned for the first time since Laurel had left. "I'll do that, Mom."

He threw some logs on the fire then went to work. He opened the curtains once more and looked at the piece he had begun. He would finish those, then do the one of Laurel by the fire. But he had another in mind that would be the center piece of his showing. It might be his greatest piece ever.

Laurel's holidays were nothing more than a dark cloud of sadness with a fake smile plastered over them. She'd walked around in a daze of disbelief over Brandon turning and leaving her standing on the sidewalk. How had things between them become twisted so quickly?

When she'd poured her heart out to her cousin, her cousin agreed to let Laurel crash at her place for a couple of weeks while Laurel figured out her next move. Time and her cousin's generosity would soon slip through the hourglass while desperation crept into Laurel.

She had hung all her hopes on Ross Biggs contacting her. If Brandon wouldn't be her answer, the next best artist would be Biggs. Yet as two long weeks went by, her hopes of getting a phone call from Biggs had dwindled. Unable to wait any longer, she tried to get in touch with him but failed on every front.

Laurel had put her faith in Brandon to come through for her. Apparently, she had angered him enough he hadn't done as he said he would. Maybe she shouldn't be surprised. Isn't that what people did? Break their promises. Why would Brandon be any different?

Checking her email for the hundredth time that day, her

heart did a flip-flop when a new email appeared. It was from the Cherry Inn. They must be looking for the book. She quickly opened the message. The email was a flyer stating B. Wheeler and Ross Biggs would be doing a two man show to benefit the Cherry Creek Academy Library on January 15th. Her heart skidded to a stop for a moment before it found its rhythm once more. The artists would be hosting a showing of new works and displaying a few special pieces. Apparently, the school had persuaded the inn to share their mailing list. Everyone was invited to attend.

She'd certainly be there. It would be her chance to clear the air with Brandon. She didn't like him believing something about her that wasn't true. Would he listen to her?

The next weekend she drove into Cherry Creek, taking care not to run over anyone on her way through town. A warmth filled her. Returning to Cherry Creek felt like coming home. Still questions plagued her. Would Brandon listen to her? Let her say what she came to say? She pulled into the parking lot of the Academy. The lot was completely filled. Laurel wasn't surprised at the attendance. Others like her would be excited to see that Brandon had returned to work. She finally found a parking space.

Laurel took a moment to adjust her sweater dress. Her hand trembled as she applied lipstick. This was one time she needed to look her best. To rally as much confidence as possible.

People mingled around the library looking at the art. Laurel searched the room for Brandon. Her nerves were strung taut with anticipation. Everything in her ached to see him. She had missed him desperately. Unable to locate him, she strolled around the room enjoying Brandon's and Biggs' work.

She recognized Brandon's unfinished pieces that were now beautiful, completed pieces of art. He had a few new sculptures. One in particular drew her close. It was a woman standing in front of a fire much as she had stood the morning after they had made love. He must have been working day and night since she had left. Each piece exuded beauty and inspiration. Biggs' work was amazing, but it was Brandon's that kept her enthralled.

"I was worried you wouldn't come." Brandon's much-loved voice reached her ear from close behind her.

Her heart did a tap dance. "I wouldn't miss an art event like this."

"I was counting on that."

She turned. He looked wonderful with his close-cut beard and sports jacket. A nice mixture of suave and mountain man. "You planned this?"

Brandon nodded. "Yeah. I had the inn email you. I was afraid you might not come if I invited you after the way I treated you."

"I'm the one who gave you the idea that I'd do anything to get you as a client. But the more I got to know you, the more I realized how special you are, as an artist, but more importantly, as a person. I didn't go to bed with you to get a piece of artwork out of you or to make you feel obligated to be my client. I should've told you how I felt about you Christmas Eve. That it didn't matter to me if you worked again or not. You are really what matters to me."

"That's nice to hear."

She put a hand up. "But I wasn't the only one who messed up. You broke your promise to put me in touch with Ross Biggs."

"I did—"

Laurel's eyes widened. Before he could say anything further, a man she recognized as Ross Biggs walked up. "You must be Laurel." He offered his hand. "I owe you an apology. I was supposed to call you a week and a half ago about representing me, but I was under the gun to get some pieces finished for this show. I didn't want to let Brandon down. By the way, you come highly recommended as an agent." He grinned at Brandon. "Here is my private number." Ross handed her a card. "Call it on Monday and we'll make plans to meet."

Laurel's heart jumped. Brandon had kept his promise after all. "I'll do that." Ross was called away and she turned to Brandon with a smile on her face. "You kept your promise."

"I told you I always do."

Laurel was so engrossed in Brandon, she didn't see another man approaching.

"Laurel."

She whirled around coming face to face with Joe. Of course, he was here. He would have seen the media around the show and not miss the chance to snag Brandon or Biggs for himself.

Joe looked beyond her to Brandon. "I'm Joe Willis. I'm with the Antwan Art Agency. I'm so excited to see your work again. It has been too long."

Brandon ignored Joe's hand and stepped beside her, his hand coming to rest around her waist offering her moral support. "Thank you. I was inspired or I might never have worked again."

Laurel couldn't help but be satisfied at the look of trepidation on Joe's face.

He cleared his throat and addressed Brandon. "I was wondering if we might talk about the agency representing you sometime."

"I already have representation." He looked at her and smiled.

She leaned into Brandon's side. Her gaze met his. "Thank you."

Brandon's focus returned to Joe. "Don't bother with asking Biggs either. We're both going with Laurel."

Joe's face darkened. "Then Laurel, I'd like to offer you your job back. I'm sure Mr. Antwan would agree."

"No thank you." Her voice rang out clear and confident.

Brandon squeezed her waist in solidarity.

Joe shifted his weight, acting unsure. "Uh, I could see you get that promotion."

Laurel shook her head. "I have something better in mind."

"Like what?" Joe demanded.

"I'm going to open my own agency. I can do anything the Antwan Art Agency can do for my clients." She smiled at Brandon.

Joe looked between them. "I doubt that. Neither of you will change your minds?"

She and Brandon shook their heads while looking at each other, having already turned their backs on Joe. He stomped off in a huff.

"That was very satisfying." Her chest hurt her heart was so full.

"Glad to hear it. I'd never do business with a man who couldn't see how special you are. His loss is my gain." He took her hand. "Come on, I have something I want to show you." Brandon led her to a small stage where something sat on a pedestal with a piece of material covering it.

Laurel had been so engrossed in seeing Brandon, she hadn't noticed it. "What's this all about?"

"I have a new piece I wish to unveil."

"Okay, but why I'm I up here?" She gave the gathering crowd a nervous look.

He whispered in her ear. "Because it's dedicated to you." His voice rose. "Ladies and gentlemen, could I have your attention." Brandon waited as people joined them. "I would like to introduce you to the woman who changed my life both personally and professionally, Laurel Marsh. It's because of her that this show is being held. I have one special piece I'd like to unveil. Unfortunately, this particular piece isn't for sale but I'll be doing many others in the future that will be available. All my pieces here but this one is for sale to support this excellent cause. Thank you for coming today." Brandon whisked the material away with a flutter.

Laurel's gasp of surprise had everyone watching her. The work consisted of a piece of curved wood polished to the upmost sheen laying horizonal. Touching the highest curve was a thumb and forefinger. The placard beneath the piece read: Love.

Her chest tightened. It was Brandon making love to her. The emotion in the piece almost took her to her knees. Oh, how she loved the man. He had to have done this work after he'd left her on the street. Her eyes filled with moisture.

He moved to stand next to her.

"It's us," she whispered.

Brandon nodded, his gaze intent on her.

"It's amazing. The most beautiful piece I have ever seen."

"You mean it?" His eyes still held a speck of uncertainty.

"I'd never lie about that. I certainly don't lie about good art. Your talent is still showing through. There's a little more genius to it. Something about it I like even better."

"It's how I feel about you." His thumb and finger brushed her hair back at her temple. "Please forgive me. I said things I shouldn't have ever thought."

Brandon's injured hand cupped her face. He wasn't hiding it, hadn't the entire time. Pride welled in her. The man was so strong.

"It's yours."

"Mine?" She searched his face.

"I want you to have it. So that every time you look at it, you'll know how I feel about you." Brandon directed her away from the crowd and toward a door. "Let's find some privacy. Is the cabin okay?"

"I didn't bring clothes or shoes to tromp through the snow."

He smiled, one that reached his eyes. "That's never stopped you before. Don't worry, I've got that handled."

A few minutes later, he'd seen her to a four-wheel drive truck and lifted her into the cab. He drove out of town to a single parking spot on the side of the road. There he changed into his boots. He came around the truck and lifted her out, carrying her to a waiting sled.

Laurel couldn't help but be impressed, and a little overwhelmed.

Brandon tucked a heavy cover over her then picked up the rope on the front of the sled and pulled. It started to snow as they made their way to the cabin. He carried her inside. Setting her on her feet, he looked at her for a long time, as if memorizing her features.

"I missed you so much. I'm so sorry for what I said. Please forgive me. I love you."

She cupped his face and kissed him. His arms came around her and pulled her tightly against his chest as if he'd never let her go. She grinned. "I know. I saw it in the sculpture." She kissed him. "You've proven it more than once today. Now it's my turn. I've been in love with you since Christmas Eve."

He kissed her deeply.

She shivered.

"You're cold. Come over by the fire." He turned her around.

There, next to Brandon's recliner, sat a floral overstuffed armchair like the one she had described. Her chest hurt with emotion as she blinked to see through the moisture blurring her sight. "Oh, Brandon." She threw her arms around his neck. "You fill my heart."

"I hoped it might encourage you to share the cabin with me. And now with you planning on opening your own agency, you could do that here in Cherry Creek. What do you think?

"I can't think of anything more wonderful. The first thing I'm going to do while sitting in that comfy chair is share our love story in the little green book before I return it."

He kissed her deeply. "Before you do that, I have other ideas about how I want you to spend your time."

"How's that?" she asked in her most innocent voice.

He nibbled at her neck "I intend to show you how much I love you."

"Sounds perfect because I love you too."

THE END

About the Author

Susan Carlisle is the author of over 40 books of fiction and nonfiction. She writes romance for HarperCollins's Harlequin imprint medical line. Her heroes are strong, vibrant man and the woman that challenge them. She loves castles, traveling, afternoon tea and reads voraciously. Get to know Susan at www.SusanCarlisle.com

Once Upon a Christmas Secret

TERRA WEISS

One

HIS NAME IS ASHER. RIGHT? OR IS IT ASHTON? OH, NO! I'M completely blanking—clearly, I'm nervous. Anyway, it doesn't matter because this date is over. I mean, zero chemistry. Zip.

I cock my head, studying him. In fairness, he does look like his profile picture. Brown wavy hair. Nerd glasses, but in an ironic way. Tall. A lawyer, like me. I mean, that's not nothing. I should really give him a chance.

Asher-Ashton takes a hefty swig of his extra hot eggnog latte loaded with nutmeg and whipped cream before letting out a long, "Mmmm." Then a big, "Ahhh."

I shift in my chair. Why did I decide to meet another Binder match? *Why?*

As Mariah Carey's *All I Want for Christmas* plays in the background of Queen Bean, my go-to coffee shop below my apartment in Atlanta, I know *exactly* why.

The holidays. I didn't want to spend them alone, especially this year.

Asher-Ashton sets his cup down, and there's whipped cream on his nose when he says, "Look, I want to fast-track this thing, Dakota."

"Dawson," I correct, blinking. I'm offended that he's forgotten my name, and the irony is not lost on me.

"Oh, that's right." He barks out a laugh. "I'm also meeting up with a Dakota later, so it's hard to keep it all straight. Know what I mean?"

My fingers twitch, overwhelmed with the urge to hit the "/tp" keys to teleport. Clearly, I've been playing too much Minecraft. I punch it out on my lap. /-t-p! /-t-p! /-t-p!

I smile and say, "I do. You're an in-demand fella."

"I absolutely am. Anyway, Dawson, let's get right to it." He taps his fingers together. "I want two kids, one of each, and I'd like the boy to have my name. He'll be the second since, clearly, I'm the first." Another bark of laughter. "But you can name the girl." He flashes a car salesperson smile while pointing at me, the cream still on his nose.

"Generous." This time, my sarcasm is thinly veiled.

"I try to be. I believe the woman should have a fifty percent say, even on the man's specialties." He sits back and stretches.

This is where I do what I've practiced a dozen times—say the words:

It's been really nice meeting you, but it appears we are looking for different things. Best of luck—I'm sure you'll find everything you're looking for. Goodbye, Asher-Ashton.

Okay, I'll leave the name off since I can't remember it. But I should say the rest.

Like right now. Say it! Do it, Dawson!

My mouth opens, but my mother's voice appears in my head. *Ladies hold their tongues.*

Dread skitters up my spine, and my mouth goes bone dry. As an adult, I realize my mother couldn't have been more arcane. But it's so hard to undo a lifetime of hardcore etiquette training from the old-school wife of a senator—a senator who's an unyielding hothead. I've been taught to give and receive compliments, eat with proper manners, and say all the right things on a first meeting. Then later, at the appropriate time, I politely decline a second date.

Okay, I'll do that.

Asher-Aston slides over a packet of papers. "If we're going to be boyfriend and girlfriend, you'll need to sign this NDA. Can never be too careful, as I'm sure you understand."

I blink in shock. Again. An NDA? Is he a celebrity I don't recognize? Does he think he's Christian Grey?

I shoot a desperate glance at Roberto, the owner of the Queen Bean and my friend-slash-resident-date-ender, and he approaches the table. "Hello. Are you enjoying your coffee today?" Roberto smiles that charming smile of his—the one that sells him swaths of lattes, mochas, and cappuccinos.

"We are, thank you so much, Roberto." I give him a quick wide-eyed look, my *help* signal.

"Actually..." Asher-Ashton scowls. "I ordered mine extra hot, but it's just regular hot."

"I'm very sorry." Roberto extends his hand, his barbed wrist tat flashing in the air. "May I make you another one?"

Asher-Ashton scoots it away. "That would be nice, thank you."

Roberto nods, giving me a shielded thumbs down before taking away Asher-Ashton's mug. I've worked out a deal with Roberto that he's to go behind the counter and call my phone. Then, I'll pretend it's a partner at my firm, and rush away with a work emergency. However, a crowd enters the shop, and Roberto says, "Excuse me," before spinning on his heel and rushing to the register.

Crappity crap! Now what? Panic floods me, and suddenly I can't suck in enough air. Beads of sweat appear on my temple, and the coffee shop seems to be shrinking. I need out of this. STAT.

Asher-Ashton puts his hands to his chest. "So, Dawson. Let me tell you some things you definitely need to know about me before signing the contract." He proceeds to ramble on... and on. About his work schedule, grooming habits, and no, please no. *Please, don't go there.* "And," he continues, "I prefer coitus in the evenings after a shower. You know, no morning breath."

Coitus?

"Wow. That's specific." I muster a smile and stand, taking my purse with a jittery hand. "I have to go to the restroom, if you'll excuse me." I promised myself I wouldn't do this anymore, but I can't breathe. This is Armageddon.

I scurry to the bathroom, not locking the door so other customers can still use it. Then I climb on the toilet, unlock the window before nudging it open. It seems more stuck than usual, and I realize it *has* been a while since I've done this.

When it finally gives, I inhale. Ahhh... fresh air! I toss my purse out, hearing it land with a thud before I throw my body into the window well. I swing one leg over before the other, and my jeans catch. I unsnag them before lowering myself to a hang. Then, I drop to the ground.

I land on my feet, barely, and grab my purse. After I spin around and see Roberto standing there, arms folded, a squeal escapes. "You scared the crap out of me! What are you doing out here?"

"Waiting for you. You lasted longer than I thought you would, actually." His head is cocked, like this is so standard, it's boring. And since he's seen me do this a half dozen times before, I guess it is.

"Why?" I brush off my pants and sling my purse over my shoulder. "Look, this time it was bad. Like bad, bad. He wanted me to name our son Asher-Ashton the Second."

Roberto winces. "What?"

"Never mind."

Roberto sighs wistfully. "I'm here because I promised to give you this." He sighs as he holds out an envelope. "It's from Eleanor."

"Eleanor?" At the sound of her name, tears sting my eyes. Heaven knows, crying is all I've done the past year since I lost my very best friend to a brain tumor. My voice is unsteady when I ask, "She left me a letter?"

"She did." Roberto's baritone voice croaks. "Eleanor's putting you in check from the grave."

I press the letter to my chest and close my eyes, picturing her face, her smile. No one else has ever loved me, the real me, the way Eleanor did. I still miss her so much my bones ache. I take a breath, placing my finger under the flap and carefully nudging it open. Through misty eyes, I read:

Not again, Dawson!

If you're getting this letter, it means Roberto just caught you climbing out the bathroom window. Which means you just had another Binder date and are on the run from whatever disaster was unraveling inside.

I know this letter is probably going to make you cry, and although I can't stop you, I hope you don't. Know that wherever I am, I'm looking down on you, my brother, and my parents. I hope I'm smiling at how proud I am of you. If I'm NOT smiling, then listen up, Dawson Hope Wright.

I'm guessing it's probably getting close to Christmas because, knowing you, you didn't get on Binder for a while after I died. I bet you did that stay-in-the-house-and-isolate-yourself thing for a while. Then, you thought about getting on Binder, and maybe you even chatted a bit, but then logged off. Now that it's almost been a year since I passed, you're thinking that the holidays are approaching, and it's time to get your butt on a date. Am I right?

I smile through my tears. Yes. She's right. Eleanor is always right.

Assuming I am, which, come on, when am I not? Here's what I need you to do. It's going to be a particularly tough holiday season for you. I really hope I didn't croak right before Christmas. I'm crossing my fingers that I make it just in time to screw up the Super Bowl, actually. Because, yuck.

She passed on December twentieth, so she didn't make it to her goal. That saddens me more, if that's possible.

Nevertheless, I didn't have control of this one, but you know me —I'm taking control where I can. I'm going to make sure that you and my family have a special holiday this year.

And that means that you, my loyal friend, need to travel to our blessed hometown of Cherry Creek, Tennessee. You must spend the week leading up to Christmas and Christmas Day with my parents and, yes, my brother.

Ugh. Eleanor's twin brother, Sawyer, is my enemy and the flaming jerk hole who crushed and humiliated me. But in fairness, it's not like I have plans for the holidays. My parents, who now live in New York when my father took office, are on a holiday cruise.

I understand that this is a big ask, but I did die, after all, so can you really say no?

No—I can't refuse my dead best friend.

I didn't think so. Once you get to my parents' house and you've complimented my mom's festive dinner and my dad's ridiculous Christmas display, Sawyer will give you instructions on how you both can get your last Christmas gift from me.

My heart squeezes. I got one more gift from Eleanor? My eyes read quickly:

You're welcome.

If you've forgotten, my dear Dawson, I love you like the sister I never had. I will love you forever, no matter where I am. Please know that I'm making you do this for a reason—a reason I'm not at liberty to share with you... yet. But I had secrets, even from you and Sawyer, and now, I need your help.

Love you to the moon and beyond,

Eleanor M. Quinn

Two

After parking my car on the street, I trudge through the snowy sidewalk to Eleanor's parents' house.

I glance up the hill to see my old house, a large Victorian mansion with a pool and the best views of the lake. It's a beautiful estate, the nicest one in the Lakeside Homes neighborhood, but I don't miss it. Studying its off-white pillars and tan shutters, I have no desire to see it up close. And, I'm actually relieved to be heading to Eleanor's house, which always felt more like home than my own.

Walking up to her place, I grin. It has to be a fire hazard with so many Christmas lights. I swear you could see it from the moon. I'm glad Eleanor's father still decided to take this Christmas as seriously as ever. I feel inspired—we should all attempt to figure out how to do the holidays without Eleanor, thinking of her through the family's traditions. It saddens me, but if being here can give us all a bit of reprieve from our grief, then it's worth it.

On the front porch is the signature backside of Eleanor's brother, which is quite appealing, unfortunately. My lip curls.

Sawyer Quinn. My arch nemesis growing up and the thorn in my side in Vanderbilt's pre-law program. Whatever I did he had to do better, and he just *had* to be totally obnoxious about it. Not to mention he's the guy who let me down when I needed him most.

If it weren't for Eleanor, who loved us both dearly, we probably would've killed each other. Which doesn't bode well for us spending the next five days together *through* Christmas day. Honestly, I'm not sure what Eleanor was thinking, but I trust my best friend. And of course, I'll honor her last wish.

Sawyer says, "I had a really great time with you tonight, Katie."

When I realize he's on the porch with a woman and appears to be at the end of a successful date, I hesitate. I do *not* want to see this. But if I head back to the car, they're going to see me.

Katie giggles. "I had a great time with you, too."

Then I hear lip smacking sounds. Seriously? Sawyer's got a date on a *Tuesday* afternoon? How do I have such impeccable timing? Also, I want to puke.

After Katie lets out a moan, I realize I *have* to do something. All three of us will be forever scarred if this goes any further.

I clear my voice as I stomp my feet to bring attention to myself. I may not be able to confront strangers, which sucks being a lawyer, but I've never had any problem facing off against Sawyer. He's the one person I can do that with, and I'm not sure what that says about me or him.

I'm extra loud when I say, "Hey, how's it going? I'm not interrupting anything, am I?"

Sawyer yanks his hands from under Katie's shirt, and she brings her arms to her side to hold her bra in place, which clearly has been undone.

"Um, you kinda are." Katie looks at me, her eyes bulging.

Extending my hand to her, I say, "Hello. I'm Dawson."

She returns the shake, keeping her elbow to her side, and she sort of looks like a penguin. She fumbles for words before she finally says, "Katie."

"So nice to meet you." I look at Sawyer and smirk. "I see you're still living up to your name, Bra Claw."

Katie looks back and forth at Sawyer and me. "Bra Claw?"

I smile brightly and bat a hand. "Just an old college nickname."

Sawyer lets out a forced chuckle. "College was forever ago, Beer Barfer."

I gasp. "That was only *one* time, and it was after a keg stand."

"Yet the name stuck all through college—bummer for you." He shrugs.

I sigh, turning to Katie. "I'm so glad to see that Sawyer found someone. You seem great."

"Oh, this is just a first date." Katie fidgets.

The boldness I have around Sawyer engulfs me, and I nod toward him with a smile. "Then you should know, Katie—if you stay the night, you'll have to share Sawyer with Mr. Bugsby. His lovie—all growing up."

Sawyer laughs that humorless laugh of his, dry yet still charming. "Aw, Dawson, you're just a funny bunny, aren't you?"

"What's so funny? Mr. Bugsby's great." I wink at Katie when I say, "But he might be due for a bath."

Katie points to her car. "Well, shoot. I have to get going. My family is expecting me for dinner."

"I'll call you," Sawyer says, desperate.

"Okay, then," she says nervously, backing up. "Bye."

I want to tell Katie she's dodging a bullet, but that'd be crossing a line. Instead, I give her a wave. "Bye, Katie. Merry Christmas."

Sawyer turns to me, flashing those fiery emerald eyes—the same ones that woo every straight woman but me. He scowls. "We're about to spend a lot of time together, and remember who you're dealing with, Dawson. You sure this is how you want to play it?"

"Oh, this is definitely how I want to play it." It's been an excruciating year, and I need some excitement in my life.

"Then game on."

We walk inside, and the smell of the real Christmas tree, apple crisps, and baking bread hits my nose all at once, and my stomach growls. Along with the Christmas lights, stockings, and a beautifully decorated tree, the place envelopes me like a warm hug.

But then I see the baby poop brown and flowery couch—the place Eleanor and I used to watch movies together, and it guts me. I squeeze my eyes shut, taking a deep breath before I look at Sawyer. "Your parents really are the most welcoming hosts. What happened to you?"

Flashing me a hurt look that I know is feigned, he says, "What? Just because I don't decorate my apartment?"

"*Decorate*? Last year when I was there, you had no furniture. Or food. Just a lawn chair and blowup mattress that was surely forced to take on more than it could handle."

"I have a real bed now. Memory foam, with loads of rockin' memories."

"Eww."

We're interrupted by Maryann, Eleanor and Sawyer's mother, who comes into the living room and pulls me into a hug. "So good to see you, Dawson." She holds me extra long, and I don't mind, as I've needed it. Since Eleanor passed, I don't get hugs from anyone. Eleanor was my family since I'm an only child, and my politician parents spend their life baby-kissing and attending charity events. Maryann pulls away. "How is everything going in Atlanta?"

"As well as can be expected," I say, even though that's not exactly true. Besides desperately missing my best friend and roommate, I'm struggling at my job. I used to love it, but it's been difficult since a new partner took over. He's known throughout Atlanta as "The Crusher," and for good reason. He not only "crushes" in the courtroom but in the office too, snapping orders and demanding impossible tasks in unreasonable time frames.

And then there was my Binder date, who was already naming our children before I climbed out the window. "How are the Christmas decorations coming? They look amazing." I'm careful not to ask how Christmas is going because I already know the answer to that—not well because how could it? How could anything be okay without Eleanor here? How will it ever be okay again?

Maryann bats a hand. "You know Steven. He almost bankrupts us with the electric bill every year." She chuckles, but then her voice turns quiet. "Truth be told, we almost didn't do it this season, but we agreed—we'll do it for Eleanor." Maryann glances up the stairs as if looking for her daughter. For a moment, the room fills with grief, but then she claps her hands together and perks up. "Steven loves it, though, so I just always pray he doesn't fall off the roof."

"That sounds like a job for Sawyer." I flash Sawyer a toothy grin, and he shoots me a scowl. By unsaid agreement, we've joined forces to keep this hard time as light as possible for Maryann.

"That's a good idea, Dawson." Maryanne looks at Sawyer. "You should help your father with the lights."

Sawyer's mouth curves. "I'd love to help Dad with the lights, Mom. Thank you *so much*, Dawson, for offering me up."

"Hey, it's why I'm here, and I'll be here. Through Christmas."

Eleanor's mom waves toward the kitchen. "Well, I hope you're both hungry because we have a table of food, and we're just about ready to eat. So, come on in and bring your appetite."

"Thanks, Mrs. Quinn."

Three

AFTER DINNER, SAWYER MOTIONS ME INTO THE PANTRY, AWAY FROM Maryann and Steven. He's holding a white envelope and wearing a mischievous expression. "Eleanor's instructions said to wait for you before opening this one. I didn't want to upset mom and dad, so I thought we could open out here." We're shoulder to shoulder, thigh to thigh, when he pulls out the single sheet of paper with four lines. Together, we mouth the words.

Dawson and Sawyer,
It's time to forage.
Go to the place
We keep our storage.

We look at each other for a second, an old spark of excitement flaring to life, then it's on. Sawyer and I race to the attic, as whoever gets there first somehow wins, like we're still teenagers. Or maybe grade schoolers? I don't know, but Sawyer has the tendency to bring that out in me.

In the corner is a Christmas gift, wrapped to perfection in shiny paper and adorned with beautiful bows, as Eleanor wouldn't have it any other way. However, there's a thin layer of dust on it, something Eleanor couldn't control. Sawyer and I slow down in synchrony, as if we need to savor this tiny connection to her. I go to it first and run my finger over the paper before brushing the dust away. I don't want my heavenly best friend to cringe, in case she's looking down.

"You don't have to do that, Dawson." Sawyer's voice is soft. "Eleanor won't get on you about it, I promise."

I swallow hard. "Right."

Sawyer looks down. "I still do it too."

Wow. Did he just open up to me? This is new, and honestly, it isn't the only thing different about Sawyer. Light creases line the corners of his eyes now, and those shiny emerald eyes are now shadowed with flecks of gold. Things that actually make him even more stunning, if that's possible, because they make him more real. Perfectly imperfect.

What the heck? Get it together, Dawson.

Sawyer reaches under the bow and touches a piece of paper. "So. What is this?"

"It has to be another note, right?"

He pulls his finger away. "You read it."

"No, you. Finders, readers."

He blinks. "Good one."

"Thanks."

Sawyer groans. "This is going to be a long Christmas break." He places a finger under the dry edges of the envelope, making a snapping sound as it breaks free.

In Eleanor's perfectly written handwriting, it says,

Dear Sawyer and Dawson,

I'm so glad to see that you both made it to Cherry Creek for Christmas. In order to open the gift's first padlock...

"Wait. It's locked?" I tear the paper off the box, unveiling a plastic storage container with a built-in padlock. "Seriously?" We keep reading.

You must complete challenge one: go to the academy and dance in Cherry Creek's production of The Nutcracker Suite.

Sawyer throws the note down. "No way."

I pick it back up and keep reading Eleanor's words out loud.

Way, Sawyer. And I know what you're both thinking. Why, Eleanor, neither of us does ballet, or performs for that matter. Yes, I know this about the two of you, but fortunately for you, I got permission from Françoise, the director of the play, because I was dying. She and I agreed you could both be mice, a role that requires the minimum level of skills. Skills that you two will learn together. But don't think you're getting off easy—at the end of the performance, Sawyer, you're going to have to lift Dawson into a twirl that must earn cheers.

"This is not a fun game, Eleanor." Sawyer flops his head back, but then we both continue reading.

You have a few days to learn this dance, so I suggest you put this note down and get your bums to the studio and learn your part so that you may wow the crowd. All the proceeds from ticket sales go to cancer research. And just so you know, if you're thinking about trying to get out of this, I was going to play the role of Clara this year, so I want my big moment to be yours. Don't let me down, I'm watching from above.

Love you to the moon and beyond,

Eleanor M. Quinn

Sawyer pinches the bridge of his nose. "If she wasn't dead, I'd kill her."

"Me too." We both stand and stare at the box for a moment as Eleanor memories swirl around us. "But we're doing this, right?"

Sawyer nods. "Heck, yeah, we're doing this." He walks away and starts shuffling through the stack of boxes in the corner of the attic. He raps his knuckles on the box. "What do you think is in here?"

"Something to remind us of Eleanor? Memorabilia? Or a million dollars because she was a secret bank robber."

"I'd rather have the memento. Remember Eleanor's handmade Christmas ornament? The green dog she made out of clay in third grade?"

"Yes." I smile. It was a tiny replica of the Shih Tzu dog she wanted from the shelter, but textured with leaves and painted green because she wanted to name it Broccoli.

Sawyer says, "We can't find it, and we wanted to keep the tradition and put it on the town tree. Maybe it's in the box."

I join him. "It's kind of a big box for an ornament."

"Probably. But I've run out of places to look."

After Eleanor made the ornament, she decided to hang her ornament on Cherry Creek's Christmas tree downtown on Christmas Eve that year, then made a wish that the dog would be hers. Apparently, her parents couldn't say no, so, sure enough, they secretly adopted the dog that afternoon before the shelter closed for the holiday break. Of course, Eleanor named him Broccoli.

Every year after, Eleanor always hung the dog ornament on Cherry Creek's Christmas tree on Christmas Eve, even though the official tree decorating ceremony for the town is on Thanksgiving Day. For everyone else, after they finish their Thanksgiving dinner, they make their way to the front of the courthouse where families bring special ornaments to hang on the tree. My family used to hang ones that belonged to my grandparents when we lived in town, but that was years ago now.

But not Eleanor. She did it her own way, like everything else in her life. Eventually, the entire Quinn family joined her in the tradition, making new ornaments for new wishes.

I grab another box and start shuffling through it, but it's not Christmas stuff. It's old clothing. We have to find it—especially now that Eleanor is gone. Cherry Creek's tree ornament tradition is all about memories of times past and loved ones who are no longer with us, and Eleanor's belongs there now more than ever.

Sawyer has a defeated tone when he says, "We looked and looked for it—we've already gone through all the Christmas stuff. It's probably lost, but I can't bring myself to give up on it."

"Of course you can't." I move to a different box.

I'm determined to find it.

After going through the entire attic with no success, we call it quits. It's bedtime, and I'm exhausted.

I'm staying in Eleanor's room, which is bittersweet. I walk in, my eyes taking in the glass case filled with her ballet trophies. Photos of all of us in designer frames hang neatly on the wall. And numerous Beanie Boo stuffed animals are neatly placed everywhere, left just as it was when Eleanor lived at home.

I set my suitcase on the silk shimmering off-white bedspread, fit for a queen. Eleanor had exquisite taste, even in high school. And she knew how to bargain shop, so she bought designer linens at outlets. I run my hand over it, smiling wistfully. Eleanor taught me how to be thrifty, but my decor never looked as good as hers. I guess you can't teach someone taste.

My phone buzzes, and I check it to see a text from The Crusher. It says,

Crusher: *Where is the briefing for the Bradford case?*

Me: *I emailed it on the tenth, sir. I also put a hard copy on your desk.*

Crusher: *where?!*

Me: *In your incoming basket, sir.*

My first time in court, I tanked. I could hardly open my mouth, and I thought they'd fire me. When they didn't, I ended up thriving on a team I loved. But then my boss quit, and Mr. Morgan, The Crusher, took her place.

When Mr. Morgan doesn't respond to my last text, I move on, hoping his silence means he found what he needed. I'm also dreading working on this case. Mr. Bradley, a seventy-six year-old man, fell on wet slippery tile at the five-star hotel we're representing. He broke bones and is currently in a wheelchair, and he's seeking well-deserved compensation for pain, suffering, and medical expenses. But we're defending the hotel, so it's my job to prove that his fall was due to his own instability, not negligence on the part of the hotel. But from what I've found, it was their fault—they had unmarked wet tiles in the lobby.

It makes me sick to think about it, so I set it aside and focus on what I can do here and now. That's when an idea pops into my head on how to find the broccoli dog ornament: why don't I put a message on NeighborhoodBuzz.com, in the Cherry Creek zip code, asking if anyone's seen it? The town tree is taken down the day after New Years, and it's possible the ornament was returned to the wrong person last year. I have a picture of it on my phone, somewhere, so I do a search. Eleanor is hanging it on the tree, pre-diagnosis, unaware that it would be the last time she participated in the tradition.

When I find it, I log onto the site and post my message with the picture, hoping someone will find it amongst their Christmas things.

When I'm done, I step over to Eleanor's vanity and see a card with hand drawn hearts sitting in front of the mirror. I'm curious but feel weird about snooping. However, the "love you forever and always" scribbled on it piques my interest. Eleanor had several casual relationships but was never serious with anyone.

Not that I know of, anyway.

I decide against picking it up—it feels wrong.

After a knock at the door, Sawyer's voice echoes from the other side. "Can I come in?"

"Sure."

He opens the door and steps inside. I have this knee-jerk reaction of guilt, like we're doing something wrong. I was never allowed to have boys in my room growing up, and somehow, being here, back in Eleanor's room like this, is making me feel like a teenager again.

Sawyer wrings his hands. "You okay staying in here?"

I nod slowly. "Yeah. Actually, I am, which surprises me. I feel closer to Eleanor."

"Good." His eyes pan the room. "It's hard not to, isn't it?"

"Yeah." Curiosity is getting the best of me, so I say, "There's a card on her vanity that says, 'love you forever and always.'" I point to it. "Do you know who that's from?"

His face puzzles before he turns and looks at it. "No idea."

"I didn't feel comfortable reading it." I gnaw at my lip.

"I do." Sawyer darts over and picks it up.

"Sawyer!" I scold, rushing over and knocking it out of his hands. "It seems private."

"She had it sitting out. It's not even hidden. I think that means it's okay."

"Fine."

He picks it back up and reads it aloud. "Hey, bunny." He stops, his lip curling. "Bunny? Are you kidding me?"

"Keep going." Now I'm *really* dying to know.

He clearly sees that, so he darts away.

"Oh, no you don't." I chase him, grabbing him by the shirt and pulling him back to snatch the note. He turns to run away again, and he trips over my foot. We both tumble onto the bed, me falling flat on top of Sawyer's chest.

We're both laughing, but my body isn't. It's feeling zings of electricity and... well, it's liking this.

But I'm definitely not.

When I go to climb off of him, I get tangled in his arms and legs and end up slipping off the silk bed onto the floor. I land with a thud.

In an instant, I see Sawyer's face over mine. "You okay?"

I bust into another chuckle, and Sawyer joins me. I love his laugh. It's so contagiously melodic and heartfelt, and it makes me laugh harder. I leap up, brushing myself off and recomposing myself. I act like I'm turning and walking away when I whiz around and snatch the card from his fingers.

"Hey, not fair!" He makes a grab for it, but I've got it, and I'm already heading for Eleanor's bathroom. When I'm inside, I manage to shut the door and lock it.

I cry out, "Dawson, one. Sawyer, zero!" before opening the card and reading,

Hey Bunny,

We only have two days left, so I plan to make the most of every minute we have together to take in that beautiful face and stunning soul.

A click of the doorknob draws my eyes up, and I see the lock pop open. Sawyer swings the door open, rushing inside holding a bent bobby pin. "You honestly thought you could keep me out of here?"

"Hey, I could've been using the bathroom!" I feign an offended look.

He rolls his eyes, his palm up. "Let's call a truce. Please. Hold up the letter, and we'll both read it. Together."

"Fine." My curiosity has now trumped my need to one-up Sawyer. I hold it up and continue reading.

This week flew by. I guess that's what happens when you meet

your soul mate. And you are mine, Eleanor Maryann Quinn. Know
that wherever we are, my heart is always with you.

Always and forever,

A

"A!" I cry out. "Who the heck is 'A'?"

"No idea."

"I can't believe it." I turn the card over. "When was this written?"

"No idea." Sawyer sounds almost offended. "My sister had a serious boyfriend we didn't know about."

I fold my arms. "And now we need to figure out who it was."

Four

We arrive at the Cherry Creek High School auditorium first thing in the morning, and it's hard to be here knowing I won't see Eleanor dancing beautifully on the stage anymore. I have so many memories in this space, and almost all of them include her. Our high school graduation was here. Most of Eleanor's performances were here, and I'd come to cheer her on as she danced expertly, giving it her heart and soul. I, on the other hand, have never had any rhythm, nor the desire to dance on stage.

At this moment, I can't help but be a little miffed at Eleanor because this is seriously the last place on earth I want to be... dancing with *Sawyer*. Yet here we are.

An attractive woman with a ballerina's body and a commanding presence approaches us. I realize it's Françoise, the woman Eleanor said would be directing the play. It's been years since I've seen her, and she's only become prettier with age.

"Welcome, Dawson and Sawyer. We've been waiting for you." Françoise looks Sawyer up and down, cracking into an approving smile.

Oh, great. She's going to be swooning over Sawyer. "Nice to see you again, Françoise," I say.

"It truly is." Sawyer uses his wooing tone, returning the smile. But he's a bit off and not his usual super confident self. He probably feels the same way about this place as I do.

Françoise says, "All right. We have two remaining practices, tomorrow and Friday from eight to eleven a.m."

Sawyer frowns. "For three hours?"

"Yes." She nods. "And a dress rehearsal on Friday, the same time. Now let's not waste minutes. We can't have you two ruining my show, now can we?"

Sawyer walks out on the stage. "You've got it, Fran."

Wow, he's on a nickname basis with her? What's that about?

When he stands there like a dude without any sense of movement, I tilt my head and say, "Sawyer, you look more ready to attend a Star Trek convention than attempt ballet."

"Haha, Dawson."

"Hello." A deep voice echoes from behind me. I turn to see a very fit, very attractive man smiling at me. "You must be Dawson." He extends his hand.

"Yes." Now it's *my* smile that's dazzling. "And you are?"

"Dante. I'll be training you while Françoise works with Sawyer. This way, you'll both be learning from an expert."

Well, well, well. This might not be so bad, after all.

"Sure Dante, let's get to work." I step into position.

Dante takes me through the basic steps. When he twirls me around like he could do it in his sleep, I giggle and lean into his chest, which feels like chiseled iron. As it turns out, he's part of a professional ballet company out of Nashville.

I see Sawyer side-eying us before going into a basic plié with Françoise. When he almost falls, she finds this funny.

Actually, I do too, even though I've almost bit the dust a

time or two as well. That doesn't stop me from saying, "You need knee pads and a helmet, Sawyer? Doing a bend can be a dangerous activity."

He narrows his gaze. "You know, maybe I do. But at least I have rhythm. You dance like SpongeBob."

I gasp. "Take that back."

"Never, Beer Barfer."

"Humph." I turn back to Dante, saying, "Turn the music on again." I'll prove I have moves. When the music starts, I attempt a pirouette with everything in me. I spin right into a fall, hitting the hard wooden floor with an echoey thud, a burning sensation ripping through my knee.

When I look at it, it's already red and bloody, like a rug burn. *Great.*

Sawyer's face is serious when he says, "You okay?" as he rushes over.

But Dante steps in front of him, offering me his hand. I take it with a big smile. "I'm fine."

Sawyer looks a bit peeved as he nods before walking away.

Once we're practicing again, I realize Eleanor's training plan was quite brilliant. Now that Sawyer and I are with separate partners, our competitiveness takes over as we fight to outdo each other with each turn and spin.

I'm laughing and having a good time with Dante, but I already know he's not my type. He's a bit too smooth and proper, which is actually Eleanor's type, if I'm being honest. I'm sad she isn't performing as Clara this year so these two could've met, as they would have hit it off, big time.

This gives me a thought. "Hey, Dante, do you have a nickname that starts with an A?"

"A nickname. My goodness, no." He says this like I asked if he has lice. I cross him off the list. I guess he's not Eleanor's secret A.

Our practice is going peachy... until it's time for Sawyer and I to dance together.

That's when everything falls apart. As we stumble and move out of time, Françoise darts ahead of us, showing us how to walk on our toes. And after a few failed twirls, I start to wonder how he and I are going to get out of this thing alive.

Especially because when we mess up, Françoise says, "Again," each time with more frustration and vigor than the last.

She must say it another million times, or it feels that way, and I'm exhausted, thirsty, and dead sick of Sawyer and his three feet.

After I stumble for the umpteenth time, he says, "You know, Dawson, I don't want to be here any more than you do, but you gotta try."

"I *am* trying. Why don't you learn where to put your big fat feet so I don't trip over them?"

We lock fiery gazes, and Sawyer seems more than happy to stare me down. But right now, I hate looking into his eyes because he's gazing at me with such intensity, I want to envelop him into a hug and never let go.

Sawyer and I have been in plenty of stare-downs before, but whatever's happening right now is different. As we look into each other's eyes, my stomach twists into a wicked knot. I yearn to sit with him and talk, all night long, laughing at ridiculous things and talking about our dreams.

Eleanor and I used to do that, which now, looking back, is painful because Eleanor would never get to realize any of those dreams. Traveling abroad. Spending a year hiking through Argentina. Going to Australia just to see the koalas.

"Hey, you with me?" Sawyer's voice is Charmin toilet paper soft, and I realize my eyes have misted over.

"Yeah, just got a bit dizzy," I croak out, separating myself from his arms. "Plus, you're annoying the crap out of me." I laugh, trying to play off my weirdness.

"Yeah, I'm a little dizzy too," he whispers.

I blink. What was *that*?

His finger touches my chin, and I tilt my head to meet his eyes again. They are glazed when he says, "Let's do this, okay? For her."

I manage a nod.

He shakes his head, smiling when he says, "Now if you'll just follow my lead, then maybe we'll get somewhere."

His playfulness spurs me to focus. I grab his arms and step into position before saying, "If you want me to follow your lead, then be a leader." I smirk. I won't let Sawyer see how his words affect me. And if I'm being real with myself, how his words have always affected me. Because if he does, I only stand to get hurt, and worse than the time he crushed me. I steel myself and say, "Okay. For Eleanor."

"There we go. Now—let's start from the top."

We go back into our sequence, and although it's nothing special, we're making progress. We stay long after the other dancers have left, and when we're finally ready to go home for dinner, I'm famished, but feeling good. We've accomplished *something*, and we'll only get better as the days go on. I'm sure that we manage something presentable by showtime.

Françoise has an ear-to-ear smile when she says, "Sawyer, can you stay behind? I want to go over a few more moves with you." She shrugs. "Then I'll give you the code to unlock Eleanor's first padlock."

First padlock? Sawyer and I share a knowing glance—leave it to Eleanor to go big or go home.

"Sure." Sawyer sounds just a little too enthusiastic, but his voice is softer when he turns to me and says, "But Dawson, can you make it home okay—"

"Your parent's house is a three-minute walk away, Sawyer." I hitch a thumb backward. "I did it a million and one times growing up, and it's still light out."

"I'll give you a ride home," Dante cuts in, grabbing his duffel bag. "I'm headed that way."

"Thank you so much, Dante." I give him a polite smile, but it's all for show. My heart's not in it.

"Oh, okay," Sawyer says hesitantly. "I'll see you at home later, Dawson."

For the holidays, Sawyer is staying at his parent's house, even though he's got an apartment downtown. It was part of Eleanor's instructions to him, so I *will* see him there... if he comes home tonight. "Bye."

When Dante and I reach the parking lot, I turn and give him a genuine smile. "Thank you again for the offer, Dante, but I'd really prefer to walk. The air is so crisp right now, and I'd like to clear my head. It's only a few minutes away, in the Lakeside Homes." I point ahead.

His gaze follows my finger. "You sure?"

"Yes, thank you." I really want to be alone, and I have zero interest in Dante.

As I walk back to Eleanor's parent's house, I can't get past how all this made me feel. Why do I care that Sawyer's staying late with Françoise? I mean, he *really* needs the extra help, and I have to follow his lead. Plus, he's just so dang irritating. That said, he also makes me feel something I haven't felt in a long time. Maybe ever. Which is probably the reason that none of my dates go anywhere if I'm being real with myself.

But I have to push all that from my mind because it's absolutely ridiculous.

It's *Sawyer*, my best friend's twin brother, the obnoxious, always-there pest, and a person I only have to tolerate for four more days.

Five

The next day, after our morning ballet practice, Sawyer and I head to downtown Cherry Creek. We're ready to take on Eleanor's next challenge, which sounds far easier than trying to perform in The Nutcracker Suite. But it's not remotely fun.

When Sawyer got home last night, he told me the code, and we opened the tote to find Eleanor's next message, along with a nested smaller storage tote with a padlock.

I was too proud, or maybe too scared to ask how the rest of his time with Françoise went. I know that means something about my growing feelings, but I'm not ready to deal with that yet. Maybe ever.

I pull at my green tights and look at the oncoming traffic, hoping no one recognizes me, although I know better. Of course they will.

"Eleanor went too far this time. For real." Sawyer tugs at the crotch of his tights, which are even snugger than mine—and showing off every inch of his exquisite body. Sawyer looks good in just about anything, but not his green elf hat has a red and white furry ball that hangs in front of his left eye.

I laugh before popping a stick of gum in my mouth, needing

it to keep me occupied while I stand here doing nothing. "You know I don't want to do this *at all*. But seeing you in that outfit kind of makes it worth it. Can't wait to hear what your cronies have to say."

As if the universe hears me, a car slows down and pulls up. Barney, a high school classmate of ours, rolls down the window, and says, "Hey, Quinnzy, nice outfit. It looks like you've really gone downhill since your star quarterback days."

The whole town knows Sawyer was headed for college football until an injury ended his career. But he's really smart, so he went to Vanderbilt on scholarship with Eleanor and me.

"Very funny, Barney." Sawyer approaches the window and wags his finger. "At least we're out here trying to raise money for shelter animals and do something good for the planet. You should try it."

Barney puffs his chest. "Hey. I'm doing the world good by just existing."

Sawyer scoffs playfully. "You should consider sterilization."

I have to hold back a chuckle at that one.

Barney roars in laughter. "And—Sawyer for the win. Hey, let's grab a beer soon, okay?"

"You got it, Barn. I'm always up for a beer. Even if it's with you." Sawyer taps the hood of the car before stepping away.

Barney looks at me. "So, Dawson. You're in town. Are you Sawyer's flavor du jour for the holidays?"

"Come on, Barn, you know better than that," I huff, indignant. "Just here helping raise money for shelter animals, too."

"Well, if you're not busy being a do-gooder later, come on by my house. Ma made her famous pecan pie." He winks.

Oh, boy. "Thanks, Barn. But all this do-gooding is exhausting. I'm gonna hit the hay."

"Right on." Barney salutes us. "You both have a Merry Christmas."

"You too." I wave.

Barney rolls up the window and drives away.

I blink before looking at Sawyer and saying, "Let's be grateful Barney J. Blecker doesn't have any names that start with A."

"Amen to that." Sawyer scrubs his chin. "I can't stop thinking about who it could be. Andy, Archer, Alan?"

My face puckers. "Nope, nope, and nope."

"Right." He blows out a long sigh. "Well, you got your wish, Dawson. A day full of people laughing at me in tights."

"Please. Barney just thought I was *your* 'flavor du jour.' Anyway, it'll all be worth it if we help save animals." In Eleanor's note, she said that the shelter was in dire need last year, but we found out that the situation is even worse this year. Overcrowding has made it so animals have to be euthanized at a higher than normal rate, not that any rate is acceptable. We need to raise enough money to fund expansion. "And Eleanor was right, as always. This is a worthwhile thing to do." I start snapping my gum—something I always tell myself I'm not going to do—yet I can't stop myself once the gum's in my mouth. I hear my mother's voice: *Don't you dare snap that gum, young lady,* and I feel rebellious and free.

Sawyer holds out his hand, palm up. "Hand it over. You know you can't handle chewing gum."

My lip curls. "It was just one snap. I'll be good from now on."

"You always say that, but after the snap comes the series of pops that never end." He wiggles his fingers. "Hand it over. It's gonna scare away donors."

I hate that he knows me so well. "Fine." I acquiesce, but only because this means Sawyer must hold my already-been-chewed gum in his hand. When it lands on his palm, I give it a good squish. "Dare you to chew it on the way to the trash bin."

Sawyer can never say no to a dare. He stares me down, not saying a word as he pops the gum in his mouth and chews with vigor all the way to the can on the street. Then he hocks it straight into the bin.

"Nice shot," I say.

"Thanks."

Time to get to work. I swing my sign around and try to put some *umph* in it. It's an arrow pointing to the donation stocking that says, "Your Donations Save Animals!"

But it's cold out here, and when it starts to snow, Sawyer and I end up doing elf dances to stay warm, which actually works in our favor as we draw attention to ourselves. Once we get people's interest, we have a laminated photo album of animals that are up for adoption in hopes of finding them good homes.

"Hey, Denise, long time no see," Sawyer says to a woman holding bags from the 5 & Dime. "How about getting Jared and Ethan a new dog for Christmas?"

After I give Denise a wave and a greeting, she walks over and flips through the pictures. "The boys want a dog so badly, but I've been hesitant because I'm not sure they're ready for the responsibility."

Sawyer points to a Corgi and says, "But look at this one. He's three, and he's the best. I have a video I took of him, too." Sawyer presses play on his phone, and it shows the Corgi fetching a ball.

Denise squeals and says, "Okay. He's adorable, and he's exactly who we've been looking for."

Sawyer takes the bags from her and carries them to her car that's parked on the street in front of us. Once she unlocks the door, he loads them into the trunk. After he shuts it, he says, "Now, go. You have to get him now because he's on the list to be put down. It's an ugly situation with space." Sawyer's tone is dire, and his genuineness makes his argument even stronger.

She groans. "Okay. You've convinced me. I'll go get him now. You're a very persuasive person, Sawyer Quinn. But we already knew that, didn't we?" Denise winks as she steps into her car.

When she drives away, Sawyer shoots me a smug smile. "Sawyer for the win."

My competitiveness with him boils to the surface, as usual, and I say, "I can do better. Easy peasy." I start to walk away.

"What?" His face drops. "Where are you going?"

"None of your business. You stay and work this corner. You've clearly got East Main covered. I'm going to West Main." I shuffle away, my elf shoes making V-shaped tracks in the snow.

When I approach the Cheery Cherry Bar, I tug down my elf top to show some skin and paint on my best smile. I'm going to drum up so much money Sawyer is going to cry. Like the baby he is.

When two burly guys in flannel coats get out of their Jeep and approach the entrance to the bar, I realize I don't know them, which is going to make my job harder. I thought I knew everyone in this town, but I have been away for a long time. Still, I've got a job to do, so I'm smiling big and ready to be something I'm not: pushy. "Hello, there. How are you two today?"

They return glowing smiles. The one with rosy cheeks says, "Howdy, elf. What can we do you for?" He chuckles, glancing at his friend wearing a knitted cap.

I laugh back, spying Sawyer in the distance, approaching with his signature scowl. My smile falls away. "This time of year is really hard for animals on the streets. They need in out of the cold, and I'm here to make sure they get adopted, or the shelter gets everything they need to give them the care they need." My eyes automatically squint when I say, "I'm doing this in memory of Eleanor Quinn. Did you know her?"

"We sure did." The knitted-cap guy shuffles his feet. "So sad. She was a force in this town."

"She was my best friend," I whisper. "And one of her last wishes was to save the animals this year. So, what do you say? Any amount will help." I hold out my stocking.

"Aw, dang it." The guy reaches for his wallet, handing me a couple of twenties. His friend does the same. "Hope this helps."

"You two just saved some animals' lives. You have a Merry Christmas."

"You too, now." Knitted-cap guy gives me a nod before they both walk away.

When they enter the bar, Sawyer says, "Really, Dawson?"

"What?"

"Showing your cleavage?"

"Oh, come on. it's not like you have scruples."

He folds his arms. "What is that supposed to mean?"

"You know *exactly* what that means." Sawyer didn't show up for me on the night I needed him most. He was supposed to be my escort for my debutante ball right after college graduation. It was a momentous day for me and my parents, and I couldn't let them down. I stood outside and waited for him, but he never showed. It was mortifying when the son of my dad's campaign manager had to step in as my escort.

Sawyer's face puzzles. "Actually, I have no idea what you're talking about."

I don't want to get into all that right now. I don't feel like dredging up ancient history in the middle of the cold, so I simply say, "There were countless times where you did whatever it took to win. You didn't care what it did to me or my feelings."

He looks away, his eyes glazing over as regret flashes in

them. "Yeah, I guess you're right on that one. I did have a nasty competitive streak in me, but I always had scruples."

Now that I think about it, he did... except that one time. Which wasn't even about something competitive. But on that night, he probably got an offer for a real date and couldn't resist. However, I'm done with this conversation, so I say, "Anyway, you did good today. You're a natural at this, Sawyer."

"Because I'm a slick salesperson?"

"No, because you genuinely care about the animals. People see that."

"That's it?"

"Yep, that's it."

He quirks a brow. "No insult in there?"

"Nope. I'm just impressed. Deal with it." I manage a smile and my lips are so cold, it hurts. "Anyway, let's call it a day. It's almost dark, and I'm freezing and starving."

He shivers. "Absolutely. Let's go drop off the donation money, then get a nice dinner at Rutherford's. My treat."

"That sounds amazing." Rutherford's is the nicest restaurant in Cherry Creek, usually reserved for important days like birthdays and anniversaries.

Sawyer meets my gaze. "And you can talk to me about whatever it was that you just referred to. I need to know."

I blow out a long sigh. I can't believe he forgot about it. "All right."

As we approach the doors of the shelter, Marlene, a volunteer, darts outside and over to us. "Sawyer, Dawson, we need your help. A pregnant stray was brought in, and there are complications with her labor. It's late, and all our volunteers have left for the day. Sawyer, I know you've done this before because you used to volunteer, and the vet needs all the hands he can get."

Six

As we rush into the Cherry Creek animal rescue center, I feel a shiver of nerves. I'm not exactly cut out for nursing sick animals or birthing puppies, but I have to help. Also, I can't let myself get too attached to the animals—I have a way of doing that, and I'm not allowed to have pets in my apartment.

"You ready for this?" Sawyer asks under his breath.

"As ready as I'm going to be," I mumble.

We walk through the center, and the place is empty. It's just the animals in their crates for the night. I shoot Sawyer a scared look—gone is my wish to simply deliver the donation funds and play with the animals.

Marlene rushes us to the back. "The vet's here doing an emergency C-section, and we're gonna need your help getting the puppies through it. There are six, and we need all hands on deck to stimulate them as they're born."

I nod, my stomach clenching more. "We'll help. Just tell us what to do."

"Thank you." She exhales in relief.

"Of course." Sawyer nods.

We walk into the operating room and Dr. Lopez, Cherry Creek's veterinarian, looks uncharacteristically disheveled. "Thanks so much for coming, Sawyer and Dawson." He pats the mother pup, who looks like a Maltese. "Lucy Bell's been in labor for hours and no babies."

Concern's etched on Sawyer's face. "Poor girl."

Once we're in position, Dr. Lopez puts Lucy Bell under anesthesia while Marlene fetches the supplies. Speaking to him, Marlene says, "I couldn't get a hold of the nurses, but I left messages."

Dr. Lopez blows out a breath, shrugging. "All right. Looks like we're a four-person show, so everyone, let's give it all we've got."

Sawyer and I both nod, our faces paling.

Once the supplies are set up, and Lucy Bell is asleep, I stand ready. Her poor tummy is bursting with babies, and Dr. Lopez says that's why there's a problem—there's simply too many of them for her small size.

After the doctor makes his incision, he looks at us with heavy eyes. "I gotta warn you, with this many puppies and this long of labor, there's a good chance some or all of them won't be alive."

I nod, having flashbacks to the day I lost my puppy, Blazer. I was seven, and it was the worst day of my life up to that point. A dizziness rushes through my head, but I'm older and stronger than I was then, and life has made me more equipped to handle these situations. At least, I hope.

Sawyer grabs my hand and gives it a squeeze, and I instantly feel better.

The doctor hands Marlene the first puppy, and she demonstrates how to clean him and rub him, telling us that now is *not* the moment to be gentle. These babies need to be turned upside down and shaken to clear their airways. Marlene continues, "When the puppies don't travel naturally down the birth canal, they usually need stimulation to breathe."

Nerves explode in my stomach, but these adorable creatures need me. I resolve myself to do everything in my power. When the second puppy comes, Sawyer takes him.

I take the third, and she's the cutest thing I've ever seen. She's all black, with streaks of white in her paws and a white tail. I'm in love.

We hope by the time the fourth arrives, Marlene's puppy is breathing so she can take that one.

Mine has blue lips, which clearly isn't a good sign. As I've been instructed, I shake the puppy upside down and clear her mouth of the fluids that are keeping her from breathing. "She's not moving," I say to Marlene.

"Just keep going, hon. It may take a good solid half hour for this to work."

"Okay." This is *way* more stressful than I imagined, as the life of this creature I'm holding entirely depends on me. "Come on, sweet baby. You can do it."

Marlene calls out, "Puppy one is breathing."

There's an echo of cheers and a gigantic sigh of relief from me.

"Way to go, Ms. Marlene," Dr. Lopez says, keeping his eyes on his surgery. "Now I have puppy number four ready for you."

I get back to my critical job, alternating between rubbing and giving CPR to my pup. "Still nothing," I say, my voice shaky. She's smaller than the other pups.

"Just keep going. Don't stop until she's breathing, in and out." Marlene is calm but firm.

"Yes, ma'am." I keep at it, becoming more desperate as I go.

"Fifth one is here." Dr. Lopez calls out.

"Number two still isn't breathing." Sawyer's tone is dire.

"Neither is number three," I add.

"Dang it. Dawson, you take number five and I'll work on number two," Marlene says. I do as instructed, and we switch puppies.

I take the little boy, heartier than my sweet girl. I hope I can help this one, but now, I'm doubting myself. I get busy, rubbing and shaking. I start CPR sooner this time, as that's what Marlene's doing.

Sawyer says, "Pup two is breathing!"

We all let out a cheer, but I'm shaken as I watch Marlene work on my little girl. Sawyer moves beside Dr. Lopez, waiting for puppy number six.

I'm focused and busy on my boy when Dr. Lopez says, "Sixth puppy is already breathing!" Excitement is clear in his voice as he rushes the puppy to the basket with the other breathing puppies.

I give Marlene and Sawyer a smile, and they have a sparkle in their eyes.

This is quite the roller coaster ride, and I have a whole new respect for veterinarians and vet nurses. When my boy takes his first gasp, my heart fills with a joy I didn't think was possible after what just happened. "Puppy four is breathing!" I announce.

Things are looking up.

I need help with Lucy Bell." Dr. Lopez's tone is dire. "Her pulse is dropping."

Marlene hands me my sweet girl, saying, "I don't think this one's gonna make it, hon," before rushing to the doctor.

I take her, resolving to do anything to make that not true.

Their conversation becomes a hum in the background while I work on this puppy, desperate. We're approaching that half hour mark with her, and I don't want to think about what happens after that. "Come on, little warrior, you've got this." I speak to her in that calming way I've just learned by watching Sawyer. And I keep talking to her as I go.

I hear Dr. Lopez say, "Lucy Bell is stabilized," but I don't look up. I'm too focused on what I'm doing.

My little girl's mouth moves.

Adrenaline pumps through my veins as I say, "There you go, Warrior. I knew you could do it."

Her chest is moving in and out. Then she's squeaking.

"Warrior is breathing!" I call out, tears of joy in my eyes. I look up to see everyone watching me with pride.

"Warrior, huh," Sawyer says.

"Yes." I sniffle, holding her to my face. "In every way."

"Well, then. We've got six breathing puppies here." Dr. Lopez smiles. "Great job, everyone." His smile is glowing, but it falls away when he returns to Lucy Bell, saying nothing as he stitches her up before bringing her off anesthesia.

When the stress is over, Marlene bursts into tears before pulling each of us into a hug. There's not a dry eye in the room, and I'm so glad this pressure cooker situation ended on a joyous note. When Lucy Bell's awake and resting, we put the puppies on her teats so they can feed. Dr. Lopez says it won't be until tomorrow before she's awake enough to be a present mother, so Marlene is staying the night with the new family to make sure the babies are eating.

As we're about to leave, Marlene holds out a folded note. "I was supposed to give you this after I collected donations, but you two went above and beyond. Here's the code from Eleanor to open the next padlock. And thank you so much for your help. Truly."

"Of course." Sawyer takes the paper and stuffs it into his

pocket. We know the drill by now. We'll enter the code on the next lock she has on her box, hoping that this time, it will be the last challenge.

Sawyer and I are exhausted as we leave the clinic, but happy. Deeply, truly happy—something I wouldn't trade for anything. Something that seems to happen here far more than it ever did in Atlanta.

Once we're sitting in the car, Sawyer glances at me adoringly. "You were incredible in there." Then he turns on the ignition.

"So were you." He was, in every way.

"Thank you." He sighs. "Rutherford's is closed now. Actually, everywhere is closed now except the Cordial Diner."

"Hmm. I'm not in the mood for diner food, and your mom has amazing leftovers in the refrigerator."

"She does, doesn't she?"

"Yup."

I study him, my friend, my enemy, so stunning, but also thoughtful and caring. And much more mature than he was before. I never saw his heart, so raw, like I did tonight helping save the animals. I take in those eyes. That face. The light scar on his chin he got when he fell off his dirt bike when he was eleven. I want to touch it—touch *him*. How can I not after what we just went through together?

With the motor running, he just sits there, staring at me. His eyes are glistening, and his voice is low, raspy when he mutters, "You're beautiful, Dawson Wright."

His words catch me off guard, knocking the wind from my chest. Sawyer Quinn thinks I'm beautiful. I could say that I would've never guessed, except that's not entirely true. Over the years, we've had plenty of these moments where electricity crackles in the air between us, and I've yearned for more of him.

But I've never thought to go there because Sawyer is lava, and when you get too close, you get incinerated.

I manage to say, "You're not so bad yourself," before turning my gaze straight ahead because having this kind of exchange with Sawyer is freaking me out.

Seven

WHEN WE GET HOME, WE BEELINE IT TO THE REFRIGERATOR AND START pulling things out. Without a word, we open Tupperwares and grab forks. We eat right in front of the refrigerator, not bothering with plates or sitting down. "This is so good," I say, after swallowing a huge bite of cold mashed potatoes.

"Right?" Sawyer's got the Tupperware of the lasagna, and after a few bites each, we switch. It hits me how natural this is, having zero manners.

Once we finish our feeding frenzy, we head up to the attic, ready to open the third padlock.

My phone buzzes, and I check it to see it's The Crusher.

Crusher: *I need a disclosure agreement by tomorrow morning.*

Me: *Mark Chenning is responsible for that, sir.*

Crusher: *Mark is busy with his family. I need you on this right away.*

I groan, taking a seat on the couch in the attic.

Me: *I'm out of town for the holidays, sir.* On approved vacation I don't add.

Crusher: *It's due Saturday morning.*

"What's up?" Sawyer sits next to me.

"My new boss." I scrub a temple. "We call him The Crusher, and next week, we have an emergency deposition. He's just barking out his usual orders."

I don't tell Sawyer he's demanding that I work on something due Christmas Eve. I'll have to stay up late tonight and tomorrow night because I can't miss the Quinn's special dinner and tradition of heading to the Christmas tree downtown to hang their decorations and make their wishes.

The tradition that Eleanor started with the broccoli dog ornament, which is still lost, and I haven't heard anything back from NeighborhoodBuzz. I'm glad I didn't tell Sawyer and get his hopes up about it since no one answered.

Sawyer's brows furrow. "That sucks. I know you've had a terrible year, but I at least thought you liked your job."

"Yeah. I used to. Not anymore." I wring my hands.

"We need another attorney here in Cherry Creek." His mouth tilts. "If you want to take cases about disputed property lines and alleged hog theft."

My mouth curves. "Actually, I wouldn't mind a pay cut if I enjoyed work again. It'd also be nice to be making a difference in the community."

"Well, I love my job as a small-town attorney, and that's why." He taps his fingers together.

"I can see that." I always thought we were complete opposites, but the more time I spend with Sawyer now, the more I realize we're becoming more alike. I decided to go the corporate law route because my parents talked me into it with promises of their subsequent pride and joy, which didn't exactly pan out. I thought Sawyer was taking the hard road with a job as a public defender, but now, I realize that maybe he was onto something. The older I get, the more I realize that happiness and fulfillment mean more than family obligation. And, living in a place like

Cherry Creek is definitely a simpler lifestyle, which I used to think I didn't want.

Now, I'm not so sure.

I hold up Eleanor's letter, saying, "We should find out our fate."

Sawyer squeezes his eyes shut. "We should."

When we unfold the note, we anxiously read,

Hello Sawyer and Dawson,

Good work getting donations for the shelter! I'm sure the staff was thrilled to have your help. Marlene needs all she can get.

Challenge number three: in order to get the code that opens the next padlock, you must first go to the library and get a book. You can't check it out, but you do have to find it. I've hidden it behind my two favorite books. Good luck, and may you both win.

"This one sounds weird." I set the note down.

"Definitely weird." Sawyer sighs. "But at least not difficult, embarrassing, or cold."

I chuckle. "Very true."

Eight

SAWYER AND I JUST FINISHED THE DRESS REHEARSAL FOR OUR
performance tomorrow, and now, we're at Cherish Cafe with
the book Eleanor made us find, which was hidden behind
Catcher in the Rye and Wuthering Heights. The book in my
hands is intriguing, to say the least.

There title is *Once Upon a Christmas Kiss*. The stories inside
are handwritten. It has no dust jacket and a forest green linen
cover with a mistletoe imprint. There are one or two loose
threads at the edges, and it's a bit worn but in good condition.
There's something mystical about it.

But I have no idea what Eleanor wants us to do with it other
than read it, so we sit at a red bistro table, side-by-side, and
thumb through the entries.

Sawyer says, "Great. A bunch of love stories—just what I've
been wanting to spend hours reading."

"But they're handwritten. It's so charming."

"That's worse, Dawson. Are we reading other people's
diaries? Because if that's the case," he hesitates, looking
upward, "I am *not* reading this. I'm drawing a line, Sister."

I point at a page. "Hold on. It says here that the book is a

Christmas legend. Come on, Sawyer, you gotta get into a legend. How cool is that?"

"Not cool." He takes a nibble of his sandwich, turkey on rye.

But together, we read the backstory: many years ago, the director of Cherry Creek Academy, a private school here, wrote a fairy tale version of the story of her parents falling in love at Christmas. While writing this book, she fell in love and planned to marry on Christmas Eve. The headmistress gave a copy of the book to her dear friend, a teacher, with a handwritten note inside. The next year, that teacher read the book and fell in love, so she added her own note in the book and left it in the school library. It was not registered in the library system, and over the years, the book has made a circuitous path through the citizens of Cherry Creek. Year after year, people found their true love at Christmastime—when they had the book. The rumors of the power of the book grew until it became a town legend.

Sawyer says, "So, if someone possesses the book at Christmastime, they'll find their true love."

"And Eleanor wanted us to have it. I guess we could both use it." I shrug.

"Right. Eleanor wanted us to find our soul mates." Sawyer rolls his eyes. "She always was a romantic at heart."

"But you see what she's doing, right? Even in death, she's trying to take care of everything that's important to her. At first, I thought it was about the causes she loved, but she's including her people, too. Us." I take a bite of my spinach and strawberry salad with pecans.

"Yeah. I think you're right." Sawyer sips his black coffee.

"It was a nice thought, but I hardly doubt my problems with love can be solved by possessing an old book."

"You don't have problems with love, Dawson. You have problems opening yourself up and being vulnerable."

I shoot Sawyer a glare. His comment annoys me, but I can't

help but wonder if what he's saying is true. I'm not about to admit that to him, so I say, "Me? What about you? Mr. Player. Bra Claw."

"Fair enough. Maybe I see the problem in you because it's something I struggle with myself."

I look to see the sarcasm etched on his face or a teasing flicker in his eye, but there's nothing. His expression is serious. It hits me that maybe Sawyer's being honest with me for once. "It means a lot that you admitted that to me."

He stares out the restaurant window, which has a gorgeous view of the snowcapped mountains. "I've had to take a hard look at myself and my decisions this past year, and I don't want to live that way anymore. I do want to make Eleanor proud, living in a way I can be happiest."

I didn't realize just how much I wanted that until this trip, and even more now as I hear Sawyer say it. I'm tired of the loneliness—having no one to tell how how I really feel, or just how much my heart aches. "I want that too."

Sawyer taps his fingers together. "I'd like to find love. I'm not sure how because I've never really gone about it the right way before, but I guess recognizing that is a good first step."

"Great first step. But it seems like you were hitting it off with Katie." I take a sip of Cherish Cafe's eggnog, which is bursting with nutmeg and surely a zillion calories. I don't dare bring up Sawyer's alone time with Françoise, as that was supposed to just be an extra practice session. I don't want to seem presumptuous.

Sawyer shrugs, sighing. "Katie. She's somebody one of my lawyer friends said I should meet because she checks all the boxes. Cute, smart, motivated, wants children. Lives here in Cherry Creek."

"So, what's the problem?"

"I dunno. She just doesn't make me feel anything. You know?"

Boy, do I ever. In fact, his words hit so close to home, that pang of that familiar dread hits my gut. I search my brain for some sarcastic retort that I'd usually say to Sawyer, but I realize that's the opposite of what I'm supposed to be doing right now. So, I go for honesty instead. "I think that might be my problem, too. I don't know if something's wrong with me. Well, outside of what I already know, which is to do everything possible not to become my parents." I manage a smile.

"I don't even have that excuse because mine are awesome. They have this amazing marriage that I'd love to have."

I tap my finger on my cup, deciding to allow myself to be vulnerable. Just a little. "Do you think it has to do with the fact that growing up, no matter what you did, you never felt quite good enough? I only ask because that's how I felt with my parents."

"Hmm." His eyebrows furrow in thought as he stares out the window again. He meets my eyes when he says, "Well, I had a twin sister that was literally perfect at everything. And she was the nicest human being and philanthropist. So, yeah. I think sometimes I had to play the bad egg because I would've never succeeded as the good egg."

My heart clenches, and I find myself feeling empathy for Sawyer. *Again.* This better not become a habit. "Eleanor was pretty perfect, wasn't she?"

"She was. And I know they say it's hard to remember the bad things after somebody passes, but I never had many complaints when she was alive. You know what they say—I just think she was too good for this earth."

"Very true. She just was."

Our eyes meet, and an unspoken understanding passes between us. It's one of being friends or siblings with somebody who was so good deep inside, neither of us could measure up. Maybe Sawyer and I have always had a lot more in common than I ever realized, and right now, I feel myself leaning into him. Moving into his smell, his scent of cedar and tea tree oil. Longing to be closer to feel his warm skin.

Our gazes lock, and for once, it's not because we're in a stare down. I've never liked to admit it, but I could get lost in Sawyer's deep green eyes, and I'm letting that happen right now.

I'm trying to fight my feelings for him, but it's getting harder by the day. And right now, I almost don't care. My body is aching for his closeness, and I—

"Can I get you both anything else?" Scarlett, the owner of the cafe, materializes at our table, yanking me back to reality.

Jeez. I hope she didn't notice the way Sawyer and I were looking at each other. This small town likes to talk, and the last thing Sawyer needs is to get caught up in the rumor mill.

"I'm good, Scarlett, thank you. Delicious as always," Sawyer says before glancing at me. "What about you, Dawson?"

It takes me a beat for my brain to find any words. "Yes, I'm all good, too. Thanks, Scarlett. It was wonderful."

"Sure thing." When Scarlett hands the bill to Sawyer, I add my credit card on top of Sawyer's and say, "Split it in half, please," making it clear that this is *not* a date.

When Scarlett walks away, I look back to the book, flipping through it to find the next note from Eleanor. I hold it up, still folded. "Looks like we have our next challenge."

Sawyer lets out a groan. He points to the envelope, his voice quiet when he says, "Eleanor says we need to read this one in private."

I turn it over to see her warning, written neatly on it.

What in the world does she have in store for us next?

§.

Since we're downtown, I go with Sawyer to pick up a few last-minute gifts for his friends and family. I already have my presents under the tree, but I'm enjoying helping him. Lately, everything we do together is fun.

When we get home, Maryann insists we sit down for dinner. It's after that when we finally make our way to the attic for privacy. This time, nerves are getting the best of me as I unwrap the next nested present and slowly unfold the letter.

Dear Dawson and Sawyer,

If you're reading this letter, I'm so very proud of both of you. It means that you got the book from the library, you got donations for the shelter, and you're practicing your Nutcracker Suite performance. I hope you're doing well, but I'll just take that you're doing it at all.

I bet none of it was easy. I should know—it's what I did every year. But at the end, I felt whole again. Because, quite honestly, the holidays were never an easy thing for me. Even after my diagnosis, doing these traditions was important to me, maybe more important. You both were with me every step of the way, which made every minute of my life fuller and richer. Okay, well, maybe not every minute. I'm talking about your disgusting burps, Sawyer, and Dawson, that gum popping addiction you have. Regardless, I feel okay leaving this earth with no regrets except for one, although I shouldn't call it regret because if I were to do it again, I'd do the same thing. So maybe it's just something I would've done in a parallel universe.

There's something I never told either of you. Last year, when I went to Nashville for that winter ballet training program, I fell for my teacher, and he fell for me. His name is Anders Dante McKay, and he's the most amazing man I've ever met.

"Dante!" I cry out. "Our ballet teacher? But he said he didn't have a nickname."

Sawyer's face twists. "In fairness, Anders is his first name, not a nickname. It *has* to be him—he's from Nashville." Sawyer goes wide-eyed. "Wow."

It was love at first sight, and we spent time together outside of the program. We were clearly falling for each other, but I didn't tell him about my diagnosis. But I had that book I made you both get from the library. I'm sure by now you realize it's a collection of stories about real people and how they met their true loves after they were in possession of the book at Christmastime. Anders and my love story is not in the book. Maybe it should be, but it can't be there. However, I want you to know it.

Anders is funny, charming, witty, and with just one small catch of my gaze, seems to understand everything about me in a way no one ever has. We knew from that moment we met on the dance floor that we were going to be inseparable, and we were, even after long, hard hours of practice. Adrenaline gave us the energy to take a walk around Nashville or go for a coffee break. Remember that grungy cafe we loved in college? We went there daily. Anders isn't perfect, but he was definitely perfect for me, and I was perfect for him. At the end of the training program, he proposed to me, and I so desperately wanted to say yes. I didn't though. I didn't want to tie him to my fate, so I pushed him away. But I would've done anything to experience loving Anders wholly and fully. Instead, I told him no, and I didn't tell him why. I lied and said I wasn't ready, which couldn't have been further from the truth. The truth was that I knew I had an expiration date, and I loved him too much to have him go through losing me. It was all more than I could take, so I ended things. But now I need your help. Please give Anders this letter. It explains everything. I know he's going to be in Cherry Creek helping direct the Nutcracker perfor-mance you're both in, so by now, you surely have met him. He needs to know that he'll always be my one and only true love, and I won't be his, and that's okay. Since I only got one, I'm so glad it was him. I just couldn't bring myself to have the "sick" conversation with him, and I selfishly wanted him to remember me as the vibrant, healthy dancer he met that one winter.

Tears in our eyes, Sawyer and I look at each other. I don't have words for this moment, and it seems like neither does Sawyer. A moment that's heart-splintering, but one where I see that I have the chance to find love and share my life with a partner—something Eleanor knew wasn't in the cards for her.

"I'm so lucky," I utter.

"Me too." Sawyer stares into my eyes. "And we should stop wasting the precious moments we have here on this earth." He runs a finger over my cheek, and electricity buzzes through me as I lean into him. Our lips are a breath apart, and my skin turns to gooseflesh. I want to kiss Sawyer. I want to know what it's like to touch his lips.

"Dawson," he says.

"Yes," I whisper.

We're three inches apart, then two, then one when my phone buzzes.

Then it buzzes again. It's The Crusher. Ugh. What does he want *now*? I worked late last night and got him the disclosure agreement this morning, a day early.

Crusher: *Emergency, Dawson. Bradley deposition has been rescheduled for 26th, and we need you back in the office on the 25th for discovery.*

The twenty-fifth?

I punch back a response. *Can we discuss this? That's Christmas day, and I'm still out of town.*

Not to mention that this year, Christmas falls on a Sunday.

My boss doesn't text again, and I hope this means he understands I won't be in the office on the twenty-fifth. But the exchange has yanked me back to the real world—the one where

I live and work in Atlanta, and Sawyer lives and works here in Cherry Creek. If we allow ourselves to get physical, it'll only lead to more hurt when I leave. "We should read the rest of Eleanor's letter. Get her next challenge," I say, my voice croaky.

"Right."

We both look back at the paper, but my hands tremble as I try to catch my breath. I don't know it's from what almost happened with Sawyer, or the news from The Crusher. Both?

Challenge number four, your final challenge, is the easiest one. Get the broccoli dog ornament, which you're going to hang on the town's tree on Christmas Eve, anyway. The instructions to where to find your final letter and presents from me are inside.

Love you to the moon and beyond,

Eleanor M. Quinn

There's a silence, tension building in the air as the realization hits.

"Oh, no." Sawyer rakes a hand through his hair. "That ornament. Which is lost. Now what?"

I swallow hard. "I don't know." I feel sick inside as reality dawns on me. There's no way we'll be able to get to our gifts from her.

So, really, this is our final letter from Eleanor. Shivers mixed with grief and gratitude shimmer down my body, and it feels like I'm saying goodbye all over again. Sawyer must feel it too because he takes me in his arms and we hug, a gripping embrace, for so long, our heartbeats sync.

It's a dragging, painful moment before I pull away, trying to focus on the positive. "At least we got to do all the challenges Eleanor wanted, and now we can finish the most important part—giving Dante the letter from her."

"I guess." He stares into the distance, his jaw clenched. "I'm not ready to let go."

I squeeze my eyes shut to fight off another tear that's about to escape. "I'm not sure we'll ever be ready to let go. Gifts or no gifts."

"That's probably true."

"So, let's be glad for all the things we did get from her this Christmas. So much more than I even expected," I say, but my heart is broken, and by Sawyer's face, so is his.

Nine

IT'S PERFORMANCE DAY. AND CHRISTMAS EVE. WE'RE BACKSTAGE, AND I think I'm going to cry. I look at the mouse head I have to put on, and just the thought makes me feel like I'm suffocating. Glancing at Sawyer, I swallow back a wave of nerves when I say, "I'm gonna hurl."

"You're not gonna hurl." After studying my face, he says, "You are a little green. If you're going to do it, do it now. Do *not* barf in the mouse head." His arm swings around me, which is so comforting after everything we've been through this past week. But I know there's much more to it than that.

"No barfing in the mouse head," I repeat.

"I want you to close your eyes and think about the happiest memory you have." He cocks his head as he studies me. "Got it?"

"Yes. That's not even a hard one. Remember that summer when you, me, Eleanor, and some college friends went to that beach house? We spent the days in the ocean and the nights by campfire talking, drinking, and laughing?"

"Of course, I remember that trip. It was one of my favorites too."

I inhale a deep breath, trying to steady my nerves. "Why was it your favorite?"

He looks at me, and I swear there's adoration in his gaze when he says, "The company."

Something in my stomach flutters, and this time, it's not nausea. By the way he's looking at me and the tone of this voice, I'm pretty sure he was referring to me. And I'd be lying if I said the reason I thought it was such a wonderful vacation wasn't about him, too. We'd buried the hatchet for the trip, and he and I really connected. "You taught me how to surf." I laugh before I say, "Well, you taught me how to ride on a surfboard for a second before I spectacularly plunged beneath the waves."

"You weren't bad." He shrugs. "You weren't good."

I'm laughing again, and suddenly, the nausea has abated. "I'm feeling better."

"You can do this, Dawson. We've practiced it a million times. And even if you don't, who cares? You're going to be in disguise. Just bat a paw and crawl off the floor." He moves my paw for me. "Like this."

"Crawl off the floor. Wave a paw. Great advice." My words say one thing, but Sawyer is right. We are in disguise, and even if folks recognize us, they know we're here for Eleanor. They won't care if we mess up. And that eases my nerves.

We put on our heads and make our way onto the stage. When I look at the sizeable crowd, the nausea hits full force. So much for feeling better. I see white stars, literally, but I take a deep breath and focus on Sawyer as we do the steps that we've done so many times this past week. He actually takes the lead like he's supposed to do, and I get into the rhythm and stay there—as long as I'm focused on him.

We take a misstep, but we're both laughing as we catch right back up with the others. Once again, we're having fun, and I realize I love being around a person who makes things feel great even when they're not.

The audience cheers as our group exits, and I realize that I actually enjoyed that. It's nice being on stage when it means being part of something bigger than myself.

When we're backstage, we pull off our mouse heads and take a breather. Other dancers rush around us to get into position on the stage next, and when they're gone, I flash Sawyer a smile and give him a high-five. "That was acceptable."

He nods with enthusiasm. "Definitely acceptable. Might I venture to say it was decent?"

"That might be pushing it, but maybe." I even out my breathing. "Now all we have left is that troublesome lift at the end of the show." In practice, we only nailed it two times in the dozens of times we tried it.

We put our heads back on and make our way onto the stage where we go into a few twirls before positioning ourselves for the lift. I step away, ready to take my run, and I think about all the times I watched others perform this show. I feel so inadequate, but then I remember that it's Sawyer that has to do most of the work, and I trust him. He pulls through in a tight situation. He always has, and he will again.

I get into a good run to make sure I give Sawyer enough momentum. When he takes me into his arms, he lifts me high in the air, like I am made of air and feathers. Then he holds me over his head like he could do it with one pinkie.

When he finally sets me down, I'm still walking on air as I try to gracefully exit the stage. When I see the audience, I realize we're getting a standing ovation.

I'm quite certain that our dance wasn't that impressive, so I'm guessing the cheers are because I didn't do a face plant, and most folks know we did this in three practice sessions. They're clearly proud of us, and I'm pretty proud of us too.

Backstage, we rip our heads off and fall into an embrace, my entire body tingling from euphoria and a complicated set of emotions that I can't fully place.

My eyes mist, and I croak out, "You were amazing out there, Sawyer."

"You were amazing, too. You *are* amazing."

I'd love to share this moment with Eleanor, but then I realize that if she was here in the show, we would've never been in it. It's one of those bittersweet moments that feels like a silver lining that's shining light on our darkest of years. Dancing in this production was something I would've never chosen, but now that I've done it, I'm so grateful I did.

I pull away, touching Sawyer's cheek. In a teasing tone, I say, "I swear you had super strength out there."

"That was just my regular strength. I'm a machine."

"I'm glad to see your ego's still firmly intact." I wink because I know and he knows that's not true. I don't know if it ever was. His ego was for show, shielding the pain and insecurities that he's always shouldered. Now that he's finding himself, it's melting away.

I pull into another hug, taking in *all* of him, his strong arms, his empathy, and his soul, which seems to see mine, even when I can't.

I don't want to leave Sawyer, not tonight. Maybe not ever. I'm falling for him, and maybe I didn't have that far to fall because I've always loved him. Like Cherry Creek, he's my home —more now than ever.

I have to write my boss and tell him I'm not going to be in the office until the day after Christmas. If he doesn't like it, so be it.

I'll just have to take a leap of faith.

❦

Sawyer and I bring Dante into a dressing room so he has some privacy. When Sawyer holds up the letter from Eleanor with his first name, Anders, written in her distinctly perfect handwriting, Dante's eyes mist.

"My sister wanted you to have this." Sawyer holds it out. "She had some things she wanted you to know."

Trembling, Dante doesn't take the letter.

I touch his shoulder. "I get that it's hard. As you know, she left us letters too. But I took mine, and I'm so glad I did. I think you will be too."

He nods, reaching out with an unsteady hand to take it. "I can't believe this."

"I couldn't either." Sawyer's mouth curves wistfully. "But it's how I ended up here. And it's made my life so much fuller and complete. I have a feeling it will do the same for you."

"I'm sure it will." A tear rolls down Dante's cheek. "So, you two know we were in love." He shakes his head. "I still love her. Always will."

Sawyer pats his back. "She felt the same. When she left, she was protecting you."

Dante swipes the tear away. "Of course she was. She was always thinking of everyone other than herself."

"Yeah." My voice turns croaky. "She was."

Dante holds the letter to his chest. "Thank you both. So much. This means everything."

I know it does. I know because all the letters Eleanor left me have meant the same thing. "You're welcome. And it was an honor training under you."

When we leave, Sawyer has to drop me off at his parent's house before heading back to his apartment for something.

After he pulls into the driveway, he shoots me a serious look. "We should talk about what's happening between us."

None of my usual doubts creep into my head, and without thinking, I say, "Okay. Let's talk. After dinner." I'm shocked at my own words.

Ten

I'm not waiting until after dinner to talk to Sawyer. Instead, I'm going to his apartment and telling him how I care for him, deeply. Maybe I'll even use the "L" word.

I'm floating as I step out of my car. His place is above the downtown shops, and I'm on the sidewalk in front of them. The storefronts are decorated in greens and reds, the street lamps are adorned with garlands, and the smell of Sal's Pizza floats in the air. As I make my way past the Gifts and Bits, I peer in the window at their gorgeous holiday display of presents placed in a bed of fake snow below a Christmas tree. Amongst the perfectly wrapped presents are items to buy, like Cherry Creek souvenir stuffed animals.

My eyes flick up, and that's when I see them. Inside is Sawyer with Françoise, and they're standing at the counter and laughing. I study them, and it becomes clear they are discussing some sort of gift to be purchased. She points at the display, then claps while nodding enthusiastically.

Sawyer is buying her a gift? Maybe to say thank you for all her help to get us ready for the show?

That has to be it. Right?

I'm desperately trying to convince myself of that when Françoise pulls Sawyer into a hug.

I stand frozen as I stare at the two of them in an embrace, the implications hitting my brain one after the next.

They both love Eleanor. They both live here in Cherry Creek. They both belong here. I don't, and my life is in Atlanta. My job and my apartment are there.

And, actually, what was I thinking? I've never told Sawyer how I feel, nor has he verbalized that he sees me as anything more than a long-time friend. Maybe I misread his signals?

And how would Sawyer and I realistically get together, anyway? Would I just leave my world behind and hope Sawyer has given up his playboy lifestyle for me? And how did I completely forget how badly he hurt me, and how he didn't show up for me when I needed him most?

Hearing those words in my head, I realize how absolutely ridiculous I was being. I was flying high on euphoria and hormones after our performance, and I'm glad I didn't embarrass myself by professing my love. None of what I thought or felt was real.

As if the universe hears my thoughts, my phone buzzes. When I check the screen, I see that, of course, it's a text from The Crusher.

Crusher: *We need you in the office, eight a.m. sharp tomorrow morning. No excuses—this is the most critical case of the year.*

I stare at the text, my eyes going blurry as they mist over. For a few precious hours, I got to believe in the fairytale—the one where I escape my life and start over with Sawyer by my side.

But his life is here, with someone like Françoise, and mine is in Atlanta keeping my job and paying the bills. That's reality.

Another piece of reality is that I'm not getting anything else from Eleanor. The last clue that would've led Sawyer and me to our gift from her is lost. There's nothing more for me here—I've completed all of Eleanor's tasks, and my heart has grown, just like she wanted.

As I walk back to my car, I text my boss and let him know that I'll be there.

I rush back to Sawyer's parent's house, as I need to get my stuff packed up and head out as soon as possible. I don't want to be driving through the snowy parts of Tennessee after dark, and leaving today is the only way I'll be able to get into the office that early.

After I collect my things, I find Marianne in the living room putting more presents under the tree. When she sees me with my luggage, her face drops. My voice is weak when I say, "I'm so sorry I have to leave, but it's a work emergency and if I don't go, I'll lose my job."

"Oh, dear." She stands, brushing away a wisp of her hair as she approaches me, taking my hand in hers. "Well, we'd sure love for you to stay, but of course, we understand if your job is on the line." She pulls me into another one of her amazing hugs, rubbing my back. "We'll miss you terribly but will be looking forward to hearing from you soon." Pulling away, she pats my cheek. "In case you don't already know it, you're welcome here anytime. It doesn't have to be a holiday. This is your home now, okay?"

Her words warm my heart. "I do feel at home here, and I can't wait to come back. Thank you—for everything."

Stephen pats my back and wishes me well before I head out the door and back into my car, stepping into the driver's seat after putting my luggage in the trunk. My mind spinning, I can't help but think back to the book that Eleanor had us take. Maybe it will help us find love. Sawyer is with Françoise and maybe, just maybe, I'll meet somebody when I get back to Atlanta.

Anyway, I need something to believe in. It's almost

Christmas after all. After I start the engine, I text Sawyer and tell him I have to leave, but I don't hear back from him. It's just as well.

I pull away, not looking forward to the four-hour drive I've got in front of me, but it's definitely better to do it now and get a decent night's sleep before getting up at six a.m. I don't even want to do the discovery for this case—I hate seeing a big corporation take advantage of an injured, elderly man. But it's my job.

Heading toward the highway, I go through downtown, passing the big, beautiful Christmas tree in front of the courthouse. The one I was supposed to stand in front of tonight and hang an ornament and make my wish. I didn't have one anyway —I couldn't bear to do it without Eleanor. At the stoplight, I study the courthouse—it's such a pretty bricked building with large Roman pillars. It makes me remember the time Eleanor and I put a time capsule inside the wall behind a loose brick in the side of the building. We pinky-swore to wait until we were thirty to dig it up, but we opened it a few years back when Eleanor got sick. It had our Furbies, Barbies, and our tween diaries, which talked about how we were in a fight because we both wanted to marry Zac Efron. We got a good laugh opening it.

Those were the days, and they're gone now, and I can't help but feel nostalgia for those moments that I thought would never end.

My phone buzzes. It's Sawyer, and I don't answer because I don't feel like talking to him right now. I need time to recover from everything that just happened.

He calls several more times, but I let it go to voicemail. Then he sends me a string of texts, but I don't read them.

I just can't right now.

An hour and a half in, I'm listening to the hum of the tires against the road and being careful to avoid the ice patches. The full moon's illuminating the night sky when my phone rings through the car speakers, and I jump. The dashboard screen says that it's an unknown Tennessee phone number. Is Sawyer trying to call me from someone else's phone to get through? I don't know, but something tells me to answer it, so I do. "Hello?"

"Is this Dawson?" It's a woman's voice.

"Yes."

"This is Cindy Thomas. I have the broccoli dog Christmas ornament that belonged to Eleanor. I'm so sorry—my boys took it off the tree last year thinking it was ours. I just found it with the wrapping paper."

My breath stops in my chest. When I finally manage to inhale, I say, "Oh, wow. You have it?" My vision blurs, and I fight to keep my focus on the road.

Cindy sighs. "Yes. I'm sorry again, but can I bring it to you after Christmas? I'm trying to get Christmas Eve dinner cleaned up and presents wrapped for tomorrow."

Without a beat of hesitation, I say, "Is it alright if I come get it? It's a really important part of the Quinn family Christmas Eve tradition."

"Sure, of course. I'll text you my address."

"Thank you so much. I'll be there in an hour and a half."

"Sure." Cindy's voice goes soft. "I'm sorry again, Dawson."

"It's okay. I'm just thrilled you found it."

I take the first exit off the highway and turn around. Once I'm safely heading back, I call my boss, expecting to leave him a voicemail. I already know what I'm going to say. *Tomorrow is Christmas, and I have family obligations. I'm sorry.*

He answers with, "Dawson Wright."

"Hello, sir." My voice shakes. I *cannot* confront him like this.

"I hope you're in Atlanta. We could use your help tonight if you can get to the office."

I sit, staring at the road ahead, not able to open my mouth. I can't find my words. This is what happens when I try to confront authority.

Speak, Dawson. Speak!

Mr. Morgan's tone is razor sharp. "We need you to dig up every medication Mr. Bradley was on. We hope to show he fell due to dizzying side-effects."

But that's not even close to the truth! I *hate* this case. And now I know why The Crusher answered—he wants something from me, of course.

"Mr. Morgan, I'm sorry..." I squeak out before my throat goes dry.

"Dawson, this isn't up for debate. You're in the office at eight a.m. tomorrow, or you're fired."

My mouth opens, and the words flood out. "Thank you for this opportunity and experience, Mr. Morgan. I have learned a great deal working for you. But I cannot sacrifice important time with my family."

"What are you talking about? Your parents are on some cruise," he says, indignant.

"Not all family is blood. And they need me right now. And, actually, I need them too. So, I won't be in the office tomorrow."

"Well, then. You're fired."

"That's completely unreasonable, but best of luck. Oh, and by the way, shame on you for what you're doing to that injured elderly man." I hit the button on the steering wheel to disconnect the call.

I sit, staring ahead, in disbelief at myself.

I did it! I found my words and said my truth.

And now, I've got a broccoli dog decoration to hang on the Cherry Creek Christmas tree... and my final gift from Eleanor to pick up.

Eleven

I roll into downtown, and it's so late, I missed the Quinn family dinner and tree hanging tradition. I texted Sawyer back after reading his texts telling me that he desperately needed to talk to me. I responded by saying: *meet me at the courthouse at 11:30*. We're just going to make it on Christmas Eve, and I know where our gift from Eleanor is.

I step out of my car in my coat, hat, scarf, and gloves. It's dark, it's snowing, and it's cold.

Sawyer is standing in front of the courthouse wearing all his layers, and he's smiling, relieved. I shove my hands into my pocket as I approach him. "Sorry it took me so long to write you back."

The smile falls away. "Yeah. Why was that?"

I bite my lip. "I saw you hugging Françoise. In Gifts and Bits."

"Oh, Dawson." He rakes a hand through his hair. "There's nothing between me and Françoise."

"Maybe there should be. You two seemed to be enjoying yourselves. She's single and lives in Cherry Creek."

"She's not the one I want."

My heart trips over its next beat. "No?"

"Never. She was helping me out, that's it."

I blow out a breath. "Helping you with what?"

"I can't say."

"You can't say," I parrot, my voice turning sharp. "See? This is why I can't trust you."

"Trust?" Sawyer groans. "Dawson, jeez. What happened that made you think this of me?"

I stand silent, trying to figure out why I'm angrier than I should be at all this. I can't quite grasp it, but it's bubbling just under the surface. When Sawyer says, "I don't get it. We were always competitive, but I never broke your trust."

"Are you kidding me?" I snarl, my face growing hot. "You were my date for my debutante ball, which you knew meant everything to my parents. And a lot to me. I was *desperate* to make my parents proud, and you stood me up."

"Oh, no. No, no, no." Sawyer looks like he's going to be sick, but I don't care.

I'm too angry, and I keep on. "You know, I wasn't just another one of your 'flavor du jours' you could toss aside."

His face goes beet red as his jaw twitching in frustration. "No. You don't understand, Dawson. I was on my way, and I even had flowers. I couldn't wait to spend the evening with you. Then your dad called and told me not to come—he said that you didn't want me there."

I shake my head, confused. "What? Of course I wanted you there! I wouldn't have done that to you."

"It didn't seem like you, but I knew the ball required you to have an escort. Which meant you must've found a real date—better than me, the backup guy. Anyway, what choice did I have? It's not like I could go against your dad's wishes."

Something sharp pierces my stomach, and my mind spins, the gears not quite catching as I fumble to figure out exactly what Sawyer's saying. When I'm finally able to verbalize it, I croak, "My dad's future campaign manager's son stepped up for me when you didn't show."

Sawyer cocks his head. "So, maybe your dad used that moment to get what he wanted for his career?"

"No," I say automatically. "Maybe."

"Hasn't he always done that, Dawson?" Sawyer's tone turns gentle.

I groan. "Yes." I hate that he's right.

Emotions race through me so fast I can't figure out what I'm feeling. Betrayed by my parents? Grateful that it wasn't Sawyer's fault? Furious? All of the above? "I can't believe you didn't say anything."

"Say what?" Sawyer's eyebrows furrow. "Something to make you feel like crap about changing your mind? If you had a real date, I had to step aside. I didn't like it but accepted it."

"Oh." I don't know what to say. He didn't know my dad lied to him. What was he supposed to do? When I've had a chance to sort through my feelings, I finally say, "You're right. You did the best thing you could've given the information you had. I just can't believe you didn't think better of me."

"I made assumptions. I'm sorry, Dawson."

Tears prickle the back of my eyes, but I refuse to let any fall. "Don't be sorry. I can't believe I've spent so many years being angry—thinking that you either ran off with someone else or you forgot."

"Forgot? No way. It was all I could think about. *You* were all I could think about."

His words make my heart gallop in my chest, and I look at him, and he's so beautiful in the moonlight with his sparkling eyes and dark, shiny hair. "So, that's why you pushed me away after that. You thought I didn't want you?"

"Well, yeah. If something went down between you and me,

my sister would've ended up in the middle. Boyfriends come and go, but you and Eleanor's kind of friendship lasts a lifetime." At his last words, his eyes splinter, and his tone goes hoarse when he says, "Well, they're supposed to last a lifetime."

"My friendship with Eleanor is forever, Sawyer. Don't worry about that. She helped shape who I am, and she's a part of me. But I am eternally grateful that you made sure that nothing ever went sideways between us."

He nods. "Right. And this was right after college, when your friendship was vulnerable with so many big changes. I'd never want Eleanor to have to choose between you or me—that's an impossible position. So, I never told anyone."

I put a hand over my mouth, my brain still fighting to catch up to all the information that keeps coming at me. When I've finally processed what Sawyer did and why he did it, I say, "You are the most thoughtful person I've ever known." My lips curve wistfully. "Well, besides your sister, and I can't believe all these years, I didn't know it."

"I wasn't always so thoughtful. I had my moments, and I definitely wasn't the person I wanted to be. But I'm getting there." His lips quirk up. "More every day."

I feel a lightness I haven't felt in a long time, some of the weight from the past year lifting. "I guess the silver lining of losing our rock is that it forced us to take a good hard look at ourselves and our life decisions."

"For sure."

I touch his chin and lift it to meet my eyes as I lean into him. "I like the Sawyer I see now."

"That means a lot. It means everything, actually." He flashes me that glowing smile of his before nodding toward the tree. "And related to that, I have something I *really* want you to see."

I'm floating when I say, "I do too. And me first."

§

We're in front of the courthouse, and the chill is seeping into my bones, but my heart is warm.

I wring my hands. "So, before we do this, you should know that I got fired tonight."

"I'm sorry, Dawson." He touches my shoulder. "I'm also not sorry." His lips tick up. "You can sue your boss for wrongful termination, which I'm sure you already know. And, also, I have a job for you here if you want it."

I really, *really* do want the job he's offering. And not just because it's with Sawyer, but because I want to work in a more rewarding position in a town I love. "I just might."

"And Warrior is yours. If you can take a dog. I talked to Marlene."

I gasp. "Warrior? All mine?"

"If you want her."

I put a hand over my mouth. "Thank you so much, Sawyer. I want to hug you, but first—" I reach into my pocket and pull out the broccoli dog ornament before handing it to Sawyer.

Wide-eyed, he turns it over in his hands. "You got it back," he whispers. When he looks at me, his eyes shine.

I run a gloved finger over it. "Cindy's boys accidentally took it home last year." I continue, explaining how I posted the ad for it, and how she called me on my drive home. I hold up the note I found rolled inside and read it out loud. *Sawyer and Dawson, you'll find your gifts hidden in the place where time capsules are stored.*

Sawyer glances to where the loose brick still sits in the corner of the courthouse. "She put it *there*?"

I smile. "Let's hope."

We rush over, working together to tug the brick out of place. When it's removed, we see a plastic storage box sitting inside.

We pull it out and pop the lid off, finding Eleanor's folded note on top of what looks like a scrapbook.

After unfolding the letter, we read it using the light from my phone.

Now onto your present, Dawson and Sawyer. You two have spent quite a few days together. Days where you busted your buns for donations for the animal shelter, where you read a book of real love stories together (Sorry, Sawyer), and where you both finished performing as mice in the Nutcracker Suite. I do hope you wowed the crowd, but it's okay if you didn't. Now that you've accomplished all that, I have a scrapbook that I hope you'll appreciate a lot more now than you would've before this week started. When you open it, you'll see pictures of the two of you standing together, smiling and laughing. Probably at the expense of the other, but laughing together, nevertheless. You'll see more pictures of the two of you, sharing stolen glances from across the room. Pictures of the adoring gazes you gave the other when you thought no one was looking. But I was looking. There's so many of them throughout the years we spent together. These countless moments prove that what was oblivious to the two of you was completely obvious to me: you've always been madly in love with each other.

I stop reading, putting my hand over my heart because her words knock the wind from my chest and bring tears to my eyes. Sweet Eleanor, so wise beyond her years.

In this scrapbook, you'll also find quotes that one of you said about the other when you were talking to me in private. Like when you, Sawyer, said, "Don't ever tell Dawson this, but she's probably the smartest person I know." Or when you were drunk and said, "Dawson is so beautiful, and not just in the way she looks. But, man, she's so hot when her chestnut hair flows in the breeze." Okay, I might've had to paraphrase that last line because you were drunk and mumbling, but I think you both get the point. And you, Dawson, the time you said, "Don't tell Sawyer I said this because I don't want his head to get any bigger, but when we hiked the Cherry Creek mountain trail, I had tons of fun hanging out with him." Anyway, I hope by now, you've realized you should stop telling me things because... well, you can't anymore, and start saying them to each other. I hope that you already have. And I hope you two have finally figured out what I have known for so long. That you were meant to be together.

I love you both to the moon and beyond, forever,
Eleanor M. Quinn

Twelve

AFTER DROPPING THE SCRAPBOOK OFF IN SAWYER'S CAR, WE RETURN TO the tree decorated in ornaments of all shapes and colors. I hold up the broccoli dog replica and say, "I think it's time we hang this." It starts to snow, which looks magical in the glow of the streetlamps.

"Definitely time. It's almost midnight."

I step up to the tree and place the broccoli dog neatly between the Quinns' other ornaments.

"It's a shame you missed the earlier Quinn ornament-hanging ceremony, but honestly, this is so much better." Sawyer looks up to let the snowflakes fall on his face.

"I was sorry about that before, but I'm thinking I might've got the good end of the deal here." With all my raging emotions, the cold feels so refreshing on my cheeks. "And they really know how to do Christmas right in this town." There's something magical about Cherry Creek at night: the snow-brushed bricked roads, the street lamps covered in garlands, and the smell from the cookie store still wafting in the air.

We stand together, in the quiet, comfortable, like everything is with Sawyer. Finally, he shrugs and says, "I've got another surprise for you."

"I'm kind of surprised out."

"Me too, but you'll like this one." He sucks air through his teeth. "I hope. So, I didn't hang my wish ornament up earlier. But I'd like to now."

"Sure." The way he's looking at me makes my stomach flip flop.

Sawyer pulls something out of his pocket, then looks into my eyes, his mouth curving when he says, "Here's my wish." He hands me the ornament, and it's a man holding hands with a woman, and they both have briefcases. Then I realize the man has Sawyer's dark hair, and the woman has my wavy brown hair. I blink, my mind processing what this means. "This is you and me."

"Yes. Together."

My heart beats thunderously in my chest. "This is what you were picking up at Gift and Bits."

"Yes. Françoise is friends with a ceramic artist. She helped me to have this made. She thinks we belong together too."

"Wow. I got that one wrong."

He laughs. "We both got a lot wrong. It doesn't mean we can't make things right now." There's a twinkle in his eyes, the brightness of the old Sawyer back. "I want us, Dawson Wright. I'm in love with you, and I always have been."

My heart explodes at his words, and I tremble as I pull him into a hug. "I love you too, Sawyer Quinn." It's amazing to finally say the words out loud—the ones that have been true so long, I can't remember when they weren't.

I'm unable to find my voice with the overwhelming emotions that have taken over my being. Sawyer leans in until the closeness of our bodies creates a force of its own. He brings his lips a breath away from mine, making them tingle.

Sawyer is going to kiss me, and I'm having a hard time catching my breath. Even though I thought I never wanted this, I realize now that it's all I ever wanted. And it's finally happening.

His lips press against mine, gently yet firmly, as if he's afraid that if he lets go, I'll vanish like snowflakes touching the pavement. He moves his mouth, feather light as he kisses me in the way he seems to live his life now: sweet, caring, considerate. Time stops, and I let myself feel all the feelings of kissing Sawyer. His hands cradle my face as sparks fly all around us. We finally break apart breathless, gazing into each other's eyes filled with pure joy at the moment we've finally arrived at together.

He holds me so close I can hear his heart beating in rhythm with mine. We stay like this for what feels like forever—all the years of unspoken love between us floods out in a rush.

Finally, Sawyer pulls away and smiles at me. "Come on, let's hang our ornament. This is one I want to make sure comes true."

With trembling hands, I take the decoration from him and carefully place it upon the tree. "It already has."

The End

About the Author

As a lover of books with mystery, witty banter, family-friend dynamics, and all the feels, Terra Weiss does her best to provide each in her stories. She works to steer away from cookie-cutter formulas and focus on how real-life people find real-life love.

Once Upon a Christmas Wish

SUSAN SANDS

One

"THREE EGGS OVER MEDIUM, WHEAT TOAST, CRISPY BACON, AND CHEESE grits." Mr. Davis, my former science teacher from Cherry Creek Academy, hadn't changed his Saturday breakfast order since I was in high school. I knew it by heart, but he insisted on always listing the items in order.

"Yes, sir. Coming right up." I stuck my pencil behind my ear and grinned at him.

"Thanks, Kayla. How's your daddy? Haven't seen him in a few weeks." The morning regulars always asked about Daddy.

"He's great. Loving retirement, of course. He's busy helping get things cleaned up for the school's renovation. And he still helps me out here at the diner most afternoons."

"Please give him my best." Mr. Davis stroked his graying goatee. It was a habit as old as his beard, which had always charmed me.

"Will do, Mr. Davis." On my way to key in his order, I quickly refilled a few coffees, brought somebody a clean spoon, and supplied the check to another table. The sounds of utensils clanking against plates, ice rattling in glasses, and the smells of maple syrup and french fries filled the air. Since childhood, it had been the symphony of my life.

The Cordial Diner was a fixture in Cherry Creek, Tennessee. My family had owned it since before I could remember, and now I was the owner since Daddy had retired two years ago. Thankfully, he still worked afternoons to help me out. Or maybe, to make sure I was doing things right. Either way, I was glad to have his guidance.

Saturday mornings and Sundays after church were our busiest days, and today was no exception. Tourists from a four-state area filled the navy Naugahyde booths, and our regulars arrived daily without fail. I took another order for the diner's famous Cherry Cordial dessert— our customers ordered the dessert any time of day. Cherry Creek boasted a grove of cherry trees in the center of town, and the cherries were the best around.

Our cherry cordial dessert was a mix of rich chocolate cake, whipped cream, and homemade cherry compote, topped with two perfect chocolate-covered cherry cordials made by Miss Dottie at her Chocolate Shop next door.

As I entered Mr. Davis' order into our computer system, a deep and familiar voice froze me in place. "Kayla? Is that you?" My breath hitched in recognition. *It couldn't be him.* The voice was close—just behind me across the counter. I worked to calm my racing heartbeat and then turned to stare into the bright blue eyes and slightly older face of Seth Jacobs.

"Seth?" I smiled, despite my shock. "It's so good to see you." I instinctively leaned across the counter to hug him—kind of. It was more like a quick touching of hands on shoulders. But he smelled the same—like the outdoors without the sweat. Pine and flannel, exactly like I remembered.

He continued to grin and stare at me in awe as if he'd

discovered a rare edition volume in the library. He'd always loved old things. "I can't believe you're still here."

Of course I'm still here! The words threatened to spew from my lips. Instead, I maintained my happy grin and said, "Some things never change, huh?"

"It's great running into you. I'm here for work. Staying at the Inn." He pointed toward the Cherry Creek Inn, run by my best friend, Sierra.

I can't believe she hadn't given me a heads-up that Seth was back in town. "For work?"

"Yes, my company got the contract to renovate Cherry Creek Academy. I hoped you were still in town so we could catch up while I'm here."

I'd heard that he'd become a restoration architect. Old books, buildings, and any kind of historical anything gave him a thrill—or it had back when we were kids. "How long will you be in Cherry Creek?" *How long will I have to worry about running into you around every corner?* This town was like that. Not quite big enough to avoid anyone.

He shrugged. "It depends on the weather. We'll work through the holidays to get it done on schedule. We'll work on the library when the students return to classes."

Thanksgiving was in three days, and we hadn't yet gotten the expected seasonal snowfall. But the snow would come as it did every year. "Daddy has been volunteering at the school, helping to move some of the old furniture and books into storage to prep for the renovation. He didn't mention that you were the one doing the work."

"My company is SJ Renovations, so he might not have known. Mayor Gregson knows it's me, but I guess he didn't mention it to anyone yet.

The bell signaled that my orders were ready to pick up from the kitchen window. "Oh, I've got to,"—I pointed behind me.

"Don't let me keep you. I'm here for a to-go cherry cordial order for old-time's sake. The place looks great, by the way." He looked around, appreciation in his expression.

"Thanks. I'll put your order in. You can pick it up at the counter." I nodded and spun on my heel toward the pickup window. Seth turning up here was like my past slapping me in the face. I used to think I would marry Seth Jacobs when we were back in high school. I'd loved him with every cell of my body, heart, and soul. Letting him go was the hardest thing I'd ever done.

I got swept up in the diner's lunch crowd and dismissed him from my thoughts for the rest of the day. More precisely, I avoided thinking about him. As the owner of The Cordial Diner, I handled the business end of things, but I also waited tables, helped Roger in the kitchen, and served cherry pie and cherry cordial from the counter.

Daddy would be here soon to help out with the lunch rush. We were just getting some of the holiday crowd that would last until the first of January. Cherry Creek was a Hallmark-esque town with enough charm to sweep anyone off their feet. Between the gorgeous inn, the cherry grove, and all the quaint shops, our town made for a beautiful weekend getaway from Nashville, Knoxville, Chattanooga, and surrounding areas.

I wondered if I'd ever see Seth again, but I'd refused to allow myself the painful luxury of looking him up on social media. Rumors were tossed here and there from the few folks who tried to keep up with him online. No mention that he was coming back to Cherry Creek for an extended stay, though. That had been a complete surprise.

Seth had hoped he might run into Kayla while in town, but part of him wished she'd gotten out of Cherry Creek. Wished she was off having a life filled with adventures. Of course, her dad was here, as was the family business, so that was a lot to hope.

Kayla's parents, Lloyd and Mary Doyle, were rooted in the community through generations of family. They'd long taken on the selfless job of bettering the community. They'd hired teens and taught them strong work skills and values, which aligned with their mission. It was devastating to so many when Kayla's mom got sick before their high school graduation.

Kayla and Seth planned to attend The University of Tennessee in Knoxville together, but she delayed attending college to help her dad care for her mom. It was tough for Mr. Doyle to run the diner from early morning until late at night. Kayla had insisted Seth go to college without her. But she didn't join him at UT sophomore year after her mom passed. Instead, she worked at the diner and attended a culinary school nearby, commuting from home.

They'd continued to communicate for over a year, but by the time graduate school came around, Seth had accepted a distinguished internship in upstate New York, so they'd lost touch. The years and distance had eroded their bond, and while Kayla was on Seth's mind often, he was far too busy to visit Tennessee. Losing her was his greatest regret.

Coming back to renovate the Cherry Creek Academy was a dream come true. He'd been a boarding student at CCA, while Kayla attended as a local daytime student. He'd boarded because he was an only child whose career-driven parents didn't spend time with him like Kayla's parents had with her. Her family had been his family during those years.

It was evident by Kayla's expression that she hadn't known Seth was in town. He looked forward to setting things right with her while he was here. She was still as lovely as she'd been as a teen, though with more life experience and less starry-eyed hope in her brown gaze. He hated to think that he might've played a part in that.

"Seth, is that you?"

Seth was walking back from the diner to the inn when a man's voice interrupted his deep thoughts from the past. He found himself staring into the eyes of Lloyd Doyle, Kayla's dad. "Hello, Mr. Doyle. It's great to see you." They shook hands and slapped each other on the back.

"Son, it's been a minute. What are you doing here in Cherry Creek?"

Seth brought him up to speed about the reno. "Kayla says you've been helping prepare things for us over at the school."

"You saw Kayla?" Seth noticed a quick flash of worry in his eyes before it disappeared.

"Yes, just now at the diner. The place looks great, by the way."

"That's all her doing. When she took it over, she refurbished the original décor. She recovered all the booths and replaced the flooring and the counter. Then, she modernized the kitchen and put a computer system in for ordering and paying tabs. It all made my head spin, but it was exactly what The Cordial needed." Mr. Doyle was clearly proud of Kayla's accomplishments with the diner.

"She's got an eye for it." Seth was also super impressed at how well it had turned out.

"I'm headed over now to help with the afternoon crowd. It's great to see you, son. I imagine we'll run into each other here or there in the coming weeks."

"I look forward to it, sir."

Two

I LOCKED THE DINER'S FRONT DOOR, TURNED OFF THE NEON SIGNS, AND flipped the sign to "closed" while we finished cleaning up. Usually, Felicity was here to help close, but one of her children had a fever. She was a divorced mother of two young boys who worked most nights and weekends. I'd also hired several teens from the school to help out during busy times so we didn't always have to clean and setups for the next day. Tonight, Daddy had stayed to help me close. I was glad it was only the two of us. We'd been doing some version of this together for as long as I could remember.

"I ran into Seth Jacobs on my way in this morning. Says he stopped by." Daddy continued mopping as he said this. Today was busy, and this was our first chance to discuss Seth's return.

"Yes. We spoke briefly." Daddy had strong opinions regarding his leaving Cherry Creek and my staying behind. He'd encouraged me to go to college, but I couldn't see how to leave home at the time—or after. He didn't blame Seth, but discussing it tended to unsettle his mood, so we rarely rehashed things from that time.

"Are you okay, Baby?" His mop stilled, and our gazes caught.

I was his baby girl and always would be. We'd been close since I was a child. Now that I was an adult, he'd stepped back a little to give me my space, but his support and love had never wavered. And Daddy knew how much I'd loved Seth back then.

"I'm fine, Daddy. I missed Seth for a long time after he left, but I've got a great life here. I love running the diner and mentoring students like you and Momma did when I was young."

"I can't help but think how different things might've been for the two of you if—" he trailed off. "I sometimes worry that you have regrets."

I shook my head. "Momma needed me. I'll never regret my time with her when she was sick. I can't go back and change things, nor do I want to. I'm content." I smiled brightly at him for good measure. The last thing he needed was for me to heap guilt on him.

"I just wanted to be sure his turning up after all this time hasn't thrown you for a loop."

I shook my head and smiled at him. "No loop. I'm good." That wasn't exactly the truth, but there wasn't any point in both of us fretting about Seth's sudden arrival in town.

As I wiped down tables, I allowed myself to fall back in time —back to when my worries were few. Back to when I'd had my future with Seth all planned. I'd enrolled as a freshman design student for the fall, and Seth would be an architect. We'd planned to synchronize our class schedules so that we could study, eat, and hang out together. Neither of us wanted to rush a sorority or fraternity because we had each other and didn't need the extra busyness of Greek life.

The future was shiny and exciting, and nothing could keep us from it. Except for learning that Momma had breast cancer —the most rare and aggressive kind. By the time she was diagnosed, it was already stage three. My parents weren't people who ran into the city to see doctors every time they got a cold—or cancer. They were too busy running the diner and being surrogate parents for the students who lived at the academy full-time that they ignored their own issues.

I'd moved from remembering the fun times to allowing memories from that awful stretch in my life to creep in—the worst time.

"Do I need to clean the grease trap?" Daddy was always willing to do the hard jobs for me.

"Roger did it this morning, so we're finished here." I handed him a slice of cherry pie from the counter and a serving of today's pot roast special that I'd asked Roger to box up.

"I'll walk you home," Daddy offered.

"No, it's okay. I'm meeting up with Sierra. She's finishing her shift in a few minutes." It was almost ten o'clock. We closed the kitchen at nine most evenings, but there were typically a few stragglers who showed up just before closing that we served coffee or dessert to while we were wrapping things up. Tonight, the diner was empty. I changed out of my work clothes before heading out since I didn't want to smell like french fries all evening.

"I'll walk you to the inn then."

I locked up and inhaled the fresh air. Daddy still lived in the same house where I grew up a few blocks away. A while back, I'd rented a cute little apartment a couple of doors down over the top of the gift store, Gifts and Bits. I'd needed some grown-up space of my own, and it allowed Daddy to live a life separate from me.

The evening was chilly but not "big coat" cold. I wore a hooded sweater over my jeans and blouse. I waved goodnight to Daddy and entered the Cherry Creek Inn. It was a gorgeous, old structure, and Sierra's grandparents had owned it before her. They'd raised her after her parents died in an accident when she was very young.

"Hey there. I'm finishing up." Sierra smiled and waved at me. She logged out of the computer at the front desk and then spoke to the employee working the night shift.

I hoped not to run into Seth while I waited. Twice in one day would be too much. Since he'd popped into the diner, my senses had been buzzing. I knew it was only our first interaction while he worked in town. He'd mentioned catching up.

"Okay. I'm all done for the evening. Where do you want to go?" We often went out for a quick bite or glass of wine at ten p.m. It wasn't unusual since we both ran businesses in town and finished our days around the same time. It was an excellent way to wind down before heading home for the evening. I'd gotten accustomed to late nights and early mornings over the years.

I suggested, "How about a drink and dessert at Rutherford's?" Rutherford's was the only fine-dining restaurant in town. There was often a crowd on Saturday evening, but by ten o'clock, tourists and locals had either gone home or returned to the inn or their privately owned vacation rentals around the area. There was a nice bar area with tables for intimate gatherings with friends. The vibe was nice, but the drinks were a little pricey.

"Sounds good." She shrugged into her jacket that hung on a coat tree by the counter.

We walked through the town square where the enormous Christmas tree would be erected by Thanksgiving day. The tree's arrival was the official kickoff to the holidays here in Cherry Creek. There was a tree lighting on Thanksgiving night, and then we all put up Christmas decorations the day after. So many of my Christmas memories had involved Seth, who was still on my mind after today's unexpected encounter.

"Sierra, I can't believe you didn't tell me Seth was back in town." I tried not to sound peeved that she hadn't given me notice. She understood how his showing up here might've upset me.

"Oh, my gosh, Kayla! It was on my to-do list all day, but we were so busy that I forgot to text or call you. Did you talk to him? What happened?"

"He came by the diner and shocked the heck out of me, for starters. I stopped breathing for a minute or two."

"I'm so sorry. He surprised me when he checked in this morning. The reservation was made under his company name, so I had no idea." She slowed her steps, causing me to do the same. "Well? How did seeing him again make you feel?"

I didn't answer right away. *How had it made me feel?* "It was like looking back into my memories. Like a lightning-fast slide show that brought to mind everything I've tried not to think about every day since Seth left."

Sierra nodded. "That makes sense. I know the two of you had some great times together."

I lifted a shoulder, trying to shrug it off. Great times and not-so-great times. "Such a long time ago, though."

We entered Rutherford's and headed toward our favorite table in the corner overlooking the nearly-empty restaurant.

"What can I get for y'all this evening?" Our frequent waiter, David, appeared as soon as we'd wrestled off our outerwear.

"Hey, David. I'll have a chardonnay." Sierra always had chardonnay.

"I'll take a White Christmas cherry martini." They'd started serving them last week. Made with cherry vodka, crème de cocoa, a splash of heavy crème, grenadine, and topped with a cherry (of course), it was my favorite cocktail. It was a tourist favorite as well. "Dessert menu?" David was already handing them to us. "I'll get these drinks started."

"Are you planning to see Seth again while he's in town?" Sierra asked as we perused our dessert options.

"I'm assuming we'll run into each other, but we didn't plan anything."

"You know, at some point, y'all will have to clear the air."

I was hoping to *not* have that conversation with him as it seemed irrelevant to the present. "But it's so much to clear. I don't think a rehashing necessary."

"Is he single?"

I lifted my eyes from the menu and stared at her. "I have no idea."

"You mean you haven't looked him up on social media?"

"No. That would be pathetic." Tempting but still kind of cringy.

"Um, no, it wouldn't. I mean, I get that you would rather not know if he's married with a few kiddos. But let's be real; everybody looks up their exes."

"So far, I haven't." I realized that was strange since it would be so easy. I guess I didn't want to know. My memories had served me well over the years.

"Well, you should before somebody else does, and can't wait to tell you all about it. Unless you would prefer an ambush, and I doubt that."

"I guess you're right. But what does it matter now?" Whether Seth was a husband and father shouldn't bother me. But Sierra had planted the seed of curiosity, and I began to wonder what his life had been like over the last decade.

Three

DADDY HANDED ME A SMALL STACK OF BOOKS WHEN HE ARRIVED FOR his shift Sunday morning. "I thought you might like some of these. I found them hidden in the back corner of the library. We're disassembling the shelves and storing the books until after the renovation."

I was a voracious reader and loved old books. That was something Seth and I'd had in common as teens, which made us both a little odd back then. While most of our friends attended football games and parties, we were often searching the library for old tomes. We had friends, but mostly we'd had each other.

Once the after-church rush had cleared, Daddy said, "I'll hang out here if you have any errands." Daddy often gave me breaks during the week so I could have some semblance of a life beyond running the diner. He had mornings to get out and do things, so after the lunch rush, I did whatever needed doing outside the diner. Plus, I had some fantastic employees who could cover for me for a few hours if I needed to be away.

"Okay. I'm going to head over to The Market to get the

turkeys and stuff for the sides." Every year, we hosted Thanks-giving dinner at my parents' house and included any students who couldn't travel home for the short holiday break. I'd continued the tradition with Daddy after Momma died. It was an open invitation to anyone in town with no family.

"You can drop the food off at the house if you want," Daddy offered.

"I will. Thanks. I'll use the garage fridge for the cold stuff, except maybe I'll brine the turkeys here." I could've stored it all in the oversized refrigerator in the diner's kitchen, but Daddy had plenty of room at the house. And that way, I wouldn't have to move things twice.

I grabbed my purse and the books Daddy brought home from CCA.

"You can take my truck if you want. It's out front." He fished the keys from his pocket and tossed them to me.

"Thanks." Normally, I would've used a small rolling cart and walked to the Market, but since I had a lot to buy today, I would need a vehicle. Plus, Daddy's house was farther from the store than my apartment.

I had a cute little red hybrid my parents had bought for me to go to college, but then Momma got sick, and we'd used it mostly for her doctors' appointments and the rare occasion that I went someplace. I seldom needed a car here in Cherry Creek, so it had extremely low mileage and was still in mint condition. We mostly used Daddy's old blue pickup to haul things here and there.

I adjusted the seat and drove the few blocks through town to The Market at the end of First Street next door to city hall. As I parked, I noticed Milton Davies headed my way from the police station. Milton was Cherry Creek's only detective, and we sometimes dated casually. Much more casually on my end than his, unfortunately. Milton'd had a crush on me since high school, and I think he'd been secretly thrilled when Seth left town after graduation. A decade later, he was unmarried and still wanted to date me.

As I climbed from the truck, Milton put out a hand to assist. I accepted his help because it was a kind gesture. "Hi there, Kayla. Heading to The Market?"

I ignored the obviousness of his question and smiled. Milton was a nice-looking guy. He still had a full head of hair and was in good physical shape. "Yes. I'm shopping for Thanksgiving dinner."

"You and everybody else. Been busy since they opened the doors this morning." He inclined his head toward the store.

"Daddy's minding the diner, so I've got a little time."

"Would you like to grab a coffee later?" he asked.

"Oh, sorry. I plan to run the groceries to Daddy's house, and then it's back to work." I hoped my expression conveyed disappointment.

"I'd love to get together soon. It's been a while since we've gone out."

"Yes, I know it has." I had to remind myself that I didn't owe him my time. I was naturally a pleaser, which was probably why I hadn't told him I wasn't very interested in him.

"Let me know if you need help loading up after you're done."

I nodded, feeling guilty about leading him on so as not to crush his feelings. "Thanks, Milton."

Milton was right about the crowd. The Market (aptly named) was the only grocery store in town, supplying residents with almost anything they might need. There was a Walmart about ten miles from Cherry Creek, but The Market was locally owned and had excellent meats, fish, and produce, though we usually bought our fresh produce from Trenton Farms just outside of town when it was in season. Their cherries, strawberries, and peaches were the absolute best.

As I rounded the endcap, heading toward the meat department with a couple of huge turkeys in my sights, a woman nearly jumped out in front of me, pretty much blocking my cart. "Hey there, Kayla. Long time no see. I heard that Seth was back in town. Have you seen him yet?"

Georgia Green's big blinky brown eyes were glued on my expression as she waited with bated breath for the town's juiciest gossip. I barely refrained from rolling my eyes at her. Tapping into my patience, I measured my words. "Hi, Georgia. Yes, his company is renovating Cherry Creek Academy."

"Are you excited? I mean, you're both single, right?" Georgia had been the town's biggest gossip since kindergarten. She was a badger in that she never gave up. She was also a mean girl who'd never truly been put in her place. Not sure what her place was, but most people didn't wish to be on the receiving end of her malice. It wasn't worth the fallout she created for those who crossed her.

"I don't know if Seth is single, but it was nice to see him."

"I'll bet that brings back all kinds of memories for you, you poor girl." Her tone was syrup and honey. Her intentions were more like battery acid and hot sauce directly to the eyeballs.

"Sorry, Georgia, I need to pick up my turkeys. I've got to get back to work." I smiled when I said it, so she couldn't accuse me of being rude.

"I wouldn't want to keep you from your hair net and french fries. Tootles." The woman's rudeness was interminable. One of these days, somebody would take her down a peg, but it wouldn't be me today.

I shook it off and rolled my basket toward the vast, refrigerated container that held what looked to be a hundred turkeys. I decided two would be a safe bet since we never knew how many people would show up on Thursday. If our numbers were smaller than expected, I could serve turkey-cranberry sandwiches as the lunch special at the diner on Friday.

We ordered weekly from a restaurant supply but tried to use as many local businesses as possible to source the diner. I smiled and nodded a greeting to pretty much everyone in the place since I'd known most of them my entire life—or thereabouts—and many were customers at the Cordial Diner as well.

I chose fresh cranberries, sweet potatoes, and green beans for the casseroles I made from scratch. I'd decided on a giant banana pudding for dessert, so I grabbed several bunches of barely ripe bananas. By the time Thursday arrived, they would be perfect for banana pudding. I'd ordered extra frozen yeast rolls with my order for the diner in anticipation of Thanksgiving. My cart was full when I checked out with Miss Joanne, the owner.

"Wow, honey. You've got quite a load here. I love how you make Thanksgiving special every year for folks without family."

I smiled. "Thanks. Let me know if you hear of anyone in need on Thanksgiving. We will deliver if necessary." On regular days, we provided our leftovers to the local shelter. And if anyone was hungry and without means, we'd kept some pantry staples just inside the diner's rear exit. So far, nobody had abused the situation, so it remained a quiet way to help those in need.

"Will do." I knew that Miss Joanne also helped feed the food-insecure folks in town. It wasn't generally discussed, but I admired her for it.

I stepped out of the store and almost mowed Seth down. "Oh, hey."

He wore faded jeans, a gray UT sweatshirt, and running shoes. "Looks like you're feeding an army. Still hosting everyone for Thanksgiving dinner?"

My stomach did a little flip as my eyes inhaled him. I noticed he'd developed a few fine lines around his eyes, but otherwise, he was still the best-looking guy in town. "Yep. We still host it every year."

As Seth was about to say something, I noticed Milton barreling our way, his gaze intently on me and my cart. Seth picked up my line of sight and turned toward Milton. Milton's eyes lit up in recognition, and the two men did a little bro hug.

"Hey, man. I heard you were back in town." Milton grinned at Seth. The two of them were best friends from the start of middle school. Seth had moved to Cherry Creek Academy in sixth grade as a boarding student, and they'd played sports together through the years.

"Yeah. I'll be here until the first of the year if everything stays on schedule. I was at school all morning with my team getting started."

"Lot of memories out there." Milton's expression appeared contemplative. He turned his attention to me then. "Can I help you load these?"

I nodded, grateful I'd scored a parking spot right up front. "Sure. Thanks."

"I'll help," Seth offered, and the two men loaded the food into the bed of Daddy's truck and finished within seconds.

Seth stepped forward. "Hey, how about I help you unload these at your dad's and hitch a ride back to the academy? I just bought several sandwiches and sent them back to the school with one of the guys in my truck." The school was half a mile from the diner, so it wouldn't take me out of my way.

I didn't know what to say besides, "Okay. I can drop you off at the school on my way back to the diner."

Milton's eyes narrowed for a split second. He perceived a competitor for my attention. "Thanks for your help, Milton. I'll see you soon."

"Sure. Anytime." Milton's peeved expression disappeared in a split second, and he refocused on his delight over running into Seth. "It was great to see you, man. Give me a shout if you get some time off. We can do some crappie fishing out at the lake if you want."

"Will do, Milton." They shook hands.

Seth came around to the passenger's side and hopped in. "So, you and Milton, huh?"

I shrugged as I put the truck in gear. "We're just friends."

"He wasn't looking at *you* like a fishing buddy."

That made me smile a little. "No, I suppose not. I think he would like us to date, but I don't want to hurt his feelings, you know?" Seth was the first person I'd admitted that to. *Why did I tell him that?*

"You always had the softest heart for people."

"I can't tell if that's a bad thing—" And what I'd said about my feelings, or lack thereof, for Milton didn't put me in the best light. "Anyway, I guess not being clear that I'm not interested in dating him is more cowardly than kind."

"I believe you meant to be kind and not hurt his feelings."

"Keep it between us, okay?" I really wouldn't want to hurt Milton's feelings, but now I realize what an injustice I'd done Milton by stringing him along and not nipping his romantic interest in the bud. Maybe I'd been hoping he would grow on me.

"Of course, I won't. Your secret is safe with me." He grinned, and my stomach flipped. I can't believe I still reacted to Seth the same as I had in high school. Did it make me pathetic that I'd never found anyone else who made my pulse race the way he always had?

I pulled the truck into the driveway at Daddy's house, and we both hopped out to unload. "This place brings back a lot of memories."

"Yes, it does. Especially since I've moved out. I'd spent my entire life in this house and can't imagine being unable to come and go here as I please."

He stared at the house for a few seconds as if remembering something. "We shared our first kiss right over there." Seth pointed to the recently-painted white swing hanging from four chains on the porch.

I followed his gaze. He was correct, and I remembered every detail. We'd been fifteen then and had just returned from the ice cream place in town. Fireflies had begun a summer's evening twinkling light show as darkness overcame the sunset, and the sounds of crickets and tree frogs commenced their evening symphony.

His eyes appeared dreamy. "I was so nervous and sweating, and you smelled like cotton candy."

Our eyes met then, and I shivered at the memory. I could picture it like no time had passed—I smelled the ice cream and sweat and remembered the anticipation of that moment. To lighten the mood, I said, "Only because I'd dripped cotton candy ice cream down the front of my shirt."

"It's something I'll never forget." His eyes cleared then, and he appeared sad, his shoulders drooping. "We were so young and hopeful back then."

"Yes, we were." I didn't have anything cute to say about that.

"I've missed you, Kayla." It was a simple but heartfelt declaration, but I couldn't say everything that raced through my mind. *I missed you so much I wanted to die along with my mom*, or

Why are you here torturing me when none of it can be undone? Or even, *Why didn't you come back for me?*

Instead, I motioned to the items in the pickup bed. "Well, we'd better get the cold stuff in the fridge."

Shaking it off, he forced a smile. "Yes." He unlatched the tailgate and gathered a load in his arms. "Lead the way."

Four

Seeing Milton again after so many years had been great, but Seth wasn't thrilled that Milton was pursuing Kayla. Of course, he had no say in what either of them did, and he realized this. Still, it was a bitter sensation.

Standing with Kayla in front of her parents' house near the old swing had caused a rush of sentimentality. Most days, he tried not to dwell on how things might have been if Kayla had gone to college with him as planned. But he was unable to block out the what-ifs today. Maybe coming back here had been a mistake. He'd genuinely believed that seeing Kayla again would give him the closure he needed to move forward. Unfortunately, it had done the opposite.

His funk continued throughout the day, and his patience wore thin. An early snowstorm out West had delayed some of the building materials. Being the coordinator of a renovation project, whether large or small, required a composed temperament—which he usually managed. He was feeling off and a bit down today, which wasn't like him.

After snapping at his foreman again that afternoon, Seth pulled off his hard hat and returned to the inn to reset his attitude. His line of work involved a lot of paperwork, and it constantly needed updating. Today was a good one for that. It was almost quitting time anyway.

As he parked his truck outside the inn, he gazed across the town square toward the Cordial Diner, where he would most likely find the source of his restlessness.

It was almost time for an early dinner, right? It *was* the best place to grab a blue plate special on the fly. He was still negotiating with himself as he pulled open the diner's glass door, its bells jingling loudly. All eyes turned in his direction, and he realized there was no backing down now.

He sat at the bar since no booths were available and grabbed a laminated menu that still boasted breakfast all day, along with patty melts, pot roast, and fried chicken. He did notice there were a few healthy options and gluten-free offerings. Kayla's cooking school background was evident in a few less "diner-ish" foods. There was an Asian stir-fry plate and a vegetarian special.

A young waiter plopped down a glass of water in front of Seth. "Hi there, what'll you have?"

"I'll take a double patty melt with grilled onions on wheat toast. Fries on the side. Oh, and a Diet Coke. Thanks." The aroma of sizzling beef on the griddle prompted a mixture of nostalgia and a deep growl from his belly since he'd skipped lunch today, despite buying sandwiches for his crew.

The young man nodded and went to key in the order.

Seth looked around then, having a moment to take in his surroundings. He spotted Kayla at the other end of the diner, speaking with an elderly lady. The woman had Kayla's arm in a claw-like grip, but Kayla was smiling and giving off no signs of impatience. She just nodded and listened.

She'd always loved working here and dealing with the customers. He'd admired that—still did. She suddenly turned, and their eyes met. She smiled, but he noticed a touch of sadness in her eyes for a split second.

As she moved behind the counter, she asked, "Has someone helped you?"

Seth nodded. "Yep. I ordered a patty melt and fries, just like in the old days."

She laughed a little. "You did love your patty melts back then."

He had a thought then. "Does my coming in here bother you?"

She appeared a little confused by his drastic switch of subjects. "Um, no. It's nice to have you here. It's—nostalgic."

"Yes, almost like stepping back in time, huh?" Seth grinned at the former love of his life.

"Almost." Kayla turned to fill a glass with sweetened iced tea, adding a lemon wedge.

Seth wanted to say more—use any excuse to spend time with her—but he could see she was busy, so he didn't comment further. But he watched her move around the diner with a natural grace he remembered so well.

As he ate, he immersed himself in the comfort of clattering dishes, the milkshake machine roar, and the aroma of all things diner. They were the sounds and smells of his happiest days.

When Kayla came around again, he put a hand on her arm. "Can we get dinner tomorrow night?"

She appeared a little shaken by his request. "I-How about you come to the house on Thursday for Thanksgiving dinner? Two-o'clock."

A thrill shot through him. "Sounds perfect. What can I bring?"

"Nothing. Just yourself." She grinned, turned on her heel, and headed to the next table with a plate of fries and a ketchup bottle.

&

After closing the diner, I walked the two blocks home, showered, and made tomato soup from a can and a grilled cheese sandwich. I could've brought home something from the diner, but I rarely did. I needed a clean slate after being around that much food all day.

I didn't allow myself to think about Seth's appearance at the diner today. Every time I saw him, it brought back both fantastic and sad memories. Inviting him to Daddy's for Thanksgiving dinner was preferable to spending an evening together in a restaurant fumbling for safe conversation topics and avoiding discussions about the past.

I sank onto my sofa, the television on low volume, and began looking through the old books Daddy had saved for me from the school library. Of course I would return them after the renovation once I'd had the chance to take a look.

As I transferred the small stack from the coffee table to the sofa, a little book slid to the floor, and I leaned down to pick it up. A spark of recognition ran through me as I spotted the cover. It was hand-bound and frayed a little at the edges, proving it had been well-loved. The title was stamped in faded gold lettering with a green cover. I could make out a sprig of what looked like mistletoe embossed just under the title, *Once Upon a Christmas Kiss.*

Curious, I flipped open the cover to find an inscription and dedication in a carefully lettered script. I recognized our former principal's name as the author. Miss Chambers must've added the volume to our school library at some point, but I don't remember ever seeing it. A story circulated around town about how Miss Chambers, who'd been single as long as we'd known her, had written a book about her parents' love story and, shortly after, found her own true love.

"To my dearest friend, Charlotte: May your heart be filled with joy this Christmas season. I leave you with my parents' long-requested true love story from years ago. May it bring you the happiness and peace it has always brought to me—and maybe a love of your own. I will miss you, sweet friend. Yours Affectionately, Elizabeth Chambers"—I then noticed several short notations and comments by other readers: "Y'all, this book is the real deal! After reading this story, I met my forever love at the Cherry Creek Post Office down the street." And "A heartfelt thanks to Miss Chambers for the romantic Christmas magic she weaved into this story. I thought I would never find that special someone, but I truly believe this book made it happen."

A few more notes and reviews were written into the margins—all proclaiming that, after reading this book, they'd found true love during the Christmas season. I was amused and skeptical at the idea that a story could be a catalyst for happily-ever-afters. None of the commenters had left a name.

I stood and stretched, then headed into the kitchen to pour a glass of chardonnay. What I'd seen so far had piqued my curiosity, and there was no way I could go to sleep without reading further to learn what the fuss was about.

Instead of settling back into the sofa, I got ready for bed. Reading before bedtime was a luxury these days. I loved doing it but had little self-control once I got lost in a story. I would set a thirty-minute timer after finishing my wine and brushing my teeth and stick to it. Five a.m. always came early.

Flannel pajamas on, I began reading. The prose was lyrical and lovely, and before long, I was hopelessly lost. My timer shut off, and I didn't reset it. I could taste and feel and see the sweet story unfold. This beautiful romance and the promise of a lifetime of love had me tearing up—and craving a happy ending for myself. A Christmas Wish. It shifted something inside my heart. I was like the Grinch whose heart grew after witnessing an emotional miracle.

I sighed as I placed the book beside me on the bed and slipped into a deep sleep, my dreams filled with magic and hope. Until my alarm went off. Suddenly, I was back to the reality of my life and the woeful lack of a happy ending thus far. But not completely. No, Miss Chamber's story had planted a seed of hope. If this Christmas miracle had happened for her and the other readers, couldn't it happen for me? After all, I wasn't *that* old. Just a little past the age where the likelihood of something so wonderful occurring was less likely.

Five

I GOT READY FOR WORK THE FOLLOWING DAY WITH A LITTLE BIT MORE enthusiasm than usual. Of course, Seth popped into my mind whenever I thought of happily-ever-afters. He always had. But maybe I should *try* to find someone to love and share my life with. Seth was out of the picture—had been for years.

He would be gone soon enough, and I would return to where I'd been for years. I was happy enough with life as I'd made for myself. So, happy enough would have to do for now.

As I walked to work, I shivered. The weather was rather gloomy today and getting colder. I wish I'd worn a heavier jacket—maybe even a heavy coat today. The new infusion of cold air made me think about the decorations I had in the storage room at the diner. We always started decorating for Christmas the day after Thanksgiving Currently, we had some turkey art from the elementary school displayed on the windows, along with our seasonal coloring sheets that young diners could display against the far wall. It wasn't a fancy display, but it linked us to the community and our customers.

I cranked the heat up a few notches when I entered the diner. Roger was already back in the kitchen working on today's special: chicken n' dumplings. The recipe had been my mom's, and it was a crowd-pleaser. Perfect for a brisk almost-winter day.

The first customers rolled in for breakfast around seven o'clock and ordered hot chocolate with marshmallows. The steaming cups smelled so good, and I anticipated we would sell many of them before the end of the day. Mondays were our slowest days, so I spent part of my morning in a booth planning the rest of the week's lunch specials. Two of our students were working today. They'd gotten off for their Thanksgiving break yesterday.

We would be closed on Thanksgiving day so our employees could be with their families or with us at Daddy's house. We'd posted a large sign on the front door stating our holiday schedule. We always closed early on Christmas Eve and didn't open on Christmas Day. Everyone in Cherry Creek knew this, but we also wanted visitors to know ahead of time.

Sierra stopped by mid-morning to grab a hot chocolate. I sat with her in a booth to chat and get off my feet for a few minutes. She shivered beneath her jacket and scarf. "Brrr. I'm freezing today."

"I know; I didn't expect this weather when I left the house. It looks like they just delivered the tree." I pointed out the front window toward the square where workers were delivering the giant Frasier Fir.

"Yes, it's huge. I'm assuming you'll go to the tree lighting tomorrow night?"

I nodded. "I haven't missed it once—besides the year I had the flu when I was ten. You?"

"Of course. After I have my Thanksgiving dinner at Chez Doyle." Since Sierra's grandparents had passed away two years ago, only months apart from each other, she spent Thanksgiving with us. "So, how are things going? I wondered if you'd seen Seth again." Sierra unwound her scarf and got comfortable.

"Yes, I've run into him a few times since he's been in town. He's coming to our Thanksgiving dinner tomorrow." I tried to diminish the effect that was having on my nerves.

"Oh, wow. That's—nice. Right?"

I shrugged a shoulder, pretending indifference. "Inviting him felt like the right thing to do, considering he's here alone for the holidays."

"You seem to be handling his being here pretty well. I think I would be a wreck if I were in your shoes. I know how hard it was for you when he left."

"It was hard. It's still hard some days, but his being back here is temporary, so I can't get too worked up about it."

Sierra grinned. "He's single, you know. I figured you hadn't looked him up yet, so it was time you knew the deal."

Her words hit me hard. Part of me wanted him to be completely safe—as in, married with kids so that I couldn't even entertain the "what ifs" when it came to Seth. I'd noticed that he hadn't been wearing a wedding ring the times I'd seen him, but not everyone who was married did.

"We talked yesterday when he came in the lobby while I was on duty. Said he was engaged a few years ago, but it didn't work out."

"Oh." I was at a loss for words. Learning that Seth was single caused my hands to sweat.

"You really should spend some time together while he's here. Bury the hatchet."

"I'm not sure if I want to go into all that with him. It's so far in the past, and he'll be leaving soon enough, and things can get back to normal." My life was normal, safe, and rarely dished out a lot of drama.

"I'm still not convinced. Nothing is impossible. Especially during the holidays."

But it was, wasn't it? I replied, "You're such a romantic." Saying those words reminded me of the book I'd read last night.

"Hey, do you remember Miss Chambers from school?" I asked.

Sierra nodded. "Yes, she was super nice."

"My dad brought a book from the old school library that she'd written."

"Oh, you mean the one that guarantees its reader true love and a happily-ever-after?" Sierra grinned. "I remember hearing about it ages ago, but I've never seen it."

I closed my eyes and inhaled, remembering the dreamy love story. "It is wonderful. Obviously, I don't believe that about the happily-ever-after stuff, but it's such a sweet story."

"Maybe I'll read it when you're done. It couldn't hurt, right?"

"I'd like to take a little more time with it and maybe re-read it. I'll hand it off to you when I'm done." I couldn't wait to revisit the little book that had captured my attention so completely.

"Sounds good. Now that I'm all warmed up, I'll get out of your hair so that you can get back to work." Standing from the booth, Sierra re-wrapped the scarf around her neck.

"Stay warm out there."

With the colder weather, I noticed that business was slower than usual, even for a Monday, so when Daddy came in, I opted to go home and take some time to prepare what I could for dinner tomorrow.

I stopped by the restroom on my way out, and when I looked in the mirror, I realized how badly I needed a haircut and color. It couldn't hurt to call my hairstylist and make an appointment while I was thinking about it. I wasn't super high-maintenance where my looks were concerned, so my hair didn't usually take up much space in my thoughts.

I dialed Marti, my hair person, whose salon I'd frequented since high school.

He answered. "Hey there, sweet cheeks. Are you finally going to let me get ahold of your head?" Marti was a friend too.

"Hi there. Yes, it's past time, isn't it?"

"What are you doing right now? I just had a client cancel last-minute."

"I was headed to Daddy's house to cook some of tomorrow's dinner. But I could come over there first, I guess." The cooking could wait a couple of hours, I supposed. I would tell Daddy I'd be there for the dinnertime rush.

"Come on over then. See you in a minute, honey."

Getting from the diner to the Cut 'n Curl only took a couple of minutes on foot, as it was just down the street from the diner. The bells on the door jingled as I entered. "Oooh, look who the cat dragged in." This came from Jimmy, Marti's partner. They'd been together as a couple since the end of high school and opened the salon right after completing cosmetology school.

"Yeah, yeah, yeah. I've already heard it from Marti." But I winked at him, taking the edge off my words.

Marti was folding towels near the shampoo bowls and motioned me over. "Let's get you shampooed, friend." He pointed to the shampoo bowl beside where he stood.

I deposited my purse on the shelf beside it and sat. I dipped my head back into Marti's capable hands. "Thanks for seeing me."

"Whenever I spot you going in and out of that diner, I want to flag you down and drag you inside. I can't wait to get my hands on your gorgeous hair. I heard Seth was back, so I assume you want the works, right?" He sounded positively giddy.

"Why would I need the works because of Seth?" Why did everyone keep acting like I was trying to somehow get Seth back in my life? I wasn't.

"Oh, girl, I've known you since we were kids. And I remember how it was with the two of you." He turned on the sprayer and proceeded to begin the shampoo.

"This isn't because of Seth. I just need a haircut." I shut that subject down but could feel myself relaxing under his massaging fingers.

"Okay, sweets. Whatever you say."

I closed my eyes, inhaling the amazing scent of the peppermint shampoo. Every time I did this, I wondered why I didn't treat myself more often.

As I sat in Marti's salon chair after my shampoo, he stared at me, squinting his eyes as he surveyed the work ahead. "So, I suggest you let me have my way."

I nodded, trusting him completely. "Go for it."

He spun the chair toward the center of the room, where I couldn't see the mirror, and he called to Jimmy, who was putting his newly folded towels on the shelf. "We're gonna need highlights and lowlights. Mix us up some 6NMG and bleach with 20 volume."

This was Greek to me, but I trusted these two to work their magic. Marti talked the entire time he was working. We chatted about pretty much everything and everybody in town. I could tell he was avoiding questions about Seth, which I appreciated. When he finished, he put me under the warm, domed hair dryer to develop my color and highlights and set a timer.

He shampooed, rinsed, and conditioned my hair and then set to cutting it. I cringed as he snipped what seemed like a *lot* of hair.

"This is going to blow your mind." He snickered as he said this, and I hoped getting my mind blown was a good thing.

Once he'd dried and styled my hair with a large-barrel curling iron, he spun my chair back toward the mirror with a flourish. "Tada, beautiful."

I covered my mouth with my hand. "Oh—wow." My hair color was still in the brown family, but it now had a cinnamon hue with a few gold streaks. The layered cut framed my face and highlighted my eyes. "I love it! Thank you, Marti."

Marti lifted a shoulder. "Of course." I could tell he was pleased with himself, as he should be.

Feeling lighter and prettier than when I'd gone in, I smiled all the way to Daddy's house. Something about a good cut and color did wonders for my mood.

Six

COOKING WAS SOMETHING I LOVED AND WAS GOOD AT INSTINCTUALLY. Attending culinary school was a great fit because I loved creating new dishes and old favorites. I made the cornbread dressing from scratch and then put together the sweet potato and green bean casseroles to prepare for last-minute heating tomorrow. I stewed cranberries, sugar, and orange juice over a slow heat until they thickened, bubbled, and cooled before transferring to the refrigerator. Then, I made the banana pudding.

After I finished the side items and dessert, I stored them in the fridge, I decided to brine the turkeys in the diner's kitchen so I could refrigerate them there. Daddy's garage fridge wouldn't hold them both, especially with all the other food inside. As I muscled the turkeys outside, I noticed a late-model black truck approach and stop at the end of Daddy's driveway, but I couldn't tell who was driving. The driver rolled down the window, and I recognized Seth.

"Need some help?" He put the truck in park and rushed over to relieve me of the two fifteen-pound turkeys. "Where do you want these?"

"Are you stalking me?" I asked, only partially joking, as I pointed to the bed of Daddy's truck.

"I wouldn't call it that exactly. I just left the hardware store and thought I'd say hello. Mr. Doyle told me you were here cooking. I've been thinking about you since our last conversation." He smiled—the one that I remembered so well.

A gust of cold wind blasted through, and I shivered and crossed my arms. "Um. Okay. Thanks for stopping by." I pointed toward the turkeys. "I need to get those into a brine at the diner before I'm back on duty for the evening shift with Daddy."

"Your hair looks fantastic."

I touched my hair on instinct. I'd almost forgotten about the haircut and color. "Thanks. Marti does work magic."

"I'll say." He continued to stare at me, which made me uncomfortable. Not because he was creepy but because I could feel myself falling into his gaze, which caused my heart to pound and my hands to sweat. Like I was still a starry-eyed teen so crazy about him, it made me giddy.

Feeling giddy wasn't helpful. "Stop staring at me like that."

"Like what?" He put his hands up in a defensive gesture.

"Like I'm your girlfriend." I still felt comfortable enough around him that I could speak my mind. Because we knew each other. That hadn't changed after all this time.

"I still like to look at you, Kayla. I always have."

"Well, stop it. It makes me uncomfortable." I narrowed my eyes at him. "You can't come back here a decade later and do that."

"I'm sorry. I'd hoped—" he trailed off.

"Don't hope. It's been nice to see you again, but I don't want to get bogged down in old memories and emotions. It won't do either one of us any good."

"It's just that I've missed you so much." He sounded sincere.

"I've missed you too, Seth." I could still be honest about

my feelings towards him. He'd been my great love, and I'd been his. But we were in different places now, both figuratively and literally. And he'd stayed gone intentionally for a decade.

"I don't live far from here, Kayla." He said this as if he'd read my mind.

"Where do you live?" I asked, genuinely curious.

"Knoxville."

His answer nearly knocked me over. "You mean you live only a couple of hours away and haven't been back even once since you left?"

"I thought I was doing the right thing by staying away—until I got a call from an associate telling me about the renovation at the school and how they were looking for a historical contractor. It was like a huge punch in the gut for me. The idea of returning here to restore a place that meant so much to me and maybe seeing you again was like a stick of dynamite. It reminded me of how great it was between us."

I could hear the hollow pain in his voice, and I closed my eyes, fighting the tears that escaped from my eyes and rolled down my cheeks. "Why are you doing this, Seth? Nothing can come of it now."

"Can't it?"

"No. And I can't believe you would put us both through this. I've got a great life here.

"I'm sorry, Kayla. I'd just hoped maybe we could try again."

"I can't put myself through that again. Please don't ask me to." I spun around, turned my back to him, and climbed up in Daddy's truck, willing him to leave. My cold hands clenched the steering wheel, but my cheeks were on fire. How dare he come back here and suggest we try again? How ridiculous. There was a gulf of time and hurt between us. Too much to even consider such an irresponsible idea. Plus, there was no way I would let myself be vulnerable to Seth ever again. One great heartbreak in my life was one too many.

I heard his engine start and saw him pull away in my rearview mirror, and I breathed a ragged sigh. I hadn't allowed myself even to consider that Seth still loved me. Or was he just trying to recapture what was long dead? Even though we'd had something extraordinary as teens, it didn't translate ten years later. Life had come along and changed everything.

Now he'd gone and done it. Seth could've kicked himself for his stupidity. He'd gotten caught up in the moment staring at Kayla like a sad puppy dog. Yes, he'd come back to do a job, but if he was honest, he'd leaped at the opportunity to see her again. Nothing in his life, not any of his professional accomplishments, had ever given him the same indescribable feeling as staring at Kayla Doyle. Kissing her. Holding her close. She'd been his one true love, and he'd blown it.

Maybe he could win her back. It would be a battle against her stellar defenses, but now that he'd begun to consider a second chance with Kayla, the idea took hold. He was here, and so was she. It would be his last opportunity to mend the line with her.

His list of regrets where she was concerned was long. Every time he'd tried to return to Cherry Creek, something had gotten in the way. Now that he was finally back, Seth realized how foolish he'd been to stay away for so many years and how he should've fought harder for a life with Kayla. She had blossomed into a gorgeous, independent woman, and he couldn't stop thinking about her. Not the girl she was but the woman she'd become.

Despite her pushing him away, he was sure she still felt

something for him too. Hopefully, it was the same something as him because now that he'd rediscovered her, he didn't think he'd be able to do as she asked and let her go again.

Maybe she wasn't yet ready to let down her guard where he was concerned, but he wouldn't give up—not until he'd lost all hope. He'd nearly married a few years ago. Jennifer had been a lovely woman, and they'd enjoyed each other's company for almost a year. He'd proposed, and they'd begun planning a wedding, but the more time they spent together, the more Seth felt like something was missing—now he realized it was Kayla. He'd finally broken off the engagement as it was unfair and unkind even to consider marrying someone unless one was completely committed for life.

Even though she'd insisted on the engagement, Seth had felt awful for inadvertently stringing Jennifer along. It hadn't ended well, and that still stung a little.

Now that he'd confirmed what he'd always suspected regarding his true feelings for Kayla, he planned to woo her with all his might. Yes, it might seem a little creepy if he turned up everywhere she was, but his intentions were the very best. He had work to do, but he'd make time for Kayla. Now that he'd spilled his feelings to her, it would give her time to think about what he'd said.

The renovation of Cherry Creek Academy was going smoothly so far. Before he'd begun the work, his team had extensively researched the original structure. Every piece of hardware, every window, and the many architectural elements had been photographed and cataloged. He'd ordered what needed replacing custom-made. Some of it was done onsite by craftsmen. These subcontractors were the very best he'd found at restoring historical elements of old buildings. Of course, things could change at any moment, so he prepared for the worst, including snow.

He burrowed down into his jacket. The cold was coming fast, and they'd probably get some on the ground in a day or two, according to the latest weather forecast.

Tomorrow was Thanksgiving, so he'd given his crew the day off. Most of them lived in the Knoxville area and would leave this afternoon to head home to their families for the weekend, giving Seth a few days to spend with Kayla. Not that she had the same plan, but he would do his best at dinner tomorrow. She'd run him off in a huff but hadn't uninvited him, which was a positive sign.

His holiday offense would begin tomorrow to win Kayla back. But first, he had a few things to do.

Seven

"THE DRESSING IS SO GOOD, KAYLA. CAN I GET THE RECIPE?" SIERRA asked. "I can't believe I don't have it already."

Since Sierra's grandparents had passed away two years ago, only months apart from each other, she'd attended our Thanksgiving dinner. She always brought something to add to the feast. Today, she'd made her grandmother's pumpkin pie with pecan streusel topping, which was to die for. "Only if you share Meme's pie recipe."

"Deal."

I had brined the two large turkeys all night in large stock pots in the diner's refrigerator. Daddy and I had gotten up super early to roast them in heavy oven bags with onions, celery, and seasonings in the enormous ovens at the diner. Nobody made a turkey like Daddy. The tricky part was transferring the very hot, roasted birds to his house once they were done. One currently graced the center of the table, with the other waiting in the warm oven for when it was needed.

A group of twenty or so had shown up. Some were students without transportation home for the holidays, and others were residents with little to no family to speak of. Most arrived with a side, dessert, or flowers for the table. The amount of food we had was incredible. "Here's to the Doyle family for feeding us stragglers." Dave Burton, the manager at the convenience store in town, raised a glass. He'd lost his wife a few years ago in a car accident.

"Here, here." Everyone raised a glass, whether wine, soda, or iced tea.

Daddy stood to address the diners. "Y'all have been our family over the years, and we couldn't do what we do without you. Thanks to everyone for making our Thanksgiving a special one." He lifted his glass.

The scene never failed to bring tears to my eyes. Our bond with this place was everything. I looked around and acknowledged our friends, old and new. When my gaze settled on Seth, I averted my eyes because he was staring back at me. I'd assumed that maybe he'd skip dinner after yesterday's awkward situation. But, no, he'd shown up forty-five minutes early to help us with the setup. And he'd brought several bottles of wine and sparkling cider in a cooler filled with ice. I'd been busy enough removing hot food from the oven, setting out utensils and filling glasses with ice to avoid having any meaningful conversation.

Now that I was clearing the table and making to-go leftover plates, I could no longer evade him, as he took the spot next to me at the kitchen counter and began to help. I stared at his hands as he transferred portions of turkey, cranberry sauce, and sweet potatoes from the roasting pans to individual containers. He had nice hands, even though they were currently encased in latex serving gloves.

"I'd like to take one of these home and stash it in my fridge at the inn if you have enough. Everything was so delicious." He stopped and raised his brows in question, the pause causing me to lose focus on the task.

"Oh, yes. Of course, there's plenty for all. We tend to overdo it with the food around here."

"Yes, I remember when we were kids, we'd bring food to the local shelter after dinner. It was always our job to distribute the leftovers."

I nodded and smiled. It was a pleasant memory. "We've got a group of young people coming over shortly to do their holiday service hours for school. They'll transport the food and pass out plates to anyone who wants or needs them."

"It's nice that y'all are carrying on the tradition. As a boarding student whose parents sometimes forgot it was Thanksgiving, I always appreciated your family including me in their holiday dinners."

Seth hadn't ever seemed angry or resentful at his parents' lack of attention, just detached from them in a way I couldn't imagine. My family fed anyone who was alone or needed a meal. "How are your parents?" I asked politely.

"My mother lives in Paris, and my father passed away a couple of years ago from a massive heart attack. They were divorced. I see Mom every year or two, depending on if she's available when I travel abroad."

"Do you do a lot of traveling?" I was curious about how his life looked now.

He shrugged. "Here and there. Mostly for consulting or architectural conferences. I usually get to Europe at least once a year for a couple of weeks."

I couldn't imagine the luxury of taking such a trip—or having the time away from the diner. "That sounds amazing."

"I could take you with me next time I go." His gloved hand covered mine, and he gazed into my eyes. He was serious.

"Where were you the last ten years? *Now* you come here and offer to take me to Europe? Do you know how hard I've worked and how much I could've used your help over the years?"

"Kayla, I wanted to be here for you. My work—it's been erratic. It's taken me all over, and for years I didn't have much control over my schedule because I worked for a big firm. Now that I'm in charge, I can schedule projects in advance."

"My work's been erratic too. And there's no way I could leave the diner for a week or two. It's my whole life." I glanced up to make sure no one was near enough to hear our conversation. But nobody paid us any mind. All were busy helping restore the kitchen and dining room to its pre-dinner state.

"Maybe it shouldn't be. You deserve some free time, don't you?"

I shook my head at his idiocy. "What I deserve doesn't translate to my reality. I took over the running of the diner from Daddy because it's our family business. It's completely hands-on."

"Yes, I know. I didn't mean to diminish your work. I just wish you had more time for yourself."

"You don't get to wish that. Only I do." I stacked the to-go containers onto a waiting tray and transferred them to an open space on the counter to clear our workspace.

"Listen, I completely understand how you feel about my leaving and not coming back. But I honestly believed you were coming to meet me at UT. Then, when you never did, I lost control of my time and followed my education and career opportunities."

"I didn't expect you to come back here to live necessarily, but I did believe you would check in on me and figure out how to make it work between us." It had been the loneliest time in my life without Seth after my mom died. "I needed you."

"I was young and stupid. Looking back, I hate myself for deserting you." His brow furrowed in an ashamed expression.

"So, I forgive you for being young and selfish. But I'm not

going backward. Reliving this with you here isn't the best use of my time."

"No, I suppose it isn't the best thing for either of us, is it?"

"Nope. After I clean up here, I have to get ready for the tree lighting." I pulled off my gloves and tossed them in the nearest open trash bag.

The annual tree lighting ceremony was the kickoff for the Christmas season in Cherry Creek. Sometime after everyone finished their Thanksgiving dinner, we made our way in front of the courthouse.

It was tradition for families to bring special ornaments to hang on the tree. These ornaments bore the dates of Christmases up until this year. Some folks had twenty or more ornaments, depending on how many years they'd participated in the tradition. It was a sentimental time and brought back memories of times past and loved ones who were no longer with us. It was a celebration of community and continuity.

With Daddy's help, I loaded his truck with collapsible tables to serve free hot cocoa, cider, baked goods, and candy canes. The Cordial Diner's logo hung on a banner in front of the table. It was a community service but also ingratiated neighbors and customers alike.

Several other local businesses set up tables alongside ours to sell or give away samples of their products. The pet hospital gave out dog treats on our left, and on the right, Miss Dottie from Dottie's Chocolates handed out delicious samples. Gifts and Bits displayed their holiday cinnamon, vanilla, and Pine candles for purchase two tables over.

As I carefully poured steaming hot cocoa and topped it with tiny marshmallows, I noticed Milton heading my way. I sighed, hoping to avoid his inevitable invitation for our next date. So far, I'd not seen Seth, which was a relief after our earlier conversation.

"Hi, Kayla. Wow, that looks great. It's gotten cold, hasn't it?" Milton rubbed his hands together.

The weather was always a safe topic. "Yes, they are calling for snow tomorrow night." I'd worn a fuzzy white beanie with my down coat and favorite red wool scarf. I had my gloves in my coat pocket, just in case.

"May I?" he gestured toward one of the cups.

"Of course. Help yourself." I offered him a candy cane, which he took and used to stir his cocoa, and then hung it on the inside of his cup.

"Hmm. This is so good," Milton said, sipping the steaming liquid.

Our small talk was comfortable and familiar, so I relaxed and enjoyed the moment. "Is your mom coming tonight?" His mom, Betty, hadn't been in great health lately.

"Not tonight. She's got a little cold, and we decided not to risk it."

"Too bad. Please give her my best, won't you?"

He smiled. "Thanks, I will."

A group of tweens approached and scooped up brownies and hot cocoa, distracting me from Milton, who continued to stand nearby. I filled more cups, and when I looked up, I saw Seth heading my way carrying a small box with a green ribbon on top.

He greeted Milton first and then turned to me. "I brought you something."

"Oh, um, thanks." He held out the box, so I took it. "What is it?" Getting gifts from Seth made me uncomfortable, especially in the middle of the town square. The gossip would likely start about Seth and me faster than a duck on a June bug. I noticed Milton step away from us and head toward the tree.

"Something I meant to give you the Christmas after I left town." I couldn't tell anything from his expression, but I was curious.

Untying the bow, I lifted the lid. It was a silver ornament, slightly dulled with time, engraved with a heart and both of our initials and the date: *Christmas 2013.* "I'd intended to give this to you the Christmas after I started college, but I'd had to go to my parents for the holidays that year because my dad had surgery."

I stared at the ornament, absorbing its meaning. It symbolized our being together for the holidays, which we hadn't been. "Why are you giving this to me now?" I couldn't tell if the tears forming in my eyes were from the cold blast of wind or the punch of emotion Seth's gift sent into my gut.

"Remember, I came in after New Year's for a couple of days on my way back to school, but you were upset that I'd missed Christmas?"

Upset? I remembered being an emotional wreck because my mom wasn't responding to chemo, and the doctors had decided to place her in hospice care. And I remembered Seth not being there for me. "I don't remember your dad having surgery that year."

"It wasn't life-threatening, but my mom insisted on my being there. I didn't tell you because you had so much going on then, and I didn't give you the ornament in January because I thought it would only remind you that I hadn't come to the tree lighting."

"It was never about the tree lighting, just so you know. I was *upset* because my life was melting down, and you weren't there. We'd made promises to each other, and you skipped out on them." I could feel myself shaking with anger. Angry that he'd been so obtuse about my emotions and angry that he was back here now, stirring up old feelings I'd dealt with long ago.

Daddy had approached and was now handling the pouring and greeting. I stepped away, and Seth followed. "I know. I've had ten years to think about my shortcomings where you were concerned. I don't always say the right things at the right time, but I do understand that I completely misinterpreted how hard and awful things were for you and your family. I'd been away from your day-to-day struggles during that time."

"I appreciate that you thought about me enough to bring this along when you came here, but it's completely insignificant now." His honest explanation soothed my angst, but he was still being obtuse. How did any of this help us now?

"You've never been insignificant to me, even if it seemed that way." It was obvious that he was sincere.

I almost leaned into him; I really almost did. But my heart needed protection at this moment, and if I became weak, it would allow Seth to hurt me again. I couldn't allow it.

"Thank you for the ornament, Seth." My tone announced that I was done with this conversation, and I stepped behind the table to resume my duties.

Seth stared at me for a long moment, then turned and walked away. Just as the countdown ended, and the Christmas season began with thousands of colored lights illuminating the enormous tree. The joy of the event evaporated the moment he'd left.

Eight

Seth's plan had blown up in his face. How could he get through to Kayla? *Could* he get through to her? Sitting on a stool at the Inn's empty bar, he pondered through two fingers of bourbon, wishing with all his heart that things weren't so messed up.

The ornament was proof that he'd intended to be with her that first year. Proof that he'd still loved her and wanted to spend his life with her, despite their being apart. But all it seemed to do was reinforce that he'd let her down at the worst point in her life.

Seth had a job to do here in Cherry Creek, so maybe he should resist his constant craving to see Kayla and concentrate on the renovation instead. Hard to do, but he still had some time here to try and figure things out.

Seth paid his tab. The bartender must be the only person in town not out hanging ornaments on the Cherry Creek Christmas tree. "Sorry, you're stuck behind the bar while everyone celebrates outside."

He smiled and pointed to his nametag, which read Jason Weinstein.

"Ah."

Being here at Christmas time brought back more than memories of Kayla. He recalled the loneliness of not having a loving, nurturing family. He'd relied on Kayla's family for a sense of home, where they discussed things openly, and nobody got stinking drunk to help deal with their problems. He laughed at the irony as he looked down at the bourbon still in his glass. Despite the current drink, he'd not gone that route. It would've been easy, but having Mr. and Mrs. Doyle as role models at a crucial time in his life had deterred such destructive behavior.

His parents had finally divorced and lived a continent apart from each other before his dad's heart attack. Not having had siblings or parents to count on emotionally, his life had become about his career. Sure, he had friends and dated some, but returning here made him realize how much he'd missed Cherry Creek. With Kayla, he'd been happy. He'd been content here in this tiny Tennessee town without much to do besides hang out with her and eating Sunday dinner with the Doyle family. And there was no better place to be during the Christmas season.

Setting the drink on the bar, he stood and slapped a generous tip for Justin Weinstein. "Thanks, buddy."

"You have a good one, sir."

Seth nodded and took the elevator up to his room on the third floor. His window faced the town square, and as he stared outside, he saw the enormous tree with its thousands of colored lights. Something shifted within him. After a decade of moving around and never feeling like he belonged, he did tonight. Even if Kayla didn't want him back.

I deboned the second turkey from yesterday's feast, reheated the large pot of cranberry sauce, and pulled out three loaves of fresh bread. The special today would be turkey-cranberry sandwiches with a side of sweet potato casserole. The second enormous pan of sweet potatoes was untouched. It should last most of the day—certainly through the lunch crowd.

Business was brisk, with folks coming in and out of the cold to warm up and grab coffee, a snack, or hot cocoa. It was tradition for all the shops and restaurants in town to put up their Christmas décor today. The place would transform by the end of the day into a winter wonderland that rivaled any Hallmark movie set. The snow was due later this evening, right on schedule for the finishing touch.

My student employees had pulled out the bins and boxes of Christmas stuff from the storage room and were busy pulling down Thanksgiving artwork and replacing it with all the shiny tinsel, greenery, and red bows we'd gathered over the years. Since the diner boasted huge plate-glass windows, the center one was the perfect place for a painted holiday mural. Brett, a senior art student at CCA, had shown me a mock-up he'd done with jolly reindeer, snow, and a big fat Santa Clause surrounded by holly and jingle bells.

I'd commissioned him to paint it across the windows in front, and he was currently unwrapping the window paints and brushes I'd bought the last time I'd gone to the arts and crafts store the next town over.

Daddy cranked up the local radio station that played nonstop Christmas music from now until the new year. A similar scene was being set all over town. One day, the movie people would stumble upon us and stare in wide-eyed wonder at the perfection of our little Christmas town.

"Wow, things are looking fantastic." Seth spoke from behind me. My surprise wasn't as great as when he'd shown up the first couple of times. Despite what I'd said to him last night, my insides still quivered a little at the sound of his voice.

"Thanks." When I turned around to address him, I noticed something different in his eyes. Where before, he'd seemed a little sad and defeated. Today, his eyes seemed brighter and happier. I decided I should apologize for making things uncomfortable and weird. "Hey, listen, I'm sorry about last night. Your gift caught me off guard."

He shook his head and smiled. "All forgiven. If you have any left, I came here for one of those turkey-cranberry sandwiches." It seems a good night's sleep did us both some good.

My relief at his not holding a grudge for my behavior last night lifted a giant burden from my heart. I'd been pushing him away so hard that I couldn't just enjoy that the best friend I'd ever had was back in Cherry Creek for now. Because, despite how crazy in love we were, he'd been my person. Despite all my reasons for shutting him down, I wouldn't look beyond today. I smiled and pointed toward the bar. "Have a seat, sir, and I'll see what we can do for you."

He grinned even bigger then as if my response thrilled him. "You bet."

A hush fell throughout the diner when someone shouted, "Look, it's snowing."

We stared out the window at the fat snowflakes falling softly outside. With the temperature below freezing, the snow would coat everything in no time.

After he'd polished off two sandwiches and a tall Diet Coke, Seth offered to salt our sidewalk out front. I hadn't thought we would need to do it until tonight for tomorrow's business day. But the snow had come in earlier than was forecast.

I pointed to the back of the diner. "Thanks so much. The salt is in the storage room."

"I remember."

It snowed the rest of the afternoon as everyone in Cherry Creek continued their holiday prep. The town was like a

Christmas snow globe as far as the eye could see with large green wreaths with red bows gracing the lampposts all over town. But, unlike a snow globe, there were real things to worry about with this much snow coming down so quickly. We had a lot of elderly folks in town who would need to be checked on, along with making sure the roadways were clear for emergencies considering the blast of arctic air that had come with the sudden snow.

Daddy emerged from the back office, his heavy down coat zipped up. "It's time to go out and check on the folks. You gonna be okay without me this evening?" he asked.

I nodded. "Do you want me to go with you?" This was something we always did together when the cold hit. I imagined the police, fire, emergency services, and many community members were already gathering at the fire station.

"No, Baby. You stay here and finish up. Seth's going to head over there with me."

I turned to see Seth zipping up his coat in preparation to join the group. It hit me then what a good man Seth was. He'd been an exceptional teen, but I could see that he'd turned out as someone to be admired, the same as Daddy.

I looked at Seth. "Watch out for Daddy. He still thinks he's in his thirties."

He gave me a thumbs up and pulled up his hood, fastening it beneath his chin. "You got it. Have the hot coffee ready when we get back."

Driving was getting dicey on the slick streets as more snow accumulated and became icy, so time was of the essence. Mr. Doyle rode shotgun beside Seth. They'd taken Seth's truck because it had four-wheel-drive capabilities, whereas Mr.

Doyle's old truck did not. "Does Miss Judy still live up on the right?" Seth asked and pointed to the little house.

"Yes, and she's our first stop. Pull in behind her car." Mr. Doyle pointed to the woman's driveway. "Her kids have been begging her to move to the assisted living, but she's stubborn. I don't blame her because I understand completely, except that she's fallen a couple of times in the past few months." Miss Judy had seemed elderly ten years ago.

They exited the truck, stepped onto the porch, and rang the doorbell. They heard shuffling and banging, and then Miss Judy opened the front door. "Hey there, handsome fellows. Want a cup of coffee?"

Mr. Doyle laughed at the woman's spunk. "Snow's getting pretty heavy. We stopped by to make sure your heat is working and see if you needed anything."

She looked past Mr. Doyle at Seth, standing just behind the older man. "Is that you, Seth Jacobs? Goodness, young man, it's been a minute."

"Yes, ma'am. It's great to see you."

"I hope you've decided to marry our Kayla, finally."

Seth didn't know how to answer that. "She's a tricky one. Maybe one day."

Miss Judy laughed. "Well, y'all can move on to the next house. I'm fine. Got plenty of food, water, and heat. Might want to check on Old Jack outside of town. He isn't getting on too well lately."

"Will do. Please let us know if you need anything, okay?" Mr. Doyle said.

The two men moved slowly from house to house, checking on the residents of Cherry Creek. They then drove the ten minutes from town to check on Old Jack. "Is Old Jack sick?" Seth asked. Seth remembered him from when they were in high school. He didn't know the man's last name because everybody called him Old Jack—even though he hadn't seemed super old back then.

"He was in the hospital recently with a bad case of gout. Glad we're getting out here before conditions get too bad."

The driveway was steep, so they took it slow as the tires slipped on the snow. "No lights on." Seth noticed this immediately once they got to the top.

"No smoke coming from the chimney either. Usually has a fire going in the fireplace. Hmm." They knocked on Old Jack's door and waited. No response. "I'm going to try the door. It's not like him not to answer," Mr. Doyle said, frowning as their boots crunched in the snow.

Seth knocked, but there was no answer. The door was unlocked, and the house was freezing. "Jack?" They went from room to room, calling the man's name.

"Let's try the barn." The big hay barn sat about fifty feet from the house. "He sometimes hangs out there." Mr. Doyle pointed to the large, weathered structure.

Chickens squawked and scattered as they opened the barn door. "Jack? You in here?"

"Over here, young fellow." The older man was wrapped in a blanket sitting beside a kerosene heater that had been around longer than either of them.

"You scared us, Jack. Why aren't you in the house?" Mr. Doyle asked.

"I was out here feeding the animals. I might've taken a little nap in my chair for a bit. When I woke up, the snow was already falling. I decided to ride it out here. Path is too slick now." He pointed an arthritic finger in that direction.

"Well, let's get you back to the house and build a fire so you can wait out the snow."

"I thank y'all kindly. I was afraid to try it myself."

They gently wrapped the woolen blanket around the man

and helped him back into his house, extinguishing the heater to prevent a fire hazard. Once they'd set the thermostat to a comfortable number and gotten a roaring fire going in the fire-place, they replenished the firewood on the hearth from outside and made sure Old Jack was set for food. Thankfully, he had a full refrigerator and several frozen TV dinners in the freezer.

"Jack, you call us if you need us, you hear?"

Jack nodded, and his eyes caught Seth's. "Good to have you back, my boy."

"It's good to be home, sir." Yes, home. This was his home.

It was slow-going as he backed the truck down the slick gravel drive, now covered in slushy snow and ice. Just as Seth managed to get back on the main road, he heard a loud crack and a splintering sound.

Nine

I WAS RELIEVED THAT SETH WAS OUT IN THE WEATHER WITH DADDY. Lately, I worried that Daddy too often took on jobs of much younger men in service of his neighbors. He didn't realize he was just as old as those he helped in the community.

The diner was cozy and fully decorated, thanks to my little staff of dedicated servers and Roger, our cook. But the weather was awful outside, and I tried not to worry about Daddy and Seth. They'd only been gone about an hour and a half, but I doubted I could relax until they were both back here, safe and sound.

This weather was beautiful but could be deadly in the wrong circumstances.

My phone buzzed, signaling a call. The screen read, Cherry Creek Medical Center. I answered immediately. "Hello?"

"Kayla, this is Jenny from the hospital. Your daddy and Seth Jacobs were in an accident."

My heart stopped beating for a second. "Are they—*alright?*" my voice hitched on a sob.

"Your daddy's okay—just some cuts and bruises. But we aren't sure about Seth. A tree fell on top of the truck on the driver's side. He needs surgery and has you listed as his emergency contact. We need you to come and sign some forms ASAP."

"I'm on my way." Relief that Daddy was okay warred with paralyzing fear for Seth. I barely remember pulling my heavy coat and boots on before I ran outside into the snow, across the town square, past the giant Christmas tree, and straight to the hospital's emergency department.

I stepped up to the desk where Jenny sat at her computer. She looked up and immediately stood, handing me a clipboard. "Here. Sign these."

I hardly read a word, knowing that Seth's surgery was delayed until I'd signed them. Jenny grabbed the clipboard the minute I'd finished. "Let me get these back there to surgery, then I'll come, and we can talk."

I turned from the desk, noticing the waiting room was nearly full. I recognized many of the folks waiting for treatment. A few were coughing. Two had sprained or broken an ankle or foot, and several more held ice packs to their heads or other extremities. I sat down in the nearest chair, waiting for Jenny to return. Bearing witness to all these injured people brought home the fact that Seth was in real jeopardy.

I pressed a hand to my heart. He *had* to be okay. I'd pushed him away and refused to listen. Now, I only wanted to see his crooked grin and hear everything in his heart. What if I never got the chance?

Jenny came around the desk toward me, and I stood. "Okay, let's go into the empty triage room to talk." She pointed to a closed door beside the big desk.

I nodded. "Thanks, Jenny."

She indicated a small chair next to an exam table for me to sit, and then she sat across from me on a rolling stool. "Here's what we know: Seth's got a head injury from one of the large tree branches coming through the window, and he's unconscious. A large cut on his head needs stitching, but they won't know how traumatic his brain injury is until they figure out how much swelling there is. The plan is to stop the bleeding and relieve any pressure with surgery."

"Brain surgery?" I croaked the words.

"Yes. I know it's scary, but he's getting the best possible care."

"Do we even have a brain surgeon in Cherry Creek?"

Jenny nodded. "Last year, we hired a neurologist who lives about thirty minutes away. Luckily, he was already here treating a seizure patient."

"Where's Daddy?"

"He's resting in a treatment room. He'll be super sore tomorrow, but otherwise, he's okay. Would you like to see him now?"

"Yes. Please." Once Jenny had told me that Daddy was okay, seeing him hadn't felt as urgent. Now that I knew Seth's condition—or kind of knew it—I wanted only to see my daddy.

Jenny led me into a hallway from the triage room. She knocked on the door, and I heard Daddy say, "Come in."

He lay there on the narrow bed, a bandage on his head and right arm in a sling. "Hi, Baby."

I ran over to his side and gently hugged him. "I was so worried about you."

"How's Seth?" he asked, concern in his gaze.

"I don't know yet. He's heading into surgery now." I tried to keep my voice from breaking, but my lip quivered.

"Oh, honey. He's a strong one. Let's focus on that, okay?"

I nodded, trying to keep my composure. Inside, I could feel myself unraveling with fear that I'd missed my chance with Seth. Our chance. The last chance. "He's got to be okay, Daddy. I love him." A single tear slid down my cheek.

Daddy smiled. "Of course you do, Baby. You always have."

᪥

Seth's head hurt. *What happened?* A beeping sound made him flinch every time it sounded. He tried to open his eyes against the bright light. "Are you with us, Seth?" A strange man's voice spoke from directly in front of him. "C'mon, open your eye."

Seth made a Herculean effort and managed to open his right eye. The other one wouldn't budge.

"Here you are. Welcome back. I'm Doctor Kingston." The man speaking wore a white coat over green scrubs. He looked to be fifty-ish with salt-and-pepper hair.

"What happened?" Seth said it aloud this time.

"You got the business end of a falling tree."

He remembered then. They'd been leaving Old Jack's place, and he'd heard a crack overhead. "It hurts."

"Totally expected. We'll get some pain meds in you as soon as we determine your condition. Right now, we need you wide awake so you can show us how you're doing."

"Where's Mr. Doyle? Is he okay? Did someone call Kayla?" *Kayla.* "I need to see Kayla."

"Kayla's in the waiting room. I'm going to sit you up a little so we can have a look, okay? Then, we'll call her in."

The movement of the electric bed sent pain radiating throughout his skull and left eye. "*Agh.* It hurts."

"Okay, let's have a look. Open your right eye." Seth opened his right eye, wondering why he couldn't open the left one.

"Good. Your pupil looks great. Tell me your name and birthday if you can."

Seth did. Dr. Kingston asked him to move his fingers and make a fist, along with a few other basic requests.

"Good. What's the last thing you remember?"

Seth told him about driving around to check on people and then about Old Jack. "I heard a loud noise but can't remember anything after that."

"That would be about the time the tree almost flattened the cab of your pickup."

"My truck?"

"Your truck is replaceable, Seth, but your brain isn't. You seem to be in command of your faculties, which is a relief. The pain will be your companion for a few days or even weeks. I'll need you to return if you notice blurred vision, pressure in your head or eye, or dizziness."

"What's wrong with my left eye?" He put up a hand to feel a bandage over it.

The doctor sighed, and Seth tightened. *Now for the bad news.* "Your eye was damaged. You'll have a nasty pirate-like scar across it, I'm sorry to say, but we won't know about your vision until you heal from the surgery. We had to call over an ophthalmologist to help during surgery. He did what he could to mitigate damage to your retina. I wish I had more and better news, but only time will tell. Don't remove the bandage until you come back to see us in a week. Until then, you'll need to take it slow and easy to avoid detaching your retina."

Seth couldn't believe what he was hearing. "I'm going to be blind?"

"There's a chance you'll recover some of your vision in that eye. You're lucky to be alive, talking, and eating with a fork at this point, considering the head trauma. An eye patch isn't the worst thing that could happen."

The doctor's words sank in. "Thank you."

"My pleasure. Now, shall we get Kayla in here?" The doctor inclined his head toward an attendant signaling that it was okay.

Kayla burst in, barely waiting for the doctor to move out of the way. "Are you alright? Oh, Seth, I was so afraid." She grabbed his hand and held it up to her cheek.

Seth smiled at hearing her voice as he turned to face her. "You were the first thing I thought about when I woke up. How's your daddy?"

She smiled at him. "He's okay."

"I might lose my vision." He pointed to his covered eye.

Kayla smiled sadly. "Better your vision than your life. I can handle you with a sexy scar."

"Can you handle me staying here in Cherry Creek?"

Her eyes widened. "You mean, you want to live here permanently?"

He nodded and then winced from the pain of it. "I don't want to pressure you, but since I've been back, I realized this is my home. This town and its people. I'm content here—even if we can't make things work between us. Are you okay with that?"

"Okay? I thought I would lose you and our last chance at being together. I love you, Seth. I always have."

Her words flowed into his heart and healed him in that instant. Seth stroked her hand, looking at her through his good eye. "I've never stopped loving you, Kayla Doyle." She leaned down and kissed his lips. He laughed weakly. "This isn't how I pictured it, you know?"

She laughed, tears in her eyes. "I don't need perfect. I just need you."

Ten

I COULDN'T BELIEVE IT WAS ALREADY CHRISTMAS EVE AS WE GATHERED around Daddy's Christmas tree, the colored lights casting a warm glow. The snow had hung around, making this white Christmas a magical one.

Seth had seen a retina specialist last week and had gotten promising news. He was starting to see light and shadows with his right eye. It would take some time for things to improve, unfortunately. So, for now, he was stuck with a healing eye patch. He had a dark red, jagged scar from the top of his head across his eye to his cheek.

"Are you ready?" Seth asked, his gaze filled with such contentment. It made me sigh with happiness.

I took his hand, and we took our seats for the annual gift swap. Every year we drew names with our employees and friends. The rule was to buy or make one gift for the recipient whose name you drew and to donate another to the Cherry Creek Community Center. It was a lovely tradition, and I looked forward to it every year.

When it was Seth's turn, he grinned. "So, I haven't had a chance to do much shopping."

"So, whose name did you get?" I asked.

"Yours."

"What a coincidence." I eyed him a little skeptically.

"Okay, maybe I did a little switching around, but nobody seemed to mind." He grinned at me as he dropped onto one knee and pulled a tiny box from his pocket. "Your dad was kind enough to help me out."

"Seth?" Despite his recent scars and injuries, I searched his gaze, loving him with all my heart.

"Since I couldn't return to Knoxville and get the one I'd bought for you years ago, Mr. Doyle assured me you wouldn't mind." He opened the lip to the red velvet box, and my heart nearly exploded with emotion and love. "Kayla Doyle, will you marry me? Finally?" His voice quivered a little as he said the words.

I stared down at my mother's wedding ring, trying to control my tears while allowing the moment's joy to settle into my soul. I stared into Seth's one good eye. "Yes, I will marry you —finally."

Seth slipped the diamond solitaire onto my finger, and I slid into his arms. The group burst into cheers and congratulations. I found Daddy's gaze. He looked so happy, yet I knew how hard this must be for him. I was his little girl.

Daddy picked up a glass from the table, where he'd filled flutes with Champagne in anticipation of this moment. "A toast, everyone. Gather 'round and grab a glass."

"To my precious daughter and her true love. May the two of you share the kind of love I had with your mom."

"Here, here." I heard voices in the background echo Daddy's sentiment, but I was so immersed in my feelings, the sound was muffled. I felt Momma's presence then—her joy that matched mine.

Seth handed me a flute of Champagne. "This was my Christmas wish."

"Mine too." I lifted my lips to his. He was my home, my love, and my forever Christmas wish.

I had a revelation as I thought about the book sitting on my bedside table. Once Upon a Christmas Kiss. I was a believer, for sure.

I could feel the magic.

The End

About the Author

Susan Sands_pulls her stories from the very Southern settings where she grew up in rural Louisiana. She is the published author of nine full-length Southern romantic novels and four novellas. Her tenth book will be released by Tule Publishing in May of 2024. Susan's novels are currently available in digital, print, and audio from all online retailers and many independent bookstores.

Once Upon a Christmas Party

CHRISTY HAYES

One

Erin Collier zipped her white parka and tucked her chin into the handmade scarf Mrs. Granger had knitted for her last year at Christmastime, dodging the bitter East Tennessee wind and a mound of dog poop someone had left steaming on the edge of the snow-covered road. She tugged on Fluffy's leash and pulled her neighbor's Bichon away from the offensive pile. "No, Fluff. Leave it, girl. We're better than that."

She also knew better than to leave that kind of mess in someone's yard for others to get in a lather about and start the Cherry Creek Reserve neighborhood grapevine humming, especially in the throes of a harsh winter when most residents were hibernating inside. With more than a little snow on the ground and the self-imposed isolation of winter upon them, it didn't take much to get the neighborhood tongues flapping. She found the extra disposable bags she carried for such occasions in her pocket and removed her mitten to dispose of the offending pile properly.

Bent over as she was with the plastic covering in her hand, Erin didn't see the large truck come around the corner until it was almost too late. She yanked on Fluffy's leash, pulling the small dog out of the road and away from the speeding vehicle. "What the ...," she said to no one in particular. Fluffy wasn't listening, not with Mr. Johnson's terrier barking at them from his perch on the couch by the sunroom window. "That truck almost ran us over."

Her indignation was short-lived when she realized the truck belonged to a moving company and had pulled onto Cordial Lane—the only street in the fifty-five plus neighborhood with a recently sold home. The former owner suffered the effects of a recent stroke, and she'd had to move into the retirement community on the other side of town. The home had only been on the market for a few days before the sold sign had gone up and the construction trucks had arrived, sending the gossip mill into overdrive with speculation over their soon-to-be new neighbor.

Erin stood, tied a knot in the baggie, and adjusted her route to get a sneak peek at CCR's newest homeowner. No sooner had she turned onto Cordial Lane when another speeding vehicle blew past, blaring its horn, and jolting Erin nearly out of her skin.

The driver of the luxury SUV didn't even slow down as the snow in his wake dusted their faces and caked their coats, leaving Erin in a fuming state of disarray and Fluffy shaking in her too-thin sweater. "Unbelievable!"

Erin wiped the snow from her eyes and would have marched right over to give the street racer a piece of her mind about speeding in a residential neighborhood filled with old people, but Fluffy had other ideas. The dog put the brakes on and whimpered when Erin tried to encourage her forward. "Come on, Fluffy. Don't you want to tell this guy off? Let him know he's not more important than his neighbors?"

Fluffy didn't care. She stood shaking in the near-freezing

temperatures and bone-chilling wind, refusing to take another step in any direction that didn't lead her home.

"Okay, okay," Erin said. "I guess I should cool off before I dress down our new neighbor." As head of the CCR welcome committee, Erin needed to calm her temper before presenting their newest homeowner with his or her welcome-to-the-neighborhood basket and recapping the lame but necessary community rules. She gave the black sports vehicle one last snarl and made her way back to Fluffy's home two manicured streets over. Fluffy would settle in for her afternoon nap and Erin could fill Mrs. Wilson in on her first interaction with their new neighbor.

Erin's phone rang just as she'd stopped to deposit the baggie of dog poop into Mrs. Wilson's trash can. She used her teeth to pull off her mitten and answered the call with a smile in her voice. "Gram. How's Costa Rica? You miss the Tennessee winter yet?"

Her grandmother gave her signature smokey laugh. "Not even a little. How are you faring, sweet girl?"

"I'm hanging in there. We had our first snow of the season a couple of days ago. It looks like you're going to miss another white Christmas."

When Louise chuckled, Erin felt a longing deep into her bones to hug her grandmother. Her grandmother was both young and young at heart, but Gram had been gone too long for Erin's comfort.

"Good," Gram said. "I've had enough white Christmases to last a lifetime. Besides, I prefer white sand Christmases—and you would too if you'd ever leave that hamlet you call home."

"It's our home, and how *could I* leave when you're never home?"

"All you have to do is hop on a plane."

"Who would water the plants?" Erin asked. "Who would

pay the bills? Who would make sure the pipes don't freeze while you're off on another adventure?"

Her grandmother had the nerve to scoff. "Sweetheart, they make automatic watering thingies. I pay my bills online, and if the pipes freeze, one of my nosey neighbors would call me and a plumber as soon as they shuffle to their phones."

Anyone overhearing their conversation would assume Erin was the seventy-six-year-old grandmother and Louise was her twenty-seven-year-old granddaughter who'd moved in two years ago and had never left. "You're lucky to have such wonderful neighbors."

"Lucky and cursed in equal measure."

"Just lucky." Erin knew all too well what it was like living alone and lonely in the frigid days of winter. "Take my word for it."

Mrs. Wilson poked her head out of the front door. "Erin, honey. Fluffy looks cold."

"Coming," Erin said to Mrs. Wilson and made her way up the driveway toward the house. "I've got to go," she said to her grandmother.

"Has that old June Wilson got you walking her mutt around the block because of a little snow on the ground?"

Erin fought to keep the frustration from her voice. "Fluffy is a purebred, Gram, and I enjoy helping our neighbors. With her arthritis acting up, it's not safe for Mrs. Wilson to navigate the slick streets."

"You keep telling yourself that and those old coots will be so busy taking advantage of your kind heart that you won't have time to do your job."

"I've got plenty of time to do my job. Besides, I need a break from the computer every now and again. If I can help a friend by walking her dog around the block, why not be a good neighbor?"

"Fine, but don't blame me if you get fired."

"I work for myself, Gram." She'd explained her online graphic design job to her grandmother a hundred times or more. "I'm not going to get fired."

"Who's getting fired?" Mrs. Wilson asked as Erin handed over Fluffy's leash.

"No one, Mrs. Wilson. No one's getting fired."

"Oh. Okay, dear." She pulled her cable-knit sweater tight around her neck. "Thank you for walking Fluffy."

"I'm happy to help."

"You're an angel sent from heaven." Mrs. Wilson blew her a kiss and closed the door against the gust of cold air.

"Like I said," Gram continued, "she's taking advantage. She convinced you she can't walk her dog around the block even though she was crowned pickleball champion last year."

"It's cold and the sidewalks are icy."

Not that Gram would know. She'd been touring Central America for over two months with her cyber-dating gentleman friend from Indiana. When Erin had dropped Gram at the Knoxville airport in early October, the leaves were still on the trees and gearing up for their epic explosion of color. Winter had been nothing more than a quiet whisper on the twilight breeze.

"Well, you enjoy the cold air and the slick roads. I've got a hot date waiting for me to go ziplining in the jungle."

Ziplining in the jungle? Erin bit her tongue to stop the lecture from leaping past her lips. The last time she'd tried to warn Gram about taking unnecessary risks during her vacations, she'd received a memorable tongue lashing in response where she was told to both mind her business and live a little. She'd taken the message to heart, even though it went against every instinct in her body.

The thought of losing her precious Gram in a pointless accident on a fool's errand to relive her youth was unimaginable. Erin's workaholic parents couldn't be bothered, so Erin had given up her no-so-great life in Atlanta to move to Cherry Creek when Gram needed help while her broken ankle healed. Getting to live with her only living grandparent, who'd always been more legend than reality, was one of the best things that had ever happened to Erin. Not only had she found a family member who loved and appreciated her for the free-spirited woman she was and not the robot her powerhouse parents wanted her to become, but she'd found an entire neighborhood of people who loved and accepted her, too.

"How is Mr. Fellows?" Erin asked about Gram's internet friend. "I hope you two are behaving yourselves."

Gram let out a cackling belly laugh, mocking Erin's prim tone. "Sweetheart, we're having the time of our lives. I'll send you a picture with the monkeys."

Gram hung up and left Erin shaking her head at the phone. "Monkeys? For the love ..."

Two

BROCK BARTLETT LOOKED AROUND THE SINGLE-STORY HOME HE'D recently purchased for his grandfather in the active adult community of Cherry Creek Reserve, inspecting the renovations completed according to his scrupulous specifications. His Nashville decorator had done a nice job coordinating the backsplash, granite countertops, and neutral but masculine interior color to change the decidedly feminine house into a home his grandfather would be proud to call his own.

Brock had to admit the place looked better than expected. When his grandfather expressed an interest in returning to his childhood hometown of Cherry Creek, Tennessee, Brock had gotten busy looking online for the perfect location. The community of Cherry Creek Reserve checked all his boxes. With its one story, open concept floor plans and amenities that rivaled Brock's downtown Nashville condo, CCR provided the perfect low-maintenance lifestyle his grandfather had more than earned. As soon as a house hit the market, Brock had bought it, sight unseen.

He'd had a bear of a time finding a reliable contractor willing to start immediately in the small mountain town. With the Christmas holidays quickly approaching, Brock heard every excuse in the book.

"I got family coming into town." *Who cares?*

"My crew is bare boned over Christmas." *Sounds like a management problem.*

"We try to slow down around the holidays." *Must be nice.*

Brock hadn't taken a vacation in years, not since his innovative substance abuse clinics had taken off and the once rocky startup had grown by leaps and bounds into every state in the nation. Thanks to his grinding pace and relentless work ethic, he planned to triple their footprint within the next year.

Once he'd finally found a company willing to do the renovations, Brock had used what he'd learned building his business —he'd sweetened the deal with a little extra cash to keep the crew on task. He wanted the job done before Christmas, so he'd have time to get his grandfather's place move-in ready before his pawpaw arrived later in the week. It was the least Brock could do to help the only relative who'd never asked him for anything.

He walked into the master bedroom ahead of the two guys carrying the king-size bed Brock would later assemble and pointed to the wall where he'd determined the bed should sit. "Set the box right there, guys," Brock said. "Right between the windows."

The room carried the chemical smell of fresh paint and new carpet, a headache-inducing combination he hoped would lessen in the next few days. Too bad the weather was so cold and snowy, or he could have opened the windows and aired the place out. Brock had his work cut out for him with the guys unloading their truck faster than he could tell them where everything went.

He shed his coat and tossed it onto an unopened box, prepared to rearrange and unpack the kitchen before the stacks of boxes created an impenetrable wall. He looked for the box cutter he'd purchased from Harley's Hardware along Cherry Creek's Main Street while retracing his steps through the house.

Considering his grandfather had grown up poor—holes in his shoes, working by age ten, going hungry when there wasn't enough food level of poor—Brock had admittedly low expectations for the town of Cherry Creek. Driving through on his way to CCR, his perception had changed. The picturesque community featured a restored theater, a handful of quaint shops and restaurants, and a gorgeous snow-covered cherry grove fronting the historic courthouse. Cherry Creek, Tennessee, looked like a postcard for homespun goodness.

Realizing he must have left the box cutter in his car, Brock sidestepped the movers and squeezed outside, his breath steaming against the frosty winter sky. He spotted the bag on his passenger seat, reached across the console to grab it, and shut the door, eager to make his way back inside. Brock startled at the booming voice bellowing behind him.

"Hello there, new neighbor," said a burly man who was standing at the base of Brock's driveway wearing a black pea coat and matching fedora with funny looking flaps over his ears. He held the leash of a black and white dog that was sniffing the snow around his mailbox.

Brock gave a quick wave and turned back toward the house.

"How's the move going?" the man asked.

Brock stopped, turned, and tried his best to be pleasant. He didn't have the time or the interest in socializing with the neighbors. "The move is going well. Thanks for asking." He attempted to escape once again.

"I'm Harry Hafner." The man pointed over his shoulder. "Two houses down. Good to have you in the neighborhood."

"It's my pawpaw's place," Brock called. He would have bridged the gap between them, but without his coat on, his fingertips were going numb. "I'm just here to facilitate the move."

"You were quick on the draw," Harry said, oblivious to Brock's discomfort and impatience. "I've got some friends who've been trying to move into the neighborhood for almost a year. This house sold before I even knew it was on the market."

You snooze, you lose. The words were on the tip of Brock's tongue. He would never have pulled himself or his family out of poverty by waiting for good fortune. He learned a long time ago if he wanted something to happen, he had to work harder, smarter, and faster than everyone else. "We caught it early."

"What's your name, son, and where are you from?"

This guy may have nothing better to do than stand around in freezing temperatures shooting the breeze, but Brock certainly did. He eyed the movers setting the couch opposite the spot he'd picked out. "Brock Bartlett, and I'm from Nashville. My pawpaw grew up in Cherry Creek."

"Is that so?"

"Yes, sir." Brock shifted from foot to foot and rubbed his arm with his free hand. If he stood outside any longer, his teeth would start to chatter. "Listen, it was great to meet you, Mr. Hafner, but I've got to run."

"Of course, of course, don't let me keep you. Tell your pawpaw welcome to the neighborhood."

"Will do. He'll be here on Friday."

Harry gave a formal tip of his hat. "I look forward to meeting him."

Brock would have sprinted up the driveway if his feet weren't halfway frozen in his new leather oxfords. He quickly walked across the yard and zipped inside, grateful for the updated heating and air unit and the blast of warm air that greeted him. His breath came out on a shudder. "Nosey old coot." He stopped the movers before they could return to the truck. "Hey, guys. How about we move the couch over here by this wall?"

The look he received told him he'd gotten to them just in time. The sooner they could empty the truck, the sooner they'd call it a day and probably hit the local tavern back in town. Their tip would reflect their less-than-enthusiastic attitude.

The guys lifted the couch, deposited it by the wall, and made their way back outside. Brock set the box cutter on the kitchen counter and started rearranging the boxes. As much as he'd like to multitask and get busy unpacking, his jaunt outside had taught him he couldn't afford to get distracted and leave the movers unsupervised.

Between directing the movers and going behind them to adjust the furniture, Brock marveled at the difference between the residents of Cherry Creek Reserve and his upwardly mobile Nashville neighbors. He'd lived in his condo for over two years and hadn't said more than three words to anyone living in his building. He hoped his grandfather was prepared for the kind of prying in Cherry Creek that his family provided on the regular —something Brock suspected was the impetus for his pawpaw's move.

Brock and Pawpaw shared a mutual disdain for the constant requests of his freeloading family. He'd rather take time off work to help his grandfather move than spend Christmas Day defending the tough love tactics he'd had to employ throughout the years whenever anyone came asking for money. Brock had done enough to get them out of their deplorable living situations. The rest was on them.

An hour and a half later, Brock watched the truck pull away from the drive and turned around to assess the damage. Boxes sat stacked three and four deep in each room, but thanks to his oversight, the furniture was where it belonged. He yanked his sleeves up to his elbows, grabbed the box cutter, and made his way to the guest bedroom.

The kitchen would have to wait. With the sun slipping closer to the tops of the white-capped mountains in the distance, he needed to set up the guest room so he'd have a place to rest his head when he eventually ran out of energy.

Three

ERIN UNLOCKED THE CHERRY CREEK RESERVE CLUBHOUSE AND scooted inside before Darlene Richardson and her flock of loyal party elves spotted her. With the neighborhood Christmas party only one week away and her co-host Mrs. Richardson down with a nasty cold, Erin had taken matters into her own hands and went to look inside the clubhouse storage closet. She had so many great ideas for this year's bash—ideas her co-host Darlene had poo-pooed—and she wanted to see what they had on hand to spice up the boring potluck Darlene had insisted they throw yet again.

She still smarted when thinking back to their one and only design meeting before Darlene had crashed hard with a cough and a cold and put herself to bed. If Mrs. Richardson had any idea how many hours Erin had devoted to planning the party and the excitement she'd quashed with her bah-humbug attitude, she might have changed her mind about all the fun activities Erin had proposed.

Who wouldn't want to participate in Christmas Carol karaoke? Or take some memorable pictures in a makeshift photo booth? Or mix things up with a lively secret Santa gift exchange? Mrs. Richardson, for one. And her gaggle of gray-haired girlfriends all stepped right in line, even though more than one of them had visibly brightened at Erin's suggestions.

Darlene Richardson had been CCR's social chairwoman for going on seven years straight. In Darlene's mind, length of tenure outstripped sheer enthusiasm and creative vision every season of the year. Darlene's my-way-or-the-highway approach to fun had intimidated the residents away from considering a better alternative.

Erin walked through the common area, envisioning the party she'd planned in her head. A microphone and stage in the corner. The neighborhood Christmas tree bursting with festive lights and sparkling ornaments and the Christmas pickle ornament hidden somewhere inside—another fun contest Darlene had mocked. A hot chocolate bar on one end of the kitchen counter and a signature mocktail station at the other. A table by the window for the gingerbread house decorating contest. She glanced longingly at the mantle above the fireplace where she'd planned to hang the baby photo collage she'd already started creating for all the residents to guess who was whom.

"Stupid Darlene and her stupid ugly Christmas sweater contest," Erin muttered under her breath. With most of the residents in their seventies, half of their winter wardrobes would easily classify as ugly. And really, how many years could Mr. Granger walk away with the prize by wearing the sweater his wife had knitted with a stuffed reindeer attached to the front?

Erin stopped short when her conscience started stinging, a phenomenon that happened whenever her mean-spirited attitude reared its ugly head. She adored Mr. and Mrs. Granger—and his reindeer sweater deserved to win every year. Outside of her social committee pigheadedness, Darlene Richardson was one of the most accomplished women Erin had ever met. Even if the party was boring, at least Darlene had agreed to continue with Erin's suggestion from last year that they collect toys for the needy children. That was something to feel grateful for.

Erin ducked into the closet when she heard the front door open, feeling foolish for hiding from a bunch of people more than twice her age. When she recognized the telltale sound of Liza Fletcher humming loudly and chewing gum, she flung the closet door open wide so it wouldn't appear as if she was sneaking around.

"Whatcha doing?" Liza asked when Erin dragged a folded cardboard box out of the closet and into the main room.

"I'm going through the leftover Christmas decorations to see what we can use for the party."

Liza sputtered and waved her hand in the air. "Why bother? Those parties are such a drag."

"Not for my lack of trying," Erin said, and then wished she'd kept her mouth shut. Liza and Darlene were friends from way back. Even though they sometimes fought like sisters, deep down they were tight as ticks.

"I know that, honey." Liza patted Erin on the shoulder. "So does everybody else. But some things around here are harder to change than the weather."

Erin didn't trust herself to get drawn into a discussion about Mrs. Richardson, so she abruptly changed the subject. "What are you doing here?"

Liza spun her key fob around her finger and chomped her wad of gum, sprinkling the stale air with the scent of spearmint. Although eighty-two, Liza had energy and sass to rival Gram's. "I can't find my yoga mat. I thought maybe I'd left it here after class last week. I was in a hurry to get out of here before Harry Hafner got a hold of my ear."

Erin choked back a laugh. "You didn't want to talk to Mr. Hafner?"

"That man ..." Liza shook her body as if she had a chill. "He's

CHRISTY HAYES

got a way of looking at me like he's seeing me naked—and I'm not a prude who doesn't mind catching the eye of a nice gentleman. But Mr. Hafner is *not* a gentleman. Anyway, I thought maybe I'd hightailed it out of here and left my mat by mistake."

"I haven't seen it, but take a look around."

"I bet that old clod took it with him so he could sniff it whenever he wanted," Liza said as she wandered away.

Erin closed her eyes and tried to snuff out the visual of Mr. Hafner holding and smelling Liza's yoga mat like a woman in his arms. Too late—the image had already formed. She cringed and brought her attention back to the box.

She rifled through bent and broken centerpieces, dented ornaments, and a pile of used candles. "Why do they keep this stuff?" she mumbled, shoving the box away and returning to the closet. She hefted another box into her arms and carried it to the kitchen, unfolded the flaps and stared inside. "What in the world is this?"

"What's what?" Liza asked, coming around the corner empty handed.

"This book." Erin carefully pulled the book from the box and stared at the forest green cover, running her fingertips over the mistletoe imprint under the title. "*Once Upon a Christmas Kiss.* It's so beautiful."

"I've never seen that before."

The binding creaked as Erin peeled back the cover and exposed the pages to the light. "It looks like a diary." She skimmed the inscription on the first page. "No, it's a story. A love story written by Miss Chambers."

Liza tilted her furrowed brow. "The old headmistress at Cherry Creek Academy?"

"Yes. I think I remember hearing about this when I was a student at the boarding school. I thought it was just a make-believe legend."

"A make-believe legend about what?"

Erin read the dedication. "Miss Chambers wrote her parents' love story down for a friend. See the inscription?"

"I don't have my glasses on. What does it say?"

"'To my dearest friend Charlotte. May your heart be filled with joy this Christmas season. I leave you with the long requested true love story of my parents from years ago. May it bring you the happiness and peace it has always brought to me —and maybe a love of your own. I will miss you sweet friend. Yours Affectionately, Elizabeth Chambers' If I remember right, Miss Chambers fell in love over Christmastime too."

Liza sputtered. "That sounds like a fairy tale."

"I thought so too." Erin flipped page after page, noting the handwritten comments in the margins. "But look at all these comments. 'This book is the real deal,'" Erin read aloud. "'A heartfelt thanks to Miss Chambers. I thought I'd never find that special someone, but I truly believe this book made it happen.' That doesn't sound like a fairy tale."

"Well, it sounds to me like either a giant coincidence or a whole lot of hooey. Trust me, honey, as a woman who's been around the block a time or two, true love doesn't come over Christmas like a gift from Santa. It takes hard work, dedication, and a truckload of luck."

"You don't believe in fairy tales?" Erin asked with more than a little sarcasm in her voice. She knew for a fact Liza had been married four times and constantly prowled for a fifth. Someone with that kind of optimism had to believe in fantasies.

"I believe that famous quote from Helen Keller that says something about how having a positive attitude gives you the faith to achieve your goal. If you believe you're going to meet the love of your life over Christmas, you're going to open your heart to the possibility. Just because some story weaves a pretty tale doesn't make it true."

"Well, that's a good point." Erin held out the book. "Why don't you take the book and read it? Maybe you'll find your one true love this Christmas."

Liza laughed and shook her curly white head. "Honey, with my luck, I'd fall head over heels for Mr. Hafner—and that ain't no fairy tale no matter how you try to spin it. Besides, I'm an audiobook girl. These old eyes get too tired to read most days. And I love listening to the different voices in my head. It's like my thoughts coming to life in the most delicious ways."

"I'm happy to record this story for you. I'm very good with computers and I like to think I've got a lyrical voice."

"I wouldn't put you to the trouble." Liza looked over Erin's shoulder and a grin sparked her wrinkles into action. "I knew it. There's my yoga mat. I did leave it here after class." She stepped around Erin and her pile of decorations to retrieve the hot pink mat. On her way out the door, she spun around, her tennis shoes squeaking in protest. "Why don't *you* take the book home and read it? You're too young to spend all your time with us old folks. You need a little love in your life before you end up like one of us."

Erin would love to spend her golden years in CCR surrounded by friends who were like family. "Happy and living your best life?"

"Alone and gossiping because we've got nothing better to do with our time. You're young. It's time you started acting like it and acting on it. If you need a fairy tale to open your heart to love, have at it, girl." Liza winked and opened the door. "That's my Christmas present to you this year."

Four

IN THE DEEPEST, DARKEST DEPTHS OF SLEEP, BROCK STRUGGLED TO ignore the annoying buzzing echoing from somewhere in the distance. He folded the pillow over his head and tried to place the maddening sound. It wasn't the buzzer in his condo ringing someone up. It wasn't his alarm—no way would he have chosen such an irritating sound. When it rang again, buzz buzz, followed by three peppy raps, Brock's sleep-addled brain knew his blessed time in bed had come to an abrupt end.

He forcibly opened his eyes and blinked around the too-bright room, trying to identify the scene. Recognition hit like a solid left hook. He was in Pawpaw's place. The guest room, specifically. He recalled stripping down to his boxers and tumbling into bed just a few short hours ago when he could no longer trust himself to handle sharp blades and operate power tools without risking life and limb.

He tossed the covers aside, set his feet on the floor, and rubbed his palms against his face. Whoever was banging on the door—he scowled at his phone—at eight fifteen in the morning, had better have a cup of coffee and a spine of steel for waking him up before he'd recharged his batteries. He felt every strained muscle in his back during his march through the maze of boxes to the front door.

He turned the deadbolt and yanked the door open wide, growling, "What?" at the trio of faces standing on his doorstep.

A woman with mink-brown hair and yellowish-brown eyes gaped at him from beneath the longest lashes he'd ever seen not manufactured in China and applied with glue. She wore a red knitted beanie with a huge furry pompom and matching gloves that complemented the rosy hue of her cheeks. She swaddled a basket of unknown objects against her puffy white parka. A couple of women old enough to be her grandmas flanked her on either side.

She looked him up and down and then marshaled her composure, closing her mouth and pasting on a smile that was as authentic as the fur on her hat. "Welcome to Cherry Creek Reserve," the younger woman croaked. "I'm Erin Collier, and this is Liza Fletcher and Patty Granger. We're from the welcome committee."

He took in the ragtag group, watched the grandmas bump elbows and gawk at the vicinity of his chest. As soon as Brock looked down, he realized he'd answered the door wearing nothing but his underwear—a greeting if there ever was one—and felt the glacier-cold breeze pelt his skin.

"Ummm," the young one said. "Would you like to put on a robe or"—she swallowed, and her eyes skittered away—"some clothes?"

Brock didn't own a robe. No self-respecting man did. However, that wasn't the point, not with his nipples freeze drying on his chest and an embarrassed woman and her pervy sidekicks watching his every move. With no other way to escape the cold, he stepped aside and waved them into the house. "Come on in."

They filed in one by one with Erin leading the way, her steps tentative and her shoulders hunched. She stopped just inside the foyer.

Brock closed the door and delved deep for his dignity, rubbing a hand over his chilled-to-the-bone flesh. "If you'll excuse me for just a moment." He didn't wait for their reply before hightailing it to the bedroom and retrieving yesterday's clothes from the floor. "Welcome committee," he mumbled under his breath. "Unwelcome committee is more like it."

He shoved his legs into his jeans and yanked the Henley over his head, grumbling as he corralled his frozen feet into socks. He contemplated dipping into the bathroom to brush his teeth but decided against it. Anyone who showed up before nine deserved to savor the smell of his morning breath.

He didn't make it out of the guest room before his conscience stopped him cold. This place was to be Pawpaw's home, and these women were his new neighbors. Being a Bartlett didn't mean much to his family, but to Brock and his pawpaw, it meant doing what was right even when you didn't want to. He pivoted into the bathroom for a quick tooth brushing and attempted to tame his out-of-control hair.

He found the ladies where he'd left them, congregating just inside the front door. With the type of greeting they'd received, he didn't blame them for not moving deeper inside the house—that and the multitude of boxes blocking their way. "Ladies, I'd offer you a coffee, but you woke me up, and I haven't found the pot in all the boxes just yet."

"That's okay," Erin said. She held out the basket in her hand. "This is for you. From us. The neighborhood, I mean."

Brock took the basket from her arms and surveyed the items hidden under a bouquet of clear cellophane. He didn't have a clue what he was looking at. "Ah ... thanks. Appreciate the gesture."

"There's an assortment of items in there from the restaurants and gift shops in town, including a bag of coffee grinds from the Cherish Café. There's also a gift card from Sal's Pizza and my favorite scented candle from Gifts and Bits."

"Plus, Erin's homemade cookies," one grandma added.

Erin's cheeks pinked adorably. "And my homemade cookies. We're sorry for stopping by so early."

"Some of us are," the other grandma said with a salacious wink at Brock. "Some of us, not so much."

"Liza!" Erin scolded, as if their ages were reversed.

The grandma that hadn't creepy-flirted with him stepped forward and squinted at his face. "You're awfully young looking for fifty-five."

Brock cracked his first smile of the day. "Ah, yeah. I'm not. This is my pawpaw's place. I'm in town from Nashville getting it set up before he arrives on Friday."

"Oh," Erin brightened, as if relieved Brock wasn't staying. "What's your pawpaw's name?"

"Ben. Ben Bartlett. I'm Brock, by the way."

"That's nice," Erin said with all the warmth of a wet blanket. What was her problem? "Where's your pawpaw from?"

"Here, originally. But he's lived outside of Nashville for the past thirty-plus years."

"Your pawpaw is from Cherry Creek?" Liza the Lecher asked. "Erin's grandmother is from Cherry Creek too. Born and raised."

"Is that so?" Brock asked with the same icy veneer as his youngest guest.

"Yep."

The way Erin popped her P told Brock all he needed to know. She didn't like him. Not one little bit. He didn't know why it bothered him so much. Other than waking him up earlier than he was ready to get out of bed, he'd never seen her before. "Well, maybe they know each other. Old friends from way back."

"Maybe," she said with her nose in the air.

"So," he said, perking up to do his own point scoring. "You live here with your grandmother?" There was no mistaking the censure in his voice.

She visibly stiffened. "Yes, I do."

"How ..." He paused, pursed his lips, and tried his best to look bored. "Exciting."

"Listen." She narrowed her eyes at him, and he mentally pumped his fist in victory. "I'm sure you haven't noticed, but CCR has a posted speed limit of twenty-five miles per hour. We'd appreciate if you and your guests would abide by the law."

Wow. She must have gotten up pretty early to shove that stick so far up her tailpipe. Brock straightened to his full height and puffed out his chest. "I'll do my best."

She fake-smiled at him and fluttered her long lashes. "That'd be great. Thank you."

They stood facing one another, their eyes deadlocked. The grandmothers stood silent like a couple of slack-jawed spectators.

"You've made some changes," the nervous grandma spoke up in an attempt to lighten the tension.

Brock hesitated before breaking eye contact with Erin. "Just a little updating. De-feminizing, if you will."

"I love the changes." Liza smiled up at him with adoration in her eyes. "So masculine. How old is your grandfather?"

Uh-oh. Pawpaw was in her sights before he'd even arrived. "He's seventy-seven."

"Is he in good health? Strong and"— she stroked her neck in a manner that made Brock want to take a shower—"handsome like his grandson?"

"He's in good shape." Brock took a deliberate step back. "Some say we favor."

"Let's hope," Liza purred.

Erin clapped her hands together like a camp counselor gathering her girls. "We need to get going."

No argument here. Brock was more than ready to hunt up the coffeepot and fish the bag of coffee out of the welcome basket and put them both to use. At least something good would come out of their unwelcome surprise. If Erin was looking for feedback—which she clearly wasn't—Brock would say little Miss Hospitality needed to work on her hospitality skills. "That's too bad," he said dryly.

Liza patted Brock's chest on her way out the door. "Be sure to tell your pawpaw I hope to meet him at the neighborhood Christmas party next week."

"Christmas party?"

"It's at the clubhouse," Liza said. "Erin's one of the co-hosts."

"Of course she is." Whoops. He hadn't meant to say that out loud. "We wouldn't miss it."

"We?" Erin asked. "You'll still be in town?"

"Disappointed?"

"Everyone's invited." Her voice turned saccharine sweet. "Just gathering a head count."

"Count me in," he said before he could rein in his runaway tongue. What was he doing? He'd planned to get Pawpaw settled and hit the road by Sunday.

"Great. Fabulous. See you then, Brick."

He licked his teeth, flaring his nostrils like a bull ready to charge. "It's Brock, actually."

"Whatever," she said and led her troop out the door.

Brock stood scowling at their retreating backs, chiding

himself for getting goaded into a spat by some snot-nosed brat who lived with her grandmother. "I need caffeine," he muttered, shutting the door. "And a lobotomy."

Five

"I can't believe you invited him to the Christmas party," Erin said to Liza as she strode down Brock's driveway and passed his fancy, too-fast car. She had to physically stop herself from kicking snow onto his tires.

"Why wouldn't I?" Liza asked, the picture of mature innocence. "He's new to the neighborhood, and we're the welcome committee. I thought that was our job."

Erin stopped short and turned back to face her neighbors. She'd been in such a snit she'd nearly left them in the dust. "*He's* not new to the neighborhood. His pawpaw is new to the neighborhood." That wasn't disappointment she felt worming its way under her skin. No way. Things in CCR were perfect just the way they were. Having another resident closer to her age wasn't appealing in the least. "Why would he want to come?" she asked. "I didn't even think *you* wanted to come."

"Well, I'm coming now," Liza said with a dramatic lift to her shoulder, reminding Erin of her theatrical past. How had someone as vivacious as Liza never made it past their community playhouse? "Go ahead and count me in."

Erin fumed, squinting against the giant ball of sun cresting the mountains in the distance. Most days, she took the time to appreciate the stunning beauty of Cherry Creek, nestled in the foothills of the Great Smoky Mountains. But after her run-in with Brock, all she could see was fire. "This is ridiculous. Can you actually see him standing around the clubhouse sipping eggnog wearing an ugly sweater? Chatting with residents without making them feel old and useless?"

The Christmas party was supposed to be an enchanting celebration of the season, not a stress-filled event where Erin spent time saving residents from Brock's putdowns and dodging his accusing stares.

"I think we should give him some grace," Mrs. Granger added. "We woke him up. Maybe he's not a morning person. Mr. Granger is a bear in the morning until he's had his coffee."

Erin couldn't believe that after the way he'd treated them, they were actually coming to his defense. "I think we could have knocked on his door any time of day and he'd have been rude."

Liza donned a cat-who-ate-the-canary grin. "But we would have missed seeing him in his skivvies."

Erin's treacherous mind flashed back to Brock in his underwear. His broad chest lightly dusted with golden brown hair, his strong muscular legs, and his tantalizing tapered waist had sent Erin's libido into overdrive. She hadn't seen that much muscled male skin since her college spring break trip to Florida. His sexy mop of bedhead and five o'clock shadow was icing on her lady parts cake. Was it any wonder she'd been less than welcoming? "Just because he's handsome doesn't mean he's nice."

"Speaking of rude ..." Mrs. Granger looped her arm through Erin's and led her back down the sidewalk. "I don't think I've ever seen you be so short with someone. Is everything okay? Did something happen to Louise?"

Erin sighed through the sting of being called out for her immature behavior. "Gram is fine. I'm sorry. You're right. I wasn't very welcoming. He went speeding through the neighborhood the other day and almost hit me and Fluffy. It set me off."

"I think the lady doth protest too much," Liza said with an annoying wink. "Did you read the book? Maybe Brock is your Christmas wish come true."

"What book?" Mrs. Granger asked.

Erin continued her childishness by rolling her eyes at Liza. She *had* read the book and every single comment in the margins. During the night, she'd considered the book's appeal might be more than just a tale well told.

All the heartfelt messages about love and completion had started her head spinning with possibilities. What if the story had actual power? What if, by reading the drool-worthy account herself, Erin could find true love this Christmas?

The first thought that hit her after Brock opened the door (when she could think again) was that maybe this was the guy —her Christmas wish come to life. Until he'd opened his mouth. "That man is a Christmas nightmare. He could barely be civil—and we came bearing gifts."

"We woke him up," Mrs. Granger repeated.

"And he paid us back by flashing us in his underwear." *Stop thinking about him in his underwear!*

"I thought he was nice," Liza said. "And I love what he's done to the house. The wall color was so warm and inviting, and the kitchen looked modern with the new granite and backsplash. He's got fabulous taste—and an adorable backside."

"Would you get your mind out of the gutter?" Erin begged. She didn't need any company as she did laps in the dirty sewer water all by herself. "He's less than half your age."

"So you've said. Maybe I'm a cougar. I've never been with a younger man."

Mrs. Granger scrunched her face like she'd bitten into a lemon. "Gross, Liza. He looks young enough to be your grandson. Don't you have a grandson?"

"I do. Several of them." She swung her gaze to Erin. "How old do you think he is? Thirty? Thirty-five?"

"I have no idea." He was old enough to strike her fancy and young enough to follow through. She admonished herself and her runaway fantasy. She would not be attracted to someone who recklessly sped through their neighborhood and stubbornly refused to apologize. No matter how good he looked in his underwear. "And I don't care."

"Liar," Liza said. "So, about this party. What can we do to jazz things up? I'd hate for Ben to get the impression we're all just a bunch of boring old fuddy-duddies."

Mrs. Granger stopped at her driveway and shook her head at Liza. "We *are* a bunch of boring old fuddy-duddies."

"Speak for yourself." Liza turned to Erin. "Seriously, what have you got planned?"

"The same potluck dinner as last year. The same ugly Christmas sweater contest. That's all."

"That's it?" Liza threw her hands in the air. "One old lady tells you no and you're just going to give up?"

"Darlene oversees the committee. She gets the final say."

"Says who? Come on, Erin. You know you're dying to sprinkle your magic dust on that boring affair."

She really did want to make it better, but at what cost? "Why me? Why do I have to do it?"

"Because Darlene already dislikes you. You've got nothing to lose."

"What?" Erin sputtered. The dastardly Mrs. Richardson strikes again. "Why?"

Liza's shrug told Erin she should already know. "She feels threatened by you."

"By me? What have I ever done?"

"You're young, and energetic, and everyone loves you."

Erin always thought those qualities set her apart and made her special. She never expected someone to use those qualities against her. "Darlene Richardson ran a division of NASA. I'm a work-from-home graphic artist struggling to pay my bills. That's … insane."

"What can I say?" Liza asked. "She's a woman. Women will always seek to destroy each other, no matter how mature we pretend to be. It's one of nature's laws."

Erin knew it was one of nature's laws for *her* generation, but she assumed at some point women would all get along. The thought was too depressing to ponder. "And you suddenly care about this party because why?"

"Because sometimes you've got to force change. Open their eyes to the possibility of more. We're old and stuck in our ways. We need a kick in the pants sometimes."

"If you feel this strongly about the party, why haven't you volunteered? The committee is always looking for members."

"Darlene is one of my oldest friends, but she's as stubborn as a mule. I don't seek out opportunities to butt heads with her when they happen so frequently on their own."

"And you think she's going to be okay with me spicing things up without her approval?"

"That's why you don't tell her *or* that gang of groupies that follows her around like she's a rock star. Sheesh. She had one meeting with the president and you'd think she actually hung the moon."

Erin swallowed. She didn't want to make an enemy in the neighborhood, but it sounded like she already had. "That doesn't feel right."

"Then talk to Darlene. I'm sure you can sway her to your way of thinking."

"How? Especially when she already hates me, and the rest of the committee will back her up."

Liza squeezed Erin's arm. "You leave the committee to me. Email me your ideas and I'll get them on our side."

"They already heard my ideas and turned me down."

"Sweetheart, trust me, I'm an actress." She swooped imaginary locks behind her shoulder and painted on a saucy smile. "I was born to play this part."

And Erin was born to be a fish out of water no matter where she landed. "I don't know, Liza. I don't want to start a war."

"Don't think of it as starting a war. Think of it as leading the troops away from the line of fire. I don't know a single person who's excited about the Christmas potluck."

Mrs. Granger raised her hand. "I am. I was going to try a new chicken casserole recipe."

"You can still bring your chicken casserole, Patty. We're talking about the entertainment."

"Does that mean Gerald can't wear his reindeer sweater?"

Liza was losing her patience by the way she sighed and pinched the bridge of her nose. "He can wear the dang sweater." She turned her back on Mrs. Granger and spoke to Erin. "So, what do you say? Let's kick this party into gear."

Six

Brock lifted the dining room blinds and peered out at the street for the millionth time that day. Friday had finally arrived, and he was beyond ready for his pawpaw to see all the work he'd done on his new home. Pawpaw had seen the listing, of course, but Brock hadn't told him anything about the renovations. He'd wanted to surprise his pawpaw and witness his reaction firsthand.

"Where are they?" He checked his watch, calculated the drive. Brock knew better than to ask his mother to transport Pawpaw from Nashville to Cherry Creek. But his mom was the only family member with a valid driver's license and Lord knew she had nothing better to do than make the three-and-a-half-hour drive. Having her here would open him up to her ridicule and scorn—but what else was new?

"Wow, fancy digs," he imagined her saying. "Must be nice to be Brock's favorite, Paw."

How many times had he suffered through her woe-is-me routine? As if her circumstances resulted from bad luck rather than the fulfillment of a lifetime of bad choices.

Brock had almost turned away when he spotted Erin in her

blinding-white coat and cherry-red hat, walking along the sidewalk with a large pot in her mittened hands. He scowled at the little busy body on her way up the street. He'd seen her throughout the week walking a variety of dogs past his house, visiting neighbors, and making herself a nuisance. Did the woman have a job or was she—as he suspected—living off her poor grandmother, laid up at home in bed?

Brock tried but failed to shake his irritation at the neighborhood gasbag who kept creeping unbidden into his thoughts. She was just like his family—leeching off her vulnerable grandmother and ingratiating herself into the lives of others for the purpose of serving herself.

Just because she could use her pretty smile and big brown eyes to soften the older residents didn't mean he couldn't see right through her act. She was a user. Just like his mom. Just like every other cousin and aunt and uncle he was unfortunate enough to call family.

He'd never seen Erin wearing anything other than that puffy white coat. Wondering what she looked like underneath gnawed at him day and night. Was she flat-chested and skinny like a teenaged boy? Full-bodied and voluptuous like Elizabeth Taylor and the other movie stars Pawpaw admired growing up? He scolded himself for wasting a second of his time on useless thoughts about a useless person. Why did he care about the shape of her body? It wasn't as if he was interested in her.

He dropped the blind and looked around the house, trying to see it through Pawpaw's eyes. Other than the recliner Pawpaw had refused to leave behind, Brock had outfitted his new home in comfortable couches and quality furniture. No more hand-me-downs for the man who'd spent his whole life barely scraping by. From now until the end, Pawpaw would only have the best. Brock would make sure of it.

He walked to the door when he heard a car pull into the

drive and spotted the rental he'd arranged for his mom. He could see the fumes from her cigarette in the enclosed cab and cursed under his breath. She knew Pawpaw was susceptible to RSV in the winter, and yet she'd smoked in the car with him anyway—even after she'd promised Brock she wouldn't. He should have hired a car service like he'd wanted, no matter what Pawpaw had said.

"She wants to see where I'm living," Pawpaw had argued for his daughter. "I don't think it's right to keep her from coming."

Brock knew it was a horrible idea to let his mom get a look at Pawpaw's new digs. If she liked what she saw—and how could she not—she'd eventually make up some sob story and be living here just like Erin. Before long, the two of them would be spending their time sharing cigarettes and swapping stories of how they'd mooched their way through life.

Brock opened the door and watched his mother toss the cigarette onto the drive. She knew Brock was watching. She knew he'd be upset. She definitely didn't care. What better way to give her son the middle finger for having the audacity to better his life and Pawpaw's without giving her another handout she'd inevitably squander.

He ignored his mother and focused on Pawpaw's face, saw happiness light his tired eyes, watched him amble up the drive, a little stiff from the long drive but otherwise no worse for wear —thank heavens. "You made it," Brock said.

"This weather sucks," his mom said in greeting. "And that car you rented has no pickup and go."

He'd deliberately rented her a no-frills four-wheel drive. "You got here safe. That's all that counts. How was the drive?" he asked Pawpaw.

"Good. There was an accident along I-40 that set us back a bit, but we're here." He crossed the threshold and looked around. "Wow. This looks different."

"I hope you like it," Brock said, suddenly unsure. "I can change anything you don't like."

"Are you kidding?" Pawpaw stroked the back of the leather sofa. "This is the nicest place I've ever stayed."

"You're not a guest, Pawpaw. This is your home."

They both pretended not to notice the sheen of tears in his eyes. Pawpaw was a real man and real men didn't cry. "I still can't believe it."

His mom shuffled her feet. "You got a restroom in this fancy place, or do I need to squat in the bushes?"

Brock directed his mother down the hall to the guest bathroom. He'd mentally tallied all the supplies he'd placed in the room, knowing he'd find something she'd swiped after she left.

"Brock, this is too much," his pawpaw said. "I can't acc—"

"Yes, you can. And it's not too much. Let me show you around and you'll see it's the perfect size. Totally manageable for you on your own." He led him into the kitchen and opened a drawer. "I put all the pots and pans here so you won't have to bend over to cook." He opened a cabinet. "Glasses and mugs here." Opened another. "Plates and bowls here." He pointed to a small drawer next to the dishwasher. "Silverware is in that drawer, and there's a spice rack next to the oven."

"There's two ovens," Pawpaw said with awe in his voice.

"Seems a little silly to me, but you know I don't cook."

"I guess I can put a casserole in one and a loaf of bread in the other." He glanced from the kitchen to the dining area to the den where Brock had mounted a sixty-five-inch TV. "I wish your granny could get a look at this place. She wouldn't believe her eyes."

"She can see it, Pawpaw. I think she's happy you're back home."

Pawpaw cleared the emotion from his throat. "I know you're right."

Brock's mom sauntered back from the hallway, glanced around with a look of disdain. "Swanky place you got here, Paw. Ol' Brocky-boy set you up real nice."

Here we go. Brock gave her a scathing glare as she prowled the den, flicking her fingers over blankets and lamps, scowling at books, and touching the plant in the corner to see if it was real. She picked up a coaster from a stack on the end table and flipped it over, probably looking for a price tag. "You must have piles of money to burn."

"I do okay," Brock said.

She cackled, flashing her stained and crooked teeth. "I'd say you do better than okay. I'd say you've got enough to go around."

"Sissy," Pawpaw said. "We talked about this in the car."

"I ain't sayin' nothing, Paw. Just giving the boy some props."

"You've used the restroom," Brock said with steel lacing his voice. "Is there anything else you need before you get back on the road?"

"Well, I—"

A knock at the door stopped his mother cold, had them all freezing in place. Brock didn't know whether to feel grateful for the interruption or irritated at whomever was delaying his mother's disgraceful departure. He opened the door to find Erin once again on his doorstep.

"Hi," she said with less vitriol in her voice than in their last encounter. "Sorry to stop by unannounced again."

"What are you doing here?" he asked.

"I saw another car in your drive and since it's Friday, I thought maybe your grandfather had arrived."

"I know you've got money to burn," his mother called from behind him. "But you're lettin' all the cold air in the house. Why don't you invite the girl inside?"

Irritated. Brock was definitely irritated at Erin's untimely intrusion. Of all the people he didn't want to show weakness in front of, it was little Miss Fake Sunshine. He stepped aside and let her enter.

"Hi," she said to his mom and pawpaw. "I'm Erin. I live in Cherry Creek Reserve with my grandmother."

"Ain't that nice," his mom said, flashing Brock with a mocking stare. She loved nothing better than embarrassing her son. "I'm Brock's mother, Priscilla." She held her hand out in an oddly formal greeting.

Erin lifted the pot in her hands as an explanation for not reciprocating the shake. "I'm so glad to meet you, Priscilla."

"You can call me Sissy."

"Okay." Erin looked at Pawpaw. "You must be Ben."

"I am Ben," Pawpaw said with a delighted grin. "It's nice to meet you, Erin."

Brock just stared at her, wondering what she was doing standing in his pawpaw's living room, inserting herself smack dab into their awkward family reunion. "Can I help you with something?"

Erin shook her head and smiled as if she'd forgotten she was carrying the pot. "Oh, this, yes." She passed the pot to Brock. "I wish I could say I made you some soup as a welcome gift," she said to Pawpaw. "I met Brock the other day when we dropped off the official welcome basket. I made some soup for a sick neighbor, but I just found out she's been admitted to the hospital."

"I'm sorry to hear that," Pawpaw said.

"I am too. Anyway, I figured with you coming into town from Nashville, you might like a home-cooked meal."

"Thank you, Erin," Pawpaw said. "That's very nice of you."

His mom got that look on her face, the one that told Brock he was going to have to do damage control. "That's super sweet of you, Erin," she said and wrapped her bony arm around Erin's shoulder. "I bet you thought a little homemade soup would help you get into my son's pants and eventually his wallet."

Erin blanched, blinking her big brown eyes.

Pawpaw shook his head. "Sissy ..."

Brock stood frozen in place. She'd more than embarrassed him. She'd rendered him mute.

"I ..." Erin stuttered and backed out of his mom's grasp. She thumped her hand against her chest. "That's not my intent. I ... I didn't even make the soup for Brock. Or Ben. I ... I just didn't want it to go to waste."

"They'll eat it, honey," Sissy said in a sexy stage whisper that made him want to vomit. "They'll eat it up good. But you should know from the get-go. I raised that son of mine on handouts, but he's not very good at sharing with others."

"That's enough," Brock said to his mother in a timbre he barely recognized. "Get your keys and get out."

She tsked at him and shook her head. "See what I mean? Not worth the effort for a pretty girl like you." Sissy brought two fingers to her lips like she was smoking a cigarette, kissed the tips, and then flicked her fingers in the air. "It's been real. But it ain't been real fun. I'll see ya later, Paw," she said as she slithered out the door.

Shame crept up Brock's neck and set fire to his face. He placed the pot on the countertop and looked directly at Erin. "I'm sorry about my mother. She's ..." *an embarrassment, a fool, the most unhappy person alive.* "There's no excuse."

"It's okay," Erin lied, inching toward the door. "It's my fault. I shouldn't have stopped by without calling."

Ben stepped forward to rescue Brock. "I'm glad you did, Erin. Brock and I appreciate the soup and your generosity."

Pawpaw didn't even try to explain his daughter's behavior. How could he?

"You're welcome. I'll leave you to get settled. Hope to see you around soon." She disappeared out the door.

Brock was tired. After four consecutive fourteen-hour days spent putting the house together and trying to run his business, every muscle in his body ached. But nothing exhausted him more than encounters with his mother. He hung his head and rubbed the all too familiar pain in his chest.

"I'm sorry, Brock," Pawpaw said. "You were right. She shouldn't have come."

"Don't apologize for her. She meant every word." He stepped into the small foyer, grabbed his coat from the rack he'd hung just that morning. "I'll be right back."

Seven

THE CHILL STUNG ERIN'S LUNGS AS SHE GULPED AIR IN AND OUT, IN AND out, trying to calm her humiliated heart. She couldn't process the events of the morning, not yet. Emotions swirled in her belly—too many to name—and left her feeling sick.

The guilt she'd felt after discovering Darlene was in the hospital for pneumonia. The soup she'd made—not with a giver's heart but with intent to bribe—felt like poison in her hands. She was on her way home to toss it down the sink when she'd spotted the car in Brock's drive. She figured she'd try to salvage the welcome committee's reputation—and her conscience—with one grandiose gesture.

The whole outing had been a colossal disaster.

"Erin!"

She heard Brock call her name and stopped walking, but didn't turn around. She didn't want to face him or listen to a lecture or worse—another apology. She didn't want to talk about what had happened until she understood it herself.

He touched her shoulder and said, "I'm sorry."

She turned and looked up into the saddest blue eyes she'd

ever seen. All the confusion she felt melded into a giant lump of pity for Brock. "It's okay. Really. I shouldn't have come by."

"No, it's not okay. What happened back there has nothing to do with you."

"Exactly. It's none of my business."

"My mother is ..." He sighed, defeated, and looked off into the distance. She could see the pain radiating from his drawn tight face. "We're not close. Obviously. Embarrassing me is like a sport to her. She doesn't like me very much."

"Yeah, I kinda figured that."

"The feeling is mutual."

Erin offered a cheerless chuckle. "I'd be shocked if it wasn't." She couldn't stand to watch him so defeated, gutted, and bleeding on the sidewalk for all to see. She had to do something, say something to get that haunted look off his face. "If it makes you feel any better, I've got one of those, too."

"One of what?" he asked.

"A mother who doesn't like me very much."

He tilted his head, his brows lifting toward his hairline. "You do?"

"I do." She never talked about her relationship with her mother. Not with anyone. But since his mother had cut him to the quick right in front of her, she figured it wouldn't hurt him to know he wasn't alone. "She wouldn't be so outright rude. She's too classy for that. Nobody does passive-aggressive like Amelia Larkin. She kept her name after she married my dad. Your classic feminist power-play."

His lips twitched. "She sounds lovely."

"Oh, she is. Just ask her."

"I'd love to. I feel as if I'm owed a little payback."

"Well, don't hold your breath. She'd rather set herself on fire than step foot back in Cherry Creek. She's better than her hometown. Soooo much better."

Brock nodded and graced Erin with a sexy half grin, firing her pesky libido right back to life. "Listen, I've got to get back to my pawpaw."

"Of course. I'll see you ... at the Christmas party, I guess."

Brock nodded but didn't move. He just stared at her with an intense look on his face that made her want to squirm. "Hey, I've got that gift card to Sal's burning a hole in my pocket. Why don't you join us—me and Pawpaw—one night for dinner? You can tell him all about the neighborhood rules and give him the lowdown on all the residents."

She'd have been less surprised if he'd picked up a stick and knocked her over the head. "Really?"

"My mom didn't just embarrass me. She embarrassed him, too. I know he'd love a chance to make it up to you."

Erin couldn't remember the last time she'd had dinner with two handsome men. "I'd love to go to Sal's with you and your pawpaw."

"Is Saturday okay?"

"Saturday is perfect."

"Pick you up at six?"

"Okay. I'll be ready." She turned, an unfamiliar mix of excitement and hope coursing through her veins, and a grin she couldn't have wiped off with a metal spatula splitting her face.

"Oh, hey, Erin?"

She schooled her features and spun around. "Yes?"

"I don't know where you live."

"Oh, ha ha, of course. I'm at 4550 Cherry Tree Lane. Second house on the left."

"4550. It's a date," he said and then immediately stiffened, shook his head, and cleared his throat. "I mean, yeah, I'll see you Saturday."

Erin's phone rang, jolting them both. *Saved by the bell.* "See ya," she said and turned to walk home, pulling the cell phone from her pocket. "Hello?"

"Erin. It's Liza. Darlene is in the hospital."

"I know. I tried to take her some soup this morning and the Wilsons told me what happened." Remorse returned but with a little less bite thanks to Brock and his friendly request. She wouldn't read any more into his invitation. It wasn't a date. He'd made that patently obvious.

"Meet me at the clubhouse," Liza said. "We've got some planning to do."

"Liza ..." Erin felt too heavy—too guilty—to plan the party. Especially with Darlene in such bad shape. "This feels wrong."

"I talked to the groupies. They admitted Darlene to the hospital as a precaution. She's going to be fine."

"It still feels wrong."

"As they say in the business, the show must go on."

Erin shuffled her feet along the sidewalk and contemplated her options. With Darlene in the hospital, it truly was up to her to be the lead hostess for the Christmas party. Why not add some spark to the party, if only to distract everyone from worrying about Darlene? "Fine. I'm on my way."

She hung up and turned left to go to the clubhouse instead of turning right to go home. She found Liza shaking her head at the contents of the storage closet. "That was quick."

"I was close when you called." Erin pulled the mittens from her hands and shoved them into her pockets.

"Do me a favor," Liza said. "If you've been picking up poop, go wash your hands." She wrinkled her nose. "It disgusts me to think of what you've touched."

"I wasn't walking a dog. I took the soup I made for Darlene to Brock and his pawpaw."

Liza's eyes flared. "You met Ben?"

"I did."

"Well, what do you think? Is he an older version of Brock?"

"He's …" Erin thought back, but could only conjure a vague impression of Ben after Brock's mother had tainted the encounter. "They're about the same height and build. Ben has a bit of a belly."

"At our age, who doesn't?" She lifted a singular brow. "Is he a Michael Douglas or a Samuel L. Jackson?"

Stumped and more than a little warm in her coat, Erin unzipped her jacket. "I have no idea what you're asking."

"Does he have hair, or is he bald?"

Erin snorted at Liza's flair with words. "He's got hair. I think."

"You probably couldn't take your eyes off of Brock long enough to form an impression of Ben."

"That's not true." She walked into the kitchen and set her jacket on a barstool. *Not* exactly *true.*

Liza followed like a dog with a bone. "You and Brock didn't come to blows?"

"No, we came to a truce. I'm having dinner with him and Ben tomorrow night."

"Well, I'll have to get your soup recipe and make a delivery of my own."

If only Erin could borrow some of Liza's confidence. "They're covered for a while, but go right ahead."

"Sweetie, men have ravenous appetites. And so should available young ladies. Are you ready to admit you're interested?"

"Liza …"

"What? He asked you to dinner."

"With his pawpaw. It's not a date."

"Maybe it's a pre-date. A getting to know you session without all the pressure."

"He lives in Nashville."

Liza shrugged her shoulders and flashed an incredulous grin. "It's a few hours away. And we live in a digital society."

"What are you suggesting? That we virtually date, like Gram and Mr. Fellows?"

"Maybe. At least Louise is getting some action."

Erin was going to have to bleach the images floating through her brain. "Ugh. Can we please focus on the party? I have actual work to do."

"Fine. I want to run into town and get a manicure at the Cut 'n Curl." She grabbed Erin's hand and stared at her nails. "You might do the same before your date."

"It's *not* a date."

"Whatever. Be your own worst enemy if you want."

Erin glanced at her short nails. She spent too much time on the computer to make a fuss. "If he doesn't like me because of my nails, he's not worth my time."

"Ah ha!" Liza howled. "I knew you were interested."

"That was not an admission. I was simply saying tha—"

"Honey, since when is being attracted to a handsome young man a crime? He's hot and appears to be financially stable. Those kinds of guys don't grow on trees—certainly not Cherry Creek trees. I say go for it. What have you got to lose?"

Liza was right. It had been too long since Erin had put any effort into finding a mate. As much as she loved living in CCR, she'd never end up with the life she'd envisioned by isolating herself with an older crowd. "Nothing, I suppose. But can we stop talking about this, please? You're going to make me nervous."

Liza mimed twisting a key at her lips. "Conversation over. Now,"—she rubbed her hands together—"what are we going to do about this party? The junk we have here just won't do. We have to go shopping."

"With what funds? Darlene controls the account."

"We'll hit the Five & Dime. It won't take much to liven this place up."

The holidays were a slow time for Erin's business. Even a trip to the Five & Dime could put her on shaky ground. "I don't know. I'm on a super tight budget." She scowled at the boxes of broken and useless items and came up with an idea. "With Gram out of town, other than the tree and a wreath I hung on the door, I haven't put out any of her Christmas decorations. I'm sure she wouldn't mind if we used some of hers."

"What does she have?"

"Garland and lights, a whole Christmas village, and tons of ribbon. I'll call her to make sure, but I don't think she'll mind."

Liza's eyes sparkled. "You know what, doesn't CCR have a crafting club?"

"I think so, but I'm not sure who's in charge."

"One of the groupies will know. Let's give them a job— make it a contest—and all we'll have to do is sit back and watch."

Erin grinned at Liza's intoxicating zeal. "You're really good at problem solving."

"I spent my life in community theater. It's more than acting. It's fundraising and finding the best way to get the most bang for your buck."

"That's it," Erin said. "I'm appointing you to the committee."

Liza looked down her nose at Erin. "You can't afford me."

"Good thing it's a volunteer position."

Eight

"I'm glad you talked Erin into going to dinner with us," Pawpaw said, shoving his arms into his coat. "We certainly owe her an apology after the way Sissy behaved."

Brock followed his pawpaw down the driveway and swallowed the nasty aftertaste of his mother's latest antics. He desperately hoped they'd bypass that discussion and have a pleasant night out. "I already apologized."

Pawpaw looked at Brock over the hood of the car. "And you were a little rude."

"I wasn't rude."

Pawpaw gave him the don't-lie-to-me-boy stare he'd mastered over the years. "You want to amend that statement?"

Brock unlocked his SUV and opened the driver's side door. "Okay, fine. Maybe I was a little rude." He got behind the wheel and started the engine. "But you weren't here when she first stopped by. She wasn't exactly friendly—and I'd never even met her."

"Erin doesn't strike me as the mean-spirited kind."

"Apparently I exceeded the speed limit on my first trip through the neighborhood. But I was trying to catch up with the movers. They'd been on the road for an hour before they bothered to call and tell me they were on their way."

"I see."

"Trust me, Erin will spell out all the neighborhood rules." He shouldn't be looking forward to spending time with her. Not after their rocky start and his continued suspicions about her reasons for living in the neighborhood. But that didn't stop him from anticipating a night in her company. "I'm not convinced she's not the neighborhood mooch looking for her next mark."

Ben scowled at him, deepening the notch between his brows. "Not every woman is like your mother, Brock."

"I know that. I just need to make sure." He hated the way Pawpaw frowned at him, a world of disapproval in his silent stare. "Besides, I figured you'd rather hear the neighborhood rules straight from the horse's mouth than log onto some silly website."

"Did you get my computer working?" Pawpaw asked.

"I did. I also printed out your passwords and put the list in your safe, along with the rest of your important documents."

"I've got a safe?"

"In the guest room closet. I'll show you when we get home." Brock pulled into Erin's driveway and put the car into park. Her house looked like all the others in the cookie cutter neighborhood with its two-car garage and faux stone facade. "I'll be right back."

Erin beat him to the punch. The whimsical wreath on her front door shimmied as she locked up the house. "Hi there," she said, wearing a bright smile and the same long white coat zipped up to her neck.

"How's it going?" Brock asked. Maybe, once he got a look at Erin's body, he would stop obsessing. With her taking up too much space in his head over the past few days, Brock realized he needed to get back on the dating train as soon as he returned to Nashville. He'd obviously neglected his love life for far too long.

He led her down the walkway with a hand on her back. "It's nice the way the neighborhood clears the driveways and the sidewalks."

"It is," she said. "I don't mind walking dogs and watering plants, but I draw the line at shoveling snow."

Brock opened the door behind Pawpaw and Erin climbed inside.

"Hi, Ben."

"It's good to see you, Erin. We really enjoyed your soup last night."

Brock closed her door and walked behind the car. His shoulders eased at hearing Pawpaw talk to Erin with excitement in his voice. He hoped he was wrong about her because it would be a lot easier to leave him in Cherry Creek, knowing someone was looking out for him.

After the short drive into town past the cherry grove with a large, decorated Christmas tree, Brock parked along East Main Street, just down from Sal's Pizza.

"I can't believe how much Cherry Creek has changed since the last time I was here," Pawpaw said.

"When was that?" Erin asked.

Pawpaw pursed his lips and peered at Gifts & Bits' colorful Christmas display. "Before you were born, I'd imagine."

"A lot can change in twenty-seven years."

Brock had wondered about her age, had pegged her for mid to late twenties. Anything younger would have made him feel like a pervert—not that he was interested. He held the door open, and they shuffled inside.

"Ciao, Salvatore," Erin greeted the mid-fifties Italian man kneading dough behind the counter.

"Bueno sera, Erin. Good to see your pretty face."

"It's been too long," she said.

The exposed brick walls and red and white checkered floors gave the place a coziness Brock hadn't expected. His stomach grumbled at the heady aroma of yeast and garlic that permeated the air. "Wow, this smells delicious."

"It is," Erin confirmed.

"Is that Vito's kid?" Ben asked Erin.

"I don't know." Erin unzipped her coat and faced the counter. "Hey, Sal. Is your dad named Vito?"

"Si, signora. Vito was my dad."

"Well, I'll be," Ben said with a face splitting grin. "I remember when Sal was just a boy."

Sal dusted his hands and approached the counter. "I'm Salvatore Bonaccorsi. You knew my dad?"

"Not well," Ben said. "I'm Ben Bartlett and this is my grandson, Brock. I grew up in these parts. Your dad used to pay me and my friends to collect bottles from the alley."

"That sounds like my dad. God rest his soul."

"I'm sorry to hear he passed."

"Going on ten years now." Sal handed the trio a stack of plastic menus. "Lasagna's our special tonight. It comes with a salad and Mama's famous garlic rolls." He winked affectionately at Erin. "Take a look and let Luca know when you're ready to order."

"Thanks, Sal."

Brock perused the menu. "What's good?"

"Everything's good. The lasagna is fantastic, but so is the pizza, and the paninis, and the chicken parmesan." She rolled her eyes adorably. "Everything."

They ordered individual meals and drinks and chose a booth along the front window. Before scooting across from them, Erin shimmied the coat off her shoulders. Brock hung it on the nearby hook while discreetly sneaking a look at her figure. She wasn't built like a teenaged boy or a Hollywood star-let, but somewhere in between. She'd paired a creamy V-neck sweater with perfectly fitted jeans. A couple of slim gold chains drew his eyes to the valley of her chest.

Pawpaw caught him looking and gave him a pointed stare. Brock ignored him and scooted into the booth.

"Y'all look a bit scrunched over there," Erin said. "Why don't one of you come sit over here with me?"

Since Brock was on the outside, he stood and took the seat next to Erin. Their legs touched beneath the table, one blue-jeaned pant to another, and neither moved to separate.

"This is such a treat," Erin said. When she spoke, her scent—something sweet and citrusy—wafted over the pungent scent of Italian herbs and cheese. "I haven't been downtown since the lighting of the tree."

"Were you born and raised in Cherry Creek?" Ben asked.

"I was raised in Atlanta where my parents live, but I went to boarding school here as a girl."

Brock inwardly cringed. Of course she went to boarding school. *This is good*, he thought. Nothing like a spoiled child-hood so different from his own to put the kibosh on his mounting attraction.

"I didn't know Cherry Creek had a boarding school," Pawpaw said.

"Cherry Creek Academy. Home of the Mudcats."

"That must have been hard," Ben said. "Living away from your parents."

"Not really." Erin stirred the ice around her cup, a melancholy look stealing the spark in her eyes. "My parents are workaholics who probably shouldn't have had a kid. My gram never left Cherry Creek, so sending me here for school was a good option for them. No fuss, no muss, and no kid to cramp their lifestyle."

"Ouch," Brock said.

"The truth should hurt, and it occasionally stings, but I got to be near Gram, so it worked out for the best." Erin sat back in the booth when Luca arrived with their food.

"I'll be right back with some drink refills," he said. "Do y'all need anything else?"

Brock looked at his plate, eyed the giant, meat-filled calzone, and couldn't remember the last time he'd been so excited about a meal. "Wow. I think I'm good."

"We're all good," Erin said. "Thank you, Luca."

He nodded and disappeared behind the counter.

Brock sliced into his calzone, watched the heat escape, and forked up a bite. "So, Erin," he said, waiting for his food to cool. "Do you ... work?"

She nodded and swallowed a bite of her personal pizza. "Yes, of course I work. Do you work?"

"Yes." He couldn't wait a second longer to taste the calzone and shoveled the bite into his mouth.

Pawpaw blinked at Erin. "Brock owns a nationwide chain of recovery clinics."

Erin halted with a slice halfway to her mouth. "Wait a minute. You're Brock Bartlett of Bartlett Recovery Centers?"

And his attraction officially flatlined. Anyone who knew his name and reputation also knew his fortune. Girls like Erin—girls raised with only the best—took one look at Brock and saw nothing but dollar signs. "You've heard of it?"

"Heard of it?" She dropped her slice, wiped her hands on the napkin in her lap, and turned to face him in the booth. "I worked for you."

Brock's jaw hinged open, and his stomach felt jittery and hot. "*What?*"

"I created your logo, your website, everything."

It took his brain more than a few seconds to start firing

again, but he started to connect the dots. "You're E.H. Collier? From Capital Design?"

"I used to work for Capital Design, but I had to quit to take care of Gram. I'm freelance now."

"I ..." He dropped his fork, his food forgotten. "I can't believe this. Sean has been trying for months to find you and Capital has been giving him the runaround."

"They weren't happy when I left, so I'm not surprised. What do you need?"

CPR. A warm blanket. A hard slap to the face. "I'm not sure, exactly. Sean handles the creative side of the business. I just know he was frustrated with whomever they assigned him after you left. He'll be ecstatic to know I've found you."

She scrunched her nose. "I'm not technically allowed to solicit business from former clients. It violates my non-compete."

"You're not soliciting business if I'm seeking you out. I mean, Bartlett Recovery is seeking you out. They can't stop us from coming to you."

"I suppose that would be okay." She chewed her bottom lip. "I just really can't afford to get sued."

"You're not going to get sued." He stared at her, at her shiny brown hair, at her open and easy smile, and quickly adjusted his image. She wasn't some freeloader living off her grandmother, but a talented designer who'd left a top firm when her family was in need. "This feels kind of surreal."

"Tell me about it." She stared at her plate before turning to him again. "Your centers are amazing. What you do for people struggling with addiction is ..."

"Inspired by Pawpaw," Brock said. "He's the one who turned his life around and taught me what it means to be a man."

"Brock—" Ben shook his head.

"It's true. I wouldn't be where I am today, thousands of others wouldn't be where they are today, without the example you set."

"I don't know about that."

Brock set his napkin on top of the table. He needed a minute to think, a timeout where he could breathe and gather his wits. "Excuse me. I'm going to use the restroom."

Nine

ERIN WATCHED BROCK WALK AWAY FROM THE TABLE, ADMIRING HIS loose-limbed gait. Physically, he exemplified her ideal type. Around six feet, he wasn't too tall or too short. He had that casual manly style totally down pat in his faded jeans and quarter zip sweater. And those eyes. A weathered blue that reminded her of the ocean during a storm.

Pawpaw said her name, drew her attention back to the table and away from Brock's backside.

"My grandson is a complicated man."

"Yes, I can tell."

"His mama did a number on him. He doesn't trust easily."

Erin leaned back against the booth, her appetite gone. "Parents have a special way of screwing up their kids."

"That's certainly true. I did a number on mine before I quit drinking."

She heard the regret in his voice, saw it in the lines fanning his eyes. "I'm sure you did the best you could."

"Even after I got sober, we barely scraped by. Working odd jobs, I could hardly put food on the table and keep a roof over our heads. Unfortunately, my kids didn't end up much better."

"At some point, everyone has to take responsibility for their own lives and stop blaming their parents. Trust me, I milked the poor-me routine for far too long."

"You're stronger than most if you've realized that at your age."

"My grandmother set a heck of an example. She doesn't suffer fools—or so-called victims—lightly."

"I'd like to meet your grandmother."

"I have a feeling you'd like her. Most people do."

"I like her granddaughter." He lifted a thumb over his shoulder toward the restrooms. "That boy credits me for his success, but it's all him. Brock's the one who broke the chain. He used his sharp mind to create a curriculum for beating addiction that's helped thousands of people break their dependence—and not just to alcohol."

"He's very impressive."

Ben lifted his brows and stared at her, reminding her of Brock. "Not so bad to look at, either."

"No," she chuckled, her face flaring hot. "He's not."

"Can't imagine why he wouldn't turn the head of a pretty girl like you."

"Ben, your grandson is very attractive. He's charming too, whenever he drops his guard long enough to relax and be himself."

"I sense a 'but' coming."

"But ..." She glanced toward the bathrooms, made sure the coast was clear. "I know his work ethic and his reputation. I've had my fill of workaholics who put their careers above everything else."

"Maybe he's never met someone who made him want to slow down."

"In my admittedly limited experience, that propensity doesn't change. Once a workaholic, always a workaholic. It's an addiction all its own."

"Men can change, Erin. Even stubborn men like Brock. My Ginny stayed with me, prayed for me longer than I deserved. A good woman can change a hardheaded man."

"She sounds like a lovely woman."

"She was the absolute best."

Brock emerged from the restroom and made his way back to the table. Erin picked up her slice and took another bite, praying their conversation wasn't written all over her face.

He sat down beside her. "Did you two solve the world's problems while I was gone?"

Ben winked at Erin. "We gave it our best shot." He looked at Brock. "How's the calzone?"

"It's great. I wish I could find a pizza place like this in Nashville."

"I've heard Nashville has amazing food."

"It does," Brock said. "If you're a foodie." He looked around the restaurant. "Sal's is more my style. Nothing fancy but really good food."

A couple approached the table, snagging Erin's attention and drawing a smile on her face. "Mr. and Mrs. Ackerman," she said as the couple passed.

"Erin," Mr. Ackerman said. "Good to see you."

"Gladys and Phil Ackerman, I'd like you to meet Ben and Brock Bartlett. Ben just moved into Sheryl Kincaid's old place."

"Well," Mr. Ackerman said. "It's nice to meet you, Ben. Welcome to Cherry Creek Reserve."

"Thank you. It's nice to meet you both as well."

Erin mined her well of knowledge about the Ackermans but came up empty. Instead, she focused on Ben. "Ben was born in Cherry Creek and moved back after many years away."

"Is that right?" Mrs. Ackerman said. "I'm born and raised. Did you graduate from the Academy or Cherry Creek high?"

"Neither," Ben said. "I dropped out as soon as I could and got my GED a few years later. School was never my thing, but I sure regretted not seeing it through."

Mrs. Ackerman smiled. "You sound like my brother, Fred. He did the same."

Ben cocked his head and narrowed his eyes. "Freddy Smyth is your brother?"

"Why, yes. Did you know Fred?"

"We used to run around as kids. Got ourselves into a good bit of trouble back in the day."

"That sounds like Fred too."

Ben blinked at his half-eaten meal, over at Erin and Brock, and finally up at the Ackermans. "Could I trouble you for a ride back to the neighborhood?" he asked.

Brock reached across the table. "Is something wrong, Pawpaw?"

"No, nothing's wrong. I'm just a little tired after the move the last few days."

"We can box up our food and go back now," Brock said. "I'm sure Erin doesn't mind."

"I don't mind at all." Especially since she had a sneaking suspicion Ben's desire to leave had nothing to do with being tired and everything to do with setting her up with Brock.

"You kids stay and have fun," Mr. Ackerman said. "We're happy to give Ben a ride. I'd love to hear about his adventures with Fred, maybe get a little ammo on my brother-in-law."

"Are you sure?" Brock asked Ben.

"I'm sure. Do you mind bringing my food when you come?"

"Of course, but—"

"No buts. Just stay and enjoy your meal—and the company." He scooted out of the booth. "I'll see you back at home."

Erin and Brock watched the three of them walk away, heard Ben give a bark of laughter as they exited the door.

"Well," Brock said. "I feel like we've been dumped."

"Sounds like your pawpaw made his first friends in the neighborhood."

"Yes, it does." Brock stood and moved opposite Erin, pulling his plate across the table. She wished he'd stayed put. He was so much easier to talk to without looking into his eyes. "That makes me happy. I thought maybe I should extend my trip into next week. Pawpaw walks around the house like he's a guest in his own home. It's going to take a while for him to settle in and relax."

"I'd be happy to check on him. Make sure he's doing okay."

"That's nice of you, thanks." He cleared his throat, seemed a little uncomfortable. "That's kind of your thing, isn't it? Helping others in the neighborhood."

"I guess it kind of is." Erin heard no judgment in his tone. "I like helping people. For the most part, my neighbors in CCR are really nice. Not everyone has family nearby, so I try to do what I can whenever someone needs a hand."

Brock nodded and chewed with a contemplative look on his face.

Erin braced for an inquisition.

"I don't mean to sound nosey," he said, lowering his voice and leaning onto the table.

Erin's stomach twisted into knots.

"But how do you strand living here with all these old folks? Don't you miss being around people your own age?"

Erin heaved a sigh of relief. She'd answered a form of his question many times over the past two years. "It's a valid question. When Gram broke her ankle and needed help, I was fed up with living in Atlanta." She thought back to her tiny apartment and her solitary life. If she'd stayed, she'd have turned into her parents—working all the time to the exclusion of anything else. "I moved there for a job I liked, but I didn't have a social outlet.

None of my close friends lived in the city, and I found it hard to make genuine connections. Neighbors didn't speak to neighbors and making friends was hard."

"I get that," Brock said. "It's easy to get lost in a big city like Atlanta."

"Don't get me started about my experience with online dating." Embarrassment heated Erin's cheeks and froze her into place. Why had she mentioned dating to a man she barely knew?

Brock winced like he agreed. "That bad?"

Shoot me now. With no way to backtrack, Erin told the truth. "The men were just so ... not what they claimed in their profile. And no one was interested in anything more than a hookup."

"That sounds bad."

"It was." She shoved a bite into her mouth and prayed he'd change the subject.

"I must admit," Brock said after a brief pause. "Cherry Creek is nicer than I expected, but can you see yourself living here forever?"

So much for casual conversation with an interesting man. Brock was as intense in person as his reputation had foretold. "I've made real friends here with people who like and appreciate me. People who know how to have a conversation. People who open themselves up to others and who aren't afraid to speak their minds. It's very refreshing. I don't know if I would find that in another town."

"But ..." He paused, setting his fork down. "What about dating?"

Her stomach did a funny flip-flop that had nothing to do with Sal's pizza. "Honestly, since I've been here, I haven't really put myself out there."

"A little gun shy?" he asked.

"I mean, even though I love living in CCR, it's a little hard to explain why I live in an active adult community with my grandmother without sounding like a total weirdo."

There was that sexy half-smile again, churning her insides into mush. "I see your point."

"What about you?" she asked. "You live in a big city. There must be lots of pretty women in Nashville."

"There definitely are. But I work too much to sustain a relationship."

Yep, just as she imagined. "Don't take this the wrong way because what you do is amazing, but that's kind of sad."

She got a full smile this time. If the half-smile flattened her insides, the full smile finished the job. "I can't argue with you there," he said. "It is sad."

"There's got to be more to life than work."

"I agree. I need to make some changes—starting with getting back out there."

"I hope you do." A growing part of her wished it could be with her, but she'd given up wishing on stars a long time ago. "When I quit my job to come here and take care of Gram, I was scared. There aren't any advertising or public relations companies in Cherry Creek. I started my business, and it was slow going for a while. It's better now, but even if it took off, I'd never work twenty-four hours a day, seven days a week. I've seen what that looks like up close and personal, and it's not pretty. If I burn out, I'm no good to anyone. The same is true for you."

"I guess I'm not as smart as you." He leaned back and rubbed his stomach, signaling the end of their heart-to-heart. She felt the pang of disappointment, but shook it away. "I'm stuffed. That was delicious."

Too bad the only guy in forever who'd sparked her interest was an unapologetic workaholic who lived far from Cherry Creek.

Ten

Brock glanced at the clock on his screen and shut his computer down for the night. Tonight was the much-anticipated Cherry Creek Reserve Christmas party, and he knew better than to show up late.

In between zoom meetings and conference calls, he'd helped Erin all week long. From lugging boxes of decorations from the back of her car into the clubhouse, stringing lights and hanging mistletoe, and shooing Liza away from his power tools, Brock felt as if he'd become an honorary member of the CCR social committee. The evening would be the culmination of a lot of work, a celebration of the season, and the embodiment of a Christmas miracle now that Darlene Richardson was on the mend and slated to arrive home on Christmas Eve.

In the week leading up to the party, Brock had taken Erin's advice to heart. A little time away from the office and a huge dose of her Christmas sunshine had convinced him his company wouldn't go careening off the rails if he loosened his grip on the throttle. In fact, the hours he'd spent with Erin had helped him come back to his job each day with a clarity he couldn't find when he never took a break.

"Pawpaw." Brock knocked on his grandfather's bedroom door. "You almost ready?"

Pawpaw opened the door, gave Brock a what-the-heck frown. "Why do I have to wear this ridiculous sweater?"

"It's an ugly sweater contest." Brock pointed to his chest. "Look at mine. It's embarrassing."

"Where did you even get these things?"

"Erin helped me find them online. If I told you what I had to pay for these with expedited shipping, you'd wear it with a smile."

Pawpaw grimaced. "It's my introduction to most of the neighborhood and you want me to wear bells and garland?"

"Grab your glasses and look at mine." Erin had laughed the hardest at the one Brock ordered for himself. He didn't care that it came with hooded elf ears and that he looked like an absolute fool—not if it meant listening to her singsong laugher all night long.

Pawpaw obliged, plucking his glasses from his nightstand and snickering like a kid. Brock hadn't seen his grandfather this relaxed and happy in a very long time. "You win. I'll keep the garland."

"I thought so." Brock put on his jacket and gathered his keys, locking the door behind them for the short walk to the clubhouse. "The temperature's dropped."

"There's a chance of snow overnight. I hope you're able to get out of here tomorrow like you planned."

"Me too. If I didn't have that big meeting on Monday, I'd hang around a couple more days, maybe work from here until after Christmas to save the back and forth." Brock hardly recognized himself or the words coming out of his mouth. Dreading work like he was back in school, delegating tasks to his employees, and shutting down at a decent hour every night to have dinner with Pawpaw and occasionally Erin.

"Sounds like you've had a change of heart about Erin."

"What do you mean?"

"She's not ingratiating herself with people for money, like you assumed?"

"No." Brock had wondered when his grandfather would get around to poking at him for his opinions about Erin. "She actually likes helping others."

"She's got a job," Pawpaw said. "And she's good at it if she's impressed Sean."

As expected, Sean was over the moon when Brock told him about Erin. Sean fired Capital Design and signed a contract with Collier Designs, LLC. "She's very good at her job."

"So," Pawpaw slowed as they approached the clubhouse's entrance. "She's a nice person who works hard and likes to help people. I can see why she gets under your skin. Plus, she's pretty, has a good sense of humor, and her cookies are the best I've ever tasted."

"That's because you've lived with Ma the last year and a half." But Pawpaw wasn't lying. Erin's cookies were fantastic.

"That's all you've got to say?"

"Fine," Brock huffed, tossing his hands in the air. "I was wrong. Happy now?"

"Yes, and strangely enough, so are you."

Brock tried to push past Pawpaw, but the old man grabbed his arm in a surprisingly firm grip. "I'm serious, Brock. She's good for you. You're good for each other."

"Pawpaw ..."

"Women like Erin don't come along every day. If you don't snatch her up while you've got the chance, someone else will. Ask me what it's like to live with regret."

Brock stared into Pawpaw's eyes and knew bluffing was out of the question. "We live in different cities." He'd calculated the two hundred and two miles and one time zone separating him from Erin almost as often as he'd envisioned kissing her.

"That's logistics—an area in which you excel."

"What are you suggesting? A long-distance relationship? Can you see her living in Nashville or me in Cherry Creek?"

"Maybe. You never know what people will do for love."

"You're jumping the gun, Pawpaw. We're not even dating."

"Do you really think either one of us would wear these stupid sweaters if it wasn't for Erin? You've been courting her all week, son. If you haven't asked her out yet, that's on you."

Brock inhaled a deep breath, let it out slowly. "I don't want to make things weird for you if she turns me down."

Pawpaw pointed at Brock's face. "I think you're afraid she won't turn you down and you'll have to give this a shot."

Busted. "What if I blow it? I'm not good at relationships. I never have been."

"When was the last time you tried?"

"Really tried?" Brock thought back over the women who'd come and gone from his life, never making a dent—never even making a mark. "Never."

"So don't blow it, okay? Just ... don't."

"That's your best advice? Don't blow it?"

"What do you want me to say? I'm a grown man wearing a jingle bell sweater. That's the best I've got." Pawpaw continued walking and left Brock stewing in his wake.

He could see Erin inside the clubhouse greeting guests and fluttering from one corner of the room to the other, her face lit up like the Christmas tree he'd helped her decorate. He rubbed the ache in his chest he got whenever he thought about leaving her behind. But could he ask her on a date and follow through, trusting her with his heart the way he was trusting her with his pawpaw? Would she even consider a long-distance relationship?

His pawpaw knew by calling Brock out, he'd force him to act on his feelings. His sneaky pawpaw knew him too well. Brock took a deep breath and headed for the party.

Erin came up behind him as he was hanging his coat on the rack. "I can't believe you bought the elf sweater," she said, holding her hand over her mouth to hide her laughter.

"You didn't think I'd do it?"

"Honestly, no. But I'm so glad you did."

The smile on her face made everything inside of him settle. If there was ever a woman who made him want to try, Erin was it. "Merry Christmas, Erin. You look beautiful in your ugly sweater."

Her cheeks colored prettily as she tugged at the hem of her sweater featuring candy cane arms and Mrs. Santa's body. "I wasn't really going for ugly since Mr. Granger wins every year."

"You mean I'm wearing this for nothing?"

She rewarded him by running her fingers over his chest, setting his heart to pounding. "You're wearing it to fit in and make the rest of us feel less ridiculous."

He'd wear whatever she asked if it meant she'd touch him like that again. Pawpaw approached and gave Erin a hug. "Merry Christmas, Erin. Heck of a party."

"Thanks, Ben. We couldn't have done it without Brock's help."

"My grandson is very handy to have around."

Brock needed to change the subject before Pawpaw asked Erin out on his behalf. He spotted Liza prowling around the room, wearing a tight red sweater and matching lipstick. "Hey, Pawpaw. Do you remember the lady I was telling you about— the one who helped Erin plan the party?"

"Yes. Lisa? Lita?"

"Liza. That's her," he nodded with his head. "Two o'clock, in the tight red sweater and curly white hair."

"Oh," Pawpaw said with a twinkle in his eye. "You didn't tell me she was so attractive."

Brock chuckled. "That's because I don't look at women your age and see them as anything other than old. That would be creepy."

"Well, that's odd. I can look at girls like sweet Erin here and think she's a beautiful woman who'd make someone a very good wife, and it doesn't make me sound creepy."

Brock glared at Pawpaw. "Actually, it kinda does."

Ever the peacekeeper, Erin graced Ben with a grateful smile. "I think it's sweet."

"So," Brock redirected Erin's attention to safer ground. "Where's the famous Gram I keep hearing about? Pawpaw wants to meet her, see if they know any of the same people."

Erin cocked her head and gave him a quizzical grin. "She's not here."

"Oh, is she sick?" He imagined an older, weaker, gray-headed version of Erin propped up in bed. "Is she homebound? The way you talk about her, I thought she was up and about."

Erin snorted and then chuckled out a laugh. "Gram is as far from homebound as you can get. She's on vacation in Costa Rica with her internet friend."

"Vacation? I thought you lived here so you could take care of her."

"I moved in to take care of her after she broke her ankle. She's all healed and on another one of her fabulous adventures. She's been gone since October."

"Wait a minute." Brock shook his head, his impression of her feeble grandmother and Erin's role in her life amending in his head. "You *choose* to live here?"

His tone got her hackles up by the way she popped her hands onto her hips. "Yes, I choose to live here. I like it here."

"That's the saddest thing I've ever heard."

Liza approached the threesome. Brock's heartburn flared at the mischievous look on her face. "Well, if you're going to stand under the mistletoe, you'd better start kissing."

Brock glanced above his head at the bushy sprig of mistletoe he'd attached to the ceiling himself. He dropped his gaze and met Erin's wild-eyed stare.

"We don't have to," she said, her voice brimming with panic.

The more she fought it, the more he wanted to kiss her—the more he needed to kiss her, if only to prove a point. "Are you scared if you kiss me, you might actually enjoy it?"

Her lips twitched. "You mean the way one enjoys a root canal?"

Man, he liked her like this—sweet little Erin giving as good as she got. *Challenge accepted.* With his eyes locked on hers, Brock lifted his hands and placed them on either side of her neck. He took his time leaning down and loitered near her lips like a man with nothing better to do than to tease and to torture. When he couldn't wait another moment, he sealed his lips to hers.

The softness of her mouth, the way her body stiffened and then yielded against his, shut his mind down and sent his senses on high alert. The smell of her skin, like sin and sunshine. The taste of her mouth, like a fiery cinnamon candy. The feel of her satin soft flesh in his hands as his palms cradled her head.

The noise of the crowd cheering brought him back to himself and back to earth. Erin clung to his sweater, her eyes closed, her lips swollen and pink. It took every ounce of self-control not to go back for more. When she opened her eyes and looked up at him, her pupils huge, he pressed his luck and said what was on his heart. "Go out with me, Erin, before your hoard of pseudo-grandparents chase me out of town with a stick."

"I thought you were leaving tomorrow."

"I am. I have a meeting on Monday morning. But I'll be back before Christmas, and I'll stay through the new year." He hadn't planned to stay that long, but for her, he'd change his plans. "What do you say?"

She blinked up at him, her lips teasing upward. "I say yes."

Eleven

ERIN FLOATED TO THE MAILBOX, WAVING AT MR. JOHNSON AND HIS faithful dog Rudy as they walked by her driveway and went on their merry way. Three days had passed since the CCR Christmas party and Brock's fly-me-to-the-moon kiss. She couldn't wipe the smile from her face. She paused before opening the box, closed her eyes, and relived the fateful moment for the millionth time since it happened.

She still couldn't believe they were dating. *I want to date you, Erin. I know I live in Nashville, and you live here, but I want to give it a shot.* He'd said it fast without taking a breath, as if he couldn't hold it inside any longer. And after that kiss and the applause from the onlookers, relief and happiness had her soaring off her feet. She'd yet to fully find the ground ever since.

She was dating Brock Bartlett. "I'm dating Brock Bartlett," she said aloud, and then looked around to make sure no one heard her babbling like a lovesick fool. They'd talked and texted every day, multiple times a day. Flirty, intimate, relationshippy conversations and texts.

She opened the mailbox and dug out the mail, chiding herself for acting so childishly. *Get a grip.* Brock was just a guy

—the smartest, most handsome, most successful man she'd ever known—and he wanted to date her. He'd promised to return to Cherry Creek before Christmas for their first official date to Rutherford's—Cherry Creek's only white tablecloth establishment. Erin had been there only once before, when Gram took her after her graduation from Cherry Creek Academy.

She flipped through the envelopes and magazines that littered her box, stopping at an official-looking document addressed to Louise Larkin. With her grandmother unreachable in the jungle of Costa Rica, Erin made an executive decision and opened the envelope on Gram's behalf.

The breath clogged in her throat as her heart slithered southward. "What?" she said after skimming the letter. "This can't be right."

She jogged inside and went straight for her cell phone, dialing Gram's number with fingers that shook with fear. Gram's phone went straight to voicemail. Erin called again and again, each time getting her voicemail.

She stood in her kitchen, staring at the document she'd placed on the counter. *Think, Erin. There must be something you can do.* She scanned the masthead and dialed the number to the neighborhood management company. A woman answered on the second ring.

"Hi. This is Erin Collier calling on behalf of my grandmother, Louise Larkin. We live at 4550 Cherry Tree Lane in Cherry Creek Reserve. She just got a letter in the mail about breaking a neighborhood covenant."

"Just a moment, please," the woman said and placed Erin on hold. She rejoined the call a few minutes later. "There's been a formal complaint lodged against the owner of 4550 Cherry Tree Lane."

"What kind of complaint?"

"Someone challenged the resident's age as too young to preside in the dwelling."

The fist strangling Erin's midsection loosened its feral grip. "My grandmother well exceeds the fifty-five and over qualification."

"Then your grandmother should have no problem proving her age and habitation at the domicile."

"How is she supposed to prove her habitation? She lives here. What more do you need to know?"

"We've had instances where the person who owns the house has passed, and younger residents stay on in violation of neighborhood guidelines. Your grandmother can resolve the issue by sending a notarized letter via certified mail confirming her occupation of the residence."

"Okay." Erin's pulse calmed. She could do this. Her grandmother would eventually check in, and Erin could get the issue handled. "Does she send it to your address here on the letterhead—the Memphis address?"

"Yes, that's the one. The letter must be dated by December twenty-second."

"December twenty-second?" Erin croaked. She had fewer than ten days to find her grandmother, get her back home, sign a notarized letter, and mail it to Memphis? "My grandmother is currently out of the country and unreachable by phone. I'm not sure I can get a notarized letter to your office by then. Is there any way to postpone the deadline until she returns?"

"I'm afraid not. If your grandmother wants to avoid a formal inquiry, she needs to provide proof of residence by the twenty-second."

Erin dropped the phone and disconnected the call, her stomach roiling. Who could have lodged a complaint—and why? As far as Erin knew, everyone loved her.

Darlene already dislikes you. She feels threatened by you. Liza's words echoed in her brain. But Darlene was still in the hospital and in no condition to lodge a complaint.

Erin's fairytale romance skidded to a halt. *You choose to live here?* Brock had said the night of the party. *That's the saddest thing I've ever heard.* Would he? Could he?

As if she'd summoned him, her phone rang, and his name flashed on the screen. She didn't want to answer and act like everything was okay—nothing was okay—and she didn't want to burden him with her problems. She needed to concentrate on locating Gram and returning her home as soon as possible.

Her phone dinged with a text.

Hey there, hot stuff. Just thinking of you. Tried to call. You're probably out walking someone's dog or picking up their prescription. 😅 I'll try you back later. XOXO.

Brock wouldn't have filed a complaint, not after kissing her stupid and sending her texts like that. Shame coated her throat for even thinking he would.

He could help you. You know he'd do whatever he could to help—and he has the resources. She tucked the thought away even though now that she'd come to her senses and determined he would never have filed a complaint, she was desperate to share the shocking development with someone who cared.

But Brock had had his fill of people leaning on him for support, of that he'd made crystal clear. Erin refused to strain their burgeoning relationship with the millstone of asking for help. And what could he do, anyway? Until she got in touch with Gram, there wasn't anything anyone could do.

Erin jumped at the knock on her door. She left the letter on the counter and walked to the foyer, checking the peephole before opening the door. Liza stood at her threshold with a box in her arms. "I'm sorry," Erin said, ushering Liza inside. "I was on my way to the clubhouse to help you and I got distracted by the mail."

"That's okay. Since you didn't officially have Louise's permission, I wanted to return her decorations before anything got lost or broken." She set the box on the counter. "What's wrong?"

Erin blinked and attempted a smile. "Nothing's wrong."

Liza scoffed, popping the gum in her mouth. "Erin, you're a terrible actress. I should know. What's going on?"

"Nothing." She placed her hand on the letter and casually dragged it away from Liza's prying eyes.

"What's that you're hiding?"

"This? Nothing, it's just junk mail."

Liza squinted her eyes. "If it's junk mail, why haven't you thrown it away?"

Erin sucked her lips between her teeth and eyed the trash can. She couldn't stomach tossing the letter into the trash when she'd only have to fish it out later. "I haven't gotten around to it yet."

"Just spill it and get it over with. I can't stand to watch this pathetic performance a second longer."

"Fine." Erin huffed, too drained and ashamed to continue the ruse. "I got a letter from the community management company. Someone in CCR lodged a formal complaint against Gram, claiming she doesn't live here anymore and I'm too young to live here alone."

"What? Who would do that?"

"I have no idea. And I've only got until the twenty-second to find Gram and get a notarized letter to Memphis."

Liza frowned, shaking her head at the letter. "What did Brock say?"

"I haven't told him."

"Why not?"

"I just got the letter and ... I don't want to bother him."

"Bother him?" Liza flattened her lips and glowered at Erin. "He's your boyfriend. He knows people."

The depths of Erin's shallowness had no bounds. At the mention of Brock as her boyfriend, she momentarily leapt off the Gram train and flung herself back onto the highway of love. *Focus, Erin*, she ordered her punch-drunk heart. "He's a busy man."

"Too busy for you?"

"Liza, listen. I refuse to be another person he has to babysit."

"But you two are in a relationship—or was all that kissing just for show?"

"It wasn't for show, but it's new, and it's fragile, and I don't want to ruin it. Please, promise me you won't say anything to Ben."

Liza's gaze skittered sideways. "We're going to lunch this afternoon. How can I not?"

"You're an actress, remember? The show must go on and all that nonsense."

"It's not nonsense. Sometimes the show literally must go on."

"Exactly. This is one of those occasions. I forbid you to tell Ben about my problem. I will deal with it on my own."

"How?"

"I have no idea, but I'll figure it out." Erin would have to, or she and Gram would end up homeless.

Twelve

Brock waited on the tarmac, toasty in his SUV, searching the sky for incoming planes. On the drive from Nashville to Memphis, he'd squeezed in three conference calls and a quick bathroom break before pulling into the private airstrip and shutting down his phone. He couldn't relax until his precious cargo was on the ground, the letter in his pocket signed and notarized and delivered by one pm. He had a date in Cherry Creek, and he didn't want to be late.

A plane materialized along the horizon, getting larger as it approached. He checked his watch, considered its direction, and figured that was the one. By the time the wheels were down, Brock spotted the familiar logo on the side of the plane and knew the eagle had finally landed. He stepped out of the car, lifting the collar of his pea coat and tucking his hands into his pockets to ward against the chill.

A woman with Erin's likeness descended the stairs wearing floral pants and a scowl he could've seen from three counties over. He approached with caution and an outstretched hand. "Louise Larkin?"

"You the one who hunted me down and plucked me out of paradise?"

"Guilty. I'm Brock Bartlett. It's a pleasure to meet you, Mrs. Larkin."

She shook her head of steely gray hair. "Am I under arrest?"

Brock's laughter was part amusement, part relief. "If you'll allow me to take your bag, I'll explain in the car where it's warm."

"It was warm in Costa Rica."

"I imagine it was." He wheeled her suitcase to the back of his SUV and hefted it inside, then opened the passenger door.

"You must be rich," Louise said when he joined her in the cab.

"I do okay."

"You own a plane and this fancy car."

"My friend owns the plane." Brock entered an address into his GPS and exited the airport. "He did me a favor."

"You got some kind of granny fetish? Cause I ain't into younger men."

Brock smothered a laugh. *This woman.* No wonder Erin never left Cherry Creek. "Mrs. Larkin—"

"You may as well call me Louise."

"Louise. Your granddaughter—"

"Erin?" She clutched her chest. "Oh, my goodness, I never thought something could be wrong with Erin. What is it? Just give it to me straight."

"Erin's fine. She's ... we're ... dating." It felt weird to say, and weirder still knowing it didn't freak him out.

She twisted in the seat to face him, a stupefied look on her weathered face. "You interrupted my vacation to tell me that?"

"I interrupted your vacation to save you both from a legal battle. If you don't have a notarized letter to your community management office by the end of the day today stating you're alive and living at 4550 Cherry Tree Lane, you may not have a home to go back to."

"What the devil is going on?"

Brock explained the story but left out an important detail he wasn't ready to share. Darlene Richardson hadn't lodged the complaint, and neither had one of "her gray-haired groupies," as Liza liked to call them. It hadn't taken much digging to discover a disgruntled neighbor had taken a poke at Brock. He hadn't decided how he wanted to handle Mr. Hafner just yet, but he would, and the man would regret the day he put two innocent women on the chopping block to settle a score.

"So, we're not in Knoxville?" Louise asked after Brock filled her in.

"Afraid not. The management office is in Memphis. After a quick stop at the bank for a notary, we'll drop the letter and I'll get you back to Cherry Creek."

Her eyes brightened. "Another ride on that fancy plane?"

"The plane was a one-time deal. You're stuck driving with me."

"That's gotta be what? Six hours?"

"Give or take."

Louise slumped back into her chair. "You must really like my granddaughter if you went to all this trouble."

After everything he'd done to find Gram and get her back, there wasn't any reason to hedge. "I do."

"Does she like you back?"

The million-dollar question. He supposed he'd find out when he showed up in Cherry Creek with Gram by his side. Would she be happy he'd stepped in and saved the day or bless him out for inserting himself into something she'd obviously deemed none of his business? "I think she does."

"Well," Louise perked up, stacking her palms atop her

crossed knees and spearing him with a pointed stare. "We've got six hours to figure it out."

§.

Erin paced back and forth in front of the window, watching for Brock's car with a mixture of excitement and dread. She couldn't wait to see him again, but she didn't know how to confess her predicament—and that she'd kept him in the dark.

Despite her best efforts to locate Gram, which consisted of calling her phone nonstop and stalking the dozens of Fellows she could find in Indiana, she'd failed. The twenty-second had arrived, and she was no closer to solving their housing crisis than she'd been when the letter arrived.

While getting ready for their date, she'd decided she had to tell Brock. He would see it on her face the moment he arrived. So many people had asked her what was wrong throughout the week. She'd stopped going out to avoid the barrage of annoying inquiries. "What's wrong?" people would ask. "Why so down?" Or her favorite, "Did you and Brock break up?"

They might be by the way she'd avoided his calls. Every time they'd talked, she'd cut their conversations short and resorted to vague texts. It was too hard to pretend things were fine, that she was working away on his account and others, counting down the hours to when she'd see him again, when her world was falling apart.

The longer she went without hearing from Gram, the more concerned she became—and not just for their living situation. Where was Gram, and why hadn't she checked in? Liza did her best to ease Erin's fears, but Gram had never gone more than a week without reaching out. Erin would never forgive herself if something had happened to Gram.

As the clock ticked toward six, Erin checked her reflection in the mirror. Regardless of the circumstances, she wanted to look good for Brock. She'd worn her favorite midnight-green satin midi dress with peep-toe heels and a bold red lipstick Liza insisted would complete the look. Her stomach seized when she heard a car pull into her drive.

She slipped her feet into her shoes, grabbed her clutch and faux fur jacket, and opened the door, only to stumble back and grip the doorframe in shock. "What?"

Gram stepped out of Brock's car wearing his oversized coat and a got-you-good grin. "Surprise," she said, patting a petrified Erin on the cheek as she scrambled into the house. "It's good to be home."

Erin couldn't close her mouth, not even when Brock leaned in and kissed her on the lips. "Hello, gorgeous."

"I don't understand." She pointed to Gram. "How did you ..."

"Your boyfriend chartered a plane." She placed her palms on her lower back and stretched. "Fanciest ride I've ever taken. I may never fly commercial again."

"How did you find her?" Erin asked Brock, her mind swirling. "How did you know?"

Brock stared at her intently, a blend of hurt and annoyance on his too-handsome face. "Why didn't you tell me?"

"I ... I didn't want to burden you with my problems."

"Erin, you have to trust me."

"I do trust you." She gripped his arms and squeezed. "It had nothing to do with trust. I don't want to be another person in your life you have to take care of. You get enough of that from your family."

He tilted his head and gave her a tiny shake. "That's what people do in relationships. They lean on each other. They ask for help and help each other. I want you to come to me with your problems, just like I want to come to you with mine."

Tears sprang into her eyes, and she launched herself into his arms. "I'm so sorry, Brock. I should have told you." She pulled back, and blinked away the tears. "How in the world did you find her?"

"It took some doing. I've got a friend who runs an adventure outfitting company out of San Jose. I called in a favor."

"I can't believe it. I can't believe she's here. But ..." she twisted around, frowned at Gram. "It's too late. We had to have the letter to the company by today."

Gram exchanged a knowing look with Brock. "Your boyfriend flew me to Memphis. We dropped the letter off on our way back to Cherry Creek." She looked around the house and out the window. "Looks like I'm going to have a white Christmas after all."

"Looks like." Erin turned to Brock, her heart thumping inside her chest. "How can I ever repay you?"

Brock stepped to her, and gathered her in his arms. "Slate is clean. We don't keep score and we don't keep secrets."

"Never again. I promise."

A knock had them turning to see Liza and Ben enter the house.

"You made it," Ben said, slapping Brock on the shoulder.

"Just in time," Brock said.

"Who's this?" Gram asked, eyeing Ben like she'd eye a piece of candy.

Ben extended his hand to Gram. "You must be the famous Gram I've heard so much about."

"Call me Louise. You're a tall drink of water."

"Hands off, Louise." Liza wrapped her arm around Ben's and rubbed him like a cat using a scratch. "I saw him first."

Gram pinched her face and crossed her arms. "You can't call dibs."

Brock pulled Erin aside and whispered in her ear. "We can make our reservation if we hurry."

"I'd like nothing more." She lifted her chin and brushed her lips against his. "I'm so happy you're here."

Brock lifted his coat from the back of the couch, his lips twisting into his signature half-grin. "The feeling is mutual."

The End

About the Author

Southerner Christy Hayes writes what she wants to read—uplifting, heartwarming women's fiction stories for all the romance readers out there who love an emotional page-turner with a good dose of family drama. There's usually a lot of love and loss, some sibling and friend dynamics, and an unexpected new beginning, but there's always a happy ever after.

Thank You

Would you like to visit Cherry Creek again soon? Look for the full-length novels telling of more happily ever afters helped by *Once Upon a Christmas Kiss*.